BLISS

J. SANTIAGO

For ordering information, please contact Angela St. James, LLC, at
www.santiagonovels.com
Visit my website at www.santiagonovels.com
Cover designer: IronDan
Development Editor: Heather Whitaker
Editor and Interior Designer: Jovana Shirley, Unforeseen Editing,
www.unforeseenediting.com

Print ISBN: 978-0-9969558-0-5
eBook ISBN: 978-0-9969558-1-2

OTHER NOVELS BY J. SANTIAGO

Lex and Lu

Five Star—Coming 2016

Thousands of young people die every single year to detectable heart conditions. SCA is the leading cause of death in student athletes—more than concussions or any form of cancer or illness combined. The standard sports physical has proven to be less than 1% effective at detecting any heart conditions. In Italy, all student athletes get their hearts checked and sudden cardiac arrest has been reduced by 89%. In our school system, kids get their eyes examined, ears tested, and backs screened for scoliosis, yet they never get their heart checked. What are we waiting for?

Bliss is a fictional story loosely based on Who We Play For. The dream is to use this powerful narrative as a tipping point behind a national movement to deliver EKG heart screenings for our student athletes. The hope is to empower heart-screening organizations across the country and inspire communities to follow.

We challenge you to turn the page and join the fight to end preventable tragedies with a heart screening organization in your community. Together, we have the power to demand heart screenings as a common sense standard of care.

With love,

Who We Play For

We all have someone or something that motivates us. It's who we play for. At Who We Play For, we are motivated by the young lives lost to SCA, and we fight to help ensure other families, teams, and communities will never know that pain. Who We Play For brings together heart-screening groups from across the country who all have their own motivations, their own stories.

Whether it's Rafe Maccarone in Florida, Brandon Goyne, Sarah Friend, and Cody Stephens in Texas, or Burke Cobb in Louisiana, we've lost too many beautiful young people to sudden cardiac arrest.

Together, Who We Play for works to inspire and empower communities to provide every student with the opportunity to screen their heart. Together, to date, we have screened over 70,000 young hearts and saved the lives of over 60 students.

FIFTY PERCENT OF THE PROCEEDS FROM THE SALE OF *BLISS*
WILL BE DONATED TO HEART-SCREENING GROUPS
ACROSS THE COUNTRY.

To Evan, Kieran, Megan, Zack, and Zane.
Thank you for sharing your stories with me.

To Tauara, Xander, Nico, and Lucas.

PROLOGUE

December 2006

J.C. Callahan shoved his shin guards into the depths of his socks and pulled tightly on the laces of his cleats. He heard his teammates moving around him, going through the rituals of pregame, attempting to stave off the sadness and anger that had been dogging them since Gabe Pryce's collapse and death. J.C. drew in a wobbly breath. He knew they were all in the same state, and maybe, eventually, that would bring comfort. But now, they were disjointed pawns lined up next to him, trying to power their way through to the state championship.

Shaking off the haze, J.C. walked out toward the field, away from the sounds of his team, away from the locker room and the memories of his fallen teammate, away from the veil of anguish. Absently, he toed a ball from the sidelines and toyed with it, the repetition soothing somehow.

In the week since Gabe's death, J.C. had kept moving—going to school, practice, games; tying his cleats; putting on his sleeves and burying his shin guards into them; walking onto the field. But he wasn't always quite sure how he'd gotten there, how he had completed his homework, how he'd made it through games.

The game tonight would be the happy ending to the tragedy that had become his life. This win tonight wouldn't erase Gabe's death, and it might not even make him feel better in the end, but in some way, deep within his shattered heart, J.C. knew this victory would be a balm for all their wounds. For Gabe, for his team, for himself—they needed the win. He could envision their story becoming a Disney movie, one of those sports stories with a happy ending after the team had overcome some tragedy.

He needed his Disney movie, and the stage would be set tonight.

"Are you ready?"

J.C. shook off his fog, stopped the ball play at his feet, and looked to the eyes of his coach. He broke the stare as he popped the ball up into his hands. "Yeah," he said.

If Coach thought his answer had been abrupt, he didn't pursue it. J.C. had tried to talk to Coach since it happened, but he found that he couldn't look the man in the eyes. Now, when he looked, he saw Coach as he had that day—across the expanse of Gabe's body, his eyes draped in fear and confusion, mirroring J.C.'s own. The memory of that afternoon had become a living, breathing entity between them.

Because J.C. only had to close his eyes to see it or let his mind wander to remember it. Gabe dying in front of him would stand as the most poignant memory of his life, and he was fairly certain that even through falling in love, getting married, having children, and watching them grow, nothing would ever be able to blot out the memory. He had to think that a victory tonight against their club teammates who played for the crosstown rival would somehow be a triumph against that memory. He'd built it up in his head this way.

It would be his Disney ending. Perhaps that would make it better. Objectively, he thought they had all the elements for a good story. They definitely had the tragedy—the death of a star athlete. It was one of those tragedies that made people count their blessings, that pulled on all those heartstrings, that had them curled up and crying in a corner. It was an event that prompted everyone to relive the days and weeks before and had them asking "what if?" *What if the ambulance had gotten there quicker? What if we'd taken a long-ago forgotten event more seriously? What if...*

They became a devastated community mourning an avoidable occurrence with kids tasting their mortality and parents throwing up prayers, thanking their God that it hadn't happened in their family.

So, there was tragedy.

Then, there was the underdog, another element for a classic sports movie. The high school on the other side of the city was a perennial soccer powerhouse - the Goliath to J.C.'s David.

Perhaps because they'd all grown up on the soccer field together, this game held even more meaning. Most of them had played with Gabe. They'd all known him. The difference between the two teams now was that they hadn't watched Gabe die, which made them lucky. So, their opponents had luck and a tradition of winning while his team had heart and desire.

Even now, moments before the game, J.C. could appreciate that his team didn't bring any beauty to the game. Fire and passion? Absolutely. But they had little finesse. They had skills from years of good coaching and traveling around the state. But it seemed secondary to the anger they had coursing through them. This game now, the one they'd grown up on, was an outlet for their grief, a necessity to quell their anger, an answer to their question of, *Why?*

As he stood on the sidelines with his brothers in grief, he acknowledged all of this, and he wanted the win. He prayed for it. He needed some sense of justice in the world.

Yes, God took our friend from us, but because we had to pay that price, we will win this game. We will go on to the state championships. We will do this for Gabe. We are playing for Gabe.

This was his last conscious thought right before game time. He knew they would call for a moment of silence. He knew he would be introduced. He knew Gabe's family would be there.

But it would all be a vague memory. The game itself would replay in his head over and over.

As J.C. prepared for his game, Maggie Pryce entered her brother, Gabe's abandoned room. She rummaged through his drawers with the cold detachment of a mortician embalming a stranger. She'd gone in there without really knowing if she was searching for anything in particular or if she just wanted a chance to be among his things. Once there though, she found his club soccer jersey hanging in the closet, the black number six stark against the white background. Her fingers lingered on it, tracing it. It brought to mind thousands of images of him in various soccer jerseys over the years, and her detachment fell away.

She pulled it from the hanger and took it with to her room. She planned the rest of her outfit around her brother's beloved jersey. Donning her jeans, she slipped his jersey over a long-sleeved shirt, pulled on her Chucks, and declared herself ready for the night.

She understood the need around her. Her parents, his teammates, his friends, his little girlfriend, his teachers, the community—they all had this profound desire to grieve. And she really did get it. But she couldn't take the oppressiveness of it. She wanted to go back to school and mourn her brother without an audience, without feeling any other person's grief more than she felt hers. When her mother had droned on and on about how much the game would have meant to Gabe, how much he would have wanted the opportunity to play tonight, and how important it was that she be there to show her support to the Apostles, she felt obligated to stay.

As she began the familiar drive to the school, she tried like hell not to remember that she had made this drive mere days before. No one had asked her if she'd been there, so she'd kept it to herself. In all the confusion of finding out about his collapse and the frantic, hopeless drive to the hospital, no one had remembered that she was supposed to pick up Gabe that day. So, no one knew that she had been there to see her brother die. Without Gabe, she wasn't sure she would ever feel normal again, as her heart limped just enough to keep her breathing and surviving but not enough for her to be fully alive.

When she found herself moving silently through the halls of her old high school, slowly making her way toward Gabe's locker, she wasn't surprised by what she found. An impromptu memorial had sprung up, one to rival the death sites of famous people. The scene gave her chills and forced her to stop her forward motion. The flowers, pictures, quotes, cards, and unlit candles—it was too much to take in. The dark hall illuminated by a measly halogen light seemed to glow with an unearthly aura. She hated it. She couldn't take other people's expressions of bereavement. She was pissed that they got to grieve for her brother in such a public way when she felt like her grief needed the security of a private space. She wanted to leave him a message or a token of a memory, but there were so many things that she needed to say and so many memories that all the halls of the school wouldn't be able to hold her outpouring.

Breathing quickly, Maggie turned and sprinted down the corridor, back toward the door where she'd entered. She couldn't catch her breath, couldn't fight the racing of her heart. She could barely contain the scream that wanted to claw its way out of her throat.

She heard the announcements coming from the field. In the back of her mind, she knew she didn't have much time to get there, to walk calmly into the middle of the soccer stadium with her parents. As she got closer, the announcer's voice became clearer, and she could make out the names of Gabe's teammates. She stopped abruptly, suddenly sure that she didn't want to go.

Leaning against the field house, one hundred yards from where her parents were waiting to walk onto the field, Maggie struggled to catch her breath.

She saw her mother looking around, and even from the distance, she could see the disappointment in the set of her mother's shoulders. Her father patted her mother's arm, and Maggie could almost hear his reassurances being whispered.

As the announcer began the tribute to Gabe and introduced her parents, Maggie slid down the side of the building, exhaustion taking hold. She listened and observed the moment of silence. From her hiding place, she watched the boys who had grown up with Gabe, play the whole game. She felt their anguish, even from so far away. Although mindful of what a victory would mean for Gabe's team, she didn't feel any excitement for it. She knew they were playing their hearts out, hoping winning would somehow make up for the death of her brother.

When the final whistle sounded and the reality of the loss trickled through the stadium, Maggie felt surprised by the satisfaction blazing through her. Part of her wanted to run through their locker room, screaming that one game or a regional final or a state championship couldn't take away the pain of Gabe's death and that what had happened on the field wouldn't make a difference. It was truly just a game.

In her twenty-two-year-old wisdom, Maggie was pretty certain that those kids, the Apostles, would just have to find a way to get through it. And they would. They would move forward, and their twenty-two-year-old selves would look back on their fifteen-year-old selves and see the foolishness of putting the hopes of forgetting death on the outcome of a game. At least, that was what she hoped for them.

Walking slowly toward his car, J.C. saw a single person sitting by the field house, her knees drawn in and her head down. The loneliness and solitude of the picture hit him. She looked how he felt—hollow and shriveled. He moved to her slowly, careful not to spook her. When he was close enough so that she could hear him, he stopped with a number of feet still separating them.

And he watched her.

Shuffling his feet to alert her of his presence, he asked, "Are you okay?"

People had been asking him the same question for the last week, and he hated it. Asking her shamed him because the sentiment seemed cheap. But even knowing that, he wasn't sure if there was any other way to ask.

She lifted her head from her knees. She pulled her hair from around her face and held it with her hand. When he realized who she was, he took a noticeable step back. Righting himself, he watched confusion and then recognition chase across her face.

She graced him with a slight smile. "I don't know. Are you?" she asked.

He almost smiled in return. Shifting nervously, he shook his head. Averting his gaze, he answered without looking at her, "Nah."

"Me neither," she whispered.

He heard movement and turned to her, watching her awkwardly get to her feet. Her movements suggested that she'd been sitting for a while. He almost moved to steady her, but he wasn't feeling very steady himself.

"Headed out?" she asked.

He nodded.

"I'll walk with you."

J.C. started forward, shuffling in his slides. He tried not to notice her, but it was difficult. Maggie was beautiful and had been the star of many of his fantasies. It was something he'd never shared with Gabe. As close as they had been, he hadn't thought Gabe needed to know he was in lust with his older sister.

They walked next to each other but didn't talk. They could have been two strangers who happened to find themselves next to each other in line.

They came to Maggie's car first, and J.C. paused just minutely, but it was enough for Maggie to notice. He met her stare, and silent communication flowed between them.

"You know?" she asked.

"Yes," he answered honestly. He wanted to lie, to pretend he didn't know her secret, but *yes* had beaten *no* to his mouth.

He watched her nod warily.

"Gabe has a big mouth...had a big mouth. Shit, he had a big mouth." Big, fat tears spilled from her eyes, and she furiously wiped them away.

"No. He just told me," he spoke rapidly.

She waved away his explanation. "It doesn't matter." Turning, she opened her car door and stepped into the V between it and the car.

He almost moved away, but he found himself turning. "You saw." He'd meant it as a question, but it came out as a statement. He needed her to know that he knew she'd watched Gabe die and he understood the horror of it.

"Yes."

"I'm so sorry," was all he could manage to say.

September 2014

Magdalena Pryce leaned back in her chair and looked out over the still waters of the intercoastal. Even from fifteen stories up, she could see the heat of the day reflecting off the glassy bay. Its smooth surface failed to calm her as she argued halfheartedly with her child's father.

The last couple of months had been filled with turmoil over their son. Nicky's desire to play travel soccer, an activity Lena had desperately wanted to avoid. It was the first real divergence in parenting Nicky that she and Mike had experienced since his birth. The breach it had caused had been difficult to navigate.

"Mike," she reminded him, "the deal was, this would be all you."

"No, Lena," he said with exaggerated patience, "that was not the deal. That was what you wanted the deal to be. This is what our son wanted—has wanted for a long time. I said I would inconvenience you as little as possible, but I really need for you to pick him up tonight. Shit, Lena."

"Fine!" she capitulated. "Where the hell am I going?"

"The fields out by Lakewood Ranch. He's on field twelve."

She glanced at her watch and groaned. "That means I have to leave now."

"Actually, you should have left five minutes ago, but you prefer arguing with me."

Point taken.

"Good-bye," she huffed before disconnecting.

Surveying her office, she reached for her backpack, grabbed her sunglasses, and logged off her computer. She still had about an hour of work to do, but she knew she could login from home later.

The drive from the west part of the city out east past the interstate would take about forty minutes. Her annoyance with Mike increased as she realized she would be late, something she hated.

She glanced at her watch and started to worry. It was already six forty. There was no way she would make it to the field close to seven. Picking up the pace, she hurried to the parking lot, threw her stuff into the Jeep, and picked up her phone to call Mike. A text message was waiting for her. Mike had already taken care of the late issue by texting the coach and the team manager. She smirked.

Damn him for knowing me so well, she thought.

When she'd put her foot down about Nicky playing soccer, she'd turned her world into a battlefield for three months. The worst of it was, Nicky had known his father was on his side, and he'd worked really hard to exploit the rift. And with her reluctance, she'd made it that much more important to her son. She couldn't be too mad about that. Of all the things Nicky had gotten from her, spotting a weakness in his enemy was one that she wished had skipped a generation, especially when it was being used against her.

As she pulled up to the fields forty-five minutes later, she cursed herself for ignoring all the soccer information, specifically the instructions on field locations. Already twenty-five minutes late, the thought of having to trudge around these fields, looking for her son, wasn't pleasant.

Taking a moment to get her bearings, she got out of the Jeep and began the trek. To her utter relief, field twelve sat right next to the gravel parking lot. A woman was standing at the corner, a Coach bag hanging from her shoulder and a toddler nipping at her feet. Her eyes widened as Lena carefully picked her way across the parking lot. The woman began to walk forward but was halted by the strength of the little girl hanging on her leg.

"Magdalena?" the woman inquired from across the distance.

"Lena, yes," she corrected tersely.

"Oh," she said, her brown eyes widening again. She explained, "All of Nick's forms list your full name. Sorry, I just assumed."

She represented everything Lena had ever imagined of a soccer mom. Her hair was cut in the popular wedge that was shorter in the back than the front, her workout clothes were coordinated, and she had this air about her that screamed efficient. Although Lena wanted to immediately hate her, as this was everything she didn't want to be, the woman's smile was kind, and there wasn't any judgment lingering in her gaze.

"No, it's fine," Lena offered, smiling and thrusting out her hand. "I am so sorry that you had to wait for me."

The woman waved her off. "No apologies. My daughter has practice now, so it was no inconvenience at all. Nick and Aiden went to watch Coach Cal. He had a game." The woman's eyes dropped to Lena's feet. "I hate to tell you this, but they are on the other side of the park. You'll never make it in those shoes."

"Shit," Lena muttered, forgetting about the sprout of a child attached to the woman's leg. "I'm sorry."

"No worries," she said. "Try as I might, I just can't always keep it clean either."

They both laughed, and for the first time since Mike had called her, Lena relaxed.

"So, where do I have to go?"

"We're here on twelve. See that far corner over there? That's where. Field two."

Taking a deep breath, Lena said, "Of course I do."

"I know you are all dressed up, but I have a pair of soccer flip-flops in the car."

Looking down at her nude stilettos, Lena realized it was either the flip-flops or go barefoot. "Do you mind?"

"No, not at all. I'll grab them for you." She picked up the child, deposited the sprite on her hip, and made her way to her minivan.

Of course it was a minivan, which completed the soccer-mom image. On the back window, she even had the stick-figure stickers of the perfect little family—a dad, a mom, a girl with a soccer ball, a boy with a soccer ball, a little girl with fairy wings, and a dog. If they were friends, she'd have told the woman to scrape those caricatures off her window.

She walked back to Lena with the flip-flops extended, but she paused before handing them over. "So, do you want to know whose feet these belong to, or are you one of those ignorance-is-bliss people?"

"Definitely *ignorance is bliss*," Lena responded immediately.

The woman cocked her head. She studied Lena for a second. "I don't think I would have guessed that," she said.

Their eyes met and held, and suddenly, Lena felt like she could tell all her secrets to this stranger.

Then, the woman laughed, lightening the mood. "Oh, I'm Sarina, by the way."

"Hey, Sarina."

"Would you mind telling Aiden to head back here soon?"

"Of course. I'll see if I can get him to walk back with us."

"He probably won't want to. He'd rather watch Coach Cal."

"Okay. Uh, thanks for the flip-flops," Lena said before going to find Nicky.

The trek across the endless green of the soccer fields was made somewhat easier with the new footwear. Lena shuffled through the grass, swinging her stilettos, as she walked to the other side of the park. It was easy to spot Nicky, his telltale fauxhawk still sticking up even after running around in the muggy heat. With his feet balanced on a ball, he was sitting on the end of a bench with his new friend next to him and an older guy on his other side.

As Lena approached them, the action on the field stopped, and the players began making their way to the bench. It obscured her view of Nicky and made it impossible to get his attention.

The grassy smell of the fields and the sweaty bodies permeated the air around her. Suddenly caught in the past, memories hit her. The years of following her brother to his practices and games danced before her, and she could no longer distinguish the men in front of her from the images of her past with her brother and his friends.

Stuck.

The guys with their backs to the field could see her standing there. Right at that moment, as she lingered between the past and the present, they could have been Gabe and his friends, the Apostles. She noticed the curiosity in their looks, but it wasn't until she heard her son that she snapped back to the present.

"Coach Cal, you shouldn't have let that guy get by you," Nicky said.

She tried not to laugh, but it was so like her son to think he knew more than everyone else. Her laughter escaped, and the relief of the dispelling memories forced it out of her mouth with more exuberance than normal. The sound drew the attention of everyone, and Nicky turned around to look at her.

Feeling awkward, she waved and said, "I'm just here to get Nicky."

Nicky blushed and rolled his eyes before turning back to the group surrounding him. But Lena received his message loud and clear. He had outgrown his nickname. Feeling her own blush creeping up her neck, she carefully took in the assessing gazes from the young men around her son.

"You got beat Coach Cal," Nicky reiterated.

"Yeah, I probably could have gotten him," Coach Cal responded with a smile for Nicky. Placing his hand on Nicky's shoulder, he moved them both toward Lena.

"I'm Coach Cal," he said, wiping his hand on his damp shirt before reaching out to her.

"Lena," she responded, taking him in.

She placed her hand in his and was struck by a sense of familiarity, but she couldn't imagine where she would have met him. She blamed it on her weird look at the past from moments before. Looking at him made her think that she wouldn't have forgotten knowing him. He was tall, well over six feet. His mahogany hair, disheveled from playing, was a longer version of Nicky's fauxhawk. Whereas Nicky's style had managed to survive practice, Coach Cal's messy locks fell unchecked onto his forehead. His dark brown eyes, straight nose, and full lips all fit together perfectly, making him easy to appreciate.

"Lena?" he asked, looking puzzled.

His question startled her, and she realized she'd been staring at him. They stood like that, touching and staring. Nicky shuffled between them, and she snapped out of it, pulling her hand out of the coach's. But she didn't stop gazing, lost a little in the dark depths of his eyes.

"Sorry I'm late," she managed to get out. She wanted to look away, but it was hard to escape the magnetic pull of him. The niggling impression of recognition remained, making her feel uncomfortable.

"It was no problem at all." He shrugged a bit. "Nick's been coaching us, and we're winning, so he can hang out after practice anytime."

She felt a connection between the two of them, and it was jarring. Nicky never had a relationship with anyone whom she hadn't known first. Coach Cal reached out to ruffle her son's hair, and Nicky ducked. Cal laughed, quickly adjusted, and managed to get his hand on Nicky's prized hairdo. They both laughed, and Lena couldn't help the discomfiture snaking through her. Their easy camaraderie, her ghostly memories, and the strange awareness of the man in front of her made her want to get away from the fields quickly.

"We need to go," she said abruptly.

Coach Cal and Nicky looked over to her, their smiles still in place. She met Nicky's gaze, and he must have sensed the change in her because his smile fell away.

"I gotta get my stuff," he said, turning away to walk back toward the bench, leaving her with his coach.

Their eyes met, and she found herself staring again. The same sense of knowing him moved through her. It was calming and disturbing all at once.

Needing to break the spell between them, she searched for something to say. "Thanks for letting him hang out with you after practice. I'm not usually late, but Mike didn't let me know that he needed me to pick up Nicky until it was almost time to get him."

"It's really no problem. He's a great kid."

"Thanks," she murmured as she looked back over to Nicky, seeking some distance from the man in front of her.

Nicky finally made his way back to them. "See you Thursday, Coach," he said.

She placed her hand on Nicky's shoulder, and they turned away from Coach Cal.

"Thanks again," she said over her shoulder without meeting his eyes.

"No problem," he returned.

Although she didn't look back, she knew he hadn't moved because a connection remained between them. She refused to turn around and make eye contact even though she could feel him watching her. Goose bumps arose on her arms, and she felt her stomach knot with tension. She wanted to laugh at the absurdity of it all, but she felt too breathless to release it.

"Why didn't Dad pick me up?" Nicky asked.

And just like that, reality smacked her in the face. "Something came up," she said.

Nicky shrugged. "I had fun. Aiden and I got to warm up Coach Cal's team."

"Shoot! I forgot to tell Aiden that his mom wanted him to come back."

"Want me to run back and tell him?"

She wanted to say no, but for some reason, she didn't want to disappoint Sarina.

"Yes, can you quickly run back there?"

He turned abruptly and took off running. "I'll get him!" he yelled.

She didn't want to turn around and watch him, but she did anyway. As she'd suspected, Coach Cal was still standing there, right where they'd left him, looking in her direction. Their eyes locked. For a moment, they just stared. Then, he smiled, and she couldn't help but smile back. When Nicky appeared in her line of vision with Aiden, Coach Cal turned back to the field.

J.C. leaned back in his chair, carefully placed his phone on the table, and ran his hand through his hair, his frustration evident. Tired after soccer, he still felt shell-shocked. He hated to even think the comparison in his head, but he experienced that same sense of disbelief and incredulity that he'd felt when Gabe collapsed in front of him. Seeing Maggie Pryce—or Lena, as she apparently went by now—had done things to him that he didn't think he'd get over anytime soon. It was unreal to think of her now when the image of her that had been locked in his brain was of a twenty-two-year-old girl in jeans and a soccer jersey. The woman who had faced him today, making his insides twist and his brain malfunction, was a goddess. The second she'd opened her mouth and the laughter had escaped, he'd known. He was still trying to reconcile her being there with a kid on his team. When she'd walked away from him, it'd hit him. He had been coaching Gabe's nephew.

All had seemed right in the world and he smiled as he thought of the serendipitous events that had put Gabe's nephew in his sphere.

But then, he remembered. He remembered he'd had an opportunity to let Maggie know who he was, and he'd withheld. It had been a fleeting but conscious thought. When he had glanced at Nick's face and then recognized her, he'd almost run to her and told her who he was. But he knew that would have been bad. He knew she wouldn't have appreciated knowing who he was. So, he'd shut it down. All he could think about was that he might have lost his only opportunity to introduce himself to her at an appropriate time. When she found out who he was, it would seem slimy and dishonest.

What was I thinking?

He had been so surprised when he saw her. The connection to Nick unknown, J.C. had lost his mind. It was the only explanation. And maybe her beauty had thrown him. Being caught in her orbit had made him stupid.

Leaning forward and dropping his face into his hands, J.C. relived every nanosecond of their interaction. He could see her sense the connection, could see her feel the chemistry. But he couldn't open his mouth, couldn't provide the explanation.

Now, he had this meeting he had to get through with his closest friends. He opened his messenger bag and pulled out an old spiral notebook where he recorded his notes. He flipped it open and looked over the ideas from the last meeting. But it all blurred on the page as he continued to torture himself by replaying his meeting with Maggie Pryce.

"You look like you just lost your best friend," Anna said from the doorway.

He looked up from the table and chuckled. "I have no idea what you're talking about."

"Uh-huh," she responded as she moved into the room. She rounded the table, placed her hand on his shoulder, and bent to drop a kiss on his head.

She sat down on his right and looked him over before narrowing her eyes. "You okay?" she asked.

"You do look like you're about to pull your hair out. What happened to you today?" Kyle added as he made his way into the room, circling around to sit on the other side of Anna.

J.C. reached up and smoothed out his damp hair, easily picturing what his nervous habit made him look like.

Anna smacked Kyle in the arm as she said, "Leave him alone."

Desperate to shift the conversation, J.C. asked, "Where's everyone else?"

With a shrug, Kyle pulled out a chair as he answered, "On their way."

Anna was a force of nature. She stood all of five feet and weighed maybe one hundred pounds, her weight almost in direct proportion to her height. She was classically blonde, one of those few people who had begun as a towhead and managed to stay naturally light. She wore her hair in a bob that ended just beneath her chin, elongating her neck and sharpening her brown eyes.

At fifteen, his best friend, Gabe Pryce, had fancied himself in love with her. Looking at her now, J.C. thought that she looked virtually the same, although more sophisticated in her carriage and manner. He wondered grimly if maybe he'd just chosen to continue to see her as Gabe had in some crazy bid to hold on to the person Gabe had thought she might grow to be. The thought depressed him.

Anna's vision for their organization, Play for Gabe, had pulled their little scholarship fund from car washes and bake sales to the next level. They had stepped up their efforts and were working toward offering free heart screenings to youth in the county. It was an exciting time for all of them.

A lot of the credit had been heaped on J.C. as the unofficial spokesman, but it was really all Anna. She'd pulled them together, held them together, and focused them in a way that J.C. hadn't had the energy to do. Play for Gabe was her future. His dreams were starting to separate from the group, and he struggled to figure out how to preserve their connection while severing the ropes that seemed to be holding him in place.

His desire to leave had happened gradually. It had taken him by surprise because it seemed as if everything since Gabe's death eight years ago occurred in a split-second fashion, like lightning following thunder when a storm was right upon you. But his new plan, which would take him away from all of them and their organization, took place in stages, like little gnats that he swatted away, laughed off, and generally ignored until he couldn't anymore.

When Fletcher, Bryce, and Max appeared soon after Anna and Kyle, he shuttered his wayward thoughts, so he could focus on their planning session. So many things were happening for Play for Gabe. The next couple of months were going to be really busy and it would be difficult to have his focus split between his present and his future.

After they hammered out some plans for the heart screening, Anna shut her laptop. She clasped her hands together in front of her and leaned forward. She looked nervous but determined. J.C.

stifled a groan, not sure of what was coming but preparing for it nonetheless.

"I know, on many occasions, we've tabled the issue of our name"—she looked at each one of them—"but we've come to the point where we need to make a change, so we can move forward."

She had made a point of addressing all of them, but J.C. knew she was really just speaking to him. Everyone else was ready—had been ready—to change their name. When they'd started talking about their nonprofit status and where the future would be taking them, they'd also decided that they needed to have a more global outlook. It wasn't just about Gabe's scholarship fund, but more fundamentally, it was about attempting to save lives through education and screening for heart issues.

"It's fine," J.C. said.

Five sets of eyes focused on him, the expression in them relaying their shock. He met each of their stares.

Am I really going to do this? he thought belatedly. Shaking his head, as if to clear it, he looked up at the ceiling, the dull fluorescent lights offering little in the way of shelter. He thought about this being his opening, his way to bow out gracefully.

He took a deep breath. He heard his exhale in the silence of the room. "I know I've been the one who's been holding out on the name issue. It's all good now."

Fletcher, the most dramatic person in the group, tossed his lengthy pale arms in the air, letting his pen fall and hit the table. "Are you shitting me?"

No one else moved. They all stayed locked in place, watching.

J.C. pulled his gaze from the ceiling and leaned forward in his chair, placing his hands on the table in front of him, mimicking Anna's let's-get-down-to-business pose. Slowly, he shook his head. "Nope."

"Why?" Kyle questioned.

J.C. turned toward him. Kyle had no poker face, and J.C. knew his change of heart on the name had taken Kyle by surprise.

"It's just time," J.C. said.

"Why wasn't it time two weeks ago when you argued us all down?" Fletcher said. "Wasn't it you who said, 'This is supposed to be about Gabe's legacy. People should know that he's the reason for this'? Didn't you say that?" Of course he threw the air quotes up and dropped his voice to try to sound like J.C.

Fletcher always managed to elicit a smile from J.C. because of his over-the-top gestures and sarcasm.

"Yep, that was me," J.C. said, self-deprecation heavy in his voice.

He really wished he could rewind a few weeks and not have argued as passionately as he had. He'd been trying, attempting, to find a way to stay in it. Changing their name, moving on from just being about Gabe, would thrust J.C. forward into a place he wasn't sure he was ready to go to.

And here he was, two weeks later, wishing he'd just kept his damn mouth shut and let it all happen.

"So, you're cool with it?" Max asked skeptically.

"Yes. You guys are right. It's time." As much as J.C. wanted to think that and let it go, he had to force the words from his mouth. "Next on the agenda?" he said, looking to Anna.

Anna was thoughtfully watching him. He knew if he looked around the table, they would all probably have the same looks on their faces. That was what years of friendship had done. Most people he knew still talked to maybe one or two people at the most whom they'd known since elementary school. The five guys around this table had all been friends since they were eight. They had suffered an unspeakable tragedy together, and they'd stayed friends. Most of the time, that thought was comforting. Because, really, what did you have to explain when you were surrounded by people who knew you best? Not a whole lot.

So, he knew they would let it drop.

"That's it," Anna said quietly.

They all sat, lost in their thoughts.

Then, Fletcher stood, clapped his hands together once, and said, "Let's go have a drink!"

And that was what they did. At least J.C. did. He wasn't really sure if they were all drunk, but he was fairly certain he'd overachieved and stretched Fletcher's drink into more than one. But it had worked. For a good three hours, he hadn't thought further than getting the drink to his mouth and swallowing. It wasn't such a bad state.

But when he plateaued, reached that point when he knew he couldn't handle any more, his hand-to-mouth-motion fixation abandoned him. He was left sitting at the bar with Anna and his thoughts. He could feel his mood shift from buoyantly carefree to depressingly drunk. Then, he felt a little proud of himself that he wasn't so drunk that he couldn't appreciate how drunk he was. Somehow, in his head, it all made sense.

But Anna being Anna, she'd just been biding her time. She'd even bought him some drinks, helping him get in this state, because she knew, like they all knew, that getting J.C. drunk was sometimes the only way to get information out of him.

He contemplated this as he sat next to her at the bar, and she leveled her brown eyes at him.

"Wanna tell me what's going on?" she said.

He recognized that she was a little drunk, too, and that helped stave off the sense of betrayal he wanted to feel at her getting him drunk.

He dropped his head and shook it. "Nope."

"You sure? You know you'll feel better if you tell me."

Again, he noted her drunkenness because she'd said it in a singsong voice, one that she'd probably used when she was little and promised to be someone's best friend if they would agree to do something they really didn't want to do. When she was like this, J.C. would notice her sharp edges.

He shook his head more deliberately, like he could fend her off with the motion. "Nothing to talk about."

"Bullshit," she said with bluster.

J.C. felt himself smile even though he was trying like mad to hang on to his resolve.

"People are so snowed by your angelic looks that they don't realize what a bulldog you are," he said with some shit behind it.

Anyone else might have been put off by his comment, but Anna basked in his grudging praise.

"Angelic, huh?" she said with a smile. "I like it." She moved more directly into his space and tapped her shoulder with his.

"Meant demonic," J.C. returned, keeping his head down. He so didn't want to give in to her, but his reluctance to talk was drowning in a vat of beer and tequila.

"Did not," she said.

Again, he noted the singsong quality of her voice. Normally, it would grate on his nerves, but for some reason, he found it cute.

He vaguely recognized that his boys had retreated. He couldn't hear them, and he brought his head up, still avoiding Anna's gaze but searching for them in the crowd.

"Gone," she said.

"Fucking conspiracy," he noted drily.

"Yep," she gushed proudly.

"I have shitty friends," he mumbled.

This made Anna laugh loudly. Then, as suddenly as it had erupted from her, she stopped. She picked up the coaster on the bar, toying with it and somehow him. "Tell me what's going on, J.C."

"I want out," he said as clearly as he could.

He was surprised when he felt better, but then he glanced over at Anna and didn't feel better. The look on her face hit him exactly as he'd predicted.

"Out?" she asked, shock radiating in her voice. Her brown eyes were wide and shimmering with the beginning of tears. She blinked and then opened her eyes, all hint of crying gone.

Like a light going off, he thought vaguely.

"Out," he confirmed.

"I don't know what that means," she said.

But she knew exactly what it meant. It meant the end of it for him. He wanted to ride off into the sunset and find something new, not live his life around this anymore. But she was going to make him say it. She would make him spell everything out—tell her what he was going to do that wouldn't involve them, explain how things would now work, and what he was willing to give up.

"I mean, when we finally get our nonprofit status and we make it through the memorial and screenings weekend, I'm done."

"Done," she repeated, drawing it out and rolling it around on her tongue like she was tasting the word.

"Yeah," he said, looking her in the eyes, assuring her of his seriousness.

"What will you do?" Her tone changed. She didn't sound angry or resigned, more like curious.

Anna always had a plan, and she knew that J.C. had one, too. But he wasn't willing to share. There were too many unknowns right now to put it out for public consumption

He shook his head, feeling the weight of it. *Yep, still drunk,* he acknowledged to himself.

"Okay," she responded.

He could hear the annoyance in her voice.

They didn't speak for a few minutes. He knew she was waiting him out, hoping the lack of conversation would inspire him to come clean with her.

With an exasperated sigh, she asked, "When will you officially tell everyone else?"

"I'm not sure. I just want to get through the next couple of months, and then I'll tell them." He felt grounded in that statement.

He didn't want the focus of the group to shift to him and his plans right now. If they thought he was leaving, they'd badger him, wanting to know, needing to be a part of it his decision.

"This changes things," she said softly.

"Yeah," he acknowledged. "But not yet."

Anna looked away from him to the other end of the bar. He figured she was lost in her own thoughts. He got it. It was a jolt, and even in his state, he could appreciate that it would take time for her to come to terms with it. But putting that aside, he felt a renewal of his earlier euphoria when he was able to enjoy his drunkenness.

This isn't so bad, he thought.

Then, Anna turned back to him—not just her head, but her body, too. She moved into him, maneuvering her legs in between his so that it went boy, girl, boy, girl. She leaned toward him, her small body pushing into his space.

Looking up at him, she said, "No, J.C." Her hands fell onto his legs, and she squeezed his thighs.

Suddenly, the warning bells in his head went off, alarms blaring.

"This changes things," she added.

He knew this was all kinds of wrong. He did not feel anything sexual toward Anna, and even in his drunken state, he was confused. Anna had seen him wade through countless women, and she'd never even batted an eyelash.

Where was this coming from?

She stopped asking questions and looked up at him with a sober gleam in her eyes. Before he could figure out of what she intended to do, she leaned forward and pressed her mouth to his.

He wasn't sure how they'd gotten to her apartment or how they'd gotten naked. But he remembered slipping inside her body and wishing that she were Maggie Pryce.

24

Anna—2010

Our first 5K is finally over, and it was incredible. The turnout was better than we'd expected. It was a simple way to continue to promote Gabe's scholarship, and most of the proceeds will go directly to the fund because the overhead was so low. It's funny how we are really getting the hang of all this fundraising stuff. I guess it helps that we are mostly all together at school now, and with unlimited access to each other, we've become a think tank. Some of the ideas we've come up with since we started Gabe's scholarship fund are amazing.

I wasn't sure what it would be like, being back together with the guys in college.

Would we still be friends? Would they still want to hang out with me?

Being a year younger than most of them, I just didn't really know how it would turn out. Part of me wanted to be somewhere by myself, to figure out who I am. You know how that goes. People from your past tend to see only what they know of you. They don't want you to change because they would have to slot you differently then. And how limiting would that be?

College, the first time being on your own, you are supposed to learn who you are, away from your parents and all their expectations for you. So, I was worried about being at the same school with everyone even though the other part of me couldn't imagine being anywhere else because of all we'd been through, because of all we'd already accomplished.

Plus, I truly didn't want to be anywhere away from J.C., Bryce, Fletcher, Max and Kyle. As hard as it is to even think this thought, Gabe's death made me special to all the boys, and I don't really want to become *un*special to them.

Even though we all grew up together, I was just a girl. When Gabe and I started dating, I was still just a girl. At fifteen, it was definitely bros over hos. The boys weren't any nicer to me. They didn't check up on me. We were all just friends in the same way we'd always been friends.

Then, *Gabe died*, and *I became one of them at that moment. They fussed over me* and, included me in everything they did. His death cemented me as an integral part of their group. Gabe's death was difficult but our coming together afterward was one of those special outcomes of the tragedy—at least for me.

As much as I wondered if I was making the right decision to go to school with them, once I got there, it didn't take me long to know. Just like at home, they took care of me. Even though I'd come to visit them my senior year, they showed me around, introduced me to people, got me involved on campus. I would see other girls looking at me, surrounded by them, and I could feel their envy. It felt good to know my place and to be secure in it. Suddenly, it didn't matter to me so much if they kept me in the same box I'd always been in because I was important.

It also made it easier to work on Play for Gabe. We were all together. At first, it'd seemed like every drunken night would end with some conversation about Gabe or what we were doing or what we were going to do.

Some of the ideas we've come up with are pretty amazing. But we'll see. We're taking baby steps.

This 5K was our first one. And based on the outcome, I think we can keep going. It's sort of overwhelming to see the impact of Gabe's passing on our town. People still remember. They remember him and the event of his death. Sometimes, it seems as if that should be enough. But most of the time, it's just a precursor to what it could be—for his death to mean something more, for us to make more of an impact.

I think that's the goal—or it will be. As a group we've talked about that a lot—about being more than a scholarship fund. But the ideas just seem to float around, and no one has grabbed hold and pulled them down to ground them in any substance. But we are all still working together, doing something to continue to move forward, each with our own our roles.

I'm an organizer and a list-maker. I guide them, taking their ideas and helping them come up with the steps to actually achieve them. With the 5K, for instance, I handled the planning, contacted vendors, and figured out how to handle the registration process.

J.C. might be the heart of the operation, but I'm the lifeblood that sustains it.

When Lena pulled into Mike and Lindsay's driveway, she turned the car off and leaned back into the seat.

She could admit to herself that she had her fair share of challenging qualities. She'd demonstrated all of them during her battle with Mike over Nicky playing soccer. Thinking about those months and the rift dividing her and Mike, she actually felt embarrassed by her behavior. Knowing all that had transpired made it that much harder to walk into their home and ask to be involved.

She couldn't, wouldn't apologize. It must have been programmed into her DNA, but she couldn't get her mouth around the word *sorry*. Instead, she would try through her actions to attempt to atone for the chaos she'd caused.

Drawing in a deep breath, she grabbed her bag and headed toward the house.

Walking inside, she heard all the kids' sounds that never failed to make her smile after a long day. Their ability to *just be* was often rejuvenating. Stepping into the kitchen, Lena found Lindsay sitting on a stool at the breakfast bar, leaning over a book, with a glass of wine in one hand.

"Have one of those for me?" she asked.

Lindsay looked up, pleasantly surprised. Standing, she walked toward Lena, gave her a quick hug, and then grabbed a glass from the cabinet. "Of course." She moved back to her perch and poured Lena some wine. "Don't take this the wrong way, but what are you doing here? I thought you had plans with what's-his-name?" She looked mischievously at Lena and winked.

It was no secret among them that Lindsay and Mike didn't really like Mark.

"Ha-ha," Lena responded before taking a healthy swallow of wine. "I do have plans, but I needed to talk to you both." She tried to sound nonchalant, like this was really no big deal.

Unfortunately, there was too much history between them, and Lindsay could read her.

Lindsay studied her. "Everything okay?"

Rolling her eyes, already playing off the importance of the coming conversation, Lena sat down. "Of course. Just need to go over some dates."

Again, Lindsay watched her, and Lena knew the assessment had commenced. Sometimes, having incredibly close friends worked against her.

Lindsay glanced at the clock. "Mike won't be here for a bit, but you already know that."

"Yeah," Lena responded, "I know. Just wanted some pregame girl time."

Lindsay nodded. "Okay." She closed her book and leaned back in her chair. "Thanks, by the way."

"For?"

"Picking up Nicky last night."

"You don't have to thank me for that. He is my son."

"Yes, he is. But we have tried to honor your wishes by handling everything. I got stuck with the girls last night, and something came up at work for Mike."

Lena waved her hand and then took another sip of wine. "Linds, you don't have to explain. No big deal." She toyed with her glass, moving it in slow circles.

"No big deal," Lindsay mimicked, a smile looming on her face. "Right."

It was the way she'd said *right* that grated against Lena's nerves. She fought the desire to say something sarcastic back to her friend. She had her opening. Lindsay had given it to her. She knew, like she always knew, what was going on, and she was subtly giving Lena the ability to have the conversation.

Damn her.

Even though she wasn't ready to start, Lena waded in. "It was weird, ya know"—she looked up from the swirl she had created in her wine glass—"being there. I think the smell hit me first. It was that sort of raw combination of dirt and grass and sweat."

Lindsay stopped smiling. "Lena," she whispered, all sympathy and conciliation laced with gentleness in her voice.

She hated Lindsay's tone of voice. Lena wasn't seeking sympathy here. Looking toward the ceiling, she attempted to gather her thoughts. "I don't think I was expecting that. I was still pissed, to tell the truth." She glanced at her friend and smiled a sad sort of smile that communicated so many things. "I had work I hadn't finished, and it was your night. And Mike was being an ass and then not an ass. I had a list, ya know?"

Again with the all-knowing smile between them.

"I had a tally of how many things I could be mad at him for. And he had to go and take some of the points back, so that pissed me off, too." She paused and took another sip of wine, gathering her thoughts. "When I got there, I somehow foolishly thought that I'd just swing in and get him, right? But I was late, which you know I hate."

Lindsay inserted a quiet, "Yeah."

"And I was wearing stilettos."

"Of course you were. When do you not?"

"Right. And I had to walk to the other side of the fields."

Lindsay laughed, and Lena knew that her friend was imagining her walking across the grass, her expensive shoes sinking into the soft ground. Lena laughed with her.

"But Sarina?" Lena waited for Lindsay's nod of acknowledgment. "She gave me a pair of slides, so I could make it across the field."

Lindsay laughed again.

"You can see me, right? In my pencil skirt and silk blouse with damn soccer slides on. You have the picture in your head?"

Lena knew Lindsay did because she was trying to control her giggles.

Shaking her head, Lena continued, "I walked all the way there, and when I got to where Nicky was sitting, I got hit with it—the smell. Fuck. I smelled him. Then, the guys that Nicky was watching morphed, and I was seeing the Apostles. I couldn't break out of the past."

Smiles and laughter left the room. Lena didn't speak for a moment, and Lindsay didn't push her.

Wanting to get through it, Lena finished her wine. "It was Nicky. It's always Nicky. He made some very know-it-all comment, and I was back."

"I'm sorry," was all Lindsay could manage to say.

"No, it's fine. I mean, it was everything and nothing I'd expected."

Neither of them spoke. Then, they heard the sounds of the kids thumping down the hall. The girls raced into the kitchen, their half-brother on their heels. They skidded to a stop, surprised to see Lena.

"Aunt Lena," the twins screamed in unison. They climbed up onto her stool, and both tried to settle on her lap.

Nicky studied her. "What are you doing here?"

"Hi yourself," Lena responded.

She kissed the girls and untangled them. She stood and made her way over to Nicky, quickly kissing him on the forehead. "Just wanted to chat with your aunt."

He shrugged, tagged Milly, and took off down the hall with the girls chasing him. Lena watched them disappear.

"I know you don't want me to say this, but I am sorry," Lindsay said.

"There's nothing to be sorry for."

"But we promised we wouldn't make you get involved with Nicky playing soccer."

"You promised because I was a complete bitch and made it impossible for you not to promise. God, in the heat of one of my many battles with Mike, I think I actually mentioned court." She shook her head, trying to shake off the memory.

"You did," Lindsay said, nodding.

"So, don't say you're sorry because let's be real…" She paused, met her friend's eyes, and winked at her. "I'm not going to."

Lindsay laughed. "Oh, trust me, I know."

"Yeah," Lena agreed. She continued, more serious now, "The thing is, I could see it—the joy on Nicky's face. He touched the ball once with his foot, and I could tell he knew what he was doing. And"—she took a deep breath—"I don't want to miss out on that."

Lindsay merely nodded.

"And who is this guy, this Coach Cal? I mean, he touched Nicky so casually, just ruffled his hair, and I could tell that my son completely and utterly trusted him. I'm not okay with someone I don't know being in his life."

"I get that."

"I mean, I know that, eventually, there will be people he'll meet that I don't know but I'm not ready for that yet."

Lindsay waited for her to continue.

"So, I need dates, and I need arrangements. And I'll take one night of practice and…" She looked up to the ceiling again because she needed another moment. She couldn't completely lose it. "And I want to be involved."

"Sure."

"No, *I told you*?"

"No. You'll get that from Mike."

Lena laughed, knowing it was true. "So, can we talk dates? I have my calendar."

Leaning against the doorframe, Mike asked, "What's going on?"

Lena and Lindsay looked up from where they sat with an empty bottle of wine and papers and phones spread out between them.

Lena glanced at the time on her phone and laughed. "Shit, I'm going to miss my date."

"No question. There's no way you're driving," Mike said.

Lena surmised that she and Lindsay must look completely drunk, if he'd made that assessment without even taking some time to talk to them.

He rolled his eyes at her when their gazes meet. "I might have had plans with my wife tonight."

Lena laughed. "You have her all weekend. And it's a kid weekend, so you weren't getting lucky."

Lindsay swatted her arm. "You can't possibly know that," she said.

Laughing at the two of them, Mike asked with a nod, "What's going on over there?"

"We are going over dates for soccer. Lena is going to pick up a night, and she wanted to get the tournament dates on her calendar."

A look of shock crossed Mike's face, and he stiffened. Relaxed Mike disappeared and a pissed off Mike turned toward her.

Lindsay started to say something, but before anything could come out of her mouth, Mike cut her off, "What's going on, Lena?"

This time, his tone set her off. This was fatherly Mike with the drop in his voice and the set planes of his face. Lena felt Lindsay stiffening beside her.

"Mike," Lindsay tried again.

Watching him ignore Lindsay, Lena suddenly realized how much she'd hurt them in the recent months. It humbled her because, really, it could have been any number of men. Thankfully, because God owed her one, it'd turned out that Mike was Nicky's father. They'd had paternity tests done to prove it. As much as she hated to admit it, Nicky's parentage had not been an easy guess. At a time when her life was out of control, she and Mike had created Nicky.

In a rare moment of perfect clarity, she threw one of those grateful sentiments to the universe, acknowledging how lucky she was that this man was the father of her child.

"What do I need to explain to you, Mike?" Lena kept her tone light because she was slightly drunk.

But Mike's demeanor didn't change. And Lena recognized it before he opened his mouth. He was truly angry with her. Watching him struggle against that anger amazed her. He'd banked it and locked it away, never breaking stride in their relationship.

"Do you know what you have put us through? What you have put Lindsay through? Lindsay stuck in the middle, between the two of us, is her version of hell. But you couldn't even recognize that. You were so damn busy being mad at me and Nick that you made it difficult for all of us. You threatened to take me to court!" The last sentence reverberated around the room, taking on a life of its own.

Lena visibly cringed, but his anger was like a sieve, draining away her sorry and leaving only her defensiveness. She felt Lindsay's hand on her arm as she stood up, preparing for battle. Turning to look at her friend, she saw the plea for peace reflected on Lindsay's face, the same look she'd given Mike when he walked into the kitchen. But it hadn't worked on Mike.

Before Lena could act, Mike pulled away from the wall and made his way toward her. He placed his hand on her shoulder and pulled her toward him into a hug.

Speaking to her in a hushed tone, he said, "I was there. I remember what you went through. I do, and I'm sympathetic. But you hurt Lindsay and our family with your three-month temper tantrum."

Lena stood stiffly in his arms, listening.

"I know this is going to be difficult for you, but it's not about you. Even though I want to throttle you, I do not want to sleep on the couch, which is what would happen if I really let you have it."

This made Lena smile sadly. Mike stepped away from her but continued to hold on to her shoulders. Gently kissing her on the forehead, he pushed her down onto the stool.

Slightly dazed by Mike's Dr. Jekyll and Mr. Hyde routine, Lena picked up her glass and took another large sip.

She saw the radiance of Lindsay's smile out of her peripheral vision and knew that Mike would be rewarded for his show of restraint.

Lena felt regret slice through her for the soccer debacle. She realized that Mike had played her like a maestro conducting his orchestra. Had he continued yelling at her, her defensiveness would have moved them in the wrong direction. He'd completely defused the situation.

Before she could think, she looked up at him and said, "I'm sorry."

He merely bowed his head in acknowledgment. "I'll have the kids start cleaning up and order some pizza."

Lindsay wrapped her arm around Lena's shoulder and leaned her head down. "It's going to be okay," she murmured.

"I hope so," Lena returned.

Silence descended between them. Lindsay moved away from her to open another bottle of wine.

Lena heard the bath running and realized how late it was. "I guess I should cancel my date, huh?" she remarked.

"Ya think? And can you get rid of him at the same time?"

"He's harmless, just a way to pass the time," Lena answered truthfully. She had no illusions about the time she had been spending with Mark. But it did give her the opening she needed to ask some questions about the other thing bothering her about soccer. "So, what can you tell me about Nicky's coach?"

Lindsay paused in the act of pouring the wine. She glanced briefly at Lena with a look that Lena was unable to decipher.

"Uh, I can't tell you a whole lot. Seems like a good guy. Was proficient with communicating his expectations at the parent meeting. The kids seem to love him, and he seems to know what he's doing. Is that what you were looking for?"

"No, not really."

Lindsay cocked her head to the side. "What else are you interested in knowing?"

"I'm not sure."

"Okay," Lindsay responded. "Am I supposed to know what to do with that?"

Lena laughed. "No. Being there was just a strange experience. And aside from how he interacted with Nicky, for a moment, I felt like I knew him. So, I guess I'm asking if he seemed familiar to you."

"No, not at all."

"Do you have to see him often?"

Lindsay narrowed her eyes. "What's going on? Did your mommy radar go off or something? If you feel weird about him being around Nicky, I'll talk to Mike about it."

Lena laughed again. "It's not that. He just made me feel different."

"Different, how?"

Huffing and rolling her eyes, Lena answered flippantly, "Like goose bumps and lightning bolts."

Lindsay's eyes got wide, but otherwise, she remained still and silent. When Lindsay had realized that she was attracted to Mike, she'd used the exact phrase. She'd reserved it for him alone. She'd never said it before, and Lena had never said it. So, even though Lena had tried to act like it was no big deal, she knew Lindsay understood that this was a big deal.

"So, if there's any way I could avoid him, I'd like that."

"Why would you want to avoid that?" Lindsay asked.

Lena quirked her brow. "How old is he?"

"He's twenty-three, and he just graduated from college."

"I figured. I just think it's a good idea if I stayed clear of him."

"Because he's young?" Lindsay attempted to clarify.

"Well, that, but more importantly, I just didn't like the way he made me feel."

"Like?" Lindsay asked.

"Out of control," she said.

Although her tone conveyed finality, Lena was sure Lindsay had heard the underlying uncertainty.

When he was younger, J.C. remembered feeling like it took forever for his first tournament to arrive. Now, as a coach, he looked at it differently. It didn't feel like he'd had enough time to get his team ready.

But as he and Bryce loaded his truck for their first tournament, he found he was eager to escape town even if his team wasn't quite ready. He'd splurged on a hotel right on the beach, hoping he could find the balance he needed after the craziness of the last week.

He was quiet on the way over, but Bryce needed to study for the LSAT, so the silent ride seemed to give them both what they wanted. They were about thirty minutes away when Bryce stopped what he was doing, and the inquisition began.

"You want to tell me what you were thinking?" he asked.

J.C. continued to watch the road, thankful for an excuse not to look at his friend.

"What?" He tried to sound confused, like he didn't know the subject Bryce was broaching.

"Don't act like you don't know what I'm talking about." Bryce paused. "Anna."

Before he could stop it, J.C. remembered waking up, hungover, with Anna wrapped around him. It had been an uncomfortable morning.

When Bryce's hand knocked him in the back of his head, he turned to glare at his friend.

"What the hell? I'm driving." It was the best protest he could manage.

"It's not just Anna. But she's the most important thing at the moment. How the hell are you going to fix this?"

"I thought I already did," he mumbled.

His conversation with Anna had been painful. She was hurt, as she should have been. But Bryce didn't see the same things in Anna that he did. Bryce liked to pretend her edges were dull and smooth when J.C. tended to see the sharp and jagged in her. With the distance of the week, J.C. could admit he'd been really messed up over seeing Maggie Pryce.

"Look, Anna and I talked. It might be awkward for a bit, but we were both drunk, and we did something stupid. She and I have already handled it. You just need to catch up," he said as he continued to drive, not taking his eyes from the road so that he wouldn't have to deal with the doubt etched on Bryce's face.

"Honestly, she said the same thing. And I think I'm the only one who knows. Just wasn't expecting to see her in your bed when I walked into the room."

"This is why I've been trying to get you to knock for years." J.C. chuckled but noted the absence of Bryce's laughter.

"Stop trying to make light of this! This changes things."

More than you know, J.C. thought.

Those three words from Bryce seemed like some kind of prophecy to J.C., and as the silence settled between them, he noted the tension and hated the unintended consequences of his actions.

Bryce let out a low whistle, and relief skittered through J.C. as they pulled up to the hotel.

"I love when you let the five-star silver spoon out," Bryce commented, the earlier exchange seemingly tabled.

J.C. just smiled. "My mom had points. She let me talk her out of them."

"I like it."

Still smiling, J.C. admitted, "Me, too."

"Does it have a bar? Please tell me it has a bar."

"It does, and I'm ready to hit it after I head down to the beach."

Bryce laughed as he climbed out of the truck. "Did you think I wanted to do that in a different order?"

"Nah."

They checked in, changed clothes, and walked down to the beach. It was hot and sticky, the kind of day where the only place to be outside was near the water. J.C. and Bryce had grown up on the Atlantic Coast, so the rolling waves seemed to be welcoming them home. They swam for a while, soaking up the water and the rays, enjoying the hotel-owned beach and its privacy. Then, they sat in the sand on the edge of the water, letting the ocean wash over them with each crest of the tide.

"You ready for that beer?" J.C. asked.

"Almost. I think I want to study for a little while longer," Bryce said as he got up to return to the hotel room.

"Cool. I'll hang out here. Just let me know when you're ready."

The unexpected time alone was not necessarily what J.C. needed. He'd managed to stay busy all week to keep the craziness of sleeping with Anna at bay.

In those few moments, before the reality of what he'd done had crashed around him, J.C. had lain awake, thinking of only one thing—Maggie Pryce. The idea that their paths had somehow converged still seemed completely unlikely to him. So many years had passed, and so many things had happened. To see her and know in an instant that he was greeting Maggie Pryce had spoken to him in some way. He knew the significance of the recognition. He just didn't understand yet what it meant.

After years of following down this path, he found that his life and his future suddenly appeared like a maze with confusing twists and turns. Why Maggie's appearance felt like the breadcrumbs he needed to find his way out, he wasn't sure. But he intended to find out.

"Coach Cal!"

J.C. turned his head toward the sound and saw Nick running along the shoreline toward him, two little girls dogging his heels. Behind them, two women were walking, casually following. Without being able to see her face, J.C. knew the woman on the left was Maggie.

He got up and walked toward Nick, holding out his fist. Nick returned the requisite fist bump.

"Is Coach B here?" Nick asked.

"He is. He just left the beach to go study," J.C. explained.

"Can you swim with me? My mom and Aunt Linds are being girlie. They don't want to get their hair wet."

J.C. tried not to laugh, but the look of disgust on Nick's face was sort of priceless.

"Who are these two?" J.C. asked as he squatted down to their level.

They were identical, but J.C. could tell immediately that their personalities differed.

One of them said quite clearly, "I'm Milly, and this is Jessie."

Two blonde-haired, blue-eyed little girls looked at him.

"I'm Coach Cal."

Milly stepped closer to him. "Can you swim?"

"I can," he responded.

"I mean, now. Can you swim with us now?"

He looked up the beach. The women were still too far away to ask, so he attempted to stall, "We should probably wait to ask your mom."

"My mom won't care," Nick said, "as long as she doesn't have to get wet."

"Well, let's wait and ask her." He stood up. "I don't want to get on her bad side," he said low so that only Nick could hear him, like it was a big secret, something confidential.

Nick nodded his head like he understood.

Knowing Nick was Gabe's nephew made J.C. want to connect with him. J.C. tried to avoid any thoughts of Nick's mother and the complications of withholding their past. He sat down in the sand with the three of them, and they started building castles.

"Mom, Coach Cal said he'd take me swimming," Nick said as soon as the women were within ten feet of their sand-castle party.

J.C. jumped quickly to his feet. "Actually," he tried to explain quickly, "we were just talking about whether or not I could swim."

He didn't think about the sand all over him or the four other people around them. Once Maggie's gaze was focused on him, he stopped thinking completely. He just took her in. Like a fragrance he couldn't get enough of, he wanted to inhale her, bask in her, be surrounded by her. When he'd seen her at the fields, she'd stunned him. Now, at the sight of her in shorts and a T-shirt with her black hair swept up in a messy ponytail, he felt almost faint.

Her face narrowed into a slightly pointed chin, accentuating the exotic shape of her dark eyes. He realized he was staring at her when he heard a throat being cleared.

Turning his head to the side, he looked toward her companion. "Hey, Mrs. Fasanelli."

"Lindsay's fine," she answered.

He could see her amused expression and knew he'd made a total fool of himself. He felt like he was fifteen years old all over again.

"You sure you're up for swimming with the three of them?" Lindsay asked.

He laughed and winked at her. "Do you think they gave me a choice?"

Chuckling, Lindsay responded, "I'm sure they didn't."

"So, can we go, Mom?" Nick pestered.

His persistence amused J.C.

He knew he had to look at Maggie again, but he hesitated, afraid to get pulled back in. She didn't speak, and J.C. knew she was waiting for him to turn toward her. When he did, he found her looking at him with a hint of a challenge reflected in her chocolate gaze and raised her eyebrows. He could tell she was questioning whether he could handle the kids, and before he realized he was answering her with a look of his own, she laughed.

Without taking her eyes off of J.C, Maggie said to Nick, "You can go swimming but just for a bit. We need to meet your father for dinner soon."

J.C. couldn't resist. He winked at her and flashed a big smile before he scooped Milly and Jessie up and waded into the Atlantic.

Lindsay waited until the kids were knee-deep in the water before she turned toward Lena and whistled low. "What was that?"

Lena looked back at her friend. "What do you mean?"

Lindsay laughed. "Um, that was hot and a bit unsettling."

"Hmm. Hot and unsettling. Unsettling, for sure."

Lindsay and Lena watched the water closely in case Coach Cal needed any saving.

"He seems to have that all under control, doesn't he?" Lindsay mused.

Lena continued to watch, sort of enthralled with his ability to handle all three of them. Even on her best day, they would exhaust the hell out of her. Coach Cal had Jessie on his shoulders as Milly and Nick swam around them, splashing at him, trying to steal his attention. He'd picked up on Jessie's reticence and found a way to get her to play with them, and it endeared him to Lena.

"What was that silent communication back there? When he got all tongue-tied and starry-eyed, I figured he would be no match for you, but then you guys had that little..." Lindsay stopped, trying to find a way to explain what she'd seen. "What was that?"

Lena smiled uncertainly. "I'm not sure. I think I threw down the gauntlet, and he picked it up."

"Yeah. I think my first assessment was incorrect," Lindsay mused out loud.

"Which assessment?"

"The one in my head."

"Which was?"

"That he's too young for you."

"Ha. Well, you might have changed your thoughts on that, but I haven't. He's way too young for me. I mean, at twenty-three, do you even have a job or a home of your own? I don't remember twenty-three. It's one of those years that's blurred with baby poop and utter sadness."

"Yeah, I have the same memories. I don't know what normal people do at that age."

"What I do know is that I didn't know anything worth sharing with anyone else. If it hadn't been for Nicky, it would have been all about me. I can't afford that in my life right now."

"I'm not sure how you are going to be able to stay away. That was some serious chemistry."

"Oh, I know. But it's not like our worlds overlap, except for at six soccer tournaments a year."

But just as Lena said that, Cal looked over at her, and their eyes locked. Even though his attention was on her, he still managed to keep the kids engaged and seemed to know exactly what each of them was doing. Watching him made her want to retract all of her reasons for staying away from him.

Lena had never really let practicality get in the way of what she wanted to do. But this decision, this line in the sand, seemed more like self-preservation than practicality. The whole mind meld thing

44

was scary. It had only ever happened once before at her brother's funeral, and it wasn't an instance that she wanted to remember.

She looked away, only to find that Lindsay was watching her, watching them.

"You are in trouble," she remarked matter-of-factly.

"No, Linds, I'm not." Glancing at her watch, Lena was relieved to find that they needed to get back to the hotel to make dinner. "We have to get inside."

Lindsay looked at her phone. "All right, guys and girls, time to get out," she called over the sound of the surf.

Lena couldn't help but smile as all four of them stopped frolicking and began making their way to the shore. Lindsay was one of those women who made motherhood look easy. Where Lena would have yelled at them, Lindsay never raised her voice, never looked frazzled, never seemed to break stride. In contrast to Lena's own experience with Nicky, Lindsay was Mother of the Year. Lena and Lindsay often joked that Lindsay had learned through the mistakes they had made with Nicky. And if Lena didn't love her so much, she would hate Lindsay.

She couldn't be sure if it was Lindsay's delivery or the help of Coach Cal, but the kids exited the water with little fuss. Nicky ran ahead, and the girls were quick to run after him, leaving Lindsay, Lena, and Coach Cal bringing up the rear.

As they made their way toward the hotel, Lena saw Lindsay glance over at her, and she winked.

Before Lena could stop the train wreck that was about to happen, Lindsay paused at the door leading into the hotel. "You should join us for dinner tonight," she said to Cal.

As they stepped into the cool air of the hotel lobby, Lena had to fight hard to keep the groan from escaping her mouth. Cal glanced back at her quickly, definitely seeking her approval. Had it been merely a asking for permission, she would have shaken her head, making him refuse. But he wasn't looking at her like that. He was staring at her with a challenge in his eyes, almost daring her to deny him. And damn if that didn't make her want to see where this would take them.

So, there she was, extending the invitation with her eyes, before she opened her mouth. "As long as you are okay with kid-friendly," Lena added.

"Is that code for nonalcoholic?" he asked, a hint of mischief making his dark eyes gleam.

Lindsay and Lena burst out laughing.

"Sobriety at dinner can be a liability with the girls and Nick," Lindsay responded.

"Count me in."

"Great," Lindsay responded. "I'll have Mike text you."

"See you later." Cal said.

By the time they made it to dinner, the list of diners had grown exponentially. The small family dinner Lena had imagined did not include Sarina's family and both coaches. But as she watched the conversations happening around her, she finally relaxed.

Over the years, Mike, Lindsay, and Lena had gotten smarter about their choice of restaurants. Now, they knew to pick places that allowed for loud, active children and included separate tables and access to games. Because of the seating arrangements, Lena had ended up clear on the other side of the table from Coach Cal, too far away for conversation and too awkward for eye contact. But she watched—a lot.

The other coach, whom everyone referred to as Coach B, shared an easy familiarity with Cal that spoke of longtime friendship. The banter between the two coaches reminded her of her own relationship with Lindsay and Mike. She was still acting as the observer when a question broke through the chatter and brought it to an expectant halt.

"You all seem so well-adjusted. How does this work?" Sarina asked Lena.

It was a common getting-to-know-you question that, with new people, Lindsay, Mike, and Lena had to field at some point. The routine was written in stone somewhere—who started the story, where the others interjected, when to pause for laughter.

So, Lena leaned in, somehow comfortable enough with this tiny crowd to take her spot on their stage. She began, "Lindsay and

I were college roommates," she said to Sarina's familiar request for an explanation of their family. "I dragged her on every adventure I wanted to take." She paused to smile at her friend, telling her with that subtle smile that she was going to go full tilt this time. "I was the typical sheltered daughter who went to college and let loose."

"Very loose," Lindsay interjected.

Pause and cue laughter.

"Yeah, pretty loose. Lots of drinking and debauchery while still managing to handle my business in the classroom."

"Only because she didn't want to end up back at home. She enjoyed the being-on-her-own thing—a lot."

"I did," Lena responded.

She took a sip of her wine and a quick look at Cal, who had zeroed in on her. The intensity of his stare both intrigued and confused her, but she had lines she needed to supply, so she whipped her eyes back to Sarina.

"So, we spent three and a half years like that—studying, partying, doing things that we hope our children will never do."

Another pause for laughter.

"Then, one night, we met Mike at a bar. He was this serious older guy, and I decided that he'd be my next Mr. One Night." Lena understood that, at this point, she was either going to lose friends or gain understanding. It was the way it worked.

But somehow, she already knew that Sarina fit in, and her husband, Jeb, seemed to also. There was no judgment here. But Lena refrained from looking at the two coaches. Belatedly, she thought that this was an inappropriate story to share with her kid's coach, but she had already gone too far. And really, it'd ended well, so maybe there was a lesson in it somewhere.

Mike picked up. "You can imagine how horrified I was to get a call a few months later. Lena explained that she was pregnant, and she was pretty sure that I was the father. December sixth changed my life."

He reached over and grabbed Lena's hand for the difficult part of the story. She continued to look down and let Lindsay pick it up.

"Lena's ultra-strict parents weren't too happy, so it was just Lena now—well, and the best friend ever."

Pause for laughter.

"Lena was pregnant, and we were seniors in college, really close to finishing. We stayed in our place but decided that when our lease was up, we'd move into Mike's house in Sarasota and make a go of this parenting thing," Lindsay explained.

Pause for comment.

Like they were all reading from the same script, Sarina asked, "The three of you?"

"Yeah. Lena was in a bachelor's and master's program for accounting. When she completed it at the end of five years, she had everything needed to sit for the CPA exam. Someone needed to help out with the baby, and since I was done with my coursework and had my degree, I offered."

"That's some friendship."

This was a new comment, not written down, and it had come out of Cal's mouth. It was delivered on a laugh, but Lena looked at him hard, annoyed at him for interrupting their flow. He met her gaze, and she figured he was judging her.

Lindsay stepped in. "At the time, Lena didn't have anyone else in her corner, and we'd been through a lot. It could have just as easily been me. At twenty-three, your life is all about you, so you can make whatever choice you want."

It was a gentle slap but a slap nonetheless, and Lena saw that it hit him right where Lindsay had intended.

"So, the three of you and an infant lived together, but there were no relations going on?" Sarina asked with a twinkle in her eye.

Lena could hug her for bringing them back to the humor in the situation.

Lena laughed. "Relations had long before been shut down. We were like *Three Men and a Baby*. We struggled that first year, and then we kind of hit our stride."

"All parents are like that. I didn't know what we were doing with our first. Complete trial and error." Sarina confirmed. "At least for us."

Lena and Sarina shared a look, understanding passing between them.

"Then, one day, I came home, and Lindsay and Mike were chatting in the kitchen while Nicky was playing with a ball, kicking it around. And there just seemed to be this denied attraction between the two of them. So, I started planting seeds in both of their heads."

"She loves taking credit for this," Mike interjected.

"I take total credit for it. Anyway, once they realized that they felt the same way, everything happened kind of quickly from there—the falling in love, the getting married, and the twins weren't too far behind. So, that's the story." She laughed and picked up her wine, needing some liquid fortitude. After placing it down, she said, "Oh, and Nicky and I moved out somewhere in between."

She completely resisted looking back at Coach Cal because she didn't want him to see how disappointed she was in his response.

"Was that hard—when you moved out?" Sarina asked.

Mike answered, "It was awful. But Lena gets pretty determined, and she wanted Lindsay and I to be able to figure our relationship out on our own. It was the right thing, but it was hard, being away from my son. I mean, getting Lena out of there was awesome."

Everyone laughed. This was the standard response, but Lena knew that Mike always felt bad saying it, so she wasn't surprised when he stood up and pulled gently on her ponytail, placing a brotherly kiss on the side of her head. He always found some way to touch her when this part of the conversation came around. They might have made a child together, but she was like his little sister now. She watched him disappear and knew he was going to get the check.

Smiling softly, she looked to Lindsay and winked.

Lindsay used to ask Lena what she thought would happen when she found someone who actually meant something to her. But Lena wasn't one to try to figure out the future. Her past had taught her that she couldn't predict anything. So, Lindsay had stopped asking, and Lena had stopped thinking that it would ever happen..

I'm an ass, J.C. thought as he and Bryce made their way out of the restaurant and back to the hotel.

He had known the beginning part of that story. Gabe had told him. The night before he'd collapsed, after their victory, as they'd sat on the beach, Gabe had told him about Maggie being pregnant.

She'd come home for Thanksgiving and told their parents. They'd kicked her out. It had been a horrible fight, and Gabe had been torn up about it, which was the only reason he'd shared it with J.C.

Gabe had one of those rare sibling relationships with his sister and telling J.C. had made him feel like he was betraying Maggie, but he'd needed to get it out. So, J.C. had listened and hadn't judged— not like he had in the restaurant when he was a complete ass.

"Cool people," Bryce remarked as they made their way back to their room.

"Yeah," was all J.C. could manage to say.

Sliding the key card in the door, he pushed it open. Walking directly to the little refrigerator, he pulled out two beers and handed one to Bryce.

Bryce popped the top and sat on the bed, swinging his legs out in front of him. "You think our parents sat around with our coaches and drank and told stories?"

J.C. leaned back on the headboard as he answered, "How else do you think they got through all those tournaments? They needed something to entertain them."

"I guess." Bryce tipped his beer back and drank deeply. "Funny to think we were this young when we all met and started playing."

J.C. could hear the whispers of reminiscing seeping through Bryce's words. He wasn't sure he was up for that tonight, but he also wasn't one to deny his friends.

"Yeah, we were tiny."

"Seems odd to start coaching the same age group. Something about coaching kids that age brings it all back. Think about if these kids stay together like we did."

"I don't want to think about that," J.C. said more harshly than he meant. He didn't want Gabe's memory with him tonight. It had been dogging him for days.

"Do you ever wonder how things would have been if he had lived? I mean, would we all still be friends? What would you be doing with your life if you didn't have Play for Gabe—or whatever the new name is going to be?"

"That's a lot of what-ifs." This was not a game that J.C. enjoyed playing.

When he thought about how they'd all stayed together and he realized they'd built their futures around finding a way to make

Gabe's death mean something, it didn't seem to make sense to attempt to think about how it could have all been different. It wasn't different. This was what life had thrown at them.

"Do you think about it though?"

J.C. leaned his head back, looking toward the ceiling for some answer. "I try not to. What's the point of that?" He could almost hear Bryce smiling. Rolling his head to the side, he looked over at his closest friend. "This conversation is depressing as hell."

"I know."

"Let's just drink beer and stop acting like girls."

Bryce laughed. "Okay." He got up from the bed and headed back to the fridge. Tossing a beer to J.C., he said, "Can we talk about the hot soccer moms then?"

J.C. couldn't help but laugh. "Sure, hot soccer moms is much safer than playing What If Gabe Lived?"

"Because that was an impressive array of talent assembled around the table tonight."

"Ha. Yes, it was."

"Makes me a little excited to think of the views I'll have from the sidelines."

J.C. laughed. "Hard to argue with that."

It was midnight when they ran out of beer and safe topics of conversation. They'd talked about strategies for their first game and discussed substitution patterns. They'd argued about college football and their hopes for their alma mater to win a national championship. They had gone over Bryce's law school options and compiled a pro-con list for his decision-making process.

J.C. was tired and a little drunk, but they had a late game the next day, and there was no reason for them to stop drinking now.

"I'll make a beer run downstairs," J.C. said.

"We can probably get a six-pack down the road for what one beer is going to cost you down there."

"I know, but neither one of us is driving."

Bryce shrugged. "Okay. But watch out for little soccer players running around."

"It's after midnight. I'll be lucky if the bar's open. I'm fairly certain there won't be any seven- or eight-year-old kids running around."

"Don't say I didn't warn you," Bryce said as he turned toward the TV.

"Famous last words," J.C. said as he strode toward the door with more beer on his mind.

On his walk down the hall toward the elevator, he realized he was drunker than he'd thought. Smiling to himself at the discovery, he pushed the Down button and waited. As he stepped into the elevator, he was somewhat surprised to find that it was occupied. He glanced up and almost groaned when he saw Lena standing there, a look of hostility on her face.

As the elevator doors closed behind him, he met her glare with a look of understanding. Before he could think about his actions, he moved in close to her, pressing her into the back of the elevator.

He reached up with his right hand and placed it on the wall behind her head. Looking down into her eyes, he said, "I wasn't judging you."

Without any further explanation from him, he could see her get it. It was almost as if they'd picked up the thread of an earlier conversation.

"It's a screening process."

"What is?" J.C. asked, confused.

"I didn't mean to put it into play tonight with you, but the question was asked. The reaction always determines who is going to stick around and who isn't."

The hostility dissipated, replaced by a matter-of-fact resignation.

J.C. dropped his hand to her cheek. The heat of her skin warmed his fingers, still cold from holding his beer.

He captured her gaze, and then he repeated, "I wasn't judging you."

Imperceptibly, she shook her head, telling him that she didn't care or didn't believe him. Even though he couldn't figure out which, his awareness of her intensified—her shuddered breath, the scent of her, the look in her eyes. He dipped his head to her left ear. His hand moved, framing her face. He felt the shiver run through her.

"I wasn't judging you. I was trying to fight the images of you being with other people."

He heard her take in an exaggerated breath that seemed to skip in the silence. Her nearness was messing with his brain. He leaned into her where his hands held her face, moving toward her mouth.

The elevator bumped to a stop. Before the doors opened, J.C. let his breath whisper across her mouth, a kiss of mingled air. Then, he grabbed her hand. Instead of heading to the bar, he moved in the opposite direction, to the door leading to the beach, Bryce forgotten. She didn't offer any resistance, so he kept moving forward.

J.C. pulled a towel from the rack as he made his way across the pool deck. They reached the gate to the boardwalk. He paused and turned back to her. He wasn't sure what he'd wanted to see when their eyes met, but blankness in her expression wasn't it. He almost stopped and let her go, but he'd gone this far, so he continued.

He walked as close to the water as he could get while still feeling dry sand. He threw the towel down and sat, bringing her with him. Bending his knees, he placed his elbows on them and leaned forward, letting the roll of the ocean calm him. They were both quiet for a few moments, letting their breathing even out, their desire cool.

"Tell me something else," he said.

He could feel her cock her head to the side, one of her mannerisms that he already knew.

"Like what?" she asked.

"Something not already patented." He heard her soft laughter but continued studying the ocean. "Some part of the story that you leave out."

"Why?"

He turned his head this time. "I want you to give me something that you haven't given to other people."

Cal intrigued Lena, wanting something she'd left out. She'd told the story enough times that it felt like there was nothing else to it, no hidden anecdotes, no unsaid words.

So, she decided on teasing. "Like an incriminating secret detail?" she asked.

Watching the glint in his eyes, she smiled. He didn't look confused at all, which was what she had been hoping for.

"Oh, you need an explanation?" he asked.

"Yes." She didn't need an explanation, but he fascinated her, and she wanted to see what he could come up with on the fly.

"All right," he responded in the spirit of her teasing. "Think of it like jousting."

Maybe the interaction in the elevator had messed with her more than she'd thought because she found herself laughing loudly.

"If I were a knight and was about to find death in a tournament, I'd look for someone to be my champion." He smirked at her. "So, come on, throw me your handkerchief."

"You're so damn cute," she said before she could even think about what was coming out of her mouth.

"Okay, now, you're just being cruel. That's just what every guy wants to hear." He shook his head in mock discouragement and then shifted his gaze back to her. "So, what've you got?"

She felt off-balance with him.

At dinner, she'd written him off. She had seen his face, the look in his eyes. The disappointment she had felt was quick and hard. Then, she'd remembered that she had nothing invested in this nor had she wanted to. But now, he was winning her over, and she didn't think she was going to fight it—at least, not at the moment.

He waited patiently, and she stalled, trying to think about what she normally doled out, wondering about the impact of pulling on the threads of old memories. There were many that she'd left waving in the wind of her mind, never finding purchase because she wouldn't give them a tether. So, this request, while invasive, made her feel a little giddy, like a child set loose with an unlimited budget in a candy store.

She'd been holding on so tightly to herself in the last few years, preserving the little pieces, keeping them safe for Nicky.

Because I've given so many pieces away.

That was what her parents had accused her of—parceling parts of her soul along with her body until all that was left was a hollow shell. At the time, she hadn't gotten it. She had still been whole then, the night of those accusations and recriminations. It wasn't until a few days later when she'd understood empty. Her parents had been a few days early with the hollow designation. Because she'd been full of all those parts of her soul, she just couldn't figure out how to get them to fit together.

Maybe, she thought *Cal could find a semblance of order.*

"The night I told my parents, we had this insane fight. I mean, I'd known they would be mad. They were Catholic, and the whole out-of-wedlock thing was too much for them. Talk about medieval."

She briefly looked at him, and he gave her a wry smile.

"Anyway, no one was really yelling. We were having this horrible fight, tearing our family apart, but everyone was just talking in normal voices. So, my little brother had no idea what he was walking into. But he'd heard enough to be really upset, and he was the first one to lose his cool. He was so mad at me for being irresponsible and upset with my parents for being unforgiving that he took off out of the house. I went after him, happy for the reprieve from my parents. We were both running. Tears were streaming down my face, and I was yelling at him to stop.

"Then, I felt this tug in my gut, and something warm started running down my legs. And my voice must have changed because he stopped immediately and came back to me. We ended up at the hospital, the two of us. I thought I was having a miscarriage. I was sure it was God's way of keeping me from getting an abortion. I couldn't help but think that this was all a blessing.

"But the doctor did an ultrasound, and the baby was, still there. The bleeding was odd, but I wasn't having a miscarriage. And once my brother saw the baby, there was no way I could have an abortion. A couple of days later, I called Mike."

Cal and Lena were quiet for a moment.

"No one knows that story."

Mike and Lindsay didn't even know. All Lindsay had known was that Lena had changed her mind when she came home, and she'd decided to have the baby. Mike was never told about her plans to have an abortion.

Cal remained quiet, which was exactly what she needed in that moment. It felt odd to talk about her brother. She rarely did it. But recently, he'd been more present. Still, something about this man tapped into her in a different way. What she'd been avoiding, what she refused to acknowledge, was that he was the same age her brother would have been right now. That alone should make her deny this attraction between them, but for some reason, she hadn't yet.

"Okay," she said, breaking the intentional silence between them, "my turn."

"Your turn for what?" he responded.

"I get to ask you a question."

"A question. Not a deep, dark secret?"

"There will be a time for a deep, dark secret, but it's not now." Now, she wanted the light banter back.

"I'm waiting," he said.

"What's your name? Because I can't keep calling you Coach Cal."

He laughed, and she could tell that her request was not what he had expected.

"Okay, my name is Jackson."

"Jackson Cal?" she said, the skepticism clear in her voice.

"No," he responded, shaking his head.

He paused, like he had to think about what he was going to say.

She nudged him with her shoulder. "Is this a difficult question? You asked for something far more difficult than my name." She laughed. She enjoyed teasing him.

"Callahan."

"Jackson Callahan. Can I call you Jackson?"

"No one calls me Jackson," he said with some wonder, like he'd never realized it before now.

"No one? Not even your mother?"

"No one."

"Perfect," she said with a wicked smile.

"Don't be offended if I don't answer," he quipped. "I probably won't recognize the name."

She laughed. "Whatever, Jackson."

"Funny," he mumbled.

"The tide's coming in, Jackson," she said on a laugh but then noticed it was true. It was also getting late.

He shifted beside her. "Yeah, it is. We've been out here for a while."

"Yes, we have, Jackson."

She could feel his light chuckle even though the sound was lost on the rolling of the waves.

He turned to look at her when he said, "That could get annoying."

And she was caught. His dark gaze locked with hers, and she belatedly noticed they had avoided looking at each other most of the time they had been here. She couldn't decide if it was a good thing or a bad thing because she couldn't look away.

All the joking washed out with the next wave, and suddenly, there was all this silence and heat trapped between them. The five seconds of contact in the elevator flashed through her mind, and she thought she could go down this path. It was an impulse, a heartbeat, a second of a thought.

J.C. felt her leaning forward, toward him. Her mouth was slightly open, enticing him with a glimpse of her tongue as it wet her bottom lip and then settled. Even in the dark of the night, he could see her decision, felt it between them. His desire to kiss her pounded through him, the physical connection so close that he could almost sink into it.

He turned his body because he knew, even before he'd tasted, that quick and light wouldn't be enough. Pulling his hand from the edge of the towel, he felt the granules of sand on the tips of his fingers, his thumb doing a quick swipe as it made its way to the nape of her neck. It was like he had extra sensory feeling as he could count each fleck of sand that fell from his hand. The slow motion of his movements increased his impatience to touch her. When his thumb made contact with her jaw and his fingers wrapped around the back of her neck, his relief escaped on a heavy sigh.

"Jackson," she whispered before moving into his kiss.

Not J.C.

His hand tightened on her neck, stopping her forward progress. But when he would have pulled away and worked for space, she kept coming, closing the gap between them. The decision taken out of his hands, her mouth met his. He fell into it for a moment, opening under her, letting her come into him.

He didn't give himself time to enjoy it. Jerking away from her, he unwrapped his hand and carefully placed it back in the sand, immediately creating distance between them. He glanced at her, expecting to see confusion but she was smiling. It was a confident smile, almost like she was telling him that she understood his hesitation. Their eerie silent communication shimmered between them.

But she couldn't possibly know what he was holding back.

Does giving her my name count even though I didn't connect the dots for her? The thought ran through his brain as he sat there, listening to the ocean beating against the sand. Next to her warmth, he was surrounded by the scent of her and the beach. *Two favorite things*, he thought.

He could enjoy being here in this place with this woman, but he understood that it had to be fleeting. A grain of sand would have a better chance of experiencing a hurricane and ending up on the same beach than he would have of surviving this secret he just couldn't seem to push out of his mouth. He'd thought or maybe hoped, that, she might have put it together without any context.

He hadn't thought she'd have honored his request to share something with him.

Who would impart such a personal story with a virtual stranger?

He thought part of the answer was because of his interloper status.

Gabe had shared many of Lena's misadventures, often with the ruefulness one might have when recounting the mishaps of a wayward puppy.

"You'll never guess what Maggie did this time," was often the start of many of Gabe's stories.

It was a little hard to reconcile Gabe's Maggie with the self-possessed Lena sitting beside him. But J.C. sensed the impulsiveness in the way she'd recounted what had to have been a painful memory. She hadn't really even seemed to think about it. He'd asked, and she'd given.

"That was probably pretty stupid," Lena remarked as she shoulder-bumped him, her voice more mischief than regret.

"Yeah," he mumbled, regretting it for more reasons than she knew. Aside from the obvious, being the fool that he was, he'd stopped kissing her.

"I'm sure there are some parent-coach fraternization rules," she teased.

He couldn't help it when he laughed with her. "Probably," he said, turning his head so that he could see her. Belatedly, he recalled that he'd dragged her out here from the elevator. "Where were you going when I hijacked you?"

She smiled at his choice of words. "Hijacked, huh? More like, yanked, but that's just semantics." She laughed again. "To the bar to meet Lindsay and Sarina."

"Sorry," he said even though the sentiment was false. "Aren't they wondering where you are?"

"Nah. I snapped a picture of your ass with your hand pulling mine forward and sent it to Lindsay."

"No, you didn't. I would have noticed."

"Nope. You were pretty intent with your pulling and hijacking." She didn't smile, and she wasn't acting like she was messing with him.

"Let me see."

"It was a snap."

"You didn't have time to Snapchat."

"You calling me a liar?" she challenged.

He stopped the banter and intently looked at her. She looked back at him just as intently. Her big brown eyes were wide with feigned innocence, and a playful smile hovered on her lips.

He didn't try to stop himself this time as he felt the impulse to kiss her. With his hands on her jaw, cradling her face, his mouth was on her, opening, delving, tangling. The roll of the ocean was gone, the beach disappearing. It was just her—the scent of her skin, the beating of her heart, the taste of her mouth. He was lost.

When she ended the kiss and he was plunged back into consciousness, she was on his lap with her feet flat on the towel, her arms around his neck, their foreheads touching.

New favorite thing, he thought, *Lena Pryce wrapped around me.*

The fact that she was now Lena in his head filled him with a heady relief. Leaning his head back, he opened his eyes to find her staring at him.

Her head was cocked to the side, and that now familiar movement made him wonder what she was contemplating. His hands were cupping her nape, and he moved, gently rubbing his thumb across her bottom lip.

"What's up?" he asked, already knowing her mind was working on something.

"How old are you, Jackson?"

There was no hesitation in the question and no teasing inflection on his name. He instantly missed the joking and already knew he going to hate the end point of the conversation.

"Twenty-three." He pulled his hands from her neck and dropped them to her sides.

"What do you do?"

"Marketing for a small organization." He hated the omission, knowing he was deepening the depth of his lie. "But I'm taking some classes, a few prerequisites that I didn't take in college, because I want to go to med school." Then, he smiled because it felt so good to actually say that out loud to someone. In his mind, sharing it with her made up for all the things he'd been withholding.

"Med school. Impressive."

He felt her withdrawing, pulling her hands free from his hair. Then, she leaned forward and placed a gentle kiss on his forehead. It was not the kiss of someone you wanted to have sex with but one you might bestow on a child before bedtime. He felt the difference and hated it.

She got up and looked down at him, her expression unreadable in the dense night. "Good night, Coach Cal."

He wanted to go after her, grab her hand, spin her around, and demand that she call him Jackson. Hell, part of him was willing to give up J.C. He wanted anything other than Coach Cal.

But he stayed and gave his attention back to the peace of the rolling ocean because he knew there could be nothing between them.

Nicky had opted to ride home with Lena. The weekend of living in a hotel room with his little sisters had proven to be enough for him. Plus, he came to her house on Sunday nights regardless, so it'd worked out best for everyone. As always, she was grateful for his presence but especially because she had a long stretch of highway to navigate, and four hours of mind-wandering would be too much. Between Coach Cal and being immersed in the soccer culture again, she was tapped out.

Nicky's presence in the backseat of her Jeep was soothing, like her second glass of wine once the first had taken the edge off of any craziness. He was sweaty and tired, hot and a little cranky, but his inane conversations and radio sing-alongs were distracting her from any deep thoughts.

They sang loudly and chair-danced to Pitbull's "Timber" while Lena tried not to think about the words belting from the top of their lungs. The fact that her almost eight-year-old knew all of the lyrics would make both of his grandmothers shudder, but she was having so much fun with him that she cranked it louder and ignored the silent recriminations in her head. She'd always been good at ignoring things.

Nicky lasted for a few more songs before the road noise and the boredom pulled him into sleep, his head bobbing under the restraint of the seat belt and the restriction of the booster seat. Marveling briefly at the noodle-like qualities of his little body, she returned her attention to the road.

When her phone buzzed, she looked down to see that Lindsay was calling her. Thankful for yet another distraction, she fumbled for her earbuds and answered her phone.

"Where are you?" Lena asked in lieu of a greeting.

"Hey, Lena. How are you?" Lindsay retorted, gently chiding her for her lack of a hello.

"Fine." She rolled her eyes and answered sarcastically, "How are you, Linds?"

"Groovy. Where are you?"

"Funny, I feel like I just asked you the same question."

"You first."

"Ninety-five south. I'm rolling my eyes, by the way."

"Shocker. We are in front of you. How did that happen?"

"We stopped. Nicky was hungry, and we're not in any hurry. Plus, Mike drives way faster than me."

"True. I'm calling because I need a favor."

"Shoot."

At Lindsay's pause, Lena felt her hands gripping the steering wheel harder.

"Can you handle soccer practice tomorrow? Something came up for the girls, and Mike has a meeting."

Lena almost laughed at the apprehension in Lindsay's voice. Instead, she sighed loudly enough that Lindsay would pick up on it and the reluctance in it. "Yeah, no problem."

This time, Lena knew Lindsay was rolling her eyes, a habit she'd picked up through all the years of their friendship.

She waited for Lindsay to call her out, but nothing came.

"Look, I know this must have been a rough weekend for you, and I'm sorry about throwing this on you at the last minute."

"Honestly, it's not a big deal."

"You just wanted me to feel a little guilt?"

"Yes."

"Shameless."

"Ha. Don't I know it?"

"So, how was it? As bad as you thought?"

"No, actually. The soccer was fine. Not any of the crazy stuff—no lingering memories or ghosts."

"Good, I guess."

"Yes. Good."

"Are you ready to tell me where you disappeared to on Friday night?"

"Thirty-six. Not bad," Lena said on a laugh.

"Huh?"

"Hours. You held out for a long time."

"Oh," Lindsay said, laughing. "Trust me, I wanted to ask, but I never had a good opportunity. I was going to come to your room last night, but then Nicky pulled the I-want-to-sleep-with-my-mom card. So, I have been *dying* over here."

"Well, there is not much to tell."

"Bullshit!"

Lena burst out laughing and then glanced in the rearview mirror to see if Nicky had awoken, but he was still passed out.

Pulling her eyes back to the road, she delved in. "There's really not much to tell. I mean, there is, but it's not going anywhere, so there's not much to say."

Lindsay laughed. "I have no idea what you just said. Sounded like Greek."

Lena sighed again, less obnoxiously. Suddenly glad about Nicky's defection to her room the night before, she was thankful that only a cellular line connected her and Lindsay now. Lena wouldn't have been able to get away with not telling her everything if they were face-to-face.

"I ran into Coach Cal in the elevator. And we had these five seconds of unbelievable contact—like Derek and Meredith in *Grey's Anatomy* hot elevator contact."

"Files on the floor?" Lindsay asked on a laugh.

"Exactly. Anyway, we went down to the beach and hung out. That was really it."

Again with the laughter. "Liar."

Lena didn't respond to that. There was a moment of silence, weighty in the absence of conversation.

Lindsay sighed before she said, "You know your lack of sharing tells me a lot."

Her comment was effective because Lena realized she was making a bigger deal out of it by not coming clean than if she'd just told Lindsay what had happened.

In a rush, the story tumbled out. "We went down to the beach. And it was like he got it, just like me—that utterly amazing calming feeling of being near the water. That was eerie, too—that he seemed to like it as much as me—even though he didn't say it. I just knew."

"Yeah?" Lindsay said, probing for more.

"I found myself telling him stuff I'd never told anyone—even you. At the same time, we were joking and laughing. And there was some kissing. Good kissing. Like forget-where-you-are kind of kissing. But then, I needed to know how old he was just because...I needed to know. So, I asked. It was better than a cold shower. And his plans for his future...it was just all too much. So, I left."

"You walked away."

"Yep. Deuces."

"Because it was too much? You got all that from one interlude on the beach?"

"Yes."

"Because he's younger than you?"

Lena huffed out her annoyance. "Because he's the same age as Gabe. I mean, you know, as the age Gabe would have been. It feels weird knowing that. And because Cal should be out being irresponsible and sowing wild oats or something."

"Not everyone needs or wants to do that, Lena."

"Well, they should. And I have a child."

"Jeez. Must have been lethal."

"What do you mean?"

"That kiss must have been lethal. How did you get from sex to involvement with Nicky?"

"I don't know." Lena took a deep breath, hoping it would calm her. "Shit. I don't know how I made that jump—except that he's already involved with Nicky."

"But you've never mixed the two."

"I know." This was why she'd asked him his age. She'd needed something to provide distance, to snap her back into reality. "That's it, Linds. I'm staying away, which will not be hard."

"Until the next tournament."

"Well, I think something might come up," she joked.

"You'd never. Nicky would be crushed. He loved having you there this weekend."

"Yeah. Nothing like actually knowing that you've done the right thing."

"You always figure it out."

"Do you think I'm crazy?"

"No," Lindsay responded. "I think you are a master at self-preservation."

"Mama," Nicky said from the back of the car, "I have to go to the bathroom."

"Gotta go, Linds," Lena said with some relief. "Pee break."

"You know, his father makes him pee in a bottle, so we don't have to stop," Lindsay informed her, giggling.

"Yes, I've heard. But I like my car too much for that. He can barely make it all in a toilet. You want me to let him pee in a bottle in my car? I don't mind stopping."

"Text me when you get home, so I know you made it."

"Yes, Mom."

"Smart-ass," Lindsay said before disconnecting.

"Mama," Nicky said once the waiter had taken their order and they'd settled in their booth, "I'm really glad you came with me this weekend."

Lena tried not to get emotional, but she felt her grip tighten on the silverware she'd been unraveling. Smiling slightly, she said, "I wouldn't have missed it."

It was a lie, and they both knew it, but he didn't call her on it.

"I loved watching you play," she told him.

"I know you didn't want me to play because of what happened to Uncle Gabe, but I'm glad you let me," he stated as he picked up his lemonade. He took a healthy sip.

Lena didn't move. The knife and fork in her hand remained almost bent in a death grip. Carefully, she laid them down on the table, picked up the napkin, and placed it on her lap. She struggled to find words. "Uh, Nicky?" she managed to get out.

With the straw clamped down between his teeth, he continued to sip on the lemonade he was balancing precariously. "Yeah?" he answered around the straw, like he hadn't just dropped an emotional bomb in the middle of their booth.

"What do you know about Uncle Gabe?" She was confused and somewhat ashamed.

She'd never told Nicky all the gory details about Gabe's death. The images of his collapse still haunted her at inopportune moments, but she'd never shared that information with him.

"That he died playing soccer. That's why you didn't want me to play."

He continued messing with his drink and the straw, and Lena fought the urge to pull it from his mouth and throw it across the restaurant.

In her head, she cursed Mike and Lindsay. She imagined storming into their house and berating them for telling her son what she should have told him when she was ready and not before.

"Who told you that?"

"Grandma. She told me about what had happened to him, so I understood why you didn't want me to play. But I'm really glad you are okay with it now."

He pulled the straw out of his drink and stuck it in his mouth, chewing on the end. As little droplets of lemonade splattered on her and the table, she reached out and swiped the straw from him.

"Stop putting things in your mouth," she snapped.

He leaned back in the seat, his physical withdrawal indicating that he knew he'd said something to make her mad.

"When did she tell you?"

He warily eyed her. It was a look she was familiar with. It was Gabe's look. Feeling like the walls were closing in on her, she took a deep breath and leaned back, mimicking his movements.

There wasn't much of Gabe in Nicky. When she had been pregnant with him, she'd thought for sure he would look like Gabe. *The Lord giveth, and the Lord taketh away…and all that.* But Nicky was really all Mike with his light-brown hair and bluish-gray eyes. He was more stocky than thin, his skin more fair than olive. Because of that, when Nicky did something that reminded her of Gabe, it always caught her off guard. It didn't happen often, but when it did, she would have to work to catch her breath.

"This summer, when I stayed with her. She showed me pictures and his soccer stuff. She showed me all his old jerseys. It's why I picked number six."

"You picked six," she repeated.

She hadn't even noticed the number, or maybe she'd chosen to ignore it.

Because ignorance is one of my great skills, she thought.

She felt off-balance and angry and betrayed and horrible.

Watching Nicky play soccer throughout the weekend had forced her to think about her brother. It was hard to compare the almost eight-year-old on the soccer field to her last memory of her brother playing.

By the time he was fifteen, watching Gabe and his teammates had brought new meaning to the phrase poetry in motion. There was an inherent beauty in a team that moved as one whose players knew where to go because they were so familiar with each other's rhythms. She didn't try to compare. She didn't try to remember.

She tried to focus on Nicky, to go all in when she'd been all out. But it was difficult, so difficult that she hadn't even noticed his number.

She was about to ask him more questions when their food arrived. Her appetite gone, she toyed with her food while Nicky dug into his mac and cheese. Her mind whirled so chaotically that she couldn't hold on to any one thing.

Six. Gabe. Memorial. Nicky. Grandma. Game. Apostles. Sudden death.

"Are you mad because I'm wearing his number?" Nicky asked.

Lena's head jerked up. She saw that Nicky had stopped eating and placed his fork down. She wondered vaguely how long he'd been staring at her, and she was tempted to stick her finger in his mac and cheese to gauge the time she'd lost.

But his question brought her focus.

"No, baby. I am nowhere near mad. I promise."

"Pinkie?" he said as he thrust his hand across the table at her.

"Pinkie." She wrapped her finger around his, and while still joined, she got up and moved to his side of the booth. Then, she disengaged their fingers and pulled him into a hug. Kissing him on the head, she reassured him, "I am not mad at you. I was just caught off guard. And I'm sorry that I made you think I was mad."

"How come you didn't tell me about Uncle Gabe?"

"I just don't like to talk about it," she answered honestly. "It hurts when I think about him."

He didn't have a response for her, and that made her feel like a coward for her answer. But it was the truth, and it had come out before she could filter it.

She leaned her head on his. "Part of your name is kind of a tribute to him."

They'd never really discussed his name, but now, she owed him something, some morsel of her soul so that he'd know she hadn't just forgotten her brother.

"His name was Gabriel, and he was named after one of the archangels. There were three."

"I know. Michael, Gabriel and Raphael."

"Right. Well, your dad kind of cornered the market on Michael. And my brother was Gabriel."

"So, my middle name is Raphael because of your brother?"

"Yep."

Nicky's face lit up like he felt special because of the connection. His light soothed over the craziness of their dinner. For the second time that weekend, Lena had shared a story that she'd kept close, hoarding it in the recesses of her memory. And she felt better because she could tell that Nicky was proud of his name and the association with his uncle.

"This is going to sound weird." Bryce said.

J.C. and Bryce had just pulled out of the hotel parking lot on their way home following the tournament. J.C. watched the road but managed to glance over at him, silently asking him to continue.

"I could be totally off on this, so just tell me if I'm being stupid or sentimental or...I don't know...weird."

"B, just tell me already."

"Does Nick's mom remind you of anyone?" Bryce asked almost sheepishly, like he was seeing ghosts or something.

J.C. drew in a deep breath, thankful for the stretch of highway that kept his eyes forward.

"I know this is going to sound strange, but she reminds me of Maggie Pryce. That's odd, right? I'm just being crazy."

J.C. still didn't speak. He should have figured that Bryce would recognize her eventually. She didn't really look much different than she had at twenty-two, perhaps a little curvier. All of their friends sort of crushed on Maggie. She was the perfect fantasy girl. She was older and wilder, but she'd hardly been around, so they'd only gotten glimpses of her. She would talk to them, but she'd seen them only as little boys, friends of her beloved brother. Because of how she felt about Gabe though, she'd paid attention to them. She'd teased them and ruffled their hair and slung her arm around their shoulders.

J.C. remembered one time, when they were twelve or thirteen, she'd been home for the weekend and shown up at a game. Gabe had scored the winning goal, and she'd been cheering loudly from the sideline. After the game, she'd run onto the field and scooped him up, hugging him. Gabe had been embarrassed. For him, it hadn't been all that cool to get tackled and hugged by his big sister. But his teammates all stood, kind of frozen, watching her. J.C. had heard their coaches chuckling, observing them all ogle her.

When he'd walked closer to the bench, he'd heard Bryce's dad say as the coaches laughed, "They'll have some interesting dreams tonight."

"J.C., that's crazy, right?" Bryce's question pulled J.C. from his memory.

"No. It's not crazy, B. It's Maggie, well Lena, Pryce," he said, delivering this startling piece of information with as little inflection as he could manage.

"Holy shit! Are you sure? I mean, how do you know? Did you ask her?"

"No. I just know."

"Have you told her that you know? Does she know who we are?"

"Nah."

Bryce reached over and grabbed J.C.'s arm. "Nick is Gabe's nephew," he said, awe apparent in his voice.

J.C. pulled his eyes from the road and smiled at his friend. "Yeah."

"We are coaching Gabe's nephew."

J.C.'s smile reflected in his eyes. "Yeah."

"Full circle, dude. Full circle."

His assessment seemed to reverberate through the car, and silence descended between them. Neither of them spoke for a time, each lost in their own thoughts. J.C. hadn't really thought about it like that, but for Bryce, it was true. Bryce's dad had coached them for a long time, so Bryce being Nick's coach was serendipitous.

"He doesn't look anything like Gabe," Bryce said after a time.

"No, he doesn't," J.C. agreed. "I think he looks just like his dad."

"Yeah, you're right.

J.C. waited, knowing that Bryce would work on the timeline. He'd figure it out soon—that Lena had been pregnant when Gabe died. Bryce would want to keep talking about it, piecing things together. And J.C. needed to decide if he would tell Bryce what had happened, what path he'd traveled down—how he'd been inside Lena's mouth, had her legs wrapped around his waist, and had pushed his hands through her hair.

"Do you realize that, when we were assessing soccer-mom talent the other night, we were talking about Maggie Pryce?"

"Uh-huh." *It's coming*, J.C. thought. *Wait for it.*

"How long have you known?" Bryce finally asked the dreaded question.

"Since the first time I saw her," J.C. answered without thinking. He surprised himself with his honesty. *But, hell, if he couldn't talk to Bryce about this, whom could he talk to?*

Bryce leaned back in his seat, dragged his hand through his hair, and worked it out. J.C. knew Bryce was trying to figure out why J.C. had known but hadn't said anything to him. Bryce would be hurt. Of course he wouldn't say that because they didn't share that kind of stuff. Eventually, he'd get mad because he wouldn't really know what to do with the hurt.

J.C. waited.

"You've known for three weeks, why haven't you said anything?"

"Because I didn't know how to deal with it."

Bryce shook his head, as if rattling things around would make the pieces fall into place.

"J.C., what the hell is going on with you?"

"I saw her at practice last week. And I don't know, man. As soon as I looked up, I knew who she was. And there was this…strange connection." He stopped and contemplated not saying the word, knowing it was a bit like Pandora's pesky box, but he moved forward. "An attraction."

Silence.

It lasted for more than a minute before J.C. realized he wasn't going to get a response.

"Then, on Friday, when you went back to study, I saw them on the beach," J.C. said.

"Them?"

"Lindsay, Lena, and the three kids. So, I swam with the kids, and that's how we ended up going to dinner with them."

Again, there was nothing from the other side of the car.

J.C. vaguely wondered, *If I don't say another word for the whole ride, then would Bryce sit there in silence, allowing the rest of the story to remain untold?* He was so tempted to find out.

"And when I went to get more beer, I saw her in the elevator and hung out on the beach with her."

Bryce instantly responded to that statement, "You hung out on the beach with her?"

"Yeah."

"What else did you do on the beach?"

J.C. knew he needed to keep talking, but he had to admit that he was nervous about telling Bryce.

"Talked…and kissed."

Nothing.

Out of his peripheral vision, he saw Bryce bang his head on the headrest, and then he turned to look out the passenger window. J.C. left Bryce to his thoughts.

When the silence continued, J.C. reached over and turned up the volume on the radio, needing to concentrate on something other than the tension between them.

Bryce turned it right back down. "Over a week ago? Like around the time you slept with Anna?"

J.C. wanted to groan. He didn't need Bryce pulling on that particular string. J.C. remained silent. He hadn't thought Bryce would get to the Anna situation until he got the whole Maggie story out of him.

"Let me recap. You met Maggie, slept with Anna, and kissed Maggie—in that order."

"Yeah," J.C. responded.

"There are so many things wrong with this." He paused and looked away.

J.C. could see the anger burning through him.

"Sleeping with Gabe's girlfriend and kissing his sister." Bryce aimed the statement toward the window, throwing it to the wind instead of at J.C., but it didn't matter.

J.C. felt the bite of it and visibly flinched.

Without any kind of response, J.C. continued to drive, his hands gripping the steering wheel hard.

"You haven't told Maggie who you are?" Bryce said like a question.

But J.C. knew it was a statement, a verdict.

"No. I was too stunned the first time I saw her. Really. I looked up from Nick, and she was standing there. I was shocked. Then, we were talking to each other, and I got stupid. There was all this stuff between us—chemistry or whatever. And I had a chance, but it slipped away before I could grab it. Then, it was too late."

"How in the hell did Anna get mixed up in all of this?"

J.C. rubbed his hand over his face, trying to scrub away the mess. "Remember the night we met as a group and went out afterward?"

"Yeah, the night you guys slept together."

"We had practice earlier that night, remember? That was the night I figure it out."

Bryce stopped talking and went back to looking out the window. J.C. went back to trying to figure out a way to clean up the mess he'd made.

Bryce and J.C. remained quiet. The radio provided a buffer between their thoughts, allowing for the quiet that had slipped between them to be like a third companion.

After they had stopped for gas and covered about one hundred miles of their drive home, Bryce crossed over the neutral zone. "Look, I don't know what's going on with you, but something is up. The fact that you slept with Anna, no matter how drunk you both were, is enough to convince me. But this other thing? It's going to blow up in your face. And it's just kind of out of character. You're not a liar. And for all of the messing around you've done, you've never lied to anyone."

It was J.C.'s chance. Bryce was giving him the opening. He just had to walk through it.

"I think I want out."

"Of?"

"Play for Gabe."

"Really?"

"I think so."

"But we've always said that you do what you can do. It doesn't have to be your life. We are all going to do different things, but we just need this to be part of what you do. It's been our theme, our motto."

"I know that. And I guess that's where I'm struggling."

"What do you want to do?"

J.C. felt off balance. Bryce hadn't sounded angry, just curious.

"I think I want to go to med school."

"Really?"

"I've been mulling it over for a while. Knowing everything we've learned over the last few years about sudden cardiac arrest, I just want to be able to do something about it."

"Isn't that what we are doing?"

"Absolutely. We absolutely are doing something about it—raising awareness, the screenings. Yes, we are. I just think I want to be on the other side of it."

"Think? You shouldn't go to med school without knowing for sure what you want to do."

"No doubt," J.C. responded with a slight laugh. "I hear you. I do."

"Are you sure?"

J.C. ran his hand through his hair, his frustration evident. "No. I'm not really sure about anything right at this moment."

"So, that night with Anna, you told her this?"

"No. I told her I wanted out. And when I said that, she was caught off guard at first. Then…well, you know what happened."

"Ah," Bryce replied.

J.C. cut a look to his side, trying to read him.

"Makes a little more sense now."

"How's that?" J.C. wanted to know.

"I've known for a long time that Anna was interested in you. We can all see it."

"Really?" J.C. had never looked at Anna in any way other than as a friend and partner in their organization. He'd never seen her act interested in him.

"Yeah, dude. She's wanted you for a long time."

"Well, I should never have gone out that night. I was messed up over meeting Lena and not telling her who I was. The last thing I should have done was get drunk and hook up with Anna."

"No question. You're an ass."

"Yeah, I get it."

"So, what are you going to do about Maggie?"

"Nothing to do."

"How's that?"

"She dipped." J.C. took a deep breath before blowing it out with a huff. "After we kissed for I don't know how long, she asked me how old I was. And that was pretty much it."

"That's good, right? I mean, how would you have explained to her who you were? Ticking time bomb."

"Yeah," J.C. answered without any conviction. "It's a good thing."

It *was* a good thing. Bryce was right. J.C. just needed to get there.

He needed to stop thinking about what it'd felt like to be around her. The last two nights, he'd been haunted by her in his sleep and slapped with reality in the morning. He knew she had felt what he felt, had loved being there with him. He knew this. It was just like how he knew that Bryce was spot-on with his assessment.

He saw Bryce looking over at him, taking him in and studying him.

"What was it like, kissing Maggie Pryce?"

He found it funny that Bryce had said Maggie's full name, like she was some celebrity they didn't know, someone who graced the pages of glossy magazines. It kept her separate from them, like when they were thirteen and she was twenty and so untouchable. But she wasn't untouchable. She was funny and engaging and beautiful. He wished like hell she wasn't who she was, that she were some random person who hadn't shared all this history with them. He wished for a lot of things.

"J.C.?"

"Heaven, B. It was like heaven."

Bryce —2007

I'm ready. I've been ready since our high school season came to a close with a loss in the regional final. I don't think I've ever been as tired as I was at the end of our season.

When I think about our high school run for the state championship, I am thankful for the outlet the game of soccer provided. It felt like I could take all of the sadness and anger and disbelief with me onto the field for every game, and I could kick its ass. For those sixty minutes, I could run and defend with my team while muddling through the darkness of Gabe's death. I would come out on the other side of the game feeling a little bit lighter, as if I were shedding the pain of his loss, little by little.

I'd still rail at God, demanding an answer to the question of, *Why?* But when it wouldn't come, I'd find that playing through it helped.

Soccer was Gabe's game. He was our emotional leader. It seems fitting to use that channel to work through his death. He would have played his heart out. He'd have found a way to forget for the duration of the game. He'd have used it, like I was using it, as a release for my disbelief.

Once our high school season ended though, I felt the collective weight of our school and community lift. We hadn't just been playing for ourselves. We had played for all of them, those who had rallied around us when we lost Gabe.

As much as I hated to admit it to myself, I couldn't wait to get back out there—this time, for my club.

I think playing with our club team will feel different. The guys on this team played with Gabe for almost as long as we've been playing. We have all of these shared experiences.

And even though they feel Gabe's loss like I do, his collapse will forever separate us. For those of us who were there—J.C., Fletcher, Max, and I who watched him lag behind in practice—we'll probably be haunted by that for a long time. Seeing our coach perform CPR is an image that is burned in my brain. So, even though Gabe's death has affected this team, there's no way that they could know what those moments following Gabe's collapse were like. That makes returning to this team a bit freeing. No matter how good it felt to play for our high school, the memory of Gabe dying in front of us stood like a sentinel outside of our stadium. You couldn't enter without acknowledging it.

I can't remember whose idea it was, but we have started a scholarship fund in Gabe's name. It helps—to do something positive with all the negative feelings, to think about something other than the loss of him. J.C., Fletcher, Kyle, Max, Anna, and I have been trying to think of ways we could raise money. It might seem simple, but people want to do something, too—something other than mourn. Our community wants to try to make sense of Gabe's passing. And in lieu of making sense of it, they want to contribute to what we are doing. So, our plans for raising money for the scholarship fund are simple. We've held a cornhole tournament, hosted a car wash, and begged our mothers to help with bake sales.

The scholarship is a good idea. As long as we can put the funds together, it will be available to one male and one female soccer player to use for college.

Here's the special part of it for me. Every year, we can remind a new generation of kids about Gabe's life and his legacy. At least then, his memory will live on. It's enough for now—something more than dedicating a season, one that came up short for us, to his memory.

Sometimes, I wonder, if we'd won, if we'd gone on to state and won the championship, would we still feel this need to do something for him? Or would the win, the title State Champion, have been enough? I'd like to think we'd still be doing this. But we'll never know.

Lena tried to ignore the conversation she'd had with Nicky. For a week, she had gone on with life—going to work, doing homework with Nicky, taking him to soccer practice—while avoiding all contact with Coach Cal. But she couldn't shake the craziness of her thoughts.

Between her errant thoughts of Jackson Callahan and her anger with her mother for telling Nicky about Gabe, she was wired with a nervous energy that made her jumpy, snippy, and pissy. She'd been staying away from Lindsay and Mike because she didn't want them badgering her about what was going on.

After she'd dropped Nicky off at their house on Friday evening, she'd found herself heading south toward her parents' house.

Not long after Gabe's death, her parents had sold her childhood home and moved to Fort Myers on the other coast of Florida. They'd splurged for a house on the water, so her father could indulge in his favorite pastimes of boating and fishing. She hadn't begrudged them their need to move on from their little beach town with its constant reminders.

Although Gabe's death had healed the breach caused by her pregnancy, her relationship with her parents was never quite right. They resented her lifestyle, and she resented their rigidity. Gabe had been who they had in common, the one subject they could agree on.

For the past couple of years, they'd had Nicky to bridge the gap. And the prickly path they usually followed had smoothed out with a different boy being the reason for the neutrality in their relationship.

As she got closer and closer to their house, she attempted to think of a way to talk to her mother without being completely confrontational. This was not her forte. She wasn't a fair fighter, and as she'd gotten older, she could acknowledge that much of the problem with her parents was actually her inability to have a rational conversation with them. But right now, she didn't know how to fix that, especially when she felt her anger brewing when she remembered her conversation with Nicky about Gabe.

As Lena pulled into the driveway, she tried to channel Lindsay, who was so good at handling confrontation. Taking a moment, she laid her head on the steering wheel, attempting to calm herself, talk herself out of thinking that she was walking into a lion's den. It was the thought of talking about Gabe that had her stomach knotted up and her head spinning.

She hadn't had a conversation with her parents about her brother since they'd arranged his funeral. Once she'd left, the night after the soccer game, she'd never looked back. It was like she'd buried her memories of her brother with his body.

Broaching this subject with her mother would be monumental. As the acid in Lena's stomach churned and her hands shook, she sat up and leaned back in the driver's seat. Then, out of nowhere, she felt calm, like the adrenaline rush had left her body to be replaced by this overwhelming sense of peace. She didn't know where it had come from, but goose bumps rose on her arms, making the little hairs stand at attention. She looked around, sure that she would see something although she wasn't sure what.

The slamming of the front door snapped her out of her reverie. Glancing over, Lena saw her mother standing by the front door with her hands on her hips and a quizzical expression. She must have recognized Lena's car because her face broke into a smile, and she rushed forward.

Lena opened the car door and came around, meeting her mother. The hug wasn't awkward even though most of theirs tended to be. Lena noted the difference and chalked it up to the lingering sense of calmness. She leaned into it and absorbed it, taking the comfort her mother was offering without even knowing why she was there.

Maybe we can find our way, Lena thought as she broke the hug.

"What a pleasant surprise," Marie said as she led Lena into the house. "I take it Nicky is with his father?"

"Yeah, it's Mike's weekend," she said, keeping her answer short and to the point.

"Are you staying tonight?" Glancing at her watch, Marie changed tactics. "It's too late for you to drive back tonight. You must stay."

Any other time, Lena would have left just for spite, to do the opposite of what her mother wanted. But the urge was missing, so she just nodded her head. "As long as you are okay with that. I can get a hotel, if I need to."

"Magdalena, don't be ridiculous. Our home is always your home."

There were so many things wrong with her mother's statement—her full name, her mother's indication that her home was always open for Lena—but for some reason, it didn't shred Lena's nerves like normal.

"Thanks. I have to get back tomorrow, but I needed to talk to you about something."

Lena followed her mother directly into the kitchen where she had been preparing dinner. There was an open bottle of wine on the counter.

"Can I have a glass?" Lena asked.

"Of course." Her mother made her way to the cabinet in the corner and pulled a wine glass from it. Filling it up, she offered it to Lena. "Your father won't be home for a while. I was actually going to eat without him and just let him heat up his dinner. So, I'm glad for the company."

Lena accepted her glass of wine and took a seat at the counter. She watched her mother continue to prep for dinner.

"I don't mean to sound ungrateful to see you, but what brings you here?"

Again, Lena found herself rolling with the comment, not letting it stick to her.

"I need to talk to you, and it needed to be in person." Lena fortified herself with a couple of sips of wine. "How have you been?"

"Good. Busy but good. Have you and Nicky decided if you are coming for Thanksgiving? That's your holiday this year, right?"

"Uh, yes, but we haven't decided yet."

"I guess it's a little far off," her mother said with a smile.

It was a gentle smile, one Lena remembered from her childhood before she'd looked for the snark behind every gesture her mother made.

"Yeah." Lena took another swallow of her wine and stood up to refill her glass. She sat back down at the counter and toyed with her glass, trying to figure out a way to talk about the subject that had brought her here.

"Are you ready to tell me what's troubling you?" her mother asked, still adhering to her task at the stove.

"I'm trying to figure out a way to bring it up and have the conversation without driving a wedge between us," Lena answered as honestly as she could.

Her mother's laughter rang throughout the kitchen. Lena tried to hold back her smile but found that she was unable to.

"I'm sorry. That wasn't very nice of me to laugh," Marie said on a giggle. "I just don't expect you to ever hold back." Then, she seemed to catch herself. "It's one of the things I love most about you—your unwillingness to compromise."

"That's what you love most?" Lena's laugh sounded brittle, even to her.

"Well, that, and the way you loved Gabe and the way you love Nicky."

Lena choked on the sip of wine she'd taken and spit it out onto the counter. "Shit," she muttered as she reached for a napkin and started to mop up the wine. She hadn't expected that. "Well, at least I have some redeeming qualities." She delivered this with a sarcastic tone and immediately regretted it.

But her mom just kept cooking and said, "You have many wonderful qualities, Magdalena."

They were quiet for a while—her mother engaged in her cooking and Lena lost in her mind, not really paying attention. Marie must have finished dinner because she was suddenly sitting across the counter from Lena.

When their eyes met, her mother reached out and patted her hand. "Tell me what's going on."

"Why did you tell Nicky about Gabe without telling me?" Lena said as calmly as she could manage.

"Ah"—Marie glanced away from her—"I was wondering when that was going to come up."

"You knew it would bother me, but you told him anyway. Then, you didn't even have the courtesy to tell me."

"But this wasn't about you, Lena."

"What was it about?" she asked.

"It was about the need to talk about my son. Your father is a lot like you. He thinks that if he doesn't talk about it or doesn't acknowledge it, that somehow makes it less tragic or less important. I'm not sure which. Which is it?"

Lena sat back in her chair, startled a little at her mother's forthright question. It normally wasn't her style.

"I don't know," Lena heard herself mutter. "I guess if I don't think about it, I don't hurt."

"Really? You don't hurt? Is that possible? How could you not hurt? You adored him."

Lena wasn't ready for this conversation. She could feel the panic beginning to amp up, her heart starting to beat faster. She wasn't sure if her mother was expecting a response, but Lena couldn't get anything out over the lump in her throat.

"He was your brother, and you two had a special relationship. But he was my youngest child. And I want to be able to talk about him. It probably wasn't right to do it with Nicky, but he can listen to me without his little world being rocked. He didn't know Gabe or love him, but Nicky is connected to him. I wish I could make you understand that without hurting you, too."

Lena didn't really know how to respond. *Who am I to dictate to my mother how she should deal with the death of her son?*

"His friends have probably dealt with it best."

"The Apostles?" Lena said this on a muffled laugh. "God, I hadn't thought about them in so long, not until Nicky started playing soccer. Only then did I remember that they existed."

Marie laughed. "They definitely still exist. They've done all sorts of things in his name. I'm sure it's cathartic for them, but for me, it's a special tribute."

"Really? Tell me."

"Tell you what?"

"What have they done? Then, I want you to tell me about your conversation with Nicky. I want to understand."

Just like that, the panic receded like a tide rolling out, creating little waves and dragging sand with it but moving in the direction it was always supposed to.

So, her mother told her. She told Lena about Play for Gabe and the scholarship fund and the organizations plans for the future. The boys had kept her parents updated on all the things they'd done. They had come to visit. They'd helped heal her mother in a way that Lena couldn't. It was both endearing and frustrating. She tried hard not to be impressed with them, but it was difficult.

Then, her mother relayed her conversation with Nicky and told Lena how Nicky had seemed to constantly find some way to weave Gabe into their conversations, providing a balm for a still smarting burn of her loss.

Lena was basking in the mellowness that a good wine and good conversation could provide. Her guard was down, and she felt peaceful.

It was how her mother slipped it by her.

"They need help. I think they need an accountant to look over their application for their nonprofit status. You should think about reaching out to them, helping them. I don't want to sound condescending, but I think it would be good for you."

And just like that, Lena found herself agreeing. "Sure, give them my contact information. Have them email me, or call the office to set up a time to meet. I'll take a look."

"Pro bono, right?"

Lena laughed. "Of course, Mom. Of course."

"Good."

They sat at the counter, ate dinner, welcomed her father when he came home, and then talked some more. It was the single longest, conflict-free conversation they'd had in her life. And it felt good.

Marie took Lena to the guest room and made sure she had everything she needed. She grabbed Lena's hand. "I'm so glad you decided to come here tonight."

"Me, too," Lena said, meaning it.

Marie turned to go but stopped just shy of the door. "Do you ever feel him, Lena?" She kept her back to Lena, which allowed

Lena to let the shock show on her face. "I mean, do you ever feel like Gabe's with you?"

"No, Mom, I don't," she said.

"You'll probably think I'm crazy, but there are times when I feel his presence, like he's giving me a sign that it's okay. He leaves me pennies."

Lena felt like she'd been hit with a jolt of electricity.

"Remember, he used to collect pennies when he was little? And he'd keep the pennies from the years when we were all born. Then, he added to it with his friends' birth years. Do you remember that?"

Lena struggled to find her voice. "Yeah."

"Well, when I have a particularly bad day or a day when I can't escape his memory, I find a penny." She laughed nervously. "Gives new mean to the saying, *Find a penny, pick it up. All day long, you'll have good luck.*"

Lena offered her a fake laugh.

"Anyway, good night, Magdalena."

Marie shut the door, and Lena sank down onto the bed. She hadn't wanted to know that last little bit because when she'd gotten out of her car, she'd noticed pennies on the ground, and that just wasn't something she was willing to deal with tonight.

Moore, Green, and Jessup, CPA, was located downtown, but it was situated so that most of the office space faced the water of the bay. It was prime real estate, but the long-ago established firm could afford it. The conference room was in the interior of the space, and thus was robbed of the tremendous view. But its mahogany paneling and beautiful art offered occupants plenty of comfort and opulence and hinted at the company's prestigious standing.

Today, Lena was thankful for the ostentatious display of the company's wealth.

It wasn't often she felt the need to impress. But since she was now about to fulfill her recently made promise to her mother, she could admit that she wanted these people to be a little awed by who she'd become. She wouldn't go so far as to say that she was the black sheep of her family, but they were from a close-knit small community. Everyone knew everyone and their business. She was fairly certain most of the Apostles' parents didn't have the best opinion of her. This was her own little episode of *Bad Girl Makes Good*. It was why she'd dressed with care this morning and blown out her hair, why she'd actually taken time with her makeup and pulled out her best sky-high heels. It explained the nervous anticipation in her belly and her overly thorough inspection of the documents the Apostles had sent over after her mother had put them in touch with Lena.

When her administrative assistant let her know that they were waiting for her in the conference room, she grabbed the documents, heaved a steadying breath, and made her way toward them. She wasn't sure what she had expected, but the lone blonde girl being swallowed up by the immense table and plush chair definitely wasn't it. Lena hid her surprise and started forward to shake the girl's hand.

She gracefully rose to her feet and held out her hand. "Anna Davies. You must be Maggie Pryce."

Lena cocked her head, slightly annoyed by the throwback name. "Actually, it's Lena, as I'm sure you know from our correspondence."

Anna blushed. "I'm so sorry," she said sincerely. "I actually practiced saying that, but you look so much like I remember you, and Maggie just came out."

Lena believed her and smiled, letting her know that she was forgiven. She glanced around the conference room. "I thought there would be more of you," she commented.

Anna regained her seat and looked anxiously at her watch. "There are. I might be early, and they are definitely going to be a late. I'm really sorry. We are normally very professional. You have to be when you are young, and people assume you are unreliable. J.C. legitimately got caught up, which means Bryce and Fletcher got caught up too, but as we speak, he are rushing to get here."

"Wow, that's a name I haven't heard in a long time," Lena remarked.

Anna gave her an understanding smile. "J.C. and Gabe were the closest of friends."

Something about her statement struck Lena as out of place, like her speech was a touch too formal and she was trying too hard.

"Yes, I remember." Lena hadn't meant to sound put out, but she did. She didn't need anyone to explain to her who had been important to her brother.

For some reason, this girl put her on edge. She vaguely remembered Anna as Gabe's girlfriend. She looked the same. If all the Apostles were lined up, however, Lena wasn't sure she'd be able to pick any of them out. She only remembered funky-smelling gangly boys whose potential future looks had escaped her at twenty-two.

She thought about Mike's adolescent pictures that she'd studied, looking for glimpses of the man he'd become. There had been so many changes, too many to attempt to picture the Apostles as they might look now.

But this girl, with her straight blonde hair and her slender body, just looked more polished and untouchable. She wondered what Gabe would have thought about her now.

"So, most of you ended up going to the same school?" Lena asked as a way to kill time.

"Yes. I mean, there aren't tons of options anyway, and it seems like, if you grow up in Florida, you already know which of the schools you want to attend."

"True."

"I don't know that it was so much planned as it just happened."

Lena laughed. "I get happenstance, trust me."

Anna returned her smile. Then, she looked at her watch, which told Lena that she was uncomfortable with the direction of the conversation.

"I know you covered it briefly in the email, but why don't you explain what you need my help with." Lena attempted a conciliatory tone and then hoped she'd nailed it.

Anna opened the leather portfolio that she had sitting in front of her. "Uh, before we do that, I think I should tell you that I didn't tell the guys who was going to help us. That probably sounds weird, but I just thought it would be easier for everyone if they didn't have any preconceived notions about this meeting."

Lena merely raised her brow.

"That didn't come out like I'd thought. When we decided we were going to move forward with our non-profit status and then realized we would need some professional help, they just left it to me to find it. I volunteered actually, but that's neither here nor there. So, they didn't ask questions. I told them to show up here, and they agreed. No one asked, and I didn't tell."

Lena shrugged her shoulders. She didn't really care. "That's fine. Look, I haven't seen any of these boys since my brother's funeral. I'm good at what I do. So, why don't we just worry about the business side of this and not get caught up in the personal stuff?"

Anna seemed to relax once Lena had let her off the hook. She pulled out her papers and started explaining, "We've been raising money since 2007. Most of that money is for the scholarship we set up in Gabe's name. To date, we've raised close to fifty thousand dollars."

"Wait. How much?" Lena was taken aback by the amount and it was reflected in her question.

"Fifty."

"Thousand?"

"Yes." Anna smiled at her. "Fifty thousand."

"Okay. Well, consider me impressed."

Anna merely shrugged. "About six months ago, we decided that we should try to get nonprofit status. So, we've slowly been working on the application."

"Okay. For a scholarship fund?" Lena asked, a little confused.

"No. I mean, we are going to continue to fund and sponsor the Gabriel Pryce Memorial Scholarship, but we are branching out."

"Branching out?" Lena wanted to take this all in stride, but she was a little overwhelmed by what Anna was telling her.

"Yes. We are going with a three-prong program."

"Three-prong?" Lena knew she was merely repeating what Anna had said, but she felt like she was hearing this underwater. She could vaguely make out the words but couldn't quite connect them.

"Right—an AED Placement Program, the Heart Health Advocacy Program that includes legislation and CPR training, and the Heart Screening Program."

"Why?"

The door opened, but Lena's attention remained on Anna.

"J.C., Lena wants to know why we'll have three programs."

"Because any of them would have saved Gabe's life," he responded.

Just then, Lena turned toward him, and their eyes met.

Bryce stepped forward, effectively breaking the staring contest between J.C. and Lena. "Hey, Lena," he said, wariness evident in his voice. Thrusting his hand toward her, he went on, "It's good to see you again." He punctuated his statement with a sweet smile.

Lena reached for his hand. "Coach B, I hadn't made the connection," she said coldly.

"Holy shit! Maggie Pryce," Fletcher interrupted, pushing forward and hugging her. "Damn, I'd have recognized you anywhere. I'm Fletcher Woodard." He was taller than everyone else in the room. His shaggy hair was combed down in an attempt to tame the craziness of his light-brown locks.

Lena should have felt unnerved, being in his embrace, but the genuine warmth she experienced from him took all the weirdness out of the hug.

He pulled away from her, but held on to her shoulders. "Holy shit. I can't believe it's you." He released her, shaking his head, as if he were waking up out of an odd dream.

"Wait," Anna said, her face showing her confusion, "Coach B?"

"Yes, Coach B and Coach Cal." Lena made a pointed effort to look at both of them and lock gazes. "They coach my son, Nicky." She tried to deliver this piece of information with as little emotion as possible, but she could feel the iciness in her tone.

Anna looked back and forth between J.C. and Bryce. "You guys…" But she couldn't seem to finish the sentence.

"Damn," Fletcher said, "you guys didn't say anything." Then, he stepped toward the table and took the seat next to where Lena had placed her stuff. A big grin split his face. "You're fucking coaching Gabe's nephew. Dude, that's so cool."

"Fletch," J.C. warned, "language, man."

"Sorry. But that's so *frickin'* cool," he said with an emphasis on *frickin'*.

J.C. and Bryce followed Fletcher's example and made their way to the table. Since Lena had set up across from Anna, J.C. and Bryce took the seats surrounding Anna as Lena sat. They settled, took out their respective tools, and were about to begin when Fletcher banged his hand on the table.

"How cool!" Fletcher smiled wide. Dropping his voice, he asked a little reverently, "Does he play like Gabe?"

Lena's throat closed up, and heat crept up her neck. She kept her head down but could see Bryce and J.C. making eye contact. She could see their silent communication as their mouths pulled up into reluctant grins.

J.C. fielded the question, "Same fire."

93

Fletcher leaned back in his chair, cackled loudly, and slapped his hands together once. "Damn right he does! Damn right."

It was too much.

Making a show of looking through her papers, Lena stood suddenly. "I left a document in my office. I'll be right back." She hurried out of the room, her heels quiet in the plush carpet of the conference room.

She longed for the sanctity of her office, but it was too far away. Dipping into the restroom, she closed the door and leaned on it, attempting to calm herself. She frantically gulped air, but the sob escaped from her throat anyway. Covering her mouth with both hands, she closed her eyes and tried to count to ten. It took her five tries, but she eventually calmed. Finally feeling steady, she opened her eyes, removed her hands, and walked toward the sink. Running the cold water, she bathed her wrists and then patted her face with her now cool hands. Cursing the hand dryer, she walked toward the toilet paper and grabbed some. She blotted her face dry and fixed the damage caused by her near panic attack.

Under control once again, she made her way back to the conference room. Opening the door, she caught the tail end of a comment by Anna.

"Could have told me," or something like that.

Touché, Lena thought.

Shaking her head and smiling at them, she said, "I must have looked right over it. It's not in my office." She was careful to avoid looking at J.C. because she thought she might hurt him if given the chance. She regained her chair.

"Anna was telling me about what you are planning to do with your organization. And I gathered from my mother that your financial documentation over the last seven years might not have been up to the IRS standard for nonprofit status. Is that correct?"

"Yes," J.C. said.

She turned her head toward him but looked right through him. She noticed him shaking his head with something like resignation or regret.

But he kept talking, "As we got into the application, we realized we needed more detailed financial information. We incorporated a couple of years ago. We have statements, but we're not sure if it's enough."

"I'm assuming you brought the records with you," she said to the room at large

J.C. answered, "Of course."

"You can leave them with me and let me take a look. Once I've gone through everything, I'll provide you with my recommendation. Until I look through what you have, I won't know what you have to provide. Once that happens, if you can get me everything I need, I can take care of the financial portion of the paperwork."

Anna pulled a manila envelope out of her embossed leather folder and slid it across the table. Lena reached forward, grabbed it, and placed it on top of her stuff.

"I can't tell you how much we appreciate this," Bryce said.

"It's not a big deal," she said, smiling tightly at him.

"So, that's it?" Fletcher asked.

Lena began to grab her stuff, and then she placed it back in the portfolio she'd brought. "Yes." She stood and looked down into Fletcher's big blue eyes. She saw his confusion and felt bad for her abruptness. "For now."

"Oh. I thought when we came in, you were talking about what we were doing. Do you want us to tell you? Are you interested in knowing?" Fletcher asked.

"I think Anna covered it," she smiled gently and reached out to touch Fletcher on the shoulder. "I have another meeting I need to get to."

She really wanted to walk out of the room without acknowledging the three people on the other side of the table, but she didn't want them to know how much she was hurting. So, against all of her self-preservation instincts, she gazed across the table and looked pointedly at each of them. She got stuck on J.C., his dark eyes assessing her. To add insult to injury, he looked damn good, dressed up in a blue oxford shirt.

"I'll be in touch," she finally said.

With as much self-possession as she could manage, she calmly left the room. With her heels now clicking loudly on the wooden hallway floor, she remembered to walk slowly because the cadence echoed in the hall. She made it to her office and then closed and locked the door. Making her way to her desk, she deliberately placed the paperwork in a neat pile.

Foregoing her chair, she moved toward her massive window. Placing her hands on it, she leaned forward, dropping her forehead on the glass, grateful for the coolness coming from the air conditioner. Her mind couldn't focus on any one of the crazy things that had happened in the last hour.

J.C. was Jackson Callahan. *Of course he was.* The weird mind meld should have tipped her off. And he didn't look surprised to find out who she was. He'd known and he hadn't said anything.

Had she really had her legs wrapped around J.C.?

She moved her head, laying her cheek on the glass.

The whole J.C. thing was bad enough. But it was what he'd said when he first walked into the room that had her head spinning.

Had he said that Gabe's death was preventable? She was pretty sure she'd heard him say that. *And what the hell was she supposed to do with that information?*

J.C. deliberately stayed in his seat. He knew if he stood up, he would follow Lena out of the conference room to wherever she had escaped to.

He itched. His fingers twitched, and his feet begged him to stand up and find her. But he knew it would be a mistake, and he'd already made too many.

He refused to speak even though he knew everyone was waiting for him to say something. An uneasy silence had descended when she walked out of the door. He avoided all eye contact, instead choosing to look down at the table and toy with the rubber bracelet around his wrist. It was the one thing he'd refuse to discard when he had to act like a grown-up in this type of meeting.

He couldn't quite figure out what to address—his anger with Anna or his unfounded annoyance with Fletcher.

Afraid to open his mouth, J.C. stalled.

He wanted to rail at Anna. *How could she have set this up without warning any of them about Lena?* Part of him thought it had been deliberate, but the other part of him knew that he hadn't asked for details, so it was as much his fault as hers.

And Fletcher. His damn mouth and his easy way with Lena had made J.C. want to punch something. Fletcher's genuine happiness at seeing her was damn cute, so endearing that even J.C. had fallen for it. But he'd almost jumped across the table when Fletcher had so casually brought up Gabe. It was how they rolled though. They didn't hold back. They'd talk about Gabe when the mood hit, when something reminded them, when they needed to feel his presence.

But J.C. was pretty confident that Lena hadn't talked about her brother since he died, and the matter-of-fact conversation had almost unraveled her.

"Well, I guess that was productive," Anna said. She made a production of packing up her stuff and standing, trying to get them to move out.

"Yeah," Bryce concurred.

J.C. felt their eyes on him, so he stood, ready to follow them out.

"I don't mean to be an ass, but why didn't you guys tell us that you were coaching Gabe's nephew? That's kinda important information," Fletcher said.

J.C. could feel Fletcher's confusion. "I don't know, man," he answered.

"How long have you known?"

J.C. flashed back to the conversation he'd had with Bryce. They exchanged a glance.

"I've known since our first tournament, so six weeks ago," Bryce said.

"Since I first saw her," J.C. admitted.

Fletcher rubbed his hand over his face. "I take it you didn't identify yourself? 'Cause she kind of looked at you like she hated you."

J.C. briefly closed his eyes. "No, I didn't say anything. I was too stunned the first time. Then, I didn't know how to go back." He shrugged his shoulders, like it was no big deal even though he felt like he'd just been gutted.

"Sucks for you," Fletcher responded. Then, he eyed J.C., as if he could see all his secrets and knew exactly what J.C. had done.

Belatedly, J.C. thought about Anna watching all of this and drawing her own conclusions. He refused to look at her.

"It doesn't seem like it matters much," Anna said.

All three of them looked at her then.

"She's going to help us, so mission accomplished."

"Yeah, mission accomplished," Bryce agreed with his eyes on J.C.

"Let's go," J.C. said.

They headed out toward the main doors.

As J.C. pressed the button for the elevator, Bryce walked up next to him. Dropping his voice, he basically whispered in J.C.'s ear, "Go talk to her. Now. I'll get Fletcher home."

He looked at his friend and knew that it was good advice. "I've gotta go to the restroom. B, you got Fletch?"

"Yep."

J.C. turned and walked back toward the restroom, mindful of the three sets of eyes watching him. He heard the elevator ding, and when the door closed, he changed direction and headed toward the receptionist's desk.

"Is Lena Pryce busy? I forgot to hand her some of our paperwork."

She looked up at him and smiled. "Hold on." She searched on her computer. "No. She doesn't have any scheduled meetings but you can just leave it with me. I'll make sure she gets it."

He withheld his groan. "Thanks but I need to explain part of it."

He thought she was going to stop him but instead, she said, "Her office is down that hallway and on the left."

He followed her directions and came to Lena's door. He wanted to just walk in, not give her a choice about whether or not to talk to him. But it was closed, so that option was taken away.

He knocked even though he was pretty sure she wasn't going to answer.

He waited, and then he knocked again.

"Lena?" he said, hoping she'd respond.

When the door opened and she stood in front of him, he was relieved. She looked unbelievably beautiful, slightly flushed, and pissed. She surprised him then by pulling the door all the way open and moving out of the way so that he could enter. She closed it behind him.

He made his way toward her desk but hesitated to take a seat, not sure how long she'd let him stay or how comfortable she'd allow him to get.

She must have seen his hesitation because she walked up behind him and said, "Take a seat." She moved around her desk and seated herself.

He sat.

She didn't relax. Her shoulders were stiff, and the hands she clasped on top of her desk showed white on her knuckles, indicating her tight grip.

"I'm sorry I didn't say anything. I was so shocked to see you the first time, and I couldn't get it out." He paused, studying her, looking for some indication of how she was feeling. When she didn't react, he continued, "And then I didn't know how to go back. I apologize."

She merely watched him with her penetrating dark gaze. "What you said when you first came into the conference room today, is it true?"

He tried to play back their meeting. "Uh…" he started, not getting what she'd asked.

"The thing about his death being preventable. I don't think you said that specifically, but I am fairly certain that was the takeaway from what you said. Am I wrong about that?"

"Oh." Rubbing a hand over his face, he drew in a deep breath. "Yes, preventable. A simple EKG would have detected the abnormality. An accessible AED would have kept him alive."

"But that's not what they told us. They said it was like a lightning strike, a rare occurrence."

J.C. was already shaking his head. "No, it's not a rare occurrence. It's fairly common. Approximately two thousand children die every year from sudden cardiac arrest, from conditions that can be detected with a simple EKG."

"So, if he'd had an EKG, he could be alive today."

"Yes."

"Thanks."

He watched her get up from her chair, walk to the door of her office, and look at him. Her eyes narrowed. "Now, get the hell out of my office."

Standing up, J.C. walked toward the door, internally debating the wisdom of attempting to talk to Lena one more time. Not one to pass up an opportunity, he stopped directly in front of her. Her hand remained behind her back, holding the knob. In her heels, she was almost eye-level with him, if she'd deign to look at him. But she didn't.

He wanted to explain one more time, to reiterate his take on what happened when he first met her. Since she was within his reach, he changed tactics. When he moved into her space, she stiffened but didn't back away. J.C.'s hand was on the nape of her neck, his thumb caressing her cheek, before he'd even realized he needed to touch her.

The words *I'm sorry* sat in his mouth, begging to escape, but he feared that if he said anything, it would break the spell between them. It seemed like a victory that she hadn't pulled away, so he moved imperceptibly closer, sucking up the space between them. Flush against her.

Then, his mouth was on hers. For a moment, she didn't respond, but he was patient enough to wait, hovering there but not. When she drew in a breath, he took advantage and moved into her mouth. The kiss was more sweet than hot, mellow rather than rough.

If she were paying attention, she would get that he was apologizing, expressing his regret. She didn't fight him, her body seemingly forgiving him. It was one of those things that could have lasted a minute or an hour. Regardless, it would always be too short in his memory.

Then, her hand settled between them, and she pushed him away. She met his gaze with an unmistakable glare. "You lied to me," she said softly.

"I did." He could argue that it had been a lie of omission, but really, what would be the point?

"Deal-breaker," she said with a glint in her eyes and a lift in her brow.

"And here I thought it was my age."

She smiled involuntarily. "Same outcome," she said with a shrug of her shoulders, like it wasn't a big deal.

"I'm sorry about Fletcher bringing up Gabe. We just talk about him, ya know? He's present in our conversations. We don't hold back. I know that it's different for you, and if Fletcher had known, he wouldn't have asked."

"You don't have to apologize for that. In the last couple of weeks, I've come to realize that not everyone has chosen to deal with his death in the way that I have. And I'm okay with that. Really."

"Yeah. Okay."

She remained within his reach, and he briefly contemplated pushing his luck by touching her again, but she appeared more fragile than she had five minutes ago. He wasn't willing to test her emotions.

"I get that. It used to bother me that you weren't interested in what we did. Took me some time to figure out that not everyone grieves in the same way. Just because Play for Gabe was our salvation doesn't mean it had to be yours."

"Your *salvation?*" she said like the word startled her.

"Maybe that's too strong of a word, but yes. It focused me, helped me think of something other than my grief." He shrugged. "So, maybe that's not too strong of a word."

"Maybe not," Lena murmured.

"It's kind of liberating, knowing the world doesn't revolve around you."

She laughed softly. "I guess I can see that."

"How do you do that?" J.C. asked.

"What?" she said with a slight tilt of her head, one he recognized in her already.

"Laugh when I know you're angry and sad."

She stayed silent for a moment, merely watching him. He'd have given anything for their weird silent communication right at this second, but he had nothing.

"Am I angry *and* sad?" she asked with enough grit in the question to make him feel the smattering of regret for killing the mood.

"Yeah, I'm pretty sure you're both right now."

"So seemingly perceptive," she murmured just loud enough for him to hear her. "Yeah, I'm pretty sure you're right. It's been kind of a crazy morning." She shrugged. "I'm angry with you, and I guess some of what I was feeling earlier was sadness. But what you just said was funny. So I laughed. In the grand scheme of things, it doesn't really matter all that much. We were just a kiss on the beach, so really, what is there to be upset about?" She shrugged again, the nonchalance of the movement telling him what she wanted him to know.

His smile faded. She reached over and planted her mouth on his forehead, much like her parting gift on the beach.

"Good-bye, J.C." She sidestepped him and returned to her desk. "Can you close the door on your way out?" she said as she took a seat in her office chair and looked at her computer.

Dismissed, he turned to leave her office. He closed the door without a sound and walked away.

Fletcher—2012

J.C. talked me into going with him to this seminar. I don't know where he found it, probably from his hours of research or something.

For some reason though, he wanted me to go with him. I'm sure it's for comic relief when he gets bored halfway through. Normally, he signs us up, and we find ourselves sitting there with all these middle-aged people.

I spend most of the morning entertaining J.C. with comparisons between the people in the room and people we know. This confirms for me that J.C. wanted me along for entertainment.

J.C. always has a reason for the things he does. I should know this, and I should have realized that he was here for a purpose. But it takes me until the end of the day to figure it out.

There's a panel of professionals, which includes the CEO of this new hospital in town and some dude from the city. We listen to the panel.

J.C. throws in a couple of pointed questions like, "Where do you start in organizing a citywide event?" and "How do you get community buy-in?"

It's actually kind of brilliant because both guys tell J.C. to find them afterward.

So, we do. We find both of them, and J.C. peppers them with questions and explains some of what our organization does and what we are hoping to do. I can tell they are reluctantly impressed with us because they freely give us their cards and are all about trying to help in any way they can.

As we leave the seminar, we're both pretty pumped. It was a good day's work.

I don't look back very often because what's done is done, but I spend the evening in a retrospective haze. It's kind of impressive—what we've done since that horrible day almost six years ago.

We were all together for so long prior to that, but watching Gabe fall on the field was like some kind of invisible cement gluing us together.

Those days leading up to the funeral and those few weeks after tested my humor skills. It was my role to be funny, to keep people laughing, to lighten the mood. While I knew that was what everyone wanted and what people expected, the first real laughter after his death was like a knife to the gut. *How could I laugh when I just saw my best friend die?*

I walked a fine line for weeks, knowing we needed the jokes but feeling guilty for trying to provide it. At fifteen though, what is there for boys besides sports, girls, and laughter? We embraced the first, clumsily made our way through the second, and attempted to find some comfort in the third.

Besides being the resident comedian, my biggest contribution was to suggest that we all shave our heads, which was kind of a big deal. My dad used to call us the All Hair Team because we liked our hair long. So, cutting it all off and shaving the number *6* into our heads was more than a statement.

It was my bright idea. And at fifteen, I was fairly impressed that I could mobilize us to do that. I'd started a movement—or so I'd thought.

Now, we were more than shaved heads and commemorative ribbons, more than bake sales and car washes. Last year, we placed three AEDs at youth soccer fields. And any one of us could spew statistics about sudden cardiac arrest. And this new idea for citywide heart screenings is crazy in its scope. The list of to-dos is completely overwhelming. But today, we moved closer.

Over the last few years, what became even more shocking was that we'd developed our own skill sets, all different but equal in some strange way. We'd grown up but not apart. It fascinated me a little.

Although deep thought isn't really my thing, I get caught up in the whole fate thing. Is this what we are all supposed to be doing? Or did Gabe's death shape us into an entrepreneur, a marketing guru, a social media expert, a fundraiser, and an organizer?

My parents had this old movie on VHS, and they used to regularly and religiously watch it. *The Big Chill* is about these college friends who get together for a funeral after twenty years. And they're all kind of surprised that they are different and not still friends even though they know each other really well and are the same. They all wonder if their dead friend's life would have been different if they'd all remained close. When I was younger, it confused me because I just wanted to tell them that things changed.

But after losing Gabe, all I could think was that we hadn't gotten that opportunity to wonder about Gabe's life.

But now I think, in twenty years, would we all still be friends, still be in each other's life? Or would we be looking around at each other, wondering what happened to our friendships?

It's depressing and definitely not part of my normal thought process. This is why thinking too much sucks and why I am thankful that my role is resident class clown.

To: M. Pryce

Subject: Information Gathering

Dear Lena,

You asked me some questions earlier today. I thought you might like to do some research on your own. I am including several good websites for you to use in case you have any additional questions. If you ever want to talk or you can't find the answers you're looking for, don't hesitate to reach out.

J.C.

It was such a short, somewhat terse email. But it haunted Lena with its tantalizing little links, links that led down a dark path, twisting and turning, impelling her toward a truth she'd attempted to avoid for eight years.

She spent hours at the computer, as if the topic were a siren's call, in the lonely hours of the night, learning about what had killed her brother and thousands of other kids every year. She knew more about the heart than she'd ever intended to know because Google searches tended to point in one direction and then move in another. She studied pictures of other children who had lost their lives, just like Gabe had. She poured over websites and foundations dedicated to finding ways to stem the tide. She read and digested research on the impact of EKGs in other countries. She was full to bursting with information that she'd never really wanted.

She hated the timing of this tournament and being stuck in a hotel. She could feel the week weighing heavily on her, like retained water that made clothes feel tight and stole bits of confidence. She must have really seemed to be a mess, like she needed a night off and a friend's ear, because Mike suggested that she and Lindsay leave the kids with him and go out.

As Lena shimmied into her skinny jeans, she banished all thoughts of J.C., a damaged heart, and a dead brother. Her brain screamed for a reprieve.

"Nicky, you ready?" When he didn't respond, she walked directly into his line of vision, blocking the TV. "Hey, are you ready to go to your dad's room?"

Nicky blinked, coming out of his TV haze. "Huh?"

"You ready to go to your dad's?"

"Miss Sarina said I could go to her room and hang out with Aiden, and Dad said it was okay."

"Whatever. Let's go though. And you need to be back in your dad's room at nine o'clock. I will tell Sarina because I am not sure I trust you to deliver the message." She kissed his head.

He laughed. "I promise, I'll leave at nine. Dad said the same thing." As he stood up, he glanced over at her. "You look pretty, Mama," he complimented shyly, making her heart squeeze.

There was nothing like a compliment from her boy to make her feel like a million bucks.

"Thanks, baby."

Nicky grabbed Lena's hand. It was one of those gestures she knew would disappear soon, so she tried to cherish the feeling of his sweaty little hand wrapped around hers as they headed out the door to Sarina's room.

The thought of coming to the soccer tournament this weekend had been oppressive. If she'd had her way, she would have opted out. The last thing she needed right now was soccer and lying soccer coaches. She'd tried really hard to convince herself that Nicky would be fine if she didn't go. And she'd been there. On Wednesday, she'd called Lindsay and said she had too much to do.

But then on Wednesday night, she'd picked Nicky up from Mike and Lindsay's house, and he'd looked at her with those damn blue eyes and said, "You're coming, right, Mama?"

Game. Set. Match.

She could totally see Lindsay coaching him to say something to sway her. But when she'd peered at her friend, she'd known by the look on Lindsay's face that it hadn't had anything to do with her.

So, here Lena was, walking down the hall of another three-star hotel, delivering her child to his friend's room.

"Wow!" Sarina exclaimed as she eyed Lena.

"I figured I might as well give it a go."

"I think I am regretting my decision not to go out tonight," Sarina answered.

"I can imagine that you won't regret it tomorrow while I'm nursing a hangover," Lena quipped.

"Well said." Sarina laughed as she opened the door wider to let Nicky enter.

Nicky gave Lena a passing glance as he headed into Sarina's room with a hurried, "Bye, Mom," and the tender hand-holding moment was gone.

Lena rolled her eyes. "Yeah, bye, buddy."

"Where are you off to?"

"I'm not sure. I left it up to Lindsay. I am just along for the ride. Not feeling up to making any decisions tonight, not even about where we go."

"Have a good time. I'll get Nick to Mike at nine."

"Great. Thanks!"

Lena headed toward the lobby to meet Lindsay. She arrived first and grabbed a seat on the hard couch. Vaguely, she thought, for next year, maybe she could take over hotel coordination for soccer, so she could pick where she wanted to stay. She desired plush rather than standard.

Leaning her head back, she closed her eyes.

When the elevator doors clamored open, she clearly identified J.C. and Bryce by the sounds of their voices. Her spot on the uncomfortable couch allowed her to see them without alerting them of her presence. They'd somehow multiplied. She recognized Fletcher but not the other two guys with them.

Probably coming to ogle Nicky, she thought.

She couldn't quite figure out how she knew their reason for showing up, but it all seemed to fit.

J.C. caught her attention. Dressed in jeans, a T-shirt, flip-flops, and a backward cap, he had a five-o'clock shadow, and he looked a little rougher—and hotter—than when she'd last seen him. His face was lit up with a smile. He was with his boys, and he was all carefree and sexy and young. She suppressed an involuntary groan.

She turned away, looking toward the opposite side of the lobby, attempting to block him. But she couldn't check the resentment. He'd cracked the shell of the insular little world she was living in with her son and Mike and Lindsay's family.

The elevator opened again, and Lindsay walked out. Lena watched Bryce and J.C. greet her with smiles and small talk. Lindsay shook hands with the unfamiliar posse.

And because Lena wanted reckless, she stood and walked toward the exit at the front of the lobby, away from the congregation of Apostles.

"You ready?" she said loud enough for Lindsay to look over at her.

Lindsay smiled and then narrowed her eyes. "Yes."

Lena tilted her head, turned, and walked through the doors without so much as an acknowledgment to the boys flanking Lindsay. Lena walked purposefully to her Jeep, and then she unlocked it and climbed in.

She thought about all the shit clouding her brain, making her feel different. She hated it. Tonight, she wanted something to regret, so tomorrow, instead of all the shitty statistics and heartbreaking stories that had taken up residence in her head, she would only have thoughts of the night before.

Lena and Lindsay were drunk. Lena had refused to drink alone, so Lindsay had had no choice in the matter.

It was late, and the cab ride home was apparently bumpier than Lindsay's stomach could take. Lena dragged her upstairs to her room, and when she walked Lindsay in, Mike glared at both of them.

Lena only managed a giggly, "Sorry," before she disappeared out of the room.

She made her way back to the elevator and leaned unsteadily against the wall, waiting impatiently. She was still antsy, like she could keep drinking if she had a reason to. The elevator dinged open. She walked directly toward it and stopped when she saw J.C. standing back against the opposite wall.

His look was wary, like he was nervous about being in a confined space with her. She met his gaze and then did a lazy perusal of him. His hat was still backward on his head, pulling his hair away from his face. She lifted her eyes back to his. Wariness was replaced with hunger.

"Hi," she murmured as she stepped into the car.

"Hi," he returned with a lift of his brow and a half-smile on his lips. "What floor?"

"Oh." She giggled.

Turning away from him, she hit the number five and turned right back around. The quick movement and the ascent of the elevator worked against her, and she stumbled a little. He grabbed her around the hips, steadying her. The same jolt of desire she had for him lanced through her. Her eyes widened, and a small gasp escaped her.

"You're drunk," he stated. He was talking to her, but his eyes kept shifting between her eyes and her mouth. His grip tightened on her hips.

Then, she felt him slightly pushing her away, making her take a baby step back. It was totally gentle, and she could see a sense of self-preservation on his face. She knew that look. She'd practically invented it.

Her anger toward him started slipping away.

"Yes, Jackson, I am."

"Ah, I'm Jackson tonight."

"J.C. reminds me of too many things—lying, for one," she said, but the bite it would have had earlier in the night was missing.

"Yeah," he murmured. His eyes dropped to her lips before skating away, looking for safer ground.

The elevator stopped abruptly. She would have stumbled, but he was still anchoring her to the floor, so just her upper body swayed. In an effort to stop it, she put her hands on his chest and leaned into him. This time, the heavy exhale came from him. She understood because her hands didn't want to leave his body. They moved up around his neck instead. Leaning in, she closed the distance and put her mouth on his. He fell into it at first, opening his mouth, pushing into hers, seeking her tongue. It wasn't sweet like their last kiss or searching and lingering like their first. It was hot and hard, all sorts of emotions moving between them.

His hands tightened on her hips, and he nudged her away from him. Releasing his grip on her, he took her hand in his and pulled her out of the elevator.

"What room?" he asked as the elevator door shut behind them.

A little disconcerted by the kiss and his abrupt halt to it, she stopped in the middle of the hall, snatching her hand from his.

"I don't need an escort," she said nastily as she opened her purse and grabbed the key card envelope.

Quickly scanning the number, she realized that she was a little disoriented. He reached out and took the key from her.

Taking her hand again, he led her in the opposite direction. When they came to her room, he opened the door and guided her inside. She glared at him, not liking the way he was handling her. It made her mad and then reckless.

He stood on the threshold, watching her. He held out the key card and the envelope to her. Grabbing it from him, she tossed it along with her purse onto the bed. Crossing her arms over her chest, waited for him to come in.

He looked at her questioningly. The invitation was obvious, but he hesitated.

"Now, you want to talk to me?" he asked, curious.

"Why did you send me that email?" she accused.

He heaved a sigh and stepped into her room, closing the door behind him. She moved farther in, and once again, she cursed the hotel because the only seating options were the two beds.

They sat across from each other, their knees almost touching. She was distracted by his nearness, and every part of her body was buzzing like it was on some kind of electrical pulse. She wanted to touch him, have some kind of physical connection so that it would ease the currents running through her. Moving forward to the very edge of the bed, her knees grazed his. It was instant relief, like grounding a live wire. She watched him as his eyes widened, and he drew in a deep breath. She almost smiled at his physical reaction. At least it was mutual.

"I sent the email because it seemed like you wanted some information," he said softly.

"I did, but it was too much," she answered, looking away from him.

"I can see that," he said as he weighed her assessment. "I didn't think about it."

They were quiet for a moment. She felt his legs shift so that he was no longer touching her.

Then, she remembered, tonight was not about answers but about regrets. She just wanted to revert, be that person who didn't have to or want to think about anyone else.

Standing, she closed the distance between them, invading his space. She stepped between his legs so that he surrounded her. His hands automatically moved to her hips, perhaps to steady her or perhaps just to touch her. She couldn't be sure which, but it didn't matter because she felt the warmth from his skin seeping into her. She tugged his hat off his head and then placed her hands on his shoulders.

He leaned back to look at her. "What are you doing, Lena?" He met her gaze, his deep brown eyes trained on hers.

"Something I'll regret in the morning," she delivered. She gifted him with a wicked grin as her hands delved into the hair at the back of his head. It was thick and soft, longer than she'd remembered.

She watched him close his eyes and lean forward so that his forehead rested on her stomach. His hands moved up her back, so she was wrapped up in him. He dipped his head, running his nose from the waistband of her jeans to her belly button. He must have felt her piercing because he groaned a little before he moved her shirt up over her navel.

He leaned back and looked up at her again for a brief second. She had no idea what he was looking for, but she knew he was seeking something. He dropped his head, pulled her forward, and ran his tongue along her navel before tugging on the piercing. The moan that escaped her was completely involuntary. She felt like she was on fire, and he'd barely touched her.

He pulled away from her again and shifted her back. Then, he stood, crowding her, making her step back, out of his way. He turned, picked up his hat, and slipped it backward onto his head. Leaning forward, he placed a kiss on her forehead—a kiss much like the one she had given him on the beach and in her office. He pulled away from her and met her gaze. Their eyes locked.

"I'm not okay with being something you'll regret, Lena," he said. Then, he headed to the door and left her.

J.C. sat on the bench next to Bryce, attempting to keep his interest focused on the game even though he found his attention being pulled toward the opposite sideline. It wasn't as if he could even see Lena's face as she was wearing a hat, some girl version of a classic baseball cap. Big fashionista sunglasses covered half of her face. So, he should have been able to block her out, but he could feel her from across the field, and it was messing with his concentration.

He'd gotten really good at not thinking about her, but today, it wasn't happening. He was blaming his lack of sleep…and maybe the memory of her kiss…the belly ring that he couldn't pass up…the wicked gleam in her eyes…her fingers in his hair. He tried hard not to think about those fifteen minutes of his life. The hold he'd had when he was awake had disappeared in his sleep where he could have her over and over.

"Coach, can I go in again?"

The plea from Aiden snapped him out of his reverie. Glancing at his watch, he noticed he was over his substitution time.

"Sure," he said. He stood up and got some of the other kids ready to go in.

With his back to the field, he didn't see it happen. He only heard a *thunk* and an "Oh, shit," muttered from Bryce.

Turning toward the field, J.C. saw Nick crumbled near the post. For a moment, he was fifteen again, and Gabe was lying on the ground, his body still. But Nick was rolling from side to side, clutching his face, and he realized that this wasn't the same thing.

J.C. jogged over to Nick's writhing form, ever mindful of Lena, who'd come out of her chair and was waiting on some signal from him to release her from her protective stance.

The ref was standing over Nick and turned to J.C. when he was close enough. "Think he's bleeding," he said low so that the kids wouldn't hear him.

J.C. knelt beside Nick. "You're not supposed to head-butt the kid," he whispered as he gently pulled Nick's hands away from his face.

J.C. saw the gash across Nick's brow and the blood on the boy's hands. Attempting to keep everyone calm, especially Nick, J.C. put his hands down near Nick's side so that the blood wasn't so noticeable.

Nick laughed. "Is it bad?" he asked.

"Well, I think you might be done for the day," J.C. said, trying to sound reassuring. But he could tell stitches were inevitable. "How do you feel about blood?"

"It's okay." Then, Nick scrunched his face up. "My blood?"

J.C. laughed. "Yeah, your blood."

"Not so good if it's mine," he said with a wavering smile.

"What about your mom and dad?" J.C. asked as he moved the corner of his shirt up and tried to mop up some of the blood.

"Definitely not my mom. She probably won't let me play anymore if I'm bleeding."

J.C. tried to stifle his laugh. "Let's not worry about that right now. I don't want you to sit up since you hit your head, okay?"

"Okay."

J.C. looked back toward the sideline. Rather than looking at Lena, he searched for Mike and waved him over.

When he saw Mike jogging over to him, he turned back to Nick. "Your dad's coming out onto the field. He's probably going to have to take you to the hospital. You need stitches, buddy."

Mike dropped down on the other side of Nick. "Banged yourself pretty good, huh?"

"Yes, sir," Nick said.

"Looks like you are going to have a shiner, too," Mike commented.

J.C. felt her before he saw her. Her proximity zipped through him before she even opened her mouth.

Leaning over Mike, Lena said, "Holy shit! He needs to go to the hospital."

"Language, Lena," Mike reminded her.

J.C. kept his eyes on Nick, afraid to look up and get trapped in her gaze. With Mike and Lena there, J.C. stood and stepped away from them.

"Hospital?" Bryce asked.

"For sure."

"I can stay and finish the game. Why don't you go with them?"

"Absolutely not. We can go after the game and check up on him. They don't need a whole bunch of people around when they get there."

Bryce sent him a sidelong look. "You sure?"

"Yes."

"Would you go if it were any other kid?" Bryce challenged.

"Yes, after the game, unless the kid's parents weren't here for some reason."

Bryce nodded. They watched as Mike gathered Nick in his arms and carried him off the field, toward the parking lot. Lena followed, contained. J.C. saw her walking away, relieved she hadn't freaked out. He couldn't begin to predict what he would have done if she had. She probably wouldn't have wanted anything from him, but it would have been hard to stand by if she'd shown any signs of being affected.

J.C. admired the way Lena and Mike interacted, but in some deep corner of his mind, he wondered what it would be like to have to compete with their relationship on a day-to-day basis. Would he be able to just be good with it, like Lindsay? Or would it bother him that Lena was so close to and comfortable with another man?

Not that it matters, he thought.

The game resumed, but it seemed to drag. All of them, coaches and players, were out of it. Thankfully, they'd had a lead when Nick went down because they couldn't seem to get anything together now. Frustrated, J.C. waited, wishing for the game to end. When the final whistle sounded, J.C. and Bryce quickly met with the team and then made their way toward Sarina.

"Have you heard from them?" J.C. asked as soon as he was close enough for Sarina to hear.

"No, but Lindsay said she would text when she had an update."

"Will you text us when you know something?" Bryce responded.

"Of course. As soon as I know, I'll let you know. I'm sure Aiden is going to want to head over there, too. Was it bad?" she asked J.C.

"Definitely needs stitches. I didn't want him to sit up, so I'm not sure if he was dizzy or if he might have had a concussion."

"Ah, I didn't even think of that."

"It was a pretty good gash to the head."

"I promise to text you when I know something," Sarina assured them.

"Thanks," they both said before heading away from the fields.

Lena was sitting in the emergency room in a little curtained cubicle with Nicky and Mike.

Lindsay and the girls had been here, too, but when it'd seemed like it was going to take a while, Lindsay had whisked them back to the hotel.

Nicky had been seen and evaluated. The emergency room doctor had deferred to a plastic surgeon because the laceration was on Nicky's face.

So, they were waiting. The nurse put the television on for Nicky, so he was perfectly content to stay where he was. His sweat had long ago dried up, and although they'd done a good job of cleaning him up, he still had some streaks of dirt and blood.

Lena saw Mike check his phone but assumed it was Lindsay. So, she was surprised when he got up and told her he'd be right back.

The chaos and concern over the last couple of hours had occupied her enough to keep her thoughts away from J.C. But with the low drone of the television and a solitary moment, she found herself thinking of him. She'd seen Nicky go down, and part of her had wanted to run out onto the field to her son, taking out anyone in her way. But Mike's hand on her arm had stayed her. She'd watched from the sideline as J.C. had calmly made his way out to Nicky. She'd seen him kneel and survey the scene. He'd taken Nicky's hands and made sure that he wouldn't panic because of the blood. She'd watched him keep Nicky calm. Seeing him with Nicky had done all sorts of crazy things to her insides, things she didn't want to think about.

The curtain pulled back, and Mike came in, saying, "Look who's here to check on you."

J.C. and Bryce walked through, heading to either side of the bed.

"How ya doing, big guy?" J.C. said as he held out his fist for Nicky.

"Hey, dude," Bryce said, following. "We just wanted to make sure you were doing okay."

"And maybe we brought you some illegal snacks," J.C. added as he handed Nicky a bag of Oreo cookies. "That's your favorite, right?"

Lena was a little fascinated. *How did J.C. know that?* she thought.

"Yeah, I love these." Nicky's eyes and face lit up. "Thanks, Coach."

J.C. nodded his head. He refused to look her way or acknowledge her.

Bryce, however, turned around from Nicky's bed and smiled at her. "Hey, Lena," he said.

Lena smiled tightly. She was touched that they'd come and impressed that they'd brought Nicky something that he so obviously loved. But J.C. ignoring her was grating on her nerves. She willed him to look up at her, but his attention remained on Nicky. She wanted to stand up and stomp her feet or do anything to get him to look her way.

She pulled her gaze away from him and found herself looking at Mike, who had a curious expression on his face, as if he'd suddenly gotten something. He studied her from across the room, and she knew he was processing whatever was in his head.

"All right, buddy, we'll come check on you when you get back to the hotel," Bryce said as they wrapped up their visit.

"You'll come see me?" Nicky asked, the hopefulness in his voice ringing clear.

"Absolutely," J.C. said. "We'll see you later."

"Sorry to bust in on you both," Bryce said as he shook hands with Mike.

"No problem at all," Mike responded. He turned to J.C. and shook his hand, too. "We'll text you when we get back."

"Thanks," Bryce and J.C. said in unison before they pulled the curtain back and headed into the hallway.

The plastic surgeon arrived right as Bryce and J.C. left. Once she'd taken a look and stitched Nicky up, they were released with instructions for his wound and potential concussion signs. The moment they drove out of the hospital parking lot, Nicky fell asleep, which gave Mike an opening that he'd apparently been waiting for because he immediately looked over at Lena.

"What's going on with you and the kid?" Mike asked.

Lena looked at him with wide-eyed innocence as she said, "What are you talking about?"

Mike shook his head. "I'm not stupid. Coach Cal did everything he could to keep from looking at you, and you did everything other than strip to get his attention. What's up?"

"Nothing," she tried for an indignant tone. She wasn't sure why she was holding back with Mike. She'd never had trouble talking to him about other men. It intrigued her somewhat.

Who am I trying to protect? she wondered.

Mike wouldn't care because Lena never mixed her relationships with her child. Unless it was important to her, she wouldn't. And Mike knew that.

"Come on, Lena. It's not like you to be tight-lipped about your dating life."

"We're not dating. Jeez!"

"Screwing?"

"No!"

Mike tilted his head. "Kissing?"

Lena hesitated. "Not really."

Mike laughed. "Not really? How do you *not really* kiss someone?"

"They are always abbreviated," she said on a laugh.

"Look, I've never interfered with your sex life, and I won't start now. But I need to say just a few things." Since she didn't try to stop him, he paused for a breath and then continued, "This kid is connected to Nick already, so whatever you do is going to affect Nick in some way."

"I'm not doing anything," she said, somewhat exasperated.

"He's a good kid. You would eat him up and spit him out."

"You're wrong there. Just ask Lindsay," she delivered with her usual sassiness.

Mike slowly shook his head. "I can see the attraction between you two. You'd have to be blind not to see that. But I just don't see anything good coming out of it. It would be complicated."

"You have no idea about complications." She stopped, knowing she was going to tell him but wishing she didn't have to. "Look, you don't have to worry. Yes, I am attracted to him— wickedly attracted to him. But he's one of the Apostles. He was Gabe's best friend. And he didn't tell me even though he knew. So, whatever it was, it's not. And it wasn't even anything. He's twenty-three, for God's sake."

"He knew Gabe?" Mike said, shocked.

"Yes. He and Bryce—we all grew up in the same town. They started this foundation in Gabe's name, and they have done all these amazing things."

"I knew they had some foundation, but I didn't know about the connection."

"Right, well, I just found out about it on Monday. I told Lindsay about it last night, over many drinks."

Mike looked over at her. "Are you okay?"

Lena shrugged her shoulders. "I don't know. I guess. I just can't really get my head around it, other than I know that I need to stay away from Coach Cal. I do know that."

"That's probably best, for many reasons," Mike warned.

She couldn't say why, but his warning, issued in his fatherly tone, pissed her off a little. And even though she could enumerate all the reasons to stay away from Jackson Callahan, it seemed like Mike had just given her a reason to do the opposite.

Lena parked her car in Mike and Lindsay's driveway and rested her head on the steering wheel before collecting herself and heading toward the front door.

It had been a hectic couple of days. One doctor's appointment had turned into three—from the pediatrician to the concussion specialist who had released Nicky and then back to the pediatrician. It had pulled her from work on Monday, which had meant a long night of trying to catch up on her accounts. It'd called for a long day on Tuesday and a late pick-up tonight. She was tired and wanted nothing more than to kiss the girls, collect her child, and head home.

She was surprised no one came running to the door when the chime had announced her arrival. Lena made her way into the kitchen and stopped when she saw the assembly with J.C., Bryce, Fletcher, and two other guys she hadn't yet met. They were all seated around the table with the kids, playing Left Right Center—their family-favorite dice game.

Lindsay saw her first, and Lena could see her friend's guilt.

She mouthed, *I'm sorry*, and then made her way over to Lena without drawing anyone's attention.

Lindsay grabbed her arm and pulled Lena back into the hallway.

"I thought you were going to be later," Lindsay said as an opening.

"Oh, that's your excuse?" Lena's tiredness took over.

"First, I don't need an excuse. This is my house, and I can have anyone over whenever I want. So, when I apologize in a second, I want you to remember that." Lindsay crossed her arms over her chest in full she-warrior mode. "This wasn't my idea. I came home, and Mike said he'd invited Bryce and J.C. over for dinner and asked if it would be okay if they brought some friends."

"You invited the Apostles over when you know all the craziness that's going on with me, and I'm supposed to just be cool with that?"

"Yes, and no. You can be mad at Mike, and I'd rather you not take it out on me."

"How about a warning? Like, *Hey, Lena, I know you are all tied up over this boy who lied to you. And I know you have to pick up your son tonight. Just a heads-up that Mike invited him and all of his little friends over.*"

"You're right, but to be perfectly honest, I didn't think you'd get here this early. I thought, by the time you got here, they would be gone, and I could explain it to you. It wouldn't have been a big deal then, would it have?"

Lena shook her head. She leaned back against the wall and closed her eyes. "I'm so tired, Lindsay. Can you just grab Nicky for me, so I can get out of here?" Opening her eyes, she looked at Lindsay, whose worry was etched into the lines on her face.

"Are you sure you want to do that? I haven't served dinner yet, which means you'll have to cook for Nick when you get home. Just grab a glass of wine, and stay for dinner."

Lena stared at her friend. The thought of hanging with the Apostles tonight after a brutal week and only a little bit of sleep wasn't something she felt up for.

For the last few days, when she hadn't been working or researching sudden cardiac arrest, she had been reliving her couple of minutes in J.C.'s arms. The last thing she needed tonight was to have to be on her toes mentally. The more she was around J.C., the more she wanted to be around him.

He'd come to see Nicky at the hotel on Saturday night, and even though the room had been full of people, she'd been completely tuned in to him. He'd interacted with all the kids and parents, made Nicky laugh, captivated her attention when she tried really hard to keep it focused on anyone but him. He'd treated her like he treated Lindsay and Sarina, like the parent of one of his players. While she had been looking at the bed and thinking about him running his tongue around her navel, he had acted like she was just another person. As much as she'd wanted to be angry with him for that, she'd found she genuinely liked him.

"I can't do this tonight, Linds," she pleaded.

"Look, I get that you're mad at him for not telling you who he was and for not explaining the connection he had with you. But they're all here to see your son. And they are good guys. So, maybe you can let this go for Nick?"

"Fine," Lena said, resignation heavy in her voice. She closed her eyes, and when she opened them, they pooled with unshed tears.

"Oh my God. Don't you dare cry on me," Lindsay said as she grabbed Lena and pulled her in for a hug.

"I'm just so damn tired."

"I'll open a really good bottle of wine. I promise, this crew will make you laugh, and you can leave as soon as dinner is over."

"I don't want to do this. I don't want to be around him."

"Afraid you won't be able to keep your hands off of him?" Lindsay quipped.

"Yeah," she whispered.

"Shit, seriously?" Lindsay said. "That was rhetorical. You weren't supposed to answer that."

Lena laughed. "Well, you asked."

Lindsay joined her. "I did. I just didn't think you'd be honest about it."

"Oh, well, like I said, I'm tired. I'm not thinking straight."

"But you'll stay, right? If I try to pull Nick out right now, you are going to have a fight on your hands."

Lena sighed long and loud. "I am going to kill Mike." Running her fingers under her eyes, she looked down at the smudges of black. "I need to fix this," she said as she held up her hands.

Turning, she made her way to Mike and Lindsay's room. She ran some water and mopped up what was left of the black on her face. Digging through Lindsay's good makeup, she fixed the mess. She wished for some liquid courage right when Lindsay showed up in the doorway with a glass of wine. She would have preferred vodka, but she took the wine with a nod of appreciation.

"I'll get dinner up right away, okay?" Lindsay said before leaving the bathroom.

"You'd better."

Lena took one last look in the mirror. Her red wrap dress was one of her favorites, so in terms of attire, she probably couldn't have done better. As an afterthought, she grabbed a hair tie and threw her hair into a ponytail. As she left the bathroom, she hoped J.C. would do something tonight to make her stop the madness of thinking about him.

When Lena entered the kitchen for the second time that night, the scene had changed. The remnants of Left Right Center had been cleaned up, and J.C., Bryce, and someone she hadn't met were helping Lindsay set up plates and utensils while Fletcher and another nameless Apostle were entertaining the kids. The clicking of her heels on the tiles drew their attention.

"Hey," she said to the room at large, going for nonchalance.

A chorus of hellos bounced around the kitchen. Lena didn't meet anyone's gaze. Instead, she walked toward the patio where the kids were playing some kind of walking tag. Nicky, Jessie, and Milly stopped long enough to plop messy kisses on her cheeks and then joined the Apostles in their game. Fletcher made sure to say hi, but she merely waved and closed the sliding glass door. Joining the dinner preparations in the kitchen, she started helping Lindsay.

Mike walked into the kitchen, found Lena immediately, and dropped a kiss on her head. "Hey, and sorry," he whispered so that only she could hear.

She leaned into him and responded with, "I hate you right now. Don't try to be nice."

Mike laughed. "Lena," he said in a normal tone, "this is Kyle. And outside are Fletcher and Max."

Lena looked over at Kyle and graced him with a smile. "Hey."

"Hey."

J.C. waded into the awkward silence that followed their introduction. "We wanted to check on Nick, and the guys wanted to meet him."

She met his eyes for a brief second and shrugged, as if it were no big deal that they were here. She wasn't trying to be a bitch, but self-preservation was at a premium.

"His eye looks better than I thought it would," Bryce said.

"It does. Our pediatrician said that the plastic surgeon did a phenomenal job," Lena responded.

"And no concussion, so will he be back at practice next week?" Bryce asked.

Lena could hear the hope in his voice.

She smiled at him before she said, "We'll see. Please don't ask him when he's coming back. He's already been hounding me."

Bryce held his hands up. "Scout's honor."

"You were so not a scout," Lena said, laughing.

"My mom kept hoping," he responded, laughing with her.

She glanced over and saw J.C. watching the exchange, his eyes glued on her. Her whole body felt his stare. She wanted to look away, but she couldn't seem to pull her eyes from him.

Lindsay bumped into her, snapping her from her J.C. haze. "You want to get the kids?"

"Of course." Lena left through the sliding glass door and ushered the kids into the bathroom to wash their hands. She needed the cool water after that staring contest in the kitchen. She was out of her mind. She wished she could come up with a graceful exit.

"Aunt Lena, will you sit with me?" Jessie asked.

"Absolutely." Lena kissed her on the top of her head.

They headed back toward the kitchen, got their food, and made their way to the table outside. Fletcher and Max were already seated outside, so Lena and Jessie joined them. Thankful for the reprieve from J.C., Lena chatted with Fletcher and Max without any mention of their shared past. Fletcher didn't try to bring up Gabe, and Max effortlessly engaged Jessie.

Lena finally relaxed, the tension over the dinner draining away. She was almost out of there, and she couldn't wait to get home.

When she went to help Lindsay with clean up, she was sent away.

"Go home. I know you're tired," Lindsay said.

Thankful for her reprieve, Lena headed back outside to get Nicky, who happened to be talking to J.C.

"Hey, buddy, we've gotta go," she said.

Nicky looked over at her and was about to argue. She could see him contemplating taking her on. There must have been something in her look because he stopped himself.

"I have to get my bag," he said before he hurried away.

"Hey," J.C. said as they both watched Nicky go.

"Hey," she responded with a tilt of her head.

127

"How are you?"

Shrugging, she said, "Fine. You know, no regrets."

He smirked at her. "Have you been waiting to say that to me?" He moved toward her, eating up the space.

"No, not at all," she lied. She'd penned that line as soon as he'd walked out of her hotel room. She'd been dying for an opportunity to use it.

"I think you're lying," he said, smiling at her.

"Nah. I haven't given it much thought."

J.C. sighed, the smile fading away, before he rubbed his hand over his face. "Lucky you," he said, watching her face.

"If I were lucky, things would have worked out differently on Friday."

He pursed his lips and nodded his head. "You think so? Drunken hook-ups your thing?"

She shrugged and pulled her lip between her teeth.

He moved closer and watched her. And she returned his stare, taking him in. He looked behind her toward the activity in the kitchen.

Then, his gaze returned to hers. "When you want it to be a beginning, not a one-night thing, let me know," he said. His gaze lingered on her for a moment before he moved around her and walked into the house.

16

"Seems like you all had a good time the other night," Anna remarked casually.

J.C. looked up from the document he'd been slaving over for the last couple of hours. It took him a second to realize she was talking about his trip to see Nick.

"We did," he answered matter-of-factly even though he felt suddenly wary. He probably should have encouraged her to come with them, but when she'd declined, no one had tried to change her mind.

"Did Maggie—crap, I mean, Lena. Did she give you any indication on when we would hear from her?"

He almost smiled at Anna's slip. When he'd first seen Lena again, it had been difficult to get his mind around that name. She'd only ever been Maggie. Now, it seemed like she was only ever Lena. He couldn't pinpoint the moment the name Maggie had been eradicated for him. It wasn't the night on the beach because he fought to get the right name out. But it was soon after when he could no longer think about her or look at her and think, *Maggie*. He remembered someone at some point telling him that you truly knew another language if you could dream in it. When he thought of her, dreamed about her now, she was Lena.

"She didn't say, but we didn't ask her when we would hear about the documents." He tried to return to his task, but he felt Anna's distraction, and it worked against him. Turning away from his laptop, he gave her his full attention. "Is something else up?" he asked.

"Is there a reason you didn't want me to go with you?" Anna replied.

"Where?" J.C. responded, feigning ignorance.

Anna rolled her eyes. "With you to see Nick."

"Why would you think that?"

"Why are you answering all my questions with questions?"

J.C. shrugged. "I didn't mean to."

Anna narrowed her eyes. "Seriously, J.C., what the hell? Why don't you want me to be around Nick?"

J.C. leaned back in his chair and held his hands up in surrender. "I have no idea what you're talking about."

"I have a theory," she said, almost on top of his response.

Without meaning to, J.C. sighed. "What theory?"

"You really don't want me around Lena Pryce."

"Why wouldn't I want you to be around Lena?"

"And there's another question."

Feeling cornered and frustrated, J.C. ran his hand through his hair, and then he stood up, out of the chair. Hating the confines of their office, J.C. found a seat on a table, getting as far away from Anna as he could get, which was only about four feet.

"Lena wasn't even there for most of it," he justified. "And I didn't know she was going to be there at all. But that doesn't explain why you would think I didn't want you around her."

"Come on, J.C. I'm not stupid."

"Pretty sure I know that."

"I get it, you know. After what happened between us, I get why you wouldn't want me around the woman you're interested in."

"Why would you think that?" J.C. asked, shocked.

"Why else wouldn't you want me around her?"

"Come on, Anna," J.C. said on a groan, his hands running through his hair, discomfort a second skin. "I thought we worked through this." He'd wanted to believe they could go back to before—before sex and Lena and Nick. He'd naively thought they could put it behind them and continue to work together.

"We did. It's all good, and I don't have a problem with any of it. But I can tell you do. Six months ago, you would have included me in all of this."

"All of what? Dinner at a player's house? That doesn't even make sense," he said, waving off her concerns with a swipe of his hand.

"Not your player's house—Nick's house, Gabe's nephew. Damn it, J.C. Don't act like I wouldn't want to know him, too."

J.C.'s eyes widened, and he looked across the small space between them, hoping for some kind of divine intervention to help him navigate this crazy conversation. J.C. tried to respond, but he waited, sure that Anna wasn't done with what she wanted to say.

"I just want things to be normal with us, and I can tell they aren't," she said.

"I'm sorry you feel that way, but I promise you, nothing is different. I'm not trying to leave you out. I invited you, remember?" he placated.

"I remember. I also remember hearing a sigh of relief when I said no," she returned.

"Okay, I definitely call bullshit on that," he said on a laugh. Feeling the crisis dissolving, he got up and resumed his seat next to her.

When he was seated, she turned toward him again. "Are you going to admit that you like her?"

Like seemed to be a small word for the enormity of his feelings. He still felt high from his five-minute exchange with her a week ago.

No regrets, he thought with a smile.

He pulled his thoughts from Lena and met Anna's knowing gaze.

"What are we, back in middle school?"

"Very funny, J.C. Just so you know, the longer it takes for you to admit, the more I'm convinced that you like her."

There was no way J.C. was going to admit anything to Anna. Although the tension had disappeared, he knew Anna didn't feel the nonchalance she was exuding. He wasn't going to step into that trap again, and he wouldn't forget to watch himself around Anna. It seemed like Lena wasn't the only girl trouble he had.

"Do you want me to reach out to Lena about the documents?" he asked, bringing the conversation full circle.

Anna shook her head as she answered, "No. I'll just send her a quick email. I don't want to harass her, but I should probably check in with her."

"How close are we to finishing this? I'm not sure there is much point in reaching out to Lena without our stuff being completed—or at least close to it."

Anna looked back at her computer. It took her some time to answer him. "Maybe seventy-five percent done? But we could be further out if Lena comes back and says we need to more financial documentation." She looked back at J.C. "That will suck, by the way."

"Yeah," he said. Leaning back in his chair, driving it onto two legs, he reached his arms back and clasped them behind his head. "Ya know that feeling at the end of a really hard semester? You've finished everything, and you have this huge sense of relief, but then you also feel like you should have something to do? There's nothing hanging over your head, no other paper to write or book to read, and it feels odd."

Anna nodded.

"I can't wait for that feeling," he said, laughing. "I can't wait until this application is done, and I can sit back and think, *I don't have anything to do.*"

This made Anna laugh hysterically. J.C. watched, puzzled.

"What?" he finally asked.

"You are so full of shit," she said around her laughter. "You won't sit for more than one day without putting your hands in the next sandbox, trying to build a castle."

J.C. righted the chair and leaned forward, dropping his elbows to his knees. "What's that supposed to mean?"

She stopped laughing, but the big smile remained, and little eruptions of giggles bubbled forth from her mouth.

"Seriously," he said.

"J.C., you are usually much more self-aware. Are you, like, in a funk or something?"

Her statement hit a little too close to home, and he suddenly didn't like where this was going. He lifted his hands up, as if to say, *Continue*, or, *What?*, or, *Go on*, since words were stuck in his throat at the moment.

"We'll finish the application. You'll survey it, deem it good, and rest—for the day. Then, the next day, you'll get up, and you'll move on to the next thing—heart screenings. This is your big push right now, right? You and Max will go to the Parent Heart Watch convention, and you'll find some way to get this to work out.

You'll mobilize the your troops, and then we'll pull this off. At the end of that day, you'll survey what we've done, and you'll rest—until the next day. The day after, you'll come up with another plan—lobbying the state legislature or Congress, for God's sake. We'll start moving in that direction. You'll finish that, then rest for the day, and move on to the next thing. If you're not moving on to the next thing, you'll get twitchy. It's like, if you are not accomplishing more than any other twenty-three-year-old can accomplish, then you won't be happy." Her eyes were lit up with her mirth.

He continued to watch her laugh at his expense while he tried not to get defensive about her J.C.-in-a-bottle assessment. It wouldn't be all bad if it were true, but he didn't see it like that. She'd made it sound like he was steering the ship while J.C. always felt like her first mate.

He turned away from her and moved back toward his computer. The best response he could generate to her description of him was, "Twitchy? Is that even a word?"

She laughed again. "Oh, yes, it is. I bet if you looked it up, it would have a picture of you when you don't have some idea germinating in your head."

For some reason, her explanation made him laugh.

J.C. and Anna were pretty much finished when a text came in from Bryce. He, Fletcher, Max and Kyle were all going out and were expecting Anna and J.C. to meet them. He held his phone out to Anna, so she could read the text. Without responding, she began packing up her stuff.

"We deserve it," she said as way of an explanation. "We got a lot done today."

J.C. didn't argue with her as he followed suit. *Busy is good*, he thought.

And they had accomplished a lot. They were now done with organizing documents, and he'd completed the narrative description of their activities. They were getting closer to completing the application for non-profit status, closer to meeting that goal.

The thought almost made him laugh as Anna's description of him flashed through his mind. He still wanted to argue points of it with her, but he was reluctant to bring up anything discordant. So, he grabbed his things and followed her out.

"You want me to drive?" Anna asked.

"Nah," he responded. "The bar's closer to my house than this."

"K," she said simply as she got into her car.

As J.C. drove to the bar, he tried to keep his mind off of Lena. *A recurring theme*, he thought.

Recently, any of his downtime had been occupied with thoughts of Lena and their interactions. The few moments in her hotel room replayed through his mind all the time, even weeks later. Seeing her last week and challenging her, he'd senselessly hoped she'd do something about it. He had been counting on her to rise to the challenge. *Silly him.*

It didn't take long for them to get to the bar. It wasn't some place they normally frequented, and he wondered briefly whose bright idea it was to try something new. Meeting Anna at her car, he walked her in. They were all there—Max, Bryce, Fletcher, and Kyle—and they had beers waiting for Anna and J.C.

"Get a lot done?" Bryce asked as he handed J.C. a bottle.

There was more to the question than work, but only J.C. and Bryce knew it.

"Actually, yes. All good," J.C. said, even though he knew things between he and Anna were far from good. He wasn't prepared to go there with Bryce right now.

"Figured it would be soon enough."

"Liar," J.C. said.

Bryce smirked. "Good at it though."

"Maybe with someone who doesn't know you."

Bryce laughed good-naturedly, and they turned back to the group.

"So, I think I gave J.C. something to think about today," Anna said.

They all turned toward her while J.C. quizzically looked at her, not sure where she was going with her statement. She looked to be in her element, all the attention focused on her.

"He is operating under the impression that he'll enjoy some downtime when we finish the 501(c)(3) application."

This statement elicited laughter from the group surrounding him, but he merely shook his head, not fighting it.

He saw Fletcher's eyes widen at something behind him. "J.C., isn't that Mark Ellington?"

Bryce muttered, "Dickhead."

J.C. smiled at his friend before he turned toward the newcomer. He did a quick perusal of the crowd behind him and turned back. "Yep, that's him. Good timing, huh? He can't avoid me in a bar."

"Pretty hard to do that face-to-face," said Fletcher.

"I'm sure he'll find a way," Anna commented.

J.C. laughed. "Probably."

J.C. and Fletcher had met Mark Ellington at a conference a couple of years ago. He'd seen the notice at school, saw Mark Ellington's name, and immediately registered for it. Mark had recently taken over as president of the new smaller hospital in town. Since his hire, the hospital had given the more established hospital a run for its money. When they had decided that they eventually wanted to sponsor a heart screening, J.C. had looked to Mark to provide some much-needed resources. Attending the conference and making the connection had been a part of his plan to get the guy on board. After the initial meeting, J.C. had had lunch with him. Then, he'd communicated with Mark via email about random various things. The moment J.C. had broached the subject of the hospital sponsoring the heart screenings, Mark had shut him down and stopped returning emails and phone calls.

Running into Mark tonight seemed like a perfect time to remind him that they knew each other.

Finishing his beer, J.C. put the empty bottle on the bar. Turning to Fletcher, he said, "You coming?"

Fletcher grinned wide. "Hell yeah," he said before draining his beer.

"This ought to be good," Kyle said.

They'd all taken their turn in lamenting about Mark's seeming disinterest in what they wanted to do. Before J.C. and Bryce had moved out of their fraternity house, they'd tacked a picture of the guy to their dartboard and used him for target practice.

J.C. and Fletcher moved toward the tables where Mark was standing with a group of people. He didn't want Mark to find a way to avoid him, as he'd seemed to be quite adept at doing.

"Hey, Mark," J.C. said as he stuck his hand forward. "I'm not sure if you remember me. J.C. Callahan. And this is Fletcher Woodard."

"Of course," Mark said as he shook each of their hands. "J.C., Fletcher, how are you?"

J.C. didn't want to give the guy a chance to get away, so he looked to Mark's date, waiting until the man had no choice but to introduce her.

Checkmate, he thought.

Mark tapped the woman on the arm, and when she turned, J.C.'s breath slipped away.

"J.C., Fletcher, this is Lena."

Damn, Lena thought as she was nudged forward.

"Hey, Lena!" Fletcher exclaimed loud enough for nearly the whole bar to hear.

He embraced her like she was an old friend, and again, she found him hard to resist.

"Oh," Mark said stiffly, "you know each other?"

J.C. said, "Yeah, we go way back."

She came out of Fletcher's arms.

J.C. merely nodded at her, glancing her way. "Lena," he said. Then, he looked back to Mark. "I was hoping to catch up with you."

"Yeah, just give me a call at my office," Mark responded, insincerity resounding through his voice.

It was loud enough for Lena to get it, and she wanted to cringe.

She watched J.C. nod, knowing he was getting blown off.

"Yeah, I'll try that," he said before turning and leaving them.

"See ya, Lena," Fletcher said with a smile. "Mark," he said, giving a nod.

Lena wasn't sure what all of that was about, but her desire to be out evaporated. She'd convinced herself to come out with Mark tonight because she needed a distraction—specifically, a distraction from the guy standing over at the bar, drinking with his friends. *How was he suddenly everywhere?* Two months ago, she hadn't seen J.C. Callahan anywhere in her little world. Now, every time she turned around, he was there, dogging her, making her want things she couldn't have.

Mark found a table and ordered their drinks. Lena fought to keep her eyes on him because they wanted to drift to the bar, toward J.C. to watch him, take him in. But she fought it—hard. It kept her from asking Mark what their exchange had been about because the last thing she needed to do was talk about J.C.

Instead, she intently listened to Mark, pretending to be interested in the guy across the table from her. When he reached for her hand and held it, rubbing his thumb across her knuckles, she allowed it. To anyone watching, she knew she looked like she was into him. At appropriate times, she made sure she leaned in and looked adoringly at him. Mark should have sensed the difference in her behavior, but he had been arrogant enough to think that she was into him before, so her increased interest didn't raise any alarm for him.

She knew she was putting on a good show because she happened to glance up and see Bryce across the bar, studying her.

Part of her just wanted to get away from Mark for a second, to soothe the unease in her stomach, so she excused herself. As she headed toward the restrooms, she looked over and saw J.C. watching her. When their eyes met, he glared at her and then looked away. She felt his withdrawal deeply, regretting her choice to go out tonight, her choice to overplay her hand with Mark, her choice to stay away from J.C.

She opened the restroom door and walked in. Anna was standing at the sink, and she met Lena's eyes in the mirror.

"Hey," Anna said, continuing to wash her hands but not looking away.

It unsettled Lena.

"Hi," she said with a smile. "Small world."

Anna shut off the sink, grabbed a paper towel, and turned around, leaning on the sink.

"Do you know that guy well?" Anna asked.

Her directness threw Lena. "Well enough," she answered.

"He's a douche bag," Anna told her.

Lena laughed loudly. "Well, don't hold back on my account," she said.

"I'm just saying in case you don't know. He's a complete ass."

Lena was too intrigued to let it go. She crossed her arms over her chest and nodded her head, giving Anna the opening she wanted.

"J.C. and Fletcher met him at a conference. He gave J.C. his card and told him to look him up. I know you don't know J.C. well, but an open invitation like that would not be passed up. J.C. called him, and they met. Mark took him to lunch. J.C. explained his idea to hold a free or low-cost heart screening for kids in the county. Your guy acted all interested, like, *Let me know what I can do*, and all that. When J.C. laid out what he needed, Mark completely shut him down. Wouldn't return his emails or phone calls. Nothing. All the resources he has access to, and he hasn't been willing to help at all."

This story didn't surprise Lena because her impression of Mark had never really been that good. He was easy. He didn't demand her attention and didn't command her thoughts. She didn't feel any pressure to introduce him to Nicky or to bring him around Mike and Lindsay. Lena didn't have to work at this. It just was.

To find out that he had promised something and hadn't delivered didn't affect her because she had nothing invested in him—until this moment. She realized she was a little put off because Mark had left J.C. hanging. She felt indignant for J.C. and wondered about her protectiveness. But she wasn't willing to put that on display for Anna, who made her uncomfortable for reasons she couldn't pinpoint.

"You really don't care about Play for Gabe, do you?" Anna asked. Surprisingly, she didn't sound accusatory. It was more factual, like she'd just figured something out.

"What makes you say that?" Lena asked, curiosity driving her.

"You've never really been interested. I guess I was just wondering why."

Lena studied the girl in front of her. She seemed fragile when looking at her, but as Lena had sensed in the conference room, there wasn't anything soft about her. And while she'd spent a lot of time over the last couple of weeks thinking about her brother, his death, and his legacy, she wasn't going to share that with Anna in a bar restroom.

"I admire what you have done in the name of my brother. It's special, and you should be proud of it."

It was a dismissal, and they both knew it. Anna would have said more, but Lena moved toward the stall and closed the door. She heard the exterior door open and close, and she breathed a sigh of relief.

I should have stayed home tonight, she thought.

Lena exited the restroom, intent on grabbing Mark and heading out of the weird twilight zone she seemed to be occupying. It had been her plan, but as she walked toward Mark, she saw J.C. and Anna talking quietly while Bryce, Max, Kyle, and Fletcher were engaged in a separate conversation.

"Let's head somewhere else," she said to Mark. She picked up her glass of wine and finished the last sip.

Mark stood, and they began heading toward the door.

She took one more glance back and then switched directions. Turning back to Mark, she said, "I just want to say good-bye." She moved them toward the bar and stepped right into the circle the six of them had created.

The looks of surprise on their faces were kind of priceless, and she had to work hard to hold back a mischievous smile.

"Hey," she said with an overabundance of enthusiasm that was foreign to her.

They all looked at her like she'd looked at them not long ago when they were at Mike and Lindsay's, like she was vaguely familiar but mostly weird. They watched her. And she returned every one of their looks with one of her own—except for J.C. She avoided him.

"Mark," she said, looking at him with feigned adoration, "I know you know J.C. and Fletcher, but I'm not sure if you know everyone else." Deliberately, she introduced all of them and made sure she left room and expectation for Mark so that he had to shake every hand. "We go way back," she said, like she was confiding some long-ago buried secret. "In fact, we all grew up in the same town."

Mark merely nodded and tried to look interested. She recognized the expression from having employed it not fifteen minutes before.

"It's nice to meet you all," he said.

"It's funny actually," she continued, center stage, "they all grew up with my brother."

Mark looked at her strangely. They'd never really been a couple, but she could tell he was surprised by the mention of a brother she hadn't thought to bring up before.

"Yeah," Bryce said, filling the momentary silence, "we went to preschool together and kind of stuck."

Lena looked over at Bryce and winked. She could tell he was attempting to hold back a smile.

"When my brother died, they started a foundation—Play for Gabe. Maybe you've heard of it?" She looked expectantly at Mark.

"Yes, I have heard of it. J.C. told me all about it."

She smiled at him, like she was encouraging a puppy to sit on command. "Amazing, isn't it? I mean, what they've accomplished." She waited for his movement of affirmation.

"Yes," Mark responded on cue.

"It just dawned on me that you could probably help them. They have been working on putting together a heart screening for young athletes." She shrugged and rolled her eyes. "I'm sure you already know that because you know everything medical that goes on in this town." *Ego stroke*, she thought.

He didn't respond at first, and she thought she'd misplayed that card.

"Not everything," he said with some arrogance, "but a lot."

"I imagine it would bring some great publicity to the hospital."

"Actually, the American Heart Association hasn't fully endorsed screenings. It's a fine line for the hospital to walk."

Lena quickly looked over at J.C., and at his slight nod of confirmation to Mark's statement, she changed tactics. "Mark, remember when I called you last week and asked you about sudden cardiac arrest, and you offered up the names of some organizations I could research?"

"There are a number of organizations across the country that hold screenings for young athletes. I am happy to send you some of their names," he said with little reluctance.

Lena smiled at him again. "I know how busy you are. Why don't you write down the contact information for your administrative assistant? I'm sure she can help get them what they need."

He slid his hand into his back pocket, pulled out his wallet, and grabbed one of his cards. Lena reached into her purse and handed him a pen. He walked to the bar and wrote something on it. He turned back and handed the card to Lena. She reached forward and held it out to J.C. Their eyes met. She winked at him and smiled.

Then, she turned back to the group. "We've got to get going. Great seeing you all." She smiled wide at them.

Mark grabbed her hand and led her out toward the door. Right before she crossed the threshold, she turned toward the group and winked again. She almost laughed but managed to hold it in. She felt a zip of exhilaration. It wasn't much, but at least she'd gotten them a contact name, someone who could help them with resources. She'd heard Mark brag enough about his administrative assistant that she was pretty sure the woman behind him ran the show.

As they came to the door leading out into the street, Mark paused. "It's raining. I'll grab the car and come get you," he said. He leaned over and kissed her on the cheek before he stepped out into the street.

Lena leaned against the wall, closed her eyes, and fought the desire to walk back into the bar to see J.C. She wondered what he was thinking about right at this moment. She hadn't specifically done it for him, but hearing Anna's story about J.C. and Mark had pushed at her in some way.

Her eyes flew open when she felt hands on her hips and a body leaning into hers. She smiled up into J.C.'s face, knowing it was him before she saw him. He moved into her space, his leg between hers. Meeting her eyes, he smiled wide. It dazzled her, stole her breath. He dropped his forehead to hers and inhaled deep, squeezing her hips where his hands rested with easy familiarity.

"I don't think I've felt so many different emotions for one person in such a short period of time. I wanted to kill you thirty minutes ago. Watching him run his fingers over your hands made me feel blind rage."

He paused and pulled her hips toward him as he pushed his forward, so they were perfectly aligned. Her breath caught in her throat and then skated up out through her mouth in a ragged exhale.

"But that little stunt there? Shit, I just don't ever know what you are going to do." He paused and moved his head away from her forehead before dropping down near her ear. "I need for you to be ready," he whispered, but the magnified sound of his voice rang through her head. "Please."

He pulled away from her as quickly as he'd invaded her space. A few feet between them felt like an ocean, and Lena longed for him to be against her again. He shoved his hand into his pocket.

"Say *go*," he said.

As he started to walk away, his right hand reached and grabbed hers. Then, he pulled away from her, his fingers leaving hers, and he turned away.

Lena looked down at her palm and saw a penny.

J.C. felt twitchy. He walked back into the bar toward his friends, but it had taken everything in him to do it. He wanted to grab Lena from the alcove where he'd left her and pull her from her date. He wanted her to stay with him and his friends because he was pretty sure they would have a blast together.

He'd never in his life felt possessive or jealous about a girl, but letting Lena leave with Mark was killing him. Tonight had tried his patience. Watching the two of them as inconspicuously as possible, he'd imagined doing bodily harm to the guy.

"Need something stronger?" Bryce said as he handed J.C. a newly opened beer.

"You have no idea," he responded.

Bryce laughed. "I think I have a pretty good idea."

He turned from J.C. to get the bartender's attention and then shoved a shot glass into J.C.'s waiting hand. Without any hesitation, J.C. threw it back.

"Thanks, man."

"No problem," Bryce said.

He looked like he had more to say, but Max stood there, eyeing J.C., so Bryce aborted whatever had been about to come out of his mouth.

"Is something going on with you two?" Max said loud enough for Fletcher to overhear and turn his attention toward them.

J.C. did a quick scan to locate Anna before he responded, "No."

Max regarded Bryce, J.C., and the shot glass. He looked over at Fletcher, who gave him some nod that J.C. knew meant something.

"Are you sure? Because there seems to be some..." Max paused.

J.C. supposed he was at a loss for a word that wouldn't make him sound like a girl.

J.C. couldn't help but mess with him. "Some, what?"

Max rolled his eyes and then looked at Fletcher for help.

"Thing," Fletcher said. "I noticed it before. You do everything you can *not* to look at her until you can't help it anymore. Then, when you do, it's all intense. And she does the same thing. But she's super nice to everyone else."

J.C. wanted to smile because Fletcher was spot-on. He didn't always give Fletcher credit for his astuteness, but he had this uncanny ability to make assumptions about people that were usually right.

Max was the observer in the group, the most reserved of them, so the fact that he'd picked up on the *thing* didn't surprise J.C. at all.

Max continued to look between Bryce and J.C. He seemed certain that if he watched them closely enough, one of them would give something away.

"Nah, there's nothing going on," J.C. said.

"Yet," Bryce mumbled loud enough for J.C. to hear.

He looked over at Bryce, who was looking right back at him with skepticism on his face. J.C. shrugged.

There wasn't anything going on with Lena, except for a couple of kisses and some intriguing conversations. He looked around again, noting where Anna was standing. The last thing he wanted to do right now was hurt Anna's feelings over something that was probably never going to happen.

But damn he wanted Lena.

He thought back to his conversation with Anna earlier in the day. Her assessment of his constant desire to always be pursuing some new lead, some challenge, made him wonder if Lena was it right now—his new thing that he wanted to conquer. The thought was comforting because he wasn't sure he would survive Lena unscathed, but he hoped he wasn't that shallow because there were too many connections between them, and the last thing he wanted was to draw her into this, only to discover he was ready to move on.

146

Or maybe the right answer for all of this was just sex. But if that had been the answer, the night in her hotel room a couple of weeks ago wouldn't have ended with "no regrets".

At this point, he was tired of thinking about it. If she showed up drunk and selling regrets right now, he'd buy without a second thought.

Fletcher grabbed J.C.'s shoulder. "Let me just say, if something were going on, I would be high-fiving you all over the place. She is one badass chick."

J.C. couldn't help but laugh at Fletcher's assessment.

"No question," Bryce commented.

"What are you guys talking about?" Anna asked, breaking from her conversation with Kyle.

Before Bryce could run interference or J.C. could think of a way out of it, Max said, "J.C. hooking up with Lena Pryce."

"I'm not hooking up with Lena Pryce," he said matter-of-factly, blotting out the image from fifteen minutes ago when he had her pressed up against the wall.

Anna's face contorted with anger. Her mouth dropped open while something in her eyes snapped with comprehension. It was almost as if she had finally figured something out. Their earlier conversation reverberated through J.C.'s mind as he watched her eyes water, tears threatening to overflow. She moved forward and discarded her beer on the bar. Grabbing her purse, she fled to the door.

J.C. went to follow her, but Bryce stopped him.

"I've got it," he said before walking out.

Three pairs of suspicious eyes turned toward J.C.

"What the hell was that about?" Kyle asked.

Of all of them, Kyle was probably the closest to Anna. They were a year younger than them. They had been home together for a year after the rest of them had graduated from high school.

J.C. didn't quite know what to do. He didn't want to lie to them, but it wasn't his place to tell them Anna's business. If she hadn't already told Kyle, she'd held back for a reason.

J.C. shrugged. "I don't know. Do you?" He turned the question back on Kyle and hated himself a little bit for it. *How did this all get so complicated?*

Then, in his mind, he saw Lena as she had been earlier tonight when she smiled conspiratorially at all of them, and he remembered why it was complicated.

Kyle shook his head. "I have no idea. She's been off for a while. But it's not like her to freak out like that. She's usually so together."

"Maybe too together," Fletcher put in. At a glare from Kyle, Fletcher held his hands up. "I'm just saying."

J.C. observed from the bar, letting his friends struggle with Anna's mystery freak-out, while he continued to feel like a complete ass for both his part in it and his silence. Downing his beer, he carefully placed the empty bottle on the bar.

"Stop. Look, Anna and I hooked up a couple of months ago. It was a mistake that we both acknowledged the next day." He didn't make eye contact with anyone. He just trudged along, as if he were doing a mindless chore, trying to get it all out. "We both apologized and moved on. You guys talking about me hooking up with Lena probably just didn't sit right with Anna."

When he stopped talking, he looked up. He saw what he'd expected—surprise, disbelief, anger. It was all there on display for him to live with. But he also felt better after telling them the truth. Holding back just wasn't his style.

"What the hell, J.C.?" Kyle said, ire apparent in his voice.

"Should have seen that coming," Max muttered.

"Damn, he really messed that up, huh?" Fletcher said to Max.

J.C. didn't really know what else to say, so he was glad for the interruption provided by the vibration of his phone. Thinking it was Bryce with an update, J.C. pulled his phone out of his pocket. It was an unknown number with one word.

Go.

"All right. I sent it." Lena sat back in her chair at the breakfast bar and smirked at Lindsay. "This is completely crazy. You know that, right?"

"What's so crazy about it?" Lindsay asked. But before Lena could respond, she continued, "Wait, what did you say in your text?"

Lena shrugged. "*Go.*"

Lindsay broke into a fit of laughter. When she finally got ahold of herself, she said, "You wrote, *Go.* That's it? No identification?"

"Do you think he's walking around, using that line, on more than one person?" Lena said with some indignation behind it.

"No," Lindsay said, still smiling. "I just think, maybe you could have been a bit more eloquent."

"I'm beyond eloquence at this point. I feel like I am stretched tight, like I could snap at any moment. He said, 'Say *go.*' So, I did. Stop giving me shit about it."

Lena shifted in her chair and held back a long-suffering sigh that she knew would make her feel even more pathetic than she already did.

Sexual frustration is a bitch, she thought.

But she knew it was more than that. It was J.C. Something about him kept pulling her in. If she were honest with herself, she'd admit that it was more than the physical attraction too. If it were just physical, it would have been over and done with by now.

But feeling her hackles rise when she'd found out about Mark blowing them off told her a lot about how she felt. She had a small inner circle, but those within it were sheltered and protected. How J.C. had provoked those feelings in her with so little effort and time even shocked her. It was how she'd found herself cutting her date short and coming to Lindsay's so late at night.

"Do you feel any better now that you sent the text?" Lindsay asked a little too gently, which earned her a glare from Lena.

"No, not really. Now, I have to wait." Lena looked over to her phone. "It's only been five minutes, but it feels like so much longer."

Lindsay smiled, and Lena could tell right away that her friend was valiantly trying to hold back her laughter.

"I'm so sorry, Lena," she said, smiling big. "I've just never seen you so...worked up and frazzled. I'm not really sure what the right word is."

"I know. It's the planning thing. I'm more of an in-the-moment kind of girl. This plotting for action is so foreign."

This time, when Lindsay laughed, Lena laughed with her.

"What the hell am I doing, Linds?"

"Why are you struggling with this? It's not like you to think so much." Lindsay shook her head. "Sorry, that didn't come out right."

Lena giggled. It was exactly what she needed, why she'd come straight to Lindsay when she had contemplated what to do. Lindsay had a way of easing her when she needed it.

"Seriously though, Lena, what has you so worked up about this?"

"He's so young, and he's who he is," she said without hesitation.

"Probably the most put-together twenty-three-year-old I've ever been around. The caveat to that statement is that I haven't been around twenty-three-year-olds since we were that age. But still, I'm sticking with my statement. And, yes, you guys have a shared history. I get how that could be hard."

"History aside, he has plans, and they don't include staying here. But I'm not leaving."

Lindsay stopped laughing. "You are fifteen steps ahead. Why are you even thinking about that? You don't even know if the sex will be good yet. You might end up excited that he has no plans to stay here."

Lena grinned. "True."

"But you still haven't really answered my question," Lindsay said. "Why are you overthinking this?"

"Do you remember what it's like?" Lena asked, suddenly serious again.

"What?" Lindsay looked quizzically her, hearing the odd bent in her voice.

"The space in between." At Lindsay's questioning stare, Lena attempted to explain, "The space between when you knew that he was someone special and when you acted on it. Do you remember those moments, days, months, between?"

Lindsay looked past her, and Lena was grateful for the reprieve.

Lena had gone from wild girl to mother in a short span of time. She'd never been in a place where she cared about a guy she was with. In terms of relationships, she was the most immature thirty-year-old ever. She almost chuckled when she thought that she and J.C. were probably on par when it came to relationships.

Lindsay reached over and put her hand on Lena's hand. "I do remember. I remember all the angst of knowing how I felt about Mike and being afraid that, if it didn't work out, I would lose you and Nicky and him. And where would I be? And I kept thinking, *Is a piece of ass really worth that?*" Lindsay bumped shoulders with Lena. "But I get it. When you put it like that, I get the weighing process, the scales. Trying to balance what you want with what you have, and see which way the scale tips. The thing is, Lena, you won't really know until you know. And if you are trying to tell me that you already know, then just say it, and maybe it will make you feel better."

Lena digested what Lindsay had said. Then, she let go of Lindsay's hand and leaned to the side to reach into her pocket. Digging deep, she extracted the penny J.C. had placed in her hand, and she dropped it on the counter. It bounced and whirled until it stopped, tails side up, directly between the two of them.

Lindsay cut her eyes to Lena. "Gabe," she whispered, as if speaking normally right then would have been sacrilegious.

"J.C.," Lena said in a normal voice. "He handed that to me as he said, 'Go.'"

151

"Oh," was all Lindsay could manage to say.

"Yeah, *oh*. So, you see, I have my dead brother. I have my mother pushing me in J.C.'s direction—inadvertently, mind you, but still. I have my child, who already thinks this guy walks on water. And I have this crazy, stupid attraction that I can't get a handle on. Do you see where my scale is tipping?"

There were no words, so Lindsay just nodded.

"And it's drawing me in, Linds—this little battle they're waging with Play for Gabe. It's pulling at me. I almost want to hang posters with them and find someone to lobby. And those boys—Fletcher and Bryce—and let's not forget Max who had Jessie eating out of his hand. There are all these fragments of my past and present scattered over the floor. And J.C. is like a magnet, pulling it together." Lena reached over and picked up the penny. "The damn penny? The penny just means *go*."

"So, go," Lindsay said as Lena's phone vibrated with a text.

Lena reached over, plucked it off the counter, and read it.

She smiled, and this time, there wasn't any uncertainty in it.

After beers, shots, and the Anna incident, it had seemed like a good idea, going to the beach—not necessarily to ease into it, but to be out together, somewhere they both enjoyed. It would be without all the pressure of a date, which J.C. wasn't sure he could pull off at this point.

Pulling up to the address Lena had texted him, he took a deep breath. He parked and was about to get out of his truck when her front door opened, and she strolled toward him. He jumped out, meeting her at the top of the driveway. Seeing her made him suddenly happy about his beach call. She was sporting a fedora straw hat that seemed to be all the beach rage these days. Her tank top was loose, so one strap rested precariously on the edge of her shoulder, and her shorts were short. The straps of her black bathing suit met and tied around her neck.

I could stand here, staring at her all day, he thought as he got to her.

"Hey," he said as he leaned forward. He dropped a quick kiss on her mouth.

"Hey yourself," she said, answering his move with a smile. "Great call on the beach. I wasn't sure what the weather would be like, but it's an awesome day to be outside. If Nicky were with me this weekend, we definitely would have ended up at the beach."

J.C. smiled as they walked to his truck, and he opened the door for her. She swung herself in, dropping her bag on the seat.

Barrier, he thought immediately as he closed the door.

He walked around to the driver's side trying to contain his excitement. He felt his adrenaline spike when he thought about her sitting in his truck and getting to spend the day with her. He took a deep breath, attempting to calm himself, before he opened the door and settled on the seat.

"I was actually going to come up to the door and knock—you know, act like this is a real date," he said, teasing her, as he reversed out of the driveway.

She glanced over at him and captured her bottom lip between her teeth, contemplating something. He narrowed his eyes at her before he dragged them back to the road.

"What?" he prompted.

"I don't really have guys in my house," she said.

He couldn't help it. He whipped his head toward her. "Huh?" he said stupidly.

"Habit, I guess. But I don't bring dates into my house. The dates always start and end somewhere else."

She hadn't even hesitated on the last part, and it made J.C. grip the steering wheel a bit harder.

"I'm just really careful about anyone being near Nicky."

"Smart," J.C. said. He liked that she her son first, but it made him a little sad for her. And he wondered if she'd ever been into someone where she let go emotionally. "So, Mark has never been here?" It slipped out of his mouth before he could stop it.

Her laughter rang out in the cab. "Oh, J.C., do you really want to go down that path?"

He felt a smile tugging at his lips. It was tempting. He shrugged, like he wanted to give her the choice to divulge any pertinent information. He could feel her eyes on him, and he knew she was studying him.

"Probably not," he responded. Out of his peripheral vision, he saw her nod.

"Good, because if you'd asked that, I'd have done something stupid, like asked what the deal was with you and Anna. It's probably best if we let some things stay unsaid."

His flinch was automatic.

"That's what I thought," she muttered.

J.C. almost went into an explanation. *But, really, what could he say?*

He wanted to tell Lena that seeing her had messed with him, turned him inside out, and he'd reached for any tether to keep him tied to where he was. But it wasn't Lena's fault that he'd stumbled into Anna's bed, and it would have sounded like that. Hell, it sounded like that in his head.

"What do you normally do on the weekends when Nick's with his dad?"

"You always call him Nick, even with me," she observed.

He laughed. "Yeah, I'd feel disloyal to my main man if I called him a name that makes him cringe when it slips out of you in public."

Lena laughed, too, and he was glad she hadn't taken offense.

"I know I have to stop, but I just can't get to *Nick* yet. It means he's more boy than baby, and after that, it'll all be downhill." She shrugged then. "I know it's inevitable, but he still lets me get away with it at home, so I'm pushing it to the limit."

"Why doesn't that surprise me?" he teased.

She laughed again, but this time, it was throaty and sexy, and he had a hard time keeping his eyes on the road.

"To answer your question, when Nicky's not with me, I'm actually at Lindsay and Mike's often. We spend a lot of time together, even when it's my weekend. We're family, and we move as one. It's hard for people to get, but I wouldn't change it."

"When you have to make decisions about Nick, do the three of you make them?"

"No. Lindsay is really good about bowing out. Even when Mike and I could both use her help, she insists that we have to work through it without her, which is stupid because we both end up going to her separately anyway."

"Have you ever not agreed?" He looked over at her.

Their eyes met, and she glared at him a little.

"Way to keep it light on the first date," she said.

He laughed. "Sorry. It just fascinates me a little."

"Why?"

He so wasn't ready to go there, but he found himself talking anyway, "It's obvious how close you all are. I just wonder what it would be like for all of you if another person were involved." He held up one hand, almost in surrender. "Not for any reason, other than curiosity."

155

"That killed the cat," she said without any real rancor. "I don't know what it might be like. We've talked about it, but no one has gotten even close, so it doesn't seem worth it to worry too much about it."

"Because you haven't let anyone get close?" he asked.

"No."

"No?" he asked.

"No."

When she didn't elaborate, he let it go. He wasn't sure if he was trying to gauge his chances or her willingness. And why he was even thinking about it, he wasn't sure.

When she'd texted him back last night, part of him had been tempted to try to see her right then, to get to her house before she could change her mind so that he could sink inside her and put them both out of their misery. But he knew the physical was only a mere fraction of it, a manifestation of all the things she made him feel and want. It provided a barricade for his feelings. Once he barreled through it, he didn't think he'd be able to hold back.

If he couldn't control his feelings but she could, he wondered where the hell that would leave him.

"Hello, J.C.?" Lena reached out and tapped his shoulder.

He looked over at her, and she wanted to stop the drive to just be able to get lost in his eyes, lost in him. She could see that hanging out with him today was a good idea. It let her off the hook—sort of. Although she'd been disappointed last night when he suggested a date today, she appreciated the time between when she'd made the decision and when she'd had to act on it. It'd allowed her distance and an emotional safeguard. Last night, there would have been no talking, no questions, no attempt to fortify her emotions. Last night and this morning, she had done it all. She knew the space she needed to survive him.

"Just thinking," he answered vaguely.

"I guess that's the way it has to be right now, huh?" she said.

He pulled into a private beach access and parked the truck. He turned his body toward her. "What does that mean?"

God, I suck at this, she thought.

His undivided attention was focused on her, and she was thankful for her foresight to drop her bag between them.

"It means that we have to dance around whatever pops into our head, filter it so that it's fit for general consumption."

He full-out laughed with his head back. When he stopped, he smiled at her, full wattage, and she felt a little fascinated by it.

"If I shared what I'd just been thinking with you, you'd run for the hills."

"What makes you say that?"

"You wouldn't even let me come to your door."

She shook her head. "That was just habit."

"Habit? You mean, it was a part of your defense mechanism."

"I've never needed a defense mechanism until you," she flung out into the space between them.

She watched him take it in, and the atmosphere in the cab of the truck changed instantly. His lips parted, like he was going to say something but then forgot. He shifted forward, picked up her bag, and carefully set it on the floorboard at her feet.

Then, he reached out and planted his hands on her waist and pulled. His mouth landed on hers before she could even evade, and before any thought surfaced, she had her hands in his hair. Her lips parted on her own, and his tongue thrust into her mouth. She scrambled to her knees, never breaking the kiss, wanting to be flush against him. He helped by lifting her and shifting her legs, so she straddled him. It was awkward because of the limited area, but his hands crawled up her tank top, caressing her bare skin and pulling her in so that the space between them ceased to exist.

He took her mouth in a fierce kiss, as if he could absorb her if he kissed her hard enough. And she met him kiss for kiss, stroke for stroke. She forgot everything—her location, her position, her tenuous hold on her feelings for him. Her hands found the bottom of his shirt, and she yanked up, attempting to get rid of it so that they could be skin-to-skin.

Sucking her lower lip between his teeth, he nibbled on it and then pressed for one more kiss before moving his hands back down, resting them on her hips. He dropped his head in the crook of her neck and lazily placed a kiss in the hollow of her throat. "Shit," he murmured against her skin.

She laughed lightly, attempting to catch her breath and her sense of reality.

He pulled away from her and looked up so that their eyes met. "You going to let me into your house later?"

The question threw her for a second because she hadn't really come back down from the kissing and touching. Images and sensations crowded her brain, making it difficult to think coherently. She knew what he was asking, what he wanted. And she wanted it, too. She wanted the beginning.

"Yes," she said simply, doubt removed.

His hands flexed on her hips. Whether involuntary or not, she couldn't tell. He continued to gaze at her in a way she found slightly disconcerting. She wanted to look away but found she couldn't. He didn't say anything after her concession, and she wondered what he was thinking about.

It struck her—as she sat wrapped around him, trying like hell to figure out what was going on inside his head—that she'd never had to wonder before. She'd always known what was expected from the guys she was with because she'd always set the expectations, which were few.

This new order, this wondering and caring, was so much harder than her previous interactions, and she briefly thought, *Am I ready for this?*

There was something rather comforting in not caring what someone thought of you. The whole ignorance-is-bliss attitude had governed her life, allowing her a certain kind of freedom. Looking at J.C., feeling this uncertainty, reminded her why she hadn't done this.

Suddenly, J.C.'s hands were on her neck, his fingers on her nape, his thumbs caressing her chin. He pulled her mouth to his and placed a soft kiss on her lips.

"Let's go to the beach," he said.

He lifted her off his lap and placed her on the seat. She stretched out her legs, enjoying the ability to straighten them. Grabbing her bag off the floorboard, she opened the door and jumped down from the truck, appreciating the physical distance from J.C. She walked quickly down the well-worn path between the sea oats toward the water.

Dropping her beach bag, she flung off her hat, tank top, and shorts, and then she ran toward the water, longing for the coolness to distract her from all this chaos in her brain. She went in as far as she could, and then she dived in and started swimming toward the buoy.

J.C. was right behind her, following. They raced, and Lena got caught up in the competition.

They hit a sandbar, and she put her feet down, making her way through. As she was about to hit the edge of the shallow, he reached out, catching her around the waist, and he pulled her under. She came up, sputtering and laughing, the release of the tension immediate and heady.

They stayed like that, on the sandbar, splashing each other. She didn't think about him shutting down in the car or the unspoken promise of the night to come. She just enjoyed him and his antics, laughing in a way she usually reserved for Nicky, Lindsay, Mike, and the girls.

When the sun started to dip and the chill began to seep in, they made their way out of the water.

When J.C. suggested dinner, Lena agreed—not because she was particularly hungry, but because the only other option was to go to her house. Although she had said yes earlier in the day, his withdrawal in the truck had smacked her in the face once she left the water behind.

The night air was cool enough for Lena to pull on her sweatshirt, the warmth of the beach long forgotten.

She and J.C. were both relaxed and enjoying the conversation, not merely pushing against time in an effort to get to the finish. They knew what the conclusion of the day entailed, and though they were both ready, the easy flow between them was real, tangible.

"Tell me about it," Lena said after the waitress had delivered another beer.

J.C. grabbed his beer. "It? Can you be more specific?"

"We haven't really talked about Play for Gabe since I found out."

He leaned back and took a sip of his beer. "Okay, what do you want to know?" If he were wary of talking about it with her, he didn't give it away.

"How it all happened, how you got to where you are."

"That could take a while," he said with a shrug.

But she felt reticence from him for the first time.

"We've got time," she said. She wasn't sure why she felt this need to talk about this now. It wouldn't really change anything, and she'd never been interested before, as Anna had so bluntly pointed out.

"Okay. You know how it started, right? You've got the bare bones?" At her nod, he continued, "When we got to college, we were still doing the same thing, but eventually, we started to think about how we could use Gabe's legacy for something more than scholarship funds. It took us a while, a lot of beers, and a couple of years to come up with the plan. After looking through the research and the stories of other people who had lost loved ones to sudden cardiac arrest, the way seemed pretty self-explanatory."

Lena nodded. "AED placement and more widespread screening?"

"Screening, period. Thousands of young people die every year from sudden cardiac arrest. A good percentage have structural issues, like Gabe, who had hypertrophic cardiomyopathy, which makes some of the deaths preventable and a worthy cause, I guess." His voice took on a different note.

She watched him from the other side of the table as his gaze became a little sharper. He was knowledgeable and passionate about it, and the more he spoke, the more she could see it. It made her wonder about his med school plan and why that was even on the board. Although she wanted to ask, she didn't want to do any more heavy talking.

"It used to make me mad," he said, shifting gears.

"What's that?"

"Your lack of interest."

His candor impressed her even though what he'd said pissed her off a bit. She could only manage an, "Oh," before she looked away from him, not sure where this conversation was going.

"For a while anyway. I can't remember when I forgave your apathy, but I remember feeling lighter because of it." He'd been looking away from her, as if the only way he could get those words out was if she wasn't in his direct line of sight. "Does that make you mad?" he asked, bringing his eyes back to hers.

She was sure he could see her anger. "Probably."

He laughed then, the same laugh from the truck that had hit her in the gut. "Kind of condescending of me to tell you how to grieve, huh?"

J.C. saw her. No matter where he was looking, he always seemed to know where she was.

She couldn't help the smile. "A little."

"I know. I told you that because I want you to get where Play For Gabe came from. I guess it started as a way to grieve, ya know? Once soccer was over and I still had all this anger I couldn't relieve on the field, it was a good way to funnel the grief. I think that's how it started, but now, it just is. I'm sure everyone who has ever lost someone close to them wonders what life would have been like—what would have been different, what would have been the same—if the person hadn't left them. Sometimes, I think that, but it's rare. I don't spend my time wondering how things would have been if Gabe had lived. Some aren't meant for this world, and there was a goodness about him that seemed otherworldly. Or it seems so now. I don't know if I tell myself that to make me feel better about it or if it's true. But if the memory of his goodness pushed me, us, in this direction, then I'm going to ride it so that we can maybe change someone else's story."

Lena looked away and let loose the breath she hadn't realized she had been holding.

She signaled the waitress, and as the girl made her way over, Lena pulled some cash from her wallet. She wasn't sure how much they'd spent, but she thrust the money into the girl's hand.

She stood up and looked over at J.C., amused at the curious expression on his face. His eyes were narrowed again.

"Let's go," she said, holding her hand out to him.

He scooted the chair back as his hand slid into hers. She pulled him through the restaurant, eager to get home, away from people. Her body was buzzing with awareness of him, and the tension between them suddenly amped up. He didn't say a word as she led him out, but she knew his cognizance had heightened also. She wasn't sure what had happened or what had hit her so directly out of everything he'd said. But the tightrope they'd been walking over the last few weeks snapped, and the only safety net in sight seemed to be trailing behind her.

"In a hurry?" he teased as they made their way through the parking lot.

She stopped and tugged on his hand so that they were toe-to-toe. She reached up with her free hand and grabbed him around his neck, pulling him forward to meet her mouth. She opened immediately and invaded his mouth with her tongue, demanding a response. And he gave it by dragging her against him, getting wrapped up. She broke the kiss on a moan, untangled her hand from his nape, and began quickly walking toward the car.

"A little," she murmured.

"Me, too," he said.

They made it to Lena's house in record time. When they climbed out of his truck and made their way to the front door, J.C. tried to take in something about her home. He was sure there were discoveries in this house for him to uncover, to find the parts of her that she kept hidden. But he could only focus on her as she opened the door wide for him. He walked past her into the foyer, and he heard the door close behind him.

Then, his brain shut down.

He turned around and grabbed Lena, pushing her back against the door that held everyone else at bay. In response, she wound her fingers through his hair and pulled his mouth down on hers. After that, he took control of the kiss, moving into her mouth, into her space, letting loose all the desires he'd held on to since he saw her on the soccer field those few months before. Her moans of acquiescence, passion, and pleasure filled the space around him, trying his patience.

He broke the kiss to discard her sweatshirt and tanktop. He stepped back and looked her over as she stood there, merely in her bathing suit top and shorts, the belly-button ring teasing him with full access. He dropped to his knees, bringing his mouth even with her navel. Licking around the ring, he flicked his tongue over it, eliciting a long, drawn-out moan and a shudder from Lena.

His hands caressed up and down her legs, smoothing, squeezing and memorizing. Her hips started to move, enticing him to want more. And he did. While the door was appealing, he wanted to be able to lay her out and feast with his eyes and hands.

Running his hands up the length of her legs, from her ankles to the apex of her thighs, he moved his fingers from back to front and pressed, making her sputter with need.

He stood and briefly kissed her hard on her mouth. "Room," he said, it sounding like a demand.

Her languid eyes opened, and she lazily pulled away from the door. Clasping J.C.'s hand, she led him through a family room and kitchen to a room in the back of the house. The moment she pulled him across the threshold, he was on her. His arms wrapped around her waist, and his mouth was on the back of her neck, nipping at her. He felt out of control, like he was going to explode if he didn't do something quickly.

He moved her toward the bed and released her. Grabbing her hips, the place he liked holding her most, he turned her toward him.

"I can't slow down," he murmured into her ear before he lightly bit down on the lobe.

She laughed breathily, like a gasp. "Who says I want you to?" She pulled him forward, down on top of her, on the bed.

She moved so that he was cradled between her thighs, and he thought he was going to lose his mind. She reached up and undid the tie on her bathing suit strap so that he was free to roam. It felt like every plane he traversed, every spot he touched, he branded as his. He was almost religious in his worship of her body. His mouth moved down from her throat toward her breasts, her nipples waiting, begging for his mouth and touch. He answered the call, her siren's moans driving him on, as he moved over her in a way that seemed desperate to him.

When he reached her shorts, he paused, taking a breath, as he looked her over. She was beautiful and lush.

His brain kept screaming, like a chant, *Mine, mine, mine.*

But he hadn't made her his yet. Discarding her bottoms, he slipped between her legs and inhaled before his mouth found her, owned her. He drove her on, and when his fingers found her, too, he felt her body give way, yielding to him. He watched her come apart, and he thought he was going to lose it right then, like a horny teenager.

"Jackson," she moaned.

His name on her lips was almost like a caress itself, and he rose up, moving fast. He claimed her mouth in a searing kiss. His tongue licked into her, pushing her taste back at her, sharing his find with her like a prize.

Her arms and legs were wrapped around him, but she let go, like she suddenly realized that the barrier of his clothes still existed. He sat up on his knees between her legs. She pulled up, grasping the bottom of his shirt, helping him lift it over his head. He reached down and unbuttoned his board shorts. He had to leave her to get them off.

He did that and pulled a condom from his pocket before tossing it at the foot of the bed. He was about to roll it on when she pushed forward on the bed. Her feet hit the floor, and she was directly in front of him. Moving toward him, she reached around his hips, grasped his ass, and pulled him forward so that her mouth could wrap around him.

His exhale was audible and bounced around the room, and then it was outdistanced by his moans. His need to be inside her ramped up, but it was hard to hold on to a thought. He reached down and closed his hands over her arms. "Lena," he said, "God, you feel good." He had to stop talking to catch his breath. "But I need to be inside you now."

She released him and leaned back, allowing him space to roll on the condom. Then, he reached down, grabbed her right leg, hooked it around his back, and plunged into her without any finesse. It shocked both of them, and they stopped, each getting used to the feel of each other.

Then, like an orchestrated moment, their eyes met, and they smiled wickedly at each other.

"Amazing," Lena said at the same time as J.C. said, "Incredible."

They smiled again before J.C. started to move, and all thoughts ceased. Their rhythm matched as their bodies moved as one, reaching for each other, fulfilling the promise they'd glimpsed with every touch and kiss and conversation. His hands were on either side of her, allowing him to drive into her.

As they moved toward their climax, he reached for her hands, and she grasped his, as if she'd been waiting for him to connect with her in another way. The simultaneous touch heightened everything, and they came with their lips locked, their hands entwined, their legs tangled, and their hearts beating as one.

22

J.C. woke up alone. As intimate as the night had been, he found himself surprised that he hadn't felt Lena get out of bed, hadn't sensed her retreat. He rolled onto his back, looked up at the ceiling, and smiled. His last memory of the ceiling was when his eyes had practically rolled back in his head as Lena had taken control and ridden him, hard.

Was that round two or three?

He couldn't quite remember the sequence. That was probably because each time had been better than the one before. Their familiarity had allowed greater access, pleasure, and the in-between—the talking, the caressing. The teasing had brought comfort. He felt like he'd won the lottery. He'd gambled so little, and he was coming away so much richer.

He looked at the clock and noted how early it was. Reaching over he turned on the light.

Last night, he hadn't taken note of anything that wasn't Lena. He could pinpoint every freckle and beauty mark on her body. He'd traversed every inch of her. He'd traced the tattoo on the upper right corner of her butt, her tribute to Gabe, a flowing scroll of the words *Brother Mine* and the date of his death. He'd noted every scar from the stitches she had on her knee to the battle scar of Nick's birth, as she'd so lovingly referred to as the telltale sign of her C-section. He'd memorized the look on her face as she'd climaxed and the small little moans she'd made in her sleep.

What he hadn't noticed was the room where they'd ended up. So, he looked around. He remembered there wasn't a bathroom, which seemed to be a small inconvenience the night before. Now, it felt wrong because the master bedroom should have its own bathroom. He hadn't seen anything on the walls. But now, he saw that only stock pictures of the bay and beach graced the rather plain gray room. There were no pictures of Lena and Nick, no personal knickknacks, and it seemed sterile.

He rolled to his side and slid off the bed, scooping up his board shorts. He dressed as he made his way to the bathroom. He took a quick shower and then went in search of Lena. He walked quietly through the house.

Lena had explained that her grandparents had given the house to her when they decided that they didn't want to take care of the lawn anymore, and they'd opted for a retirement community not far away. It was an old craftsman-style home with some upgrades that must have been done over the last few years.

The wooden floors were well-worn, and he hit a couple of creaking spots. Briefly, he thought that Nick would have to memorize the pattern if he ever wanted to sneak out. The thought made him smile. He crept into the room right off the kitchen and noted it as Nick's. Here, he saw personal effects, pictures, and odds and ends that would fascinate an eight-year-old boy.

J.C. turned from the room and continued down the hallway, back toward the front of the house. Lining the walls, were pictures of the duration of Nick's life but nothing of Gabe. He looked at each one in the dim light of the morning. The faces were familiar to him now—Lindsay, Nick, Mike, Jessie, and Milly. This was Lena's family.

When he saw the door at the end, he stopped. He knew what he was going to find on the other side, and he wasn't sure what or how to feel about it. Before he could make up his mind one way or another, he pushed lightly on the door to her room. He stood, leaning against the frame, taking in the sight before him. This was her haven, her protected inner sanctuary.

The way Lena was curled up in the middle of her king-sized bed was already familiar to him as she had been snug against him in the same exact position not long ago. Perhaps he needed to wonder about what had chased her from the bed they shared—or more importantly, why she'd directed them to the guest room and not hers the night before. But he couldn't quite bring himself to do it.

Instead, he stepped into the room and sat on the edge of the bed, the side she faced. He leaned forward and lightly ran his fingers down her cheek and across her lips, noting the still there fullness of all their kisses. He enjoyed knowing he'd been there.

She stirred and looked up at him without any surprise or guilt in her eyes. "Hey," she murmured.

"Hey," he answered. "It's early, but I'm going to head out."

She turned her head to the side, presumably looking for the clock. She groaned slightly and then turned back to him. She pushed herself up into a sitting position, fighting the grogginess. "Okay," she said as she rubbed her hands over her eyes.

J.C. couldn't help it. He reached over, cupping her nape, and he rubbed across her jawline with his thumb. She leaned into his hand, not fighting it, even though she'd left him in the night. For a split second, he contemplated asking her what had happened. But it all seemed a little too complicated for a five a.m. conversation, like too many walls to climb. And there was something about the afterglow that he wanted to enjoy.

"What time does Nick come home?" he asked.

She shook her head. "He doesn't. I go over there because we always do Sunday dinner together." She yawned again and covered it with her hand.

J.C. nodded. He wanted to have a plan to see her again, but she hadn't provided an opening.

He leaned forward and gently kissed her on the forehead. He ran through a litany of phrases he could say—*See ya, See ya around, Give me a call, Hit me up later, Deuces.* But they all sounded ridiculous, considering how close they'd been last night.

The silence between them suddenly felt heavy and expectant, but neither one of them made any move to alleviate the awkwardness hanging in the air. He felt the morning-after glow extinguish itself.

He stood smoothly and settled on saying, "Bye," before he turned toward the door and left.

When Lena awoke sometime later, she stayed in bed, staring unseeingly at the ceiling. Weak light from outside weaved through the blinds, indicating a cloudy day, which matched her mood perfectly.

When she'd startled awake in the night, sometime between rounds, she'd luxuriated in the feel of J.C.'s arms around her, his body pressed just right against hers. She'd stayed awake, wrapped up in him, reliving scenes from their night together. All that mind-melding had made for unbelievable sex, and that was what had driven her from his arms.

Rolling over, she forced herself out of her bed and went toward the bathroom. She felt like she was in some sappy movie scene as she showered, imagining J.C. touching whatever part of her body she washed, images flashing before her eyes. All she needed was a good musical score to accompany her thoughts. She smiled wickedly as she thought Maroon 5's "Animals" would do nicely.

But the smile was fleeting as she tried to deal with all the emotions behind the sex. As much as she wanted to chalk it up to amazing sex, which it had been, it was all about the sex being *with him*.

She turned off the shower but leaned against the tiles, letting the coolness seep into her body. It grounded her in some way, this contrast between the long hot shower and the still cold tile, reminding her of who she was in the hours she'd spent with J.C. in bed and the moments after when she'd run because she longed for the separation, a way to stay cold. It made her shaky with regret because she'd left the comfort of his arms and relief because she'd pulled away and erected a barrier.

When he'd asked her if she was going to let him in her house, she hadn't understood what he was really asking. But he had a way of seeing two steps in front of her. When he'd demanded a room, she'd never even contemplated letting him into hers. How he'd predicted her actions, she wasn't sure, but she imagined when he'd found her this morning in her own bed, he'd thought back to his simple yet complicated question and probably smiled ruefully.

Even now, as she stepped from the shower, dried off, and put on a robe and her necessary makeup, she felt the impact of her withdrawal, and she wished she could have acted in a different way. In the stark light in her bathroom, with her reflection staring back at her, she could admit to herself that she had no idea how to navigate J.C., and the realization was scary as hell.

She pulled on a pair of jeans and a lightweight sweatshirt in deference to the wet, soggy weather. In desperate need of a cup of coffee, she made her way to the kitchen, grabbing her phone as she went. After a quick call to talk to Nicky, she pulled out her computer and the Play for Gabe documents. She was almost done with her analysis and figured she could finish it in the next couple of hours.

She'd just gotten everything situated when the doorbell rang.

Lena never considered that J.C. would come back, so when she turned the corner into the foyer and saw him through the glass of the door, she didn't have time to think about how to stifle her reaction. He stood outside with a lopsided grin on his face and a backward baseball cap on his head, slightly wet from the persistent rain.

Her smile was quick and genuine as she opened the door. "Hey," she said, her wit deserting her.

J.C. didn't answer but rather moved in quick to kiss her, gently at first. But at her response, his hands found their spot, and he pulled her to him. Their mouths opened and tongues met. When he broke the kiss, she stepped away, allowing him access to the house.

"Hey," he said belatedly.

She turned and led him to the kitchen. Looking at the paperwork spread out on the counter, she moved toward it, pulled it back into its folder, and shut her laptop.

"Coffee?" she asked as she walked to the cabinet.

"Please. I haven't had any yet." J.C. sat at one of the stools at the breakfast bar.

Lena poured some into a mug she had retrieved. Then, she busied herself with getting milk and sugar and a spoon. She felt flustered. She knew he was watching her every move, and part of her wanted to demand that he tell her what he was thinking.

Pushing the mug across the counter to him, she finally glanced up and met his gaze.

"First morning-after?" he asked with a hint of teasing.

She pulled out a barstool and sat heavily upon it. A lick of embarrassment crept up her face and neck. With a sigh, she dropped her chin onto her fist and looked at him with a tilt of her head. "Maybe," she said.

He grinned big. It was the smile from the truck and the restaurant yesterday, the one that would make her knees wobble if she were standing. It hit her like a blow every time.

"I was going to leave you alone today," he began as he dumped a few spoonfuls of sugar into his coffee. "When I left, I wasn't going to come back."

She nodded because she had known. When he'd left, his "Bye," had sounded like a concession.

He took a sip of his coffee but watched her over the rim, his eyes never leaving hers. It was like there was a promise or a message in his stare.

"But I got home, and I didn't really feel like letting you off the hook."

This phrase had her sitting up straighter in her chair, speculatively eyeing him. "Off the hook?" she asked with a touch of ire.

Again, he had that damn grin.

"Off the hook," he reaffirmed. "Look, last night was..." He looked away from her for a second, searching for a word. "I'm not sure I have a description for it." He glanced back in her direction but not at her. "So, I get why you needed some space. I really do. I'm letting you get away with crawling out of the bed in the middle of the night."

She looked at him disdainfully. "I don't crawl."

"*Sneak, crawl, slip, leave*—different words for the same action."

This time, his big grin disappeared, and she saw some remnants of the hurt and disappointment he must have felt when he'd found her sleeping elsewhere.

"Whatever you want to call it, something drove you from me." His phrasing soothed her, a balm for the guilt she'd been denying.

He took another sip of coffee and continued to watch her as she watched him, both content to let the silence nestle between them.

Lena imagined it would be a good time for an explanation, but she realized he'd already pinpointed exactly what had happened, already reconciled it in his head. It had brought him back to her door.

He must have seen the realization in her eyes because he smiled again.

Leaning forward across the counter, bridging some of the distance between them, he said softly, "Yeah."

She smiled back, the look in her eyes softening.

"I thought about it the whole way home," he continued, as if there hadn't been any break in the original conversation, "but I wouldn't be me if I didn't go after what I wanted with a single-minded determination. And here I am."

She grinned. "And what's your plan?"

He looked toward the window and watched the steady stream of rain for a minute. "I'd like to crawl back into whichever bed you choose because I'm really not picky." He winked at her then and laughed. "But it's Sunday, and we always go to brunch on Sundays. I want you to come with me."

She tilted her head, "Brunch? With whom?"

"The Apostles, of course," he replied with a wink.

174

Lena had managed to steer clear of any one-on-one time with Lindsay, but when Mike offered to bathe the kids, Lena knew her time was up. Ruefully shaking her head, she grabbed a bottle of water, headed out to the patio, and sprawled on the chaise lounge. Leaning her head back, she closed her eyes and waited for the inquisition. She could have made it easy on Lindsay, as part of Lena longed to talk about her time with J.C., but she also felt the need to hold it close, to keep the memories locked up.

The moments ticked on, Lena heard Lindsay open the patio door and take the seat next to her but Lindsay remained quiet. When Lena couldn't take it any longer, she rolled her head to the side, opened her eyes, and lifted her eyebrows.

Lindsay shrugged.

Lena laughed. "You know me too damn well."

Lindsay merely shrugged again.

"What do you want to know?"

"What do you want to tell me?"

The question made Lena pause and think. "I'm not sure," she finally said, surprised by her response.

Lindsay smiled at her. "Well, I obviously want to know everything, but it feels weird to make you talk to me."

Lena looked at her quizzically.

In response to the look, Lindsay rolled her eyes. "The thing is, Lena, if you wanted to tell me anything, you would have come over, sat at the kitchen bar while I cooked, and spilled your guts,"

Lindsay said with an understanding smile. "But from the moment you walked in the door, I knew you weren't ready to talk about it. And don't take this negatively, but it's not your normal thing to play with the kids the whole time I'm cooking, even knowing how much you like playing hide-and-seek." She winked.

"I just don't know what to say really. It was a good day and night. He's…"

Lena could feel Lindsay's curiosity pique as she struggled to find a word.

"You're actually speechless. Wow!" Lindsay laughed, completely enjoying Lena's discomfort.

"Yeah, I guess. I'm not really sure what to share. We went to the beach, but that part of it was sort of rocky. I think we both assumed what the night would hold, but neither one of us wanted to act like we knew. Does that make sense?" She looked hesitantly as Lindsay.

"Yeah. Unspoken promise?"

"Ha. Maybe. Then, we went to dinner, and I asked him about Play for Gabe. It was like this light lit him from within. He didn't talk about it for long, but what he said—his knowledge and obvious passion about it—made me want him, like right then. So, we left the restaurant and went back to my house. And you know, the sex—well, it didn't suck."

Lindsay laughed. "Okay. It didn't suck? Not a ringing endorsement."

"I could come up with better descriptors, but I'm not sure I really have a word for it or the way it made me feel."

Lena stopped for a second.

"Really?"

"Really."

"So, what happened today?"

"We went for brunch with some of the Apostles."

"Do you think you will ever stop referring to them as the Apostles?"

"I don't know. Probably not with you," she said, smirking.

"How was that?"

"Interesting. The first couple of seconds, seeing the looks on their faces, was pretty priceless. I don't know who knew what but it was pretty obvious they were surprised to see us together. So, after those awkward moments, we had a good time."

Lindsay didn't respond. Lena sighed.

"He's their center—not their leader, by any means. He's just their cornerstone, like base. If they can just touch him, they know they are safe, like when you're little and playing a game and you just need to touch the base. And it seems like Bryce is that for him— his Lindsay. Fletcher might be my favorite because he just makes you forget anything that might be on your mind. He sweeps you away with his big personality and his little witty remarks." Lena stopped to take a sip of her water and gather the rest of her thoughts. "Max, on the other hand, I think he thinks about everything. His comments were few but thoughtful, and his observations were right on even if they were made sparingly. I couldn't get a read on Kyle." Her assessment completed, she gulped down the rest of the water in the bottle and leaned back against the chaise again. "That's what you wanted, right?"

Lena could feel Lindsay's smile even though she wasn't looking at her friend.

"Yes!" she said almost gleefully. "You know I love it when you do that."

"Well, that's about all I could come up with based on our two hours together."

"But you like them?"

"I do. But they are glaringly young. I know that sounds stupid and makes you want to roll your eyes. But you know how it is. As a parent, most of your stories are somehow related to your child. And I had to bite my tongue often to not throw out funny observations about Nicky. I knew it would only highlight our age differences."

"The parent thing is more about life experience than age."

Lena held up her hand. "Fine. I'll agree with you on that, but it's a filter that I have to have turned on when I'm with them."

"What about when you're with J.C.?"

"To tell the truth, I don't know yet. We didn't talk about much. Aside from dinner and brunch, there wasn't a whole lot of talking going on. I mean, there were whispers during the night but not any real conversations where I would know."

"You're lying," Lindsay said.

Lena greeted her assessment with silence. Just like she could pinpoint different things about the Apostles at brunch, she already knew that she could talk to J.C. about pretty much anything. She just wasn't ready to accept it yet.

"Did you have fun this weekend?" Lena asked as she and Nicky made their way home.

"Yeah," Nicky answered, the one-word response sufficient for him.

"What did you do?" she asked, wanting to know how he'd spent his time. She tried not to think about what she had been doing while he was gone.

"The usual."

She shook her head, familiar with his Sunday night responses.

"Mama, are you coming to my tournament next weekend?" he asked, suddenly animated now that he wanted a response to something.

"Yes. I am driving us over on Friday because your father has to do something for work and can't come until Saturday."

"Okay. Good," he said, excited by her response.

Even though she had tried to reassure him that she was on board with the whole soccer thing, he still felt the need to check with her every time there was an event. It never failed to remind her of her awful behavior over the summer and the damage she'd inflicted on their relationship. He'd never had a reason to doubt her before.

"When we get inside, get your lunch packed, brush your teeth, and then straight to bed. It's late."

"It's always late when we get home on Sundays," he mumbled.

She stifled a giggle because it was so true, and then she ushered him into the house.

The moment she entered, the difference hit her. The remains of the coffee she and J.C. had shared sat on the counter, a reminder of their conversation. Her laptop and files were neatly stacked, as she'd left them this morning on her way out with J.C.

While Nicky searched through the pantry for snacks, she grabbed the two mugs and hastily put them in the sink, like she needed to hide the evidence that J.C. had been there even though

Nicky was too tired to notice anything. But she'd noticed. The air in her house settled around her in an unfamiliar way, as if the presence of J.C. last night had permanently affected the molecules, altering the taste in the air.

After Lena got Nicky ready for Monday and settled for the night, she cautiously went into the guest room. It had been closed all day, and the scent of her time with J.C. hit her the second she opened the door. Feeling slightly nostalgic, she made her way into the room and sat on the bed. The sheets were still tangled, the bedspread askew. She picked up the pillow J.C. had used and inhaled, the smell of him moving through her, pelting her with images from the night before—him driving into her, her body welcoming his. She felt him all around her and was slightly unnerved by the lingering memories seemingly on replay in her head while surrounded by the smell of their actions.

Snapping out of it, she pulled the sheets from the bed. As she wrapped them into a ball to take them to the laundry, she silently praised herself for the foresight to keep J.C. out of her room. She didn't know what it would have been like to enter her room and have those memories dance around her like impatient ghosts, pulling at her clothes to acknowledge them.

Hastily stuffing the sheets and towels from the guest bath into the washer, she poured the detergent into the lid and dumped it into the drum. She knew it wouldn't help. She wouldn't be able to rid her house of him, and the thought was both disturbing and comforting.

When her phone vibrated with a text, she knew it was J.C.

J.C.: Can you talk?

She almost said no but was honest enough to admit that she wanted to hear his voice. She pulled up his number and waited for him to answer.

"Hey," he said.

"Hey."

"How was dinner?"

"Not bad."

"No Spanish Inquisition?" he teased.

Laughing, she said, "Unfortunately, Lindsay knows how to wheedle information out of me."

"Hmm. I'll have to remember that."

She leaned against the washing machine, smiling. "I think you do just fine."

"So, what are you doing?"

"Laundry."

"Oh. Very fun."

"Yeah, I had to clean up the guest room."

"I bet you did," he said on a laugh.

"I was pretty relieved it was the guest room," slipped out before she could think about what she was saying and to whom.

Her statement was greeted with silence. She wanted to take the words back or try to laugh them off, but she didn't know how to do it, so she just sat there with the quiet surrounding her, shaking her head in consternation.

Then, she heard him chuckle on the other end of the line.

"I'm sorry," she said finally. "I wasn't thinking."

"It's fine. You made it perfectly clear in the middle of the night."

"No, really, J.C. It was like sensory overload when I walked in there tonight. I wouldn't have been able to sleep very well in my room with all those reminders." She thought too late again about what she'd said and wanted to start the whole conversation over or go back and tell him that she couldn't talk.

"I guess I can take that as a compliment," he said, a hint of self-deprecation in his voice.

"Backhanded at best, but I'd much rather you take it like that," she said, wanting to die of mortification. This was why she couldn't do this kind of stuff. Having to talk to him after the intimacy of the night before was torture. She really was emotionally stunted.

"When can I see you?" he asked.

"Um, probably not at all this week. I have Nicky all week, and then we have the tournament." She knew it was an excuse. She could make it happen, but she knew that she was in way over her head. And knowing that made her want to put up every barrier within reach.

She could feel his disappointment through the phone, the mind-meld working over the cellular towers.

"Okay, Lena. I guess I'll see you at the tournament. Good night."

He disconnected before she could say anything else. She shoved the phone back into her pocket and turned on the machine.

Walking back through the house, she stopped in front of the open guest room door. As she put new sheets on the bed and straightened the room, she could almost forget what she'd done there last night. She closed the door behind her and shut it all out, J.C. included.

When J.C. had accepted the Thanksgiving invitation, he had done so with much trepidation. He'd been consistently surprised over the last ten days. Waking up alone after the night he'd spent at Lena's, her acceptance of his brunch invitation, her total engagement with his friends, and then her complete shutdown afterward, left him feeling completely bewildered. He hadn't expected her to completely avoid him during the tournament. Hell, even Lindsay's invitation had caught him off guard.

At this point, he wasn't sure what to expect.

When Lindsay asked J.C. and Bryce to join them for Thanksgiving, she had been completely honest with him. The invitation had been issued from Mike and her, not Lena. And they hadn't told Lena that they were inviting him. This time, she'd have to handle the unexpected. He definitely wasn't sure how good of an idea it was, but since she'd been shutting him down for the last ten days, he was willing to take the risk of inspiring her ire.

It wasn't normal for him to stay in town for Thanksgiving. But he had used the lead provided by Lena for Mark's assistant and had made serious headway in exploiting some resources for their first heart-screening event. He felt like leaving town right now would curb the momentum he'd built over the last few weeks. Explaining to his mother his absence for the holiday had been difficult, but Bryce had decided to stay, too, which had made it better in his mother's eyes.

He would have felt significantly better if Lena knew he was coming. She'd been pretty clear with her actions over the last couple of weeks. She needed or wanted distance. And he'd given her so much distance that it seemed the tether between them had snapped.

They'd spoken at the tournament, and he had felt her watching him even though she'd pretended to be indifferent. He imagined the difficulty for her. She'd always dictated the pace, if there were one, and to have him be in her life for reasons other than what she was comfortable with had to be hard.

The struggle for him really came down to his request for her to come into this when she was ready for more than sex so that whatever was between them had a chance to be something other than physical. He'd asked for a beginning. She had obviously misunderstood him. And although he wanted to be understanding, he found his patience waning.

That was why he and Bryce had decided to pre-party before heading over to dinner. Unfortunately, it wasn't having the desired effect, and J.C. found himself pushing down on his anger. The last sip of whiskey slid down his throat as he attempted to find his deliberate calm.

"Ready?" Bryce asked as he stood up and threw some cash onto the bar.

"Yeah," J.C. answered even though he wasn't sure he was.

It didn't take long for them to get to Mike and Lindsay's house.

J.C. grabbed the wine he'd bought and shoved one at Bryce. "Don't want you to go in empty-handed," he mumbled as they made their way to the front door.

Bryce laughed, enjoying J.C.'s discomfort. "Glad we stopped for a drink?" he teased.

"You have no idea," J.C. returned with a smile, enjoying the warmth of the whiskey as it soothed the nerves in his stomach.

Even knowing that a lot of people were going to be there didn't prepare J.C. for the noise when he walked into the house. He was grateful for the crowd because, all of the sudden, he didn't really want to have an opportunity to talk to Lena.

Bryce and J.C. made their way through the foyer and out onto the patio to get some drinks.

"Coach Cal, Coach B!" Nick ran through the kitchen and out onto the patio, a whirlwind of energy. "Can we go play soccer? Aiden is here, too, and I guess we can let the girls play." He jumped around them, speaking a mile a minute. "We can play in the backyard. My dad just put up goals."

"Okay," Bryce responded with a ruffle of Nick's hair.

J.C. took a sip of his newly opened beer and said, "Let's do it."

"This way," Nick called.

They were almost to the outside patio door when J.C. heard her.

"Nicky," Lena said, "there's not much time before dinner, so don't get so involved in your game that you give me a hard time."

"Yes, ma'am," Nick responded with a roll of his eyes that J.C. knew Lena couldn't see.

J.C. looked over at her just as she noticed him. The only indication she'd been surprised was a slight widening of her eyes that most people would have missed.

"Bryce, J.C.," she said with a nod of her head.

J.C. responded in kind and turned to walk out with Nick.

Bryce looked over his shoulder at J.C. and said, "That went well."

His eyes held a note of mischief, and J.C. couldn't help but laugh. As far as greetings went, it was a long way from friendly. That was fine and what he'd expected. But as they stripped down to their T-shirts for the four versus four soccer game, J.C. started to wonder if Lena was capable of anything more.

They hadn't played for long when they were called in for dinner with instructions to wash up before coming to the table. J.C. trailed the kids to the bathroom, dutifully washed his hands, and then followed them to the kitchen where everyone stood around the breakfast bar in the middle of the room. J.C. knew most of the people present, but there were a couple of strangers.

Lindsay took on her hostess duties and said, "We'll have our prayer, and then we'll eat. It was Lena's year to cook, so if the turkey's dry, take it up with her."

Everyone laughed, and J.C. assumed it was a running joke.

"Please join hands," Lindsay added.

Everyone stepped more surely into the circle around the bar, clasping hands. He was tempted to look around the room for Lena but managed to win the battle over his desire.

He reached out to Jessie, who had been around him since the soccer game. He grabbed her little hand in his left and leaned down, whispering, "I guess you're with me."

That elicited a giggle. Not knowing or really caring who was to his right, he blindly reached out. He didn't have to turn to know it was Lena when her hand interlocked with his. He tried to keep his focus on Jessie, who was still giggling at him. Straightening up, he shot a glance in Lena's direction, completely expecting that her eyes would be averted or that she'd be looking at someone else. So, when their gazes met, he found himself struggling to fight the jolt he'd experienced.

"Hey," he said softly, aware of the hush starting to fall through the room as Mike asked for everyone to bow their heads.

He heard the words Mike was saying, felt the wave of fellowship wash over him, while he held Jessie's fragile hand in his. Then, the prayer was over, and the noise ratcheted up. Jessie dropped his hand and took off toward her twin, but Lena held on. He turned toward her, unsure of her mood.

She stepped into the space in between them and said, "I'm glad you're here," before she released his hand and went to help Lindsay.

It was late. The crowd had lessened. Mike's work colleagues had been the first to go. Then, Sarina's family had left because they lived out past the interstate and wanted to get home before it was too late. The kids had been sent off to bed long ago.

Mike, Lindsay, Bryce, J.C., and Lena were sitting around the table, finishing a bottle of wine and drinking beer. The conversation had started with their soccer team and progressed from there. At times, J.C. thought Mike was vetting him, trying to determine if J.C. was worthy of Lena and possibly being a part of Nick's life. But then the conversation would veer, and J.C. thought he was probably being paranoid. Eventually, they came back to Play for Gabe, and he found himself looking to Lena, judging her reaction, wanting to know if it was all too much.

"So, Lena tells me she's working on the 501(c)(3) application with you?" Mike said, the inflection of his voice asking a question even though there wasn't anything to be answered.

Lena smirked, and J.C. found himself smiling at her across the table.

Bryce said, "Well, she said she'd do it pro bono, but we haven't gotten it back yet, so I'm not sure if we are supposed to slip her some money or not."

Lena laughed. "Actually, I just finished. I'll have everything to you on Monday. I left a message with Anna yesterday."

J.C. looked at Bryce, the question implicit in his stare. Bryce shook his head. J.C. tried to mask his annoyance with Anna by thanking Lena for her help.

"It wasn't a problem," she said.

Aside from her comment after the prayer, she hadn't been particularly partial to J.C. all night. But she hadn't been withholding either, so he considered it a small victory.

"How did you go from raising money for a scholarship to becoming a nonprofit with a mission?" Lindsay asked as she handed them new beer bottles.

J.C. pulled the top off and deferred to Bryce with a nod. They never really talked about the actual journey much, so J.C. was as interested in Bryce's version as everyone else around the table.

"I don't know if I can really start with the scholarship fund. I think it goes back to Gabe's death and the end of that soccer season. Looking back, not winning the regional game to go to the state championship had a profound impact on me, and I think everyone else, too. Part of me thinks that if we'd won, his legacy would have felt complete, like we'd done what we owed him and won state, doing something no other soccer team from our school had ever done, fulfilling our destiny. And maybe that would have been enough." Bryce paused, toying with the label on his beer bottle.

Then, he looked up at J.C.

J.C. saw the question in his eyes, the do-you-feel-the-same-way question. He nodded his head. "Probably," he concurred.

Then, he looked at Lena. But she wasn't really looking at Bryce or him. She was looking at space, probably remembering the game.

"Anyway, the loss made me feel like we still needed to do something, to let him know he wouldn't be forgotten. At the time, it wasn't necessarily sudden cardiac arrest and awareness and screenings. It was just this need to make an impact, to do something monumental for Gabe. Once we got to that point, where we identified that need, it grew from there."

"It's pretty awesome—what you're doing," Lindsay said quietly.

J.C. almost laughed as he and Bryce shrugged at the same time.

"Thousands of families have suffered the same tragedy, and they have the same story. And so many of the tragedies could have been prevented."

"Prevented," Lena said.

J.C. wasn't sure if it was a comment or a question, so when silence settled around the table, he wasn't sure what to do to break it.

Bryce looked questioningly at J.C. and then shuffled into the void. "Screenings. An ECG can detect up to eighty-nine percent of all conditions that can lead to SCA." He wasn't preaching. He was just putting the facts out there.

"So, let's say Gabe had an ECG. Is that the same as an EKG?" Lena looked to J.C., and he nodded. "Then, they find the abnormality. What then?"

Bryce looked to J.C., so he said, "Medication, lifestyle changes, potentially a heart transplant."

"Hmm," she said. She still had that faraway look in her eyes, like she was in another place mentally. "No more soccer," she murmured.

Bryce and J.C. both shook their heads, another in-sync moment.

But J.C. realized she couldn't see them, so he answered, "Potentially. It would have depended. Not all heart conditions lead to giving up activities. In fact, most don't."

Then, he looked toward Lindsay first and then Mike. They were closely watching Lena, the sympathy and worry apparent on their faces.

"I wonder…" she said out loud but not to anyone in particular.

J.C. wondered if she even realized she was talking.

"I wonder what he would have felt like if he had been diagnosed and had to give that up, what his fifteen-year-old self would have thought about watching life from the sidelines."

"At least he would have been around to watch it," J.C. snapped.

Lena looked at J.C., somewhat startled by his tone. She blinked, like she was coming awake. Lindsay laid her hand on J.C.'s thigh and patted him, like one would to settle an impertinent child. He looked over at her, and she smiled gently.

He looked back to Lena and found her staring at him, seeing him again.

"I don't mean that not knowing was better—or maybe I do. There's something to be said about ignorance being bliss. I mean, I can't help but think what his life would have been like if he had known—if he would have been grateful or if he would have struggled with the knowledge. When I think about the joy he got from playing soccer...I just...don't know." She shook her head like she needed to cast off the fog of the moments before. Then, she stood up and started collecting the debris on the table, signaling closing time.

When she walked out toward the kitchen, J.C. followed. She dumped everything in the recyclable can, shut the cabinet, and leaned forward, dropping her head to the counter. J.C. walked up behind her and placed his hands on her hips. She jerked up, nailing him in the chin with her head.

"Sorry," she said, turning in his arms, examining his face for an injury.

"I didn't mean to scare you," he said, keeping their bodies anchored together.

"No. I mean, for what I said. I just...I don't know where that came from." She put her arms around his neck and dropped her head to his chest.

He caressed her back, trying to comfort her.

Then, she pulled away from him and grabbed his hands in hers. "Will you come home with me?"

"Of course," he said without any hesitation.

It had been ten long days of self-denial or preservation, depending on how it was looked at. Even at the tournament over the weekend, Lena had kept her distance, trying not to appear rude. She was just another soccer parent supporting her child.

But then Lindsay had meddled. Lena hadn't dealt with her yet, but no matter the outcome, she would. When J.C. had walked into the house today, Lena's most honest first reaction had been happiness. She'd just wanted to bask in his presence. Then, when he'd left to play soccer with Nicky, she'd been mad. Keeping J.C. out, staying away, had been hard work, and with one little invitation, all the work had gone to waste. Her time of trying to increase the distance between them was a futile attempt. Slipping her hand into his for the prayer had been the most natural act of her day.

Her flip-flopping was confusing and frustrating her, so she could only imagine what J.C. thought about it.

Lena led J.C. into the house, desperate to touch him. She moved toward the room she now considered theirs and pushed him down on the bed, determined to call all the shots. She needed to feel like she was in control of something, anything. And if it were merely dictating the sex they were about to have, it would have to be enough.

He didn't argue. There didn't seem to be enough time or inclination or air for either of them to get any words out of their mouths. When he was finally inside her, relief moved through her as he did, calming her as his body claimed hers.

When it was over, J.C. pulled her down next to him on the bed, so they faced each other. His head rested on his hand, his other wandering randomly over the planes of her body. The stubble on his face aged him enough that she forgot how young he was for a moment.

"Can you tell me?" he asked.

They gazed at each other. "What do you want to know?"

"What it felt like when you lost him."

She blinked and then looked wide-eyed in her denial. "I...uh..." Then, for some inane reason, she laughed. "Wow. Way to allow me to enjoy the post-orgasmic glow."

He laughed with her, but his eyes remained serious, almost pleading in their intensity, requesting her honesty. His hand continued its lazy perusal, natural in its quest to touch her everywhere. She closed her eyes and rolled onto her back, leaving his hand suspended in the air where her hip had been. He dropped it, so it landed low on her belly. She was tempted to shimmy up, to push his attention back to the physical, putting up another barrier. He wanted to break them down, and she wasn't ready for him.

But he seemed to know that about her. Even now with the silence settling between them, she could tell he was accommodating her. It was as if Lindsay had given him her little Keys to Lena black book, and he'd studied it, like he did everything else.

"At first," she said, "it seemed surreal. I saw him lying on the ground while everyone else got up. Even now, I remember thinking, *That's so not like him*. He always seemed to have to be first. Maybe second to you was okay once in a while."

His hand stilled on her stomach, and she knew her words hit him.

"But, I didn't understand what was going on. I could see the rising panic, ya know? Everyone got frantic. I saw you take off, but I didn't know where you were going. I saw the coach leaning over him, pushing on him. And stupid though it seems now, I was kinda pissed. I thought, *What the hell are you doing to my brother?*"

J.C.'s fingers pulled into a fist. Then, his hand moved to her opposite hip, and he rolled to his back, bringing her with him, so she fit into the place near his shoulder, a puzzle piece nuzzled up to its mate, snapping into place with a satisfied sigh.

"We weren't sure what was wrong," he said simply.

In her new position, she could feel his words through his chest, and they moved into her.

"Yeah," she murmured, acknowledging his admission.

They were quiet for a time, the memory a third wheel.

She continued. "I never felt the compulsion to go to him. Now, I realize I wouldn't have been much help, probably a hindrance to all the chaos. But sometimes—the very few times I allow myself to think about it—I wonder why I didn't feel the need to go to him."

He pulled her closer, hugging her harder, knowing she needed the kind of comfort words wouldn't offer.

"But when the ambulance came, I knew. I knew he was gone, and it was like drowning. You are awake, and you know you aren't getting out of it. And you're fighting for air and trying to swim for it. But you know, in the part of you that can sense doom, that you aren't going to reach the surface. And you want to scream your frustration and curse God, wondering why he would have let that happen to you." She stopped talking, imagining the darkness. "As you fade to black, you still know. You know that you are dying, and maybe there is a way to stop it, but you're not strong enough or clever enough or good enough."

His hands on her paused, his grasp light, his breath shallow.

"That's what it felt like to me, Jackson—like I was drowning, and I couldn't save myself. It took me a long time. And I'm pretty sure Nicky saved me. Funny little trick God played on me—taking away my brother and giving me my son. Honestly, if the timing had been any different, I probably wouldn't have kept Nicky. And I would have been lost."

They were quiet for a long time. J.C. never said a word when she'd finished, and she silently wished for their weird mind-mingling. In the aftermath of her brutal memory, she needed to know what he was thinking.

She suddenly sat up, shaking them both out of their solitary thoughts.

"In the parking lot that night, you knew I was pregnant?" It was an accusation shrouded in a question. "How did I forget about that?" She looked down at J.C., taking him in, and was surprised by the smirk on his face.

"I did," he admitted. "Gabe was worried about you. I swear, he didn't tell anyone else."

He reached up and pulled her back down, fitting her back into her spot.

"I don't think I meant what I said tonight at Mike and Lindsay's, about not wanting to know," she admitted.

J.C. tensed under her, his body suddenly taut instead of languid.

"But maybe I did. I don't know. It makes me sad to think that he knew in some way, that he was walking around, thinking something was wrong but not knowing how to articulate it. What if he spent that whole day with the dreadful feeling that something bad was going to happen?"

J.C. took a deep breath and blew it out, and then his body relaxed under her. He began to stroke her back again. She melted into him, his physical presence absorbing her questions, cushioning her doubts.

"Is that why you said what you?"

"No. I said what I did because I am a firm believer that ignorance is bliss. I get your cause, and I think it's monumental and important. And this is just me, so take it for what it's worth, but I don't know that I would want to know. It would hinder me and make me scared all the time. And I wouldn't want to live like that. I wouldn't be able to forget and just live. I wouldn't want that."

J.C. didn't comment, and stillness settled between them.

She started to feel antsy, and the familiar feeling of too much intimacy crept in, making her skin itch. She pushed away from him, ready to return to her inner sanctuary, the place not breached by anyone but her. But he held her in place.

"Don't run away from me now," he said.

"I'm so not good at this, J.C. I just need...space."

"I gave you ten days of space."

"And you just forced me to relive the lowest point of my life, and you're not giving me anything back!" She'd meant to keep her voice controlled, but it rose steadily. She glared down at him, her hands on his chest, her arms straight, giving her the greatest possible distance without breaking their physical connection.

"You're not ready for what I have to give you."

She almost cried at the irony of him sounding like the big kid in the relationship. "How do you know what I'm ready for?"

"You spent the last ten days avoiding me."

"Because I don't want to do stupid shit, like share my feelings over everything. What guy doesn't want to just have sex?"

He laughed then, sidesplitting laughter. He rolled to his side and got out of bed, laughter still rumbling through him. He reached down and pulled on his jeans. He buttoned them up and then turned back toward her, his face still reflecting his mirth.

She looked up at him, suddenly serious. "What am I not ready for?"

The smile left his face, and he shook his head, denying her.

"Try me," she said, defiance in her tone.

He rolled his eyes.

"What?" she asked again.

Then, he leaned down, so his arms were surrounding her.

"After it happened, I had all this anger, so much anger that it was an effort to control it. I would hold on to it, hoard it. Then, I would step on the field, and I would bring it all out. I'd get excited because I knew that I could rid myself of it. I could let it go, do something with it, and leave pieces of it on the field. I knew, eventually, I'd leave enough of it out there that I wouldn't have any left. I would let it rush through me, and I'd use it on our opponents. In those moments, that time on the field, I would feel good and happy, balanced and whole.

"I've been adrift for a while—there, but not there. I've been all over the place in a way that is foreign to me at this point of my life. All that anger I got rid of allowed me to be this really focused individual who knew how to go after things. The med school stuff and trying to figure out my place have been weighing on me. Then, I see you again. And when I'm around you, not even just in your guest-room bed, I feel good and happy, balanced and whole.

"But you aren't there yet. You use your grief as a shield. Emotionally, you don't want to grow up because it allows you to stay disconnected and risk-free. I get it. I totally get it and you. And you know it, but you aren't ready for it."

She wasn't sure which one of them moved first, but she was suddenly in his arms, his body cradling hers, her arms around his neck, her legs around his waist. He was inside her as soon as he had shed his clothes, and before she couldn't think any longer, she consciously knew how right he was. She wasn't ready for him.

"Do you have someplace you need to be?" Lena asked the following morning as she rolled out of bed.

J.C. shook his head, reluctant to move from his spot. He couldn't quite tell if she was asking to hurry him out of her house or to perhaps propose plans. He shifted to his side, watching her, as she slipped on her dress from the night before. He liked her like this—when she wasn't trying to fight it, when she was just being herself.

"Do you?" he finally asked.

She paused in gathering her bra and underwear. "No, not really." She stood up with her loot and looked at him. "I gave some thought to doing some Christmas shopping."

"Oh," he said, his lack of enthusiasm apparent in his tone.

She laughed. "I know, I know. Black Friday is crazy, but my shopping days are limited to the weekends when I don't have Nicky." She shrugged and teased, "I bet it's still okay for you to give fraternity social T-shirts to all the people on your Christmas list."

"Yeah, right," he said with a roll of his eyes. "My mother absolutely lets me get away with that."

"Is it just you and your mom?" Lena asked, the teasing glint disappearing from her eyes.

"Yeah. My dad died the year after Gabe. But my mom is from a big family, and most of them still live there, so it's rarely quiet."

"I'm sorry about your dad."

J.C. saw her eyes take on the glazed-over sympathetic look he'd learned to hate at sixteen. It was an interesting lesson to learn so young—the futility of the words and comfort that people would try to offer in the face of death.

Nothing anyone said or did could assuage the sadness and grief of losing Gabe. When he'd lost Gabe, he'd learned to hate the phrases, *I'm sorry*, and, *Are you okay?* He understood the need to offer up those platitudes, but there was really no way to make it any better.

Gabe's death had left him blaming God and being angry. When his dad had died, he'd found himself more accepting.

"You probably don't remember or didn't pay attention, but my dad was quite a bit older than my mom. He'd already raised a family, and he had been widowed when he met my mother. So, his death was different. Don't get me wrong. It wasn't easy, but it seemed more natural, the natural order of things."

"I don't remember your parents," Lena said.

"Let's just say, my dad must have had mad skills to land my mother, who was twenty-five years younger than him." He delivered this with a wink and a smile. It was a way to put people at ease when he told them about his parents.

J.C. watched Lena's eyes get wide, and he could read the *ew* factor reflected there. It'd never bothered him when he was little. He'd barely recognized the questioning glances and knowing smirks. But as he'd gotten older, he'd understood the confusing looks when people realized his parents were a couple. Now, he could acknowledge that, if you didn't know, you might think his mother looked like she could be his father's daughter or whatever. His half-sister and half-brother were only five and seven years younger than his mother. It was just the way it was, but that didn't mean people wouldn't need time to adjust to it.

"Makes seven years seem like nothing, doesn't it?" he joked.

Finally, he got her to smile and laugh, the odd turn of the conversation straightening out.

"Yes," she conceded as she leaned over to kiss him.

He started to pull her back into bed, but she broke the kiss. It looked like she might ask more questions or dig a little deeper. Right now, it appealed to him, to have her want to know more, especially after his confession the night before.

"So, how about some Black Friday shopping and then maybe dinner?"

When her question had finally left her mouth, he found he was a little disappointed.

"Like a date?" he teased, trying to find some pleasure in her request to spend more time with him.

She rolled her eyes before she turned and made her way toward the door. "Yes, a date*ish*."

She stepped over his khaki pants crumpled in a ball on the floor. "But," she said, looking over at him, "I think we need to get you some new clothes."

He laughed. "And probably a shower and my car." He paused. Because he had her undivided attention, he said, "Although it wouldn't be bad to smell like you for the rest of the day." He looked her over from her brown eyes down to her pink toes, and he watched the heat walk its way up her neck.

"Be that as it may, I'd appreciate it if you took a shower," she said with a smirk.

"Noted," he said, chuckling.

After Lena showered, they jumped in her Jeep and headed to his apartment, so he could change.

He was slightly uncomfortable having her at his apartment. It still sang of a college student with its simplistic layout and mismatched dishes. He grabbed a bottle of water from the fridge and made sure she was comfortable in the living room on the couch his mother had given them. He didn't think Lena would be up for coming into his room. Compared to her house, his room would likely seem like a shrine to her brother. The three pictures he had of Gabe would probably seem over the top.

"Quick shower and then we can go," he said before quickly kissing her on her mouth.

He left her on his couch and made his way into his room. As he got into the shower, he thought about the kiss he'd dropped on her.

She wasn't good with the casual touches. She was completely sexy and open when she knew it would lead to sex, but his hand on her lower back and the kiss he'd just delivered were difficult for her, and he could see it in the way she shied away and found ways to avoid his touch. He figured he'd know he was more than sex to her the moment she grabbed his hand in public or leaned into him without any future promises. What he needed to figure out was if he was willing to wait around for her.

He couldn't believe he'd asked her how she'd felt when Gabe died. Her ability to articulate it, put her grief into words, had left him reeling. He would never have been able to give it words, to take those feelings and explain them to someone.

Her trusting me enough to talk to me about it has to mean something, right?

Shaking off the thought, he jumped out of the shower and quickly dressed. He was about to leave his room when the door cracked open, and Lena walked in.

"You almost ready?" she asked.

He paused near his closet and then moved toward the door, not up for another emotional discussion. But it was too late as she'd already started perusing his room, much like he'd done at her house at his first opportunity. Her curiosity should have made him happy, but he waited for her to get to the pictures.

He could tell the moment she recognized the photos. At first, she went right by them, but then she stopped and backtracked. She stiffened, her back going ramrod straight. Then, she reached out with her finger, putting it on the tiny face of Gabe in the team picture. She moved then to look at the last picture ever taken of him. J.C. could see that she recognized it because she'd been there that night, the night before he'd died. It seemed like the memory reached for her as she stepped back with a microscopic flinch.

He stayed where he was, not sure if he should say anything to her or let her lead the way. She continued to look at the pictures. Then, stepping away, she continued to look around. And he let it go because it seemed to be what she wanted, and he was willing to do whatever she needed.

As much as the thought of shopping had horrified J.C., it was over before he knew it. They found a restaurant near the beach and sat, watching the sun descend into the horizon.

"Thanks for coming with me even though you really didn't want to," Lena said with a grin.

"It wasn't nearly as bad as I'd thought it would be."

"Well, at least you'll admit it. When I make Nicky do something he doesn't want to do, he complains. Then, he'll have a great time, but he'll never admit it."

"Really?" J.C. asked, interested.

She rarely talked about Nick.

"Yeah. He's like an old man. It's impossible to get him to do stuff sometimes."

"Like what?"

"You name it. Ride his bike. Go hiking with me. Go to the beach," she listed with a smile on her face.

"Interesting. I don't see that in him, but I guess it's because of soccer."

"Yeah," she acknowledged. "I never have to convince him to go to soccer practice. But if I were to suggest he take his ball out and do something with it, he'd protest."

They shared a smile.

"The pictures in your room…they caught me off guard," Lena said, changing the subject and surprising J.C. with the direction of the conversation.

"Yeah," he said, "I tried to keep you out of there."

She smiled, possibly in appreciation of the gesture. "It was fine. I haven't…" She paused. "I haven't really looked at pictures of him in so long. He looks so young, caught in time like that. It seems weird to look at those pictures. It wasn't just because of Gabe, but I also recognized you, the boy, there."

"And he's frozen in time," J.C. said thoughtfully, like he hadn't actually considered it before.

"Yeah, frozen in time, never getting any older."

Neither of them spoke for a moment, and J.C. wondered if they would ever get to a point where Gabe wouldn't be a focal point of their conversations, if they could ever exhaust him as a subject. Then, he immediately felt guilty for the thought. If that were the only thing tying her to him, it would be short-lived, and he'd never really have the opportunity to find out.

"Let's get out of here, J.C."

He already recognized the look in her eyes, the luminosity of her growing lust reflected there for him to see, feel. He didn't hesitate to get the check and make his way out of the restaurant with her following closely behind. They didn't touch, and he wondered if she felt like him—electrified, an easily tripped wire.

Would she explode if he touched her, detonating under his hands?

He knew the trigger—memories of her past acting as an aphrodisiac for her. It was her escape. Sex with him helped her block it out—all the pain she'd boxed up and locked away.

The more they delved, the deeper he got. For now, he thought he could handle it—the sex without anything else. *What guy wouldn't be able to, as she'd reminded him yesterday?* But he wasn't sure if what they were doing was any good for either of them.

The ride home stretched between them, the short distance drawing out their longing. He didn't even attempt to make conversation because he couldn't quite hold on to a thought—other than the need he had.

They parked and headed into her house, the scene so familiar.

Groundhog Day, he thought as they walked through the door, and she led him back to the guest room.

But this time, before anything happened, she stopped him with a hand on his chest. "I get Nicky back tomorrow morning, so you can't stay."

Before he could react or even process her words, her mouth was on his, and all thoughts faded to black.

But when it was over and they lay there, panting and sweating, he remembered. And before he could think about what he was doing, he rolled out of bed and got dressed. She didn't say a word. She just watched him with a unique expression. He could see the stormy lust in her eyes had calmed, but weariness hung heavy in the air between them.

He waited for her to say something, anything, to get him to stop. But when her mouth remained closed and her eyes stayed hard, he turned and left without a word.

Lena was sitting in her office on Friday afternoon, thinking about the seven days since she'd seen or talked to J.C. The absence of him had been resting in the corners of her mind over the last week, but she couldn't bring herself to do anything to soothe over their last interaction.

With the weekend stretching out in front of her, she allowed herself a moment of indulgence. Without thinking about the consequences, she picked up her phone and texted him.

Lena: Are you around this weekend?

J.C.: No. Headed home.

It was all she got and probably more than she deserved. Although he could have and maybe even should have, he hadn't even made her stew and wait for a response.

Lena tried not to think about the look in his eyes when he'd left her the week before. In the moment, she'd only felt relief—relief to be out of his orbit, away from his light. She had forced him out and hadn't done anything to explain. So, she was really only reaping what she'd sown.

She found herself reaching for her phone, rereading J.C.'s text. She felt all the desire for him surge back through her, the lid she'd fashioned unable to hold down the emotion. Suddenly, she was on the phone with Mike, asking him to keep Nicky for the weekend.

She ran to her house and grabbed a bag for him, and then she went to drop it off with Lindsay. She saw the questions in Lindsay's eyes, but she only said she was going home.

"Not *home*," she corrected. "Just the place where I grew up."

It was one of those decisions that would further reinforce the notion of Lena's impulsiveness. She could see it on Lindsay's face and hear it in Mike's voice when she'd asked them to keep Nicky for the weekend.

When Lena refused to give Lindsay an opportunity to pick her brain, she managed to draw new lines in the sand between them, imaginary walls whose boundaries stretched around her and engulfed her in their protectiveness. Lena rarely made decisions of import without at least discussing them with Lindsay, but there hadn't been even an inkling of what she had planned because, of course, she hadn't planned it.

The drive was a blur of Pandora stations blasting from her phone through the speakers of the car, the music keeping her from thinking too much. She ignored Lindsay's phone calls. Between the music and the Starbucks, she kept herself awake and wired, so when she pulled into town, the decision to explore seemed natural. She quickly checked into the hotel but returned to her car, suddenly eager to see how her little town had grown up.

She drove from one side to the other, weaving through the streets, canvassing her old neighborhood.

She saw the ghosts of her and Gabe's younger selves at their little Catholic school with his hand clasped in hers on his first day of kindergarten, sullenness a mask for his face. Again, she could see him on his eighth-grade graduation as his crew posed for pictures to mark the rite. Before she could stop it, the memory of her last day in Christ the King—or any church, for that matter—the day of his funeral, superimposed itself over the good memories, like a thundercloud overtaking the sun. It angered her to know her memory of his death seemed to be larger than the memory of his life.

She wondered when she had let it happen, allowing the dark to blot out the light. Without meaning to, she thought of J.C. and her overwhelming need to get away from him last weekend. It seemed her course had been set those years ago when her brother was taken from her, and she was powerless to change it.

BLISS

Lena pulled away from the church without any destination in mind. She continued her tour. As she turned into the high school, she couldn't help but smile at the unintended place. Part of her dreaded this part of the trip more than the church. Their church merely represented the good-bye. Her high school was the birthplace of her worst memory.

She traversed the deserted parking lot, weaving her way toward the athletic fields. Now that she was there, she knew exactly why she'd come and where she needed to go. She parked near the entrance to the soccer, track, and football fields. Stepping out, she quietly closed the door, as if she needed to worry about making noise.

It seemed so much smaller than she'd remembered. In her mind, the stadium had taken on Disney proportions. Everything had been bigger and shinier and newer. It'd radiated its own kind of energy, one of cheering crowds, big lights, and red and blue pompoms.

But in the dark of night, it looked small, old, and underwhelming.

She stepped up to the ticket booth and pulled gently on the fence. It gave easily, and she squeezed through the opening. Picking her way around the hedges toward the track-and-field area, she walked slowly toward the end zone. She could see the field set for soccer, the goals in place, pulling the focal point from the yellow uprights.

Weaving around the goal, she marched, trance-like, to the middle of the field. When she hit the center point, she stopped, setting her right foot on the line. Then, slowly, she turned in a three-hundred-sixty-degree pivot, taking in the whole field in a panoramic view. Much like at the church, she caught glimpses of Gabe, too many to take in, even though she'd probably only seen him play a few games on this field. It was like a mind odyssey, a collage of his soccer teams, his years, his greatest hits. The poignancy of the memories kicked her in the gut, strangling her with its intensity. It was eight years' worth of withheld thoughts bombarding her, overrunning the dam she'd built and gushing over.

She didn't collapse.

She didn't cry.

She just felt.

She let it all come.

Then, she sat at center field. For a moment, she only felt the cold of the dewy grass seeping into her jeans. When she adapted to that, she lay down on her back and took in the whole of the sky. Reaching out her arms, she found herself smiling at the thought of a dew angel. She moved her arms and legs, basking in the silliness of the notion.

She stopped when her middle finger hit against something hard and cold in the grass. She didn't even need to pick it up to know what had been waiting for her. But her hand curled into a fist, scooping up the coin. She brought it to her face, merely for confirmation. She opened her hand and turned it over, palm up. With the opposite hand, she reached over, picked up the penny, and held it in front of her face.

Then, she smiled.

Lena wasn't sure how long she'd been there or when she'd drifted off to sleep, but she awoke with a jolt and found herself staring up into J.C.'s eyes.

"Hey," he said gently. He took a couple of steps back from her, presumably to give her space.

She looked around, trying to take in her surroundings. The cold of the grass had soaked into her clothes, through her skin, and into her bones.

"What are you doing here?" she asked, shaking off the fog.

He squatted down, still with the distance between them, before he answered, "Lindsay called me. She was worried about you."

Lena continued to watch him, but she sat up. He reached a hand out to her. She took it and allowed him to slowly pull her to her feet. She freed her hand from his and then crossed her arms over her chest as an involuntary shiver ran through her. J.C. must have seen it because he removed his jacket and wrapped it around her. It was immediate intimacy with its still warm feel and his smell enveloping her. She slid her arms into the sleeves and returned them to her chest. She could already sense her need for him, and keeping her hands to herself seemed important.

"Bryce drove me. Why don't you let me drive you to where you are staying? He can follow us and give me a ride home." His voice was soothing, gentle, the tone that would be used for a cornered animal.

"I can drive," she argued, an attempt at bravado, her desire to appear strong. They started walking from the field.

"I know you can," he explained, "but I'd feel better knowing you are home safe."

"You guys can follow me, if it will make you feel better, but I'm fine," she insisted, holding tightly to her control, the tone of her voice, the inflection. But she'd stopped moving, as if moving and talking at the same time were suddenly too much for her. She noticed it and made another conscious effort to do both at the same time, an orchestrated normal.

"I've got this," she reiterated.

Literally putting one foot in front of the other, Lena moved toward the ticket booth. A turnstile for her memories and foolishness of the night, she approached it as if it were the Holy Grail. If she could only make it there, she knew she could put all this behind her. She remained conscious of J.C.'s presence slightly behind her, to her left, allowing her to make her way on her own but there should she falter. But she didn't falter. She made it out of the gate, and she breathed easier.

She walked directly to the Jeep, opened the door, and climbed into the driver's seat. She silently celebrated the victory of escape until J.C. got in the passenger seat.

"Bryce is going to follow us. Where are you staying?" he asked.

"At DoubleTree," she answered.

"Do you know how to get there from here?"

The question earned him a glare. He held up his hands in surrender, and she couldn't help the small smile. She started the car, and the radio blared, prompting her to press on the volume button on her steering wheel.

"Damn, woman! You must have been jamming out," he observed.

She lifted a shoulder in response but then explained snippily, "I like loud music when I drive. It keeps me awake."

"Yeah, it'd be hard to sleep with that bass thumping."

She rolled her eyes and stuck her tongue out at him. He laughed.

Then, they were silent.

Lena couldn't help but feel a little violated. She was confused about Lindsay's call to him and his ability to find her. It made her want to ask how many places he'd looked for her and if he'd tried to call her. She wanted to feel awkward with him, but she didn't.

Neither of them spoke for most of the drive.

Then, when they were about five minutes away, he shifted in the seat and looked toward her. "You seem like you're mad at me."

It wasn't a question, so she wasn't sure what he wanted her to say. Instead, she remained quiet, content to let him wonder.

"Are you?" he said, trying again.

"Not exactly," she responded.

All her emotions were too close to the surface, which made it difficult for her to talk to him. He'd already seen too much of her, and she needed to keep parts of her to herself.

"Oh, okay," he responded sarcastically. "Thanks for clearing that up."

She wasn't quite sure what it was—the trigger in his response. Maybe it was the sarcasm, which he rarely used, but something about his words made the bubbling feelings almost boil over. She was suffocating under the weight of them, and for the first time, she thought, maybe if she talked, she'd feel relieved.

"I'm not a big fan of people seeing me weak," she said, removing the filter.

"I get that. But I don't think you're weak."

She shrugged in nonchalance but knew her hands were gripping the steering wheel harder.

"How did you find me?" she asked.

He raked his hand through his hair, seemingly reluctant to answer her. Another minute passed, but since she didn't really want to be pushed tonight, she returned the favor and waited.

"Wasn't hard, Lena."

"How many places did you look before you found me?"

He didn't hesitate this time when he answered, "None."

"That was the first place?"

"Yes."

She nodded.

"Are you okay?" he asked quietly.

She took a second to think about what he'd said. "Yes." Her answer came out strong and resounding in the car, and it made her smile. "I'm still a little surprised that Lindsay called you, and I'm kind of mad at her."

He shrugged. "I understand. But she'd been calling you and texting you all night."

Lena reached into the center console and pulled out her phone. She saw ten missed calls from Lindsay, four from Mike, and one from J.C. The number fifteen appeared in red over her little text message icon. She sighed. She put the phone back and then made the turn into the hotel parking lot.

"Look," he said, twisting to face her as she turned off the car, "with today being what it is, your request for them to take Nicky on their off weekend, and your silent phone, she just wanted to make sure you were okay."

Lena looked at him quizzically. Something he'd said hit against her chest, but she couldn't grab on to it.

Bryce pulled in next to them, and a quick zing of relief whipped through her.

No more explanations, she thought.

Lena gathered her purse, her charger, her phone, and then she turned to open the door. She heard J.C. follow on the other side.

Bryce rolled down his window and smiled at her. "Hey," he said.

"Hi, B," she returned, using J.C.'s nickname for him, as if she'd known Bryce forever.

He smiled larger.

J.C. stepped up to her. "You sure you're good?" he asked quietly.

"Yes," she said, nodding.

She stepped around him, so he could get into Bryce's truck.

Bryce leaned forward and said, "I'll feel better leaving if I know you're safely inside."

She rolled her eyes, which made them both laugh, but she started toward the lobby doors. She was almost there when it struck her—the off comment she couldn't figure out. She turned back to the truck waiting for her to go inside, and she walked toward them.

J.C. rolled down the window and cocked his head to the side.

"What about today?" she asked. When he didn't respond right away, she clarified, "You said, 'With today being what it is.'"

She watched him exchange a loaded look with Bryce.

Then, he looked back at her and responded, "Today is the anniversary of Gabe's death."

"Right," she said quickly before she turned and walked into the hotel. "Of course," she muttered to herself. "Of course it's the anniversary. I just didn't remember."

Max—2013

Even now, I still can't bring myself to walk into a church. I know it sounds stupid and immature, but I'm still a little angry with God.

Gabe and I were altar servers from fifth grade on. We tried to make sure we always got paired together even though I guess we weren't the ones taking care of it. I'm sure it was our parents.

In sixth grade, we discovered funerals. Weird, right? But it took us a whole year to figure out that if we served at funerals, we would get paid. It was only ten dollars, but at twelve years old, ten dollars seemed like a big deal.

Right before our first funeral, my dad had pulled Gabe and me aside. He told us that, if we were going to serve at funerals, it would be our duty to listen to the eulogy, to pay tribute to the family grieving by really trying to know the person. It seemed a little deep but not hard to do since we had to be there anyway, so we might as well listen.

It was one of the best lessons I learned from my dad.

Gabe and I would head to the vestibule to change after mass, and we would always talk about the person who had died. In an unspoken agreement, we'd share our impressions and feelings about the person and the people left behind.

I'm sure all of us have special memories of our own about Gabe—things each of us shared with him that no one else did. For Gabe and me, it was the post-funeral wrap-up. We never told anyone else what my father had said to us, and we never talked about it once we'd left the church. But it bonded us in a different way from everyone else.

And when I had to attend Gabe's funeral, it was all I could think about. I didn't listen to anything said. It was like my mind couldn't grasp it. All the experiences I had watching other people suffer and deal with an unexpected death and the thought of life without the person who had died withered away and left me bereft.

I vaguely remember the service. I mean, I remember carrying the casket out, and I remember the burial, but I couldn't tell you one thing anyone said about one of my best friends.

But when I left the church that day, I knew I'd never return. How could the God I'd grown up with and worshipped make us suffer in such a way?

So, the anniversary of Gabe's funeral is also the anniversary of my parting with the church.

I wasn't looking for reinforcement, but when we went to the Parent Heart Watch convention, hearing the stories from everyone there sort of hit me the same way. We were the only friends there. Everyone else had lost a child, and seeing their grief hurt something deep inside of me.

I'd think, after this long, I'd be able to accept the terror of Gabe's death, but it's still there, lurking. I know everyone else is accepting of it. It happened so long ago. But I still feel a little mad when I think about it. I can't imagine what his parents must have gone through and still go through when they look at us. I know they appreciate what we've done in his name, and they get the drive, our need to make some kind of impact. And they've been really supportive of that. But I would imagine they look with wonder at us and try to imagine who he would have been if he were still alive.

Would he still have been friends with us? Would we all still be friends?

Or maybe not. Maybe I just try to imagine what they feel like.

This was one of the better things we have done—becoming a part of this organization, reaching out to other people who have experienced the same loss. Their experience with their own organizations is going to push us forward, connect us in ways we wouldn't have been able to achieve by ourselves.

But it doesn't take away my anger at God.

The alumni game was J.C.'s favorite event. After Lena's unexpected visit the night before, he was even more excited about their tradition of hanging out for a pregame sunset. When J.C. and Anna pulled up to the beach, Bryce, Max, Fletcher, and Kyle along with some others had already arrived. He was late.

Aside from the hangover that continued to plague him, Anna had needed some help with a couple of last-minute things. As the two of them got out of his truck, J.C. did a quick inventory of the crowd, his perusal stopping on Lena sitting next to Bryce.

He wasn't quite sure how to react and was thankful she hadn't been looking at him when he discovered her presence. He hadn't spoken to her since last night. And he definitely hadn't told her about their pregame ritual, so he was really curious about how she'd come to be here. He knew for certain he didn't want her here.

"It's about time you two showed up!" Fletcher yelled, realizing they were there and drawing everyone's attention to them.

"Someone had to take care of everything for tonight," Anna retorted.

For once, J.C. was thankful for her snippiness. He smiled down at her. Placing his hand on the small of her back, he moved her forward into the fray. He was pretty certain he would have done the exact same thing even if Lena wasn't sitting with Bryce, watching his interactions with Anna, but he couldn't be sure.

"You still look hungover," Fletcher said with a smile. "I haven't seen you that drunk in a while though, so I guess I'm not surprised."

J.C. acknowledged his observation with a nod and a rueful smile. "Yeah, still hurting." And he was.

Even sleeping until noon hadn't quite cured him of the lethal amount of alcohol he'd consumed last night. He'd been pacing himself until he had gone to find Lena. Then, it had been all about drowning his confusion. He still couldn't understand what she had been doing in town, let alone on the beach with them now.

"B and I were just telling Lena that we had to get you home and into bed," Fletcher teased.

On any other day, in any other company, J.C. would have handled the teasing with a smile and probably a couple of reminders to Fletcher and Bryce about all the times he'd had to take care of them in their drunken states.

"Well, I'm sure that J.C.'s hand-holding of you two far exceeds last night," she said. Then, she looked over at Lena. "I didn't realize you would be here," she said with enough curiosity to make her sound interested rather than territorial.

But J.C. could feel the tension in her.

Lena returned her look with a wide-eyed innocence of her own. "Oh, Bryce invited me. That's okay, right?"

J.C. almost laughed at her tone, but in the interest of peace, he just smiled and said, "Of course."

Anna concurred with a nod of her own. "Absolutely."

J.C. handed Anna a bottle of water from the cooler and sat next to Bryce in the only free beach chair. He noted Lena and Max were engaged in some seemingly in-depth conversation, so he pinned Bryce with a what-the-hell stare.

"When was the last time you checked your phone?" Bryce asked.

"It's charging in the car. It was dead."

"Well, when it comes back on, you can apologize for that look you just gave me."

J.C. laughed, the strain seeping out of him. Shaking his head, he held out his fist to Bryce, who bumped it back.

"Sorry, man," he said.

The stress from the night before finally dissipated as the roll of the waves beat at the beach. J.C. got lost in the sound of the tide and the last remnants of the day sinking into the horizon. He closed his eyes for a moment, letting it all wash over him.

Of everything they had done in Gabe's name, the alumni game was the most special for J.C., and he thought, if he asked everyone else, they'd probably agree. Soccer had brought them all together. And when Gabe had died, soccer had helped them all cope with his death. It seemed appropriate that the alumni game, started at their high school only after they'd graduated, had become the focal point of the memorial weekend, and it always started at the beach.

J.C.'s eyes popped open when he felt someone sit down in front of him, moving the sand underneath his feet.

"Hey," Lena said.

She'd planted herself directly in his line of vision. Sitting cross-legged, like a little kid, she smiled up at him.

"Hi," he responded with a tentative greeting, hesitation heavy in his answer.

"I'm sorry to crash the party."

J.C. shook off the haze and leaned forward, his forearms resting on his thighs. "You're not crashing. It's not some formal thing. We just come here and hang out before the game."

Lena smiled before she said, "Yeah, that's how Bryce explained it. But still, I feel bad, surprising you like this."

He shrugged involuntarily. "No big deal."

She studied him, like she was suddenly trying to figure him out. Her scrutiny unnerved him a bit. He wasn't any different than the man who'd escorted her to the hotel last night, but the look she leveled at him felt like she was seeing him for the first time. He wanted to move his hand, reach around, and place it in his spot on her nape before pulling her forward and plundering her mouth. But he found himself resisting the temptation to touch her.

"Thanks for last night," she said softly, her eyes boring into his. "I really appreciate it, and I'm pretty sure I didn't tell you that at the time."

"Hindsight," he answered matter-of-factly.

But she shook her head. "No. Awareness."

"Of?"

She didn't answer immediately, and for a long time, he thought she wasn't going to. She kept her face turned upward toward him, but she wasn't really seeing him. In his impatience, he moved back, sitting upright in the chair and then leaning into it. It opened their conversation, pulling him away from the intimacy of the moment before and the chatter from his friends surrounding him. He heard snippets of conversations but reluctantly kept his focus split between the woman in front of him and his friends around him. If she was going to say something about what she was feeling, he didn't want to miss it, but he also wasn't going to wait for her to figure it out.

"Of you."

J.C. moved forward again, leaning down toward her.

"What did you say?" He wasn't trying to be an ass. He thought he'd heard her, but he wasn't sure, and he needed to be sure.

"I said, of you. Awareness of you and who you are."

He briefly looked around, just to gauge the conversations around them. He wanted to pull her away from the group, but this was their thing, and he wasn't going to give it up for her.

So, he leaned forward even more, close enough to kiss her if he wanted to, and he asked, "What does that even mean?" His voice sounded incredulous, even to him.

But she laughed. "I'm not sure really. I mean, it sounded good when I rehearsed it earlier." She shook her head and then dropped her eyes down to the sand in front of her, leaving J.C. with just the view of the top of her head. "I suck at this," she murmured.

"You really do," he concurred.

Her head popped back up, and when their eyes met, they both laughed.

"I know," she said, laughter still present on her lips.

He was still close to her, and the urge to kiss her overpowered him.

Instead, he shook his head, like he could dislodge the temptation. He moved back a bit, giving himself some breathing room.

"Look," he said, "I can tell that you feel like you need to get something off your chest, but this isn't the best time or place. Maybe you should take some more time to think about what you want to say, and we can try it again after the game."

He delivered his set down as gently as possible, and he could tell he'd done a decent job because she nodded her head, her eyes broadcasting her regret.

"I think that's a brilliant idea," she said softly.

"Wait. Were you planning on coming to the game?" he asked, suddenly remembering whom he was talking to and that she'd never been before.

"I was planning on it, if that's okay."

His first instinct was to think she couldn't handle it, that it was too much after yesterday.

She should wade in, he thought, *rather than jump off the high dive.*

But he could also admit to himself that caution wasn't her specialty, and if she wanted to go, then she should go. He made a note to himself to be scarce after the game. He wasn't ready to soothe her sadness again, and as much as he loved having sex with her, he needed a mental barbed wire fence to stay away from her.

"Absolutely. It would be awesome to have you there," he said, reassuring her after his brief pause. "You know your parents come every year."

She shook her head. "I'm sure they've mentioned it, but I probably tuned it out."

"Right. Well, they'll be there, too." He paused. "For better or worse."

She nodded. "Yeah." She looked around at the group and then looked back at J.C. "What's this all about?"

He smiled. "Yeah, so after Gabe's death, we spent a lot of time here, mostly drinking and talking. We'd come before games just to feel close to him, I guess. We'd tell stories and end up laughing a lot. Being here made it feel okay for a while. Now, we do it whenever we are all home but always before the game."

"Nobody has said much about him," she observed.

He smiled. "Well, they probably have, but they've been quiet about it."

"Because of me?"

"Because of you."

"Bryce said it was okay for me to come," she said, defending herself.

J.C. couldn't hold it back this time. His hand moved forward and wrapped around the nape of her neck. "It's absolutely fine. I promise you." His thumb swept along her jawline, and then he moved back, out of her space again. "When we want to talk about him, we do. It's not a big deal for us."

"I found a penny last night," she said.

J.C. smiled. "Oh, yeah?" He felt the hush around them, the perk of the ears of his friends, the zeroing in on her voice.

"Yeah. I was lying in the middle of the soccer field in the middle of the night"—she looked up at him and then over at Bryce—"as you both know." The three of them shared a smile. "Anyway, the grass was wet, and I could see the outline of my steps onto the field. I had this stupid idea to do a dew angel, and I thought, *What the hell?* Gabe would have loved this. We used to do sand angels when he was little."

She paused, and J.C. could tell she was getting lost in the memory.

"So, there I was, moving my hands and feet like a complete idiot, and my hand hit something cold and hard in the grass. I picked it up, and it was a damn penny."

"What was the year?" Fletcher asked.

Lena looked at him like he was crazy.

They all started laughing.

J.C. got it under control first. "Do you happen to know the year on the penny?"

She looked sheepishly around at them. Then, she reached into the pocket of her shorts and pulled it out. She flipped it over and said, "The year is 2004."

Kyle pumped his fist while J.C., Bryce, Max, and Fletcher groaned.

"What?" Lena asked, curious at their reactions.

"The alumni game is split up by graduation year—evens versus odds. Evens have won every year," J.C. explained.

Lena smiled. "Looks like the odds are shit out of luck again this year."

"Looks like it," he said, returning her smile. He glanced at his watch. "We've gotta go."

They stood and started packing up, gathering the cooler and the beach chairs. J.C. watched as Lena pitched in, helping load everything up. She seemed good to him, and he wanted to think she'd be able to handle the game tonight, but he couldn't help but worry. She was going from famine to feast, and he wasn't sure if she could stomach it.

When everything was loaded up and she was about to get into Bryce's car, he pulled her aside. "Are you sure you are up for this?" he asked.

She took a deep breath and looked away. Then, she met his eyes. "I know I've put you in a position where you feel like you have to clean up after me whenever Gabe's name is mentioned. And I apologize for that. But I'm good, and even if I'm not, you are going to have to let me go through this. Okay?"

He nodded his head, thankful for the exoneration.

"See you there," he said.

"Yes, you will."

"All right." He walked back toward his truck and headed out to the game.

The field looked totally different to Lena with its lights casting away the shadows from the night before and the small crowd of people dispelling the emptiness. The anticipatory energy of the people around made her thankful for this new memory of the stadium. It wasn't like she wanted one, but her previous two overwhelming associations had everything to do with sadness, and she found herself thirsty for something lighter.

She let Bryce steer her toward the sideline, and when she saw her parents, she understood why. The look on their faces when they saw her reminded her of Visa commercials—dead son, wayward daughter, surprise appearance, priceless.

"Magdalena," her mom said with a touch of awe, "what are you doing here?"

She felt Bryce's hand on her back, a touch of reassurance. Smiling briefly at him, she walked forward and gave her mom and then her dad a hug.

"Well, you got me hooked up with these jokers, and I figured I'd come see what this was all about," she delivered with a touch of her natural snark, a signal to her parents that all was right in the world. She saw the relief on their faces and silently congratulated herself for her insight.

She waited, thinking her mother would burst into tears, but it was her dad who caught her off guard when he reached for her hand and squeezed.

"It's so good to have you here," he said.

She looked up at him but then averted her eyes because his looked misty, and she didn't think she could hold it together if her father cried.

Bryce interrupted the moment by stepping in and hugging her parents. Once again, she found herself indebted to him.

"I've gotta go—ya know, help out with everything. You good?" he asked as he turned back to look at her.

She nodded, and he pulled her to him for a quick hug. He stepped away and jogged over to the check-in table.

When Lena turned back to her parents, they were watching her with a curious look on their faces, and she almost smiled.

Wrong boy, she thought.

She'd run into Bryce early in the morning at the coffee shop she'd found while walking through the Commercial District. She'd expected awkwardness, but he'd walked right up to her, bought her coffee, and directed her to a quiet table, so they could talk. It was exactly what she'd needed after last night.

She'd woken up, wanting to talk to J.C., but suddenly, it hadn't seemed fair to run to him with all her thoughts and feelings. She'd fallen into a dangerous pattern with him, and it'd become crystal clear to her what she'd been doing. The only way she could handle sex with J.C. had been if she wrapped it up in an act of forgetting about her grief. And perhaps she needed to think about it. But now wasn't the time.

"Where's Nick?" her father asked, looking around as if Nicky was hiding behind her legs.

"With Mike and Lindsay. I thought my first trip here should be handled alone before I brought him."

Her dad looked her over, studying her, as if he were seeing her for the first time. "That was probably a good idea."

Not long ago, a comment like that, somehow inferring that he hadn't expected her to be a good mother, would have shut down their interaction. But for some reason, she took it as a compliment, the way she was sure it had been meant.

"Yeah, I thought so."

"You look good," her mother commented. "And I'm glad you're here. I am still a little shell-shocked. This is the second time you've surprised me recently," she delivered with a smile.

Lena found herself smiling back.

She'd intended to respond, to maybe credit the boys with getting her there, but she didn't get a chance because a steady stream of people came to pay their respects. It seemed like everyone knew her parents, and they knew everyone. They were hugged often. She listened to them ask each individual how they were doing and how this or that plan had played out and what their future held. Her parents knew them all, almost intimately, and Lena felt decidedly out of place—until her boys came. And that she referred to them in her head as *her boys* almost prompted her to laugh out loud.

Fletcher picked up her mother and spun her around, provoking a girlish giggle from her. Then, he was hugging her dad and laughing with him. Max and Kyle followed with hugs and questions, and Lena could tell they'd kept close tabs on her parents. They knew things she didn't know, which wasn't very difficult, but again, she was thankful to this community of supporters who had gathered around her parents, helping them deal with Gabe's death.

J.C. was one of the last to make his way over, and she wondered if he'd reluctantly waited because of her or if this was what he normally did.

"Marie," he said as he gave her a tight hug. Turning to her father, J.C. embraced him also, more than the typical man hug. "Tom, good to see you."

"Is your mom coming?" Marie asked.

"She's here, helping Anna with some last-minute things."

J.C. looked over at Lena, like he was trying to tell her something, but she didn't quite get what, if anything, he was attempting to communicate.

Just as quickly, he looked back at her parents. "So, we're going to do a moment of silence at the beginning, like we do every year. Then, after the game, we'll gather midfield. And I'm hoping you'll start us off," he said, looking at her father.

Lena's dad nodded his head, a slight smile on his face. "Of course."

"Okay. I just wanted to make sure you knew the game plan."

Her mom reached out and squeezed J.C.'s hand—her gesture of thanks, Lena assumed.

"All right! Let's get this started," J.C. said, turning away from them.

"Such amazing young men," her mom murmured.

Lena wanted to concur, but she couldn't seem to form any words, afraid that if she opened her mouth, it would release something else inside of her. Lena tried really hard not to take J.C.'s obvious dismissal to heart, but she couldn't deny the hurt lancing through her. She turned to face the field, waiting for the game to begin. She followed his progress for a minute, down the sideline and then to where his team was waiting. They did some sort of huddle, and then a couple of them walked to the middle of the field to talk to the ref.

She lost track of him in the sea of blue. Bryce looked up out of the masses and smiled at her. She smiled back, but it didn't have any heart behind it. The impending moment of silence beat down on her as she waited to hear them announce it.

Lena heard the announcer start to say something, but she blocked it out. She was lost, and it wasn't because of Gabe. It was because she didn't have any connection with J.C. The realization made her breathless.

What has this boy done to me? she thought.

Then, she felt someone grab her hand, and she looked over to find J.C. standing next to her, her hand interlocked with his. She stood there, staring over at him, and he stood there, looking out onto the field. He was beside her but in his own head.

When the moment of silence ended, he looked to her and smiled. It was the brilliant smile that she had a hard time handling. Then, he was pulling her to him and moving toward her. Their mouths met softly at first before he deepened the kiss, taking from her whatever she was willing to give. But this time, she took back, drawing him in, keeping him there, stealing his soul.

He finally broke the kiss and dropped his forehead to hers. "I needed a good-luck charm," he said. Then, he kissed her quickly and ran out to the field amid cheering from both teams.

Lena avoided looking directly at her parents as they made their way to the bleachers to watch the game. She followed dutifully, her head down, the smile on her face somewhat hidden by her hair. When they found their seats, Lena felt like she'd landed in hostile territory with Anna sitting right beside her.

"Lena, I don't know if you remember J.C.'s mother, Pam?" Anna said as Lena found her seat.

Containing her smile, Lena looked past Anna toward Pam, who was sitting on the other side of Anna. "It's nice to meet you," Lena managed to say as they shook hands.

Lena could immediately see the resemblance between J.C. and his mother. It made her think of her own son and how no one had ever found any similarities between she and Nicky.

She'd expected some censure from the older woman, but instead, she received a knowing smile.

"It's very nice to finally meet you. I have heard a lot about you," Pam said.

Her comment made Lena feel more uncomfortable than Anna's perpetual glare, but she merely smiled. "J.C. looks a lot like you," she said, surprising herself.

Pam smiled at her. "So I've been told. I've just never been able to see it."

Lena laughed. "My son, Nicky, looks just like his father, Mike, and he says the same thing."

They shared a look that only mothers could, an intimate smile of the sacred sisterhood of being a mother.

"Do you have a picture of him? I'd love to see him."

Lena got up from her seat and went up one row, taking a seat behind Pam. She retrieved her phone from her little purse and pulled up a picture of Nicky.

Pam took the phone from her and stared at the picture. "He's wearing Gabe's number," she said matter-of-factly. "I would have thought he would look like Gabe," she continued, almost to herself.

"I know, right?" Lena said.

They shared another knowing glance.

Pam continued to scroll through the pictures as Lena narrated for her.

When she reached the end of the picture show, Pam placed her hand on Lena's knee. "You know how much it means to J.C. and Bryce to be coaching him, right?"

"Yeah," Lena responded, "I do."

Pam patted her knee and then turned her attention to the game. Lena put her phone away in her purse and returned to her seat on the other side of Anna.

Lena could feel the waves of resentment flowing from Anna.

"Do you want to see the pictures?" she asked as an afterthought to include Anna.

Anna looked over at her, and Lena saw a flash of something she wasn't sure she wanted to name. Whatever it was, it was gone before Anna nodded.

As Lena showed her the pictures, the game got underway. Then, she forgot about Anna's obvious dislike, Pam's open friendliness, her longtime resistance to being a part of this celebration of her brother's life. Her sole focus was on J.C. running up and down the field. It had been a little over a week since she'd basically kicked him out of her house, and she had a hard time thinking about why she'd done it.

Without any discussion with him, she knew she couldn't ever do it again. The next time, if there were a next time, she would need to make sure she was ready for him. It couldn't be like it had been. She knew that. She was hurting both of them. When they were together, she didn't think much about what would come next. She enjoyed him, who he was.

But he made her think of things she'd willfully blocked for the last eight years, and it'd become too much. The past wasn't truly the problem though. The problem was that she'd found herself thinking of a future with J.C. She'd conjure images of Nicky, J.C., and herself. She'd think about how he would mix with Lindsay and Mike. She'd wonder if she and Nicky could fit into his life and how he would handle having to consider an eight-year-old kid when he was basically a kid himself. Those were the thoughts that would drive her from his arms and keep him out of her bed.

Before she realized it, the game was ending. She glanced briefly at the scoreboard and laughed. Evens had won again. Every person in the stands made their way out to the field. Lena followed, just a passenger along for the ride. A circle formed, and she managed to stay outside of it, behind the crowd. She was just an observer, not a participant.

The boys were the last to walk over, and as they passed a few feet from her, she reached into her pocket.

"Kyle," she said, a voice caught under the din of the crowd.

He looked toward her as she flicked the penny in his direction.

"To the victor belongs the spoils," she said softly, their eyes meeting.

It was Hollywood-like in execution as he caught it one-handed, seemingly without looking at it. He held it up, caught between his fingers, displaying his prize. And they all laughed as they kept walking toward the circle. Then, they were absorbed into it, enfolded in its warmth.

But Lena remained where she was, not willing to take those final five steps to be a part of it.

When her father started speaking, she took one step, some force moving her forward. She couldn't tell anyone what he said, but his pleasure in being there, surrounded by Gabe's friends, was obvious. She relished it.

Thinking back to her conversation with her mother, she wondered if her father had saved all of his talk about Gabe for this night. Maybe for him, it was his way of grieving and accepting, looking around at the young men who would have surrounded his son and now carried him forward into everything they did, carrying his light. It made her proud of her family in a way she hadn't thought possible. Somehow, Gabe's life and his death had provided inspiration, and there was no greater gift of solace that a parent could get for a loss.

She took another step.

J.C. took over for her dad, and once again, she found herself drawn to him. She wanted him and not just in her grief. She wanted him in her life, in her child's life. And again, she felt that stab of pride. Gabe had somehow brought her full circle to J.C.

How wise was my brother to have picked J.C. and Bryce and Fletcher and Max and even Kyle and Anna for his friends?

"We thought it might be good to turn it over to you guys this year," J.C. said before stepping back out of the center.

It was then, when he moved back into the circle, that she realized she was in it, too.

It was a love letter.

It took J.C. some time as he stood there, surrounded by all these people he knew—some well, some not—before he could figure out how to describe it.

When they'd thrown it out there, like an open mic night in some random nightclub, they hadn't been sure what they were going to get—maybe no one would step up, or maybe they would, but their lines would fall flat. Perhaps that was why they hadn't ever even thought to do it. But for some reason, this year, they had.

When the words had left J.C.'s mouth, silence had greeted him.

Was it because no one was prepared? Should we have had some plants in the audience, people who knew it was coming so that they could know what they wanted to say?

Maybe the spontaneity would have disappeared, but it would have been better than the crickets from the audience.

He knew the first guy—kinda.

"I got here at two o'clock today. I had to fly standby from Seattle. I'd saved up for the last couple of months so that I could be here today. I wouldn't have missed this even if I'd had no money. I would have found a way to be here. This game is something I look forward to all year."

A lot of, "Yeah," and, "No doubt," comments followed his statement.

The guy was a year behind them in Kyle's and Anna's class. He was a good dude but not one of those people who had been involved with them on a regular basis. Somehow knowing so little about him made his testimony seem even more important, special - so score.

The next person started speaking, "I graduated from college this morning at ten o'clock. Then, I got in my car and drove home. I didn't want to miss this, even for graduation."

J.C. kept his gaze cast down, knowing eye contact right now would be difficult.

People kept speaking—different people with different experiences, some who knew Gabe and some who didn't. But the theme remained the same. This was something they'd looked forward to, they'd planned around, something they hadn't wanted to miss.

When the group dreamed it up, this alumni game, they hadn't been sure what would come of it. The tradition had never really been at their school. Getting people to come back to play a soccer game was a shaky concept at best. But here they were, all with their own reasons for being here.

It hit J.C. differently, hearing from people who hadn't necessarily been involved with what Play for Gabe did but who had found their own way to remember Gabe.

Every new person who spoke seemed to strip something from J.C., leaving him raw. It was the combination he knew. Lena standing across the circle from him, here and participating but not really with him, pulled something away from him, too.

The people around the circle continued.

"Took time off of work, so I could make it back here."

"Had to drive from Nebraska straight through to try to get here on time."

He heard snippets, small little chunks he knew he could absorb. He wondered, against his will, what Lena thought about the importance of being here.

He could barely process it. *When had this begun to matter so much to his hometown?*

In the time they had been doing Play for Gabe activities, J.C. hadn't been overly emotional. It was as if he'd experienced all the emotional upheaval in between the time he was sixteen and seventeen—two years of loss and learning from those losses. Since then, he'd managed to objectively handle things, rarely allowing any messy feelings to get in the way to cloud his thinking. But since

September, he'd been back in the space where passion, feelings, and sentiment crowded out his objectivity, like the walls had closed in and forced him to give way to another possibility.

The last person spoke, and Bryce closed it out, thanking everyone for being here. The circle broke up, and everyone moved into their positions, doing their things, breaking everything down.

But J.C. stood in the same spot, enjoying the afterglow of all the sentimentality. He felt oddly empowered, like he could do anything. In a strange juxtaposition from earlier in the day, he knew exactly whom he wanted right at this moment. And for the first time, he knew he'd be okay with any little piece of Lena.

J.C. sat on the players' bench, the cold of the aluminum a small shock to his overheated muscles. Bryce joined him, warily watching him from the side.

"It's cool, man," J.C. said as he leaned down to start untying his cleats.

He knew Bryce would need no introduction to the subject. The conversation was overdue.

"I didn't mean to surprise you like that. I figured you'd check your phone."

"It's all good." J.C. peeled off his socks and stretched out his feet, dreading tomorrow's sore muscles and remaining headache. "Shit, I'm out of shape," he said on a laugh.

"No doubt," Bryce concurred, mimicking his movements, removing gear piece by piece. "Do you want to know why Lena was here today?"

J.C. hesitated. There was no question of his desire to have been a fly on the wall this morning. But now, he wasn't really sure if he cared. Something had shifted in him during the night, and he was willing to let it all go for now and just be with Lena in any capacity she was able to handle. If he were selling himself and his feelings short, he was okay with it.

He shrugged involuntarily. "Nah."

He could tell Bryce was taken aback by his answer. And J.C. waited for it. Until Bryce released his interaction with Lena to J.C., he'd feel like he'd betrayed J.C. with the omission.

Three...two...one...

"I ran into her at the coffee shop this morning," he started as J.C. smiled. "She was nervous about seeing me at first, I could tell, but then we got some coffee and talked."

Bryce paused, and J.C.'s interest was piqued. He could tell himself that it didn't matter, but he couldn't bank his curiosity.

"Anyway, I think whatever that was last night had changed something for her. She didn't seem as..." He stopped, searching for a word, J.C. supposed. "I don't know. *Sad* is the wrong word. *Closed off* is wrong, too. I can't really describe it. It was like she'd morphed or something."

"B, it's all good. You don't need to explain why you brought her. I trust you enough. You wouldn't have had her here without a good reason." J.C. didn't want to hear anymore about Lena from Bryce. If something had changed, he deserved to hear it from her. He threw his stuff into the bag and stood up. "Let's go get some food."

Bryce didn't respond. He just merely looked up at J.C. with an unreadable expression. Finally, he stood, too. "I'll buy," he said in a conciliatory manner.

"You'll buy?" he asked.

"Yeah," Bryce responded.

He didn't elaborate, and J.C. didn't push. He wasn't going to argue with Bryce about buying, but he could tell his friend was feeling guilty.

They walked off the field, each lost in their own thoughts. As they neared the gates, Bryce slowed down and put his hand on J.C.'s arm, stopping him from leaving.

"There's one thing I need to tell you," he said when J.C. looked at him.

Rather than prompt, J.C. waited, willing him to get on with it. Bryce looked down for a moment, trying J.C.'s patience.

"What?" J.C. finally said.

Bryce looked at him with a half-smile. "So, who would you like to ride with—Anna or Lena? Because they are both in the parking lot, waiting for us."

He picked Anna—not because he didn't want to talk to Lena yet, but because Anna had ridden with him, and he didn't want to be an ass and ditch her.

As they walked toward their trucks, Anna and Lena had naturally gone to where they were supposed to, so any awkwardness was avoided.

He stopped at his mom's house to take a quick shower and then headed toward Izzo's, a pizza place where they held their post-game celebration. It was a quick, quiet ride, and he almost escaped, unscathed.

But as they pulled into the parking lot, Anna stopped him. "So, are you guys together now?" she asked.

He turned back to her. He felt bad for the way things had gone down between them, but he knew there wasn't any way to fix it at this point. "I'm not really sure. But if it were up to me, the answer would be yes."

Her eyes got a little wide and a little watery, but she held it in, and he was thankful.

"Look, I know this is difficult and uncomfortable. I hate everything happened. And I really hope we can figure out a way to get past it." He struggled a bit because he wondered if he could get over it if Lena had said the same thing to him. "I'm not sure how to get past it," he amended, "but you and I are so much more than one night. We've been friends for a long time, and I'd hate to lose your friendship."

The look she gave him burned with something other than acceptance of his offer. But then he watched her pull it all together, and he cheered her strength and her many masks. If he hadn't been in such a hurry to get out of the car, he might have paid more attention to the first look.

She shifted forward and pulled him into a hug. He hugged her back. As he pulled away, she kissed him on his mouth. She held him there for a moment before she released him. He could have protested, but it didn't seem worth it.

"Come on," he said, "let's get a beer."

Izzo's was a small restaurant with a couple of booths, a couple of high tables, foosball, pinball, and a bar. J.C. spotted Bryce, Fletcher, and Lena immediately. He also noticed a couple of unclaimed beers next to them and headed in their direction.

"Hey," he said when he reached them.

He flashed a smile at Bryce and Fletcher before he grabbed Lena around the waist and kissed her hard. Bryce and Fletcher laughed.

When he stepped away from her, he grabbed his beer and Lena's hand with his free hand, and he laced their fingers together.

They mingled for a while. Lena moved through the crowd with a quiet confidence. When he introduced her, she handled all the comments about her brother and her family with a respect that had been lacking not so long ago. She didn't shy away from talking about Gabe or Nicky. And almost everyone asked about her son.

He noticed her comfort with Fletcher and Bryce, but she seemed to have a special bond with Max. He wasn't sure what it was rooted in, but he added it to his list of questions he had for her.

J.C. only released her hand when he was reaching for a beer or shaking someone else's. After he'd made the rounds, he guided her toward the foosball table.

"Do you play?" he asked, a competitive glint in his eyes.

She smiled at him. "I do."

"Let's see if I can get one W under my belt tonight."

He dropped the ball to start the game. For the first few minutes, neither one of them said anything, focusing on the match. J.C. had a lot to say, but he didn't want to do it here. He just wanted to enjoy hanging out with her.

Lena scored a point, tying up the game. She grabbed the ball and was about to drop it when she looked up at him.

"You've been doing a lot of kissing today," she said with her head cocked to the side.

He smiled big. "You've been letting me."

She seemed to consider his statement. "Among other people," she said, a teasing smile on her face.

J.C.'s eyes got wide. "You saw that?"

"Oh, I think that was staged just for me," she responded matter-of-factly.

Something about her observation didn't sit right with him, but her nonchalance soothed the niggling sense of worry.

J.C. came around the foosball table. She turned toward him, her face lit with some new smile that he hadn't seen before. He reached out and ran the back of his hand past her belly button, nudging the ring, the spot he thought of as his own. His hands clamped down on her hips, and he pulled her toward him. He smiled the whole time as his mouth descended to hers. It was the kiss from the field, but all of his anger was gone. He opened her mouth and slid his tongue inside, mapping her. He felt her hands reach up and dive into his hair.

He heard Fletcher yell, "Get a room!"

J.C. was surprised that he could recognize anything outside of Lena, but it was like everything else was in slow motion, and his senses were heightened. He could feel something inside of her give way under him, and when he ended the kiss, he was still smiling. His forehead rubbed up against hers.

"That was just for you," he whispered.

She gave a sharp tug on his hair as she laughed. "Point taken," she whispered back.

He pulled away from her. "You ready to get out of here?" He was so ready. His skin was jumping with it. He needed her in a way he hadn't thought was possible. All the emotion, the elation from the night, had pooled in his belly, and he needed to share it with her—physically and emotionally. The high from the field remained, and the high from her intensified.

But she merely smiled at him. "Oh, I see your game, Callahan. I tied it up, and you're ready to cash it in?"

He moved his head to the side, the perma-grin still in place. "You really think you can win this? I was taking it easy on you."

She laughed, putting her hands back on the table. She leaned forward to him and raised her brow. He answered her silent request and leaned forward also.

"I'm an even," she whispered. "Seems like it's going to be my night."

He couldn't help it. He laughed loudly, oddly proud of her in her conceited moment. He loved a girl who could talk trash.

"All right, Pryce. Let's see what you've got."

J.C. closed the hotel room door behind him and leaned against it, still holding her hand. It had been like that all night—constant contact. Even across the foosball table, if there was an opportunity, he'd seized it, and she'd welcomed it. She'd met every touch with one of her own, every kiss with a response. After he'd won the rubber match, they'd left the bar, barely saying good-bye to anyone.

Now, he tugged on her hand, bringing her against him, her back to his front. She leaned her head against his shoulder and sighed into his chest. Her whole being was ready for him. He moved her hair forward, around her other shoulder, and kissed down the side of her neck. His fingers dug into her hips before they let loose to explore. She felt the gentle tug on her piercing and smiled, knowing he was claiming it, her. Her hands hit his hamstrings, right below his amazing ass, and squeezed before holding on. His right hand traveled to her left breast, and she knew she wouldn't be able to hold on for long. She needed him, wanted him in a way that seemed final.

His hands gently pulled on her shirt before he moved it up and over her head. He found the button and zipper of her jeans. He undid them and pulled her pants down, ending at her ankles. He moved around her and knelt to pull off her shoes.

"You wore similar shoes the night of our regional game," he said quietly before he tossed the shoe aside.

She laughed lightly, not really able to focus on talking or listening.

He got rid of her other shoe and her jeans in one swoop. He stood, unzipped his jeans, pulled himself free, and put on a condom before she even realized he had moved. He was down in front of her again. He dropped his obligatory kiss on her navel before tugging on the ring with his mouth, making her whimper and want.

"God, I love that ring. So damn sexy," he murmured.

Again, she merely smiled, unable to form thoughts. He ran his finger along her C-section scar, another signature move for him, and she briefly wondered what about her scar turned him on. But he didn't give her any time to think long because she was suddenly airborne, and he was inside her. Her arms wrapped around his shoulders as a moan tore from her mouth.

He paused once he was there, like he wanted to take a moment to enjoy it. "No place I'd rather be," he said.

They stayed pressed against the door, joined in the most intimate of ways. He leaned back so he could look at her. They stared at each other as so many thoughts passed between them— the mind meld. What she saw in his eyes made her catch her breath.

He looked away from her for a brief second before he turned back, kissing her, as he started to thrust into her with a tangible intensity. It surrounded her. He was loving her, and she knew it. It pulled her in, amplifying her desire and need, making her come quickly. His mouth found hers as he followed close behind.

They stayed there, against the door, catching their breaths. When her feet found the floor on unsteady legs, he dropped his hands back to her hips and pulled her against him, holding her.

"My legs are toast," he said on a laugh. He dropped a kiss on her head.

She laughed with him. "I didn't even think about that. You ran a lot tonight."

"Yeah." He released her but clasped her hand and walked with her to the bed.

He yanked the comforter down, and then he gently pushed her onto it. He stripped out of his clothes, got into bed with her, and settled her onto his chest, not allowing her room to get away—not that she would this time, but she couldn't blame him for preempting her. Rather than fight him, she melted against him, tucking her head under his chin. He locked their hands together again, before letting them rest on his stomach.

"Tonight, the game—it was amazing," Lena said.

He stiffened under her, and she realized he hadn't expected her to want to talk about it.

She smiled against him. "What you did after the game, hearing all those people talk, I can't even give it words."

His unengaged hand stroked up her back. "We've never done that before—let anyone else speak. It was pretty overwhelming. It's always been so important to us. I guess I never stopped to think about whether or not it was important to other people. You know what I mean?"

Lena didn't release his hand, but she sat up, so she could see him. "J.C., it was magical. I had goose bumps the whole time." She paused, shaking her head, looking for the words. "Do you know the feeling when you have the chills, but you're not cold? It's like you're in your body, but you're not? I was almost afraid to move because I didn't want it to go away. I wanted to stay in that moment."

His free hand reached up to cup her face. "Yeah, I get that."

She leaned into his hand, unable to tear her eyes away from his. There was so much she wanted to say to him, so many things to explain. As she stared into his eyes, she knew, even if she chose to hold it in and back, to keep everything from the last few days to herself, he would be okay with it. It made her feel like she could fly. His acceptance, his patience, his love—she could see all of it in the depths of his gaze, and while it scared her, it brought her some peace.

She dropped a kiss on his mouth, quick but meaningful. "I have some explaining to do," she said.

He pulled her back down onto his chest, his hand resuming its lazy perusal. "Maybe," he said.

She laughed. "No *maybe*. I don't feel like I have to, J.C. I want to tell you."

Something shifted with what she'd said.

He moved quickly, flipping her, pulling her underneath him. He kissed her, his mouth closing over hers, a soul-stealing deep kiss. He ended it and kissed along her jaw to her ear. "Later."

Lena woke up to the sun shining in between the curtains they'd forgotten to close the night before. J.C. was wrapped around her, their hands still joined.

"Hey," he said.

"How long have you been awake?"

"A while. Damn sun," he said.

She laughed. Disentangling herself from him, she made her way to the bathroom. She brushed her teeth and picked through the knots in her hair before throwing it up into a ponytail. When she walked back into the room, J.C. hadn't moved, except to close his eyes. Feeling a bit mischievous, she ran toward the bed and launched herself at him. He moved quickly, catching her, laughing with her. He positioned her, so she was straddling him.

"I think I'm on the injured reserved list today," he said, flexing his feet and stretching his arms.

"I bet." She looked him over from her perch on top of him.

He was beautiful and good, and she felt her heart swell with some crazy notions of forever. She shook her head, dispelling the image.

"What?" he asked, as in tune with her as always.

"Nothing," she said.

"I thought today was explanation day," he teased.

"It is," she said. "But I'm not ready to share that last thought."

"Fair enough," he said, sitting up so that they were chest-to-chest. He leaned in and kissed her. "How do you feel about surfing?"

"Now? Today?" she asked.

He shrugged under her arms, and her fingers dug into the muscles of his back, molding to the curves. "Yeah, today, before you leave."

She knew a shadow passed over her face at the thought. He reached up and soothed the line between her eyes that puckered when she thought deeply about something.

"I thought you were on the injured reserve list?" she said, trying to inject fun back into the conversation.

"I am. But the cold water will probably feel good."

"Okay," she said. "J.C.?"

He looked at her sideways before he said, "Yeah?"

"I want to give this a go—for real." She pushed the words out of her mouth before she could think twice about it. She wanted him to be in her life, and she was willing to put herself out there to get him. But it was difficult to admit, and she figured if they left this room without her saying it, she'd probably hold it in and just let him try to guess.

He pulled back a little and gave her an irresistible half-smile. "I know."

She felt startled. "How did you know?"

He paused, seeming to gather his thoughts. "Last night, you were different—more open but resolute." He laughed a little. "*Resolute* is probably not the right word. But you seemed different at Izzo's. You let me touch you all night." He paused again. "And when I was inside you all last night, it wasn't just your body letting me in. It was you."

She felt her face heat at his words. "When I came here on Friday, I wasn't sure what I was looking for. I made it to the field by rote memory. I was just there, and I wasn't really sure how I'd gotten there. But the moment I stepped onto the field, I just let it all come. Gabe's life hit me in this unbelievable kaleidoscope. No matter which way I turned, these memories unfolded in amazing Technicolor. It was unbelievably freeing. I never realized how much I held back." She paused.

"Opening my eyes to you felt as good as letting Gabe wash through me. But I couldn't tell you that on Friday night. I wasn't sure if it was even real. I needed to get through the game on Saturday night to see if I could handle it. For the first time since he died, I enjoyed hearing about him—the stories, the memories. God, those kids and their desire to be at that game last night were overwhelming in its sweetness."

She stopped again, and J.C. held tight. He didn't say anything, didn't comment. She could read it all in his eyes.

Lena wasn't enlightening him at all. He'd somehow gotten there without her explanation. But hidden there in the folds of his understanding was his complete delight in her trust in him. She could feel it pulsing between them.

"So, I want to be able to be in this with you. But I don't have any idea how to do it. I don't know how to let you into Nicky's life or to share you with Mike and Lindsay and the twins. I...I don't want to mess this up, but I know I am going to mess this up. I just don't know how to manage all of this, to open up my life for another person."

She dropped her head to his shoulder, the confession exhausting her. His hands soothed her, moving up and down her back. She could tell he was trying to figure out what to say and maybe how to say it. She knew he wasn't going to disappoint her, but she began to get impatient.

He tugged on her ponytail, bringing her face up.

"Do you remember when we were at Mike and Lindsay's, and I asked you for a beginning?"

She nodded, but she knew she looked worried because one of his hands came up and soothed the space between her eyes.

"It's all we need right now—just a start. I don't know how to do this either, so we can stumble through it together. We just need a beginning. Okay?"

"Okay."

"So, a little surfing and lunch with my mom, and then I guess you need to get on the road?"

She cocked her head to the side. "Did you just say, *lunch with your mom?*"

He laughed. "I did. I know you two talked at the game last night. You already showed her pictures of Nick. What's a little lunch?"

She groaned. "Fine. Lunch with your mom."

"And your parents," he threw in as he flipped her onto her back.

"Absolutely not," she said a little too loud.

"And Bryce." He kissed her.

"No."

"And Fletcher." Another kiss.

"No," she continued, moving her head to the side.

He grabbed her chin, gently holding her head. "And Max. I know he's your favorite, so I'll make sure you get to sit by him."

She narrowed her eyes at him. "I feel like this is a setup."

He kissed her again. "It's a tradition," he said simply.

"I hate you," she said without any heat.

"I think I can change your mind." He kissed her long and deep, stealing her breath and igniting her want.

242

"Fine," she said when she came up for air. "You win." Then, she kissed him.

"I think we're even," he murmured. "Surfing can wait."

Surfing had been fun and relaxing. On the heels of an emotional weekend, it was exactly what Lena had needed before she braved the trip home and offered up her explanations to Mike and Lindsay. For once, she was thankful for her split-second decision.

Although lunch with her parents, the Apostles, and J.C.'s mom had horrified her, it wasn't as bad as she'd imagined. They'd picked a local oyster bar with a huge deck situated on a canal, which eventually fed into the ocean.

As they finished up their meal, Lena got up to waylay the waitress, so she could pay. It wasn't until she'd taken care of the bill that she noticed her mother waiting for her near the hostess stand.

When their eyes met, her mother held out her hand to Lena and led her outside. It was warm enough to forgo any jackets but cool enough to discourage most people from eating outside. They ambled toward a railing and leaned out, overlooking the water. They stood side by side, watching. Lena felt herself getting antsy but tried to allow her mother the time she needed to say whatever it was she needed to say.

When Lena couldn't take it any longer, she leaned into her mother's shoulder, prompting her. "What's up?"

Her mother sighed but remained quiet.

"Mom," she said, impatience heavy in her tone.

"I'm glad you came this weekend," her mother began.

"Me, too."

"You've really surprised me recently. I've never been sure of what you were going to do, even when you were a little girl." Her mother paused and looked over at her, smiling. "You've always kept me on my toes."

Lena didn't know if she was supposed to take the statement as a compliment or a complaint. Rather than jump in with a pithy response, she waited for her mother to continue.

"As you got older, most of the surprises weren't ones I was very happy about."

"That's an understatement," Lena supplied with a nervous giggle.

Her mother's answering laugh soothed some of Lena's tension. "Well, I think that's the way of teenagers, right?" They shared another look. "You'll see as Nicky gets older."

"Right. I'm really looking forward to that!"

Her mother looked back out onto the water. "Remember when you came to the house not too long ago, and you needed to say something, but you weren't exactly sure how to say it?"

Lena felt her stomach drop. "Yeah, I remember."

"There's really no way for me to say what I need to say without you taking it the wrong way."

"Wow, that's quite an introduction," Lena commented, shaking her head, like she could ward it off somehow.

Her mother took an audible deep breath. "This thing with you and J.C., is it serious?"

Lena dropped her head and stared pointedly at the seemingly still water below. Three days ago, her answer would have been so different than what she wanted to answer right now. She wanted to tell her mother that she could be in deep with him. She wanted to share her vision of J.C. and Nicky and herself together. But she could barely wrap her head around what she could imagine with J.C., and she was fairly certain her mother wouldn't really be on board with it.

So, she laughed. It was this easy, somewhat girlish giggle, reminiscent of the teenager her mother could call to mind so easily. She was flippant Lena in that moment, a version of herself that her mother seemed so much more comfortable with.

"No, not really," she lied. It felt wrong in her mouth, like she'd just sucked down a lemon when she'd been expecting something sweet.

A relieved sigh slipped from her mother's mouth. The tension she released in that puff of air found its way into Lena's lungs. She inhaled it and immediately felt a pull in her muscles, a clenching around her heart.

"Good." She reached out and placed her hand on Lena's arm, rubbing gently. "I thought I was going to have to go into this long-winded explanation."

"Oh?"

"Aside from the obvious—"

"Obvious?"

"His age."

"Right. His age."

"And Nicky."

"Of course. But that wouldn't really be a problem. Nicky loves J.C.," Lena said merely for the sake of argument.

Her mother grinned. "I'm sure he does. But you know what I mean. Having a child limits what you can do. And having another man in his life would be complicated."

"Yes, it would. But, eventually, Nicky will have to deal with that—unless I'm not supposed to ever have a significant other in my life?" she asked.

"No, that's not what I mean. But it should be someone who's ready to be a father."

Lena wanted to argue. She wanted to say a lot of things to dispute what her mother was saying, but it didn't make any sense to do it now when she'd just told her mother that it wasn't serious. And right now, she had no idea what was going to happen, so there was no reason to take this any further.

"Plus, with things between J.C. and Anna, I just don't want to see you get hurt."

"Things?" Lena said, her tone belying her feigned calm.

"They're so obviously perfect for each other." There was a certain clarity in her mother's voice, an inherent belief in her tone, that pushed up against Lena's feelings for J.C. "It's why I'm thankful you aren't serious about him."

"Yeah," Lena responded, afraid to say anything more.

"We should get back inside." Her mother turned away from the railing and waited for Lena to follow.

When Lena turned toward her, she linked arms with her and moved them into the restaurant and back to the table. Everyone stood as they came in, and they made their way to the exit. Lena stood with J.C. as they watched their parents depart, but she knew he could feel the distance she'd placed between them. When they were out of sight, he turned to her, removing the space.

"You good?" he asked, studying her face.

She leaned her head forward, resting it on his chest. His arms came around her, and he pulled her in closer. She stepped into his embrace, but her arms remained dangling at her sides. He released her back, found her hands, and moved them up to rest around his back.

"That's more like it," he remarked.

She was tempted to put it out there for him, to tell him about her mother's doubts. But her reluctance to taint their weekend won out, and she kept her mouth closed.

"I've got to get back," Lena remarked into his chest.

"I know." Grabbing her hand from his back, he clasped it in his and walked her to her Jeep. When they reached the door, he maneuvered her, so her back was against it, and he leaned in, perfectly aligning them. "When can I see you?"

Twenty minutes before, she would have had a ready answer. Now, she felt the persistent need for space again. "Let's talk this week and figure it out. I have some groveling to do with Lindsay and Mike when I get back, and I probably owe them a kid-free weekend."

"True." He dropped his forehead down to hers. "I'm glad you were here this weekend."

"Me, too," she said, meaning it. Whatever happened from here, she was thankful for the past few days.

"Let me know when you get home." He captured her mouth with his, a painfully sweet kiss that left her wanting more.

He stepped away from her. She got into her car and drove away, her last glance at him filled with longing for something she wasn't sure she could have.

When Lena had left Mike and Lindsay's on Friday night, she knew she'd have to answer to them when she returned. She'd left, knowing she would need to provide them with an explanation since she dropped off Nicky without much of one. She had to pay the piper. The thought of the coming confrontation kept her mind from replaying the scene with her mother. While she really just wanted to relive the highlights of her time with J.C., she mostly anticipated her upcoming conversation.

She arrived in time for dinner. She knocked briefly before opening the front door.

"Convenient timing," Lindsay said to her.

"Sorry," Lena said before scurrying down the hall to find her child and the twins.

She needed the fortification of their hugs and giggles. After chasing them down and then wrangling them into the bathroom to wash up for dinner, she joined Mike and Lindsay for their weekly family meal. It was a boisterous affair as the kids talked over each other to tell her about their weekend while Lindsay and Mike allowed her to skate through without any searching questions or glances.

But the moment the kids asked to be excused, it started.

"Now, it's your turn," Mike said the moment Nicky, Jessie, and Milly skipped away from the table.

"Huh?" Lena said, feigning ignorance.

Neither of them said anything, preferring to stare her into submission rather than coaxing her to talk.

She procrastinated by clearing the table and loading the dishwasher. And they let her. She was merely treading water, trying to come up with the right approach, which she'd been unable to decide on during her three-hour drive. When she'd run out of diversions, she made her way back to the table and sat, eyes cast down, like a wayward teenager about to receive an overdue punishment.

"I apologize for the short notice and the disappearing act over the weekend. I owe you a completely kid-free weekend whenever you choose." She looked up then, proud of herself for getting through the awkward first step.

Lindsay continued to stare at her.

"Okay," Mike responded. "We'll definitely take you up on that. But is that really all you have to say?" He lapsed into the fatherly tone that never failed to grate on her nerves.

"I'm sorry I didn't return your calls and that I let you worry about me. I just…" She paused and looked back down at the table, feeling guilty. But the guilt didn't have anything to do with her actions on Friday. It was for not feeling bad about what she'd done.

"I needed to go there this weekend. I didn't get it at the time. It seemed like a totally impulsive action. It wasn't until Friday night when J.C. and Bryce found me that I understood why you had been worried. It just didn't even occur to me what the date was at the time." She took a deep breath. "But you're not my parents, and I shouldn't have to explain to you every action I take." The last sentence she hadn't planned, and she really didn't even know it had been living inside of her, waiting to come out.

She saw Lindsay's eyes widen, and she felt bad for throwing it out there with nowhere for it to land but in Lindsay's heart.

Mike opened his mouth to retort, but Lindsay placed a hand on his arm, effectively silencing him.

"You're right, Lena. You don't really need to explain, except for the fact that Nicky was involved. If you want to take off, by all means, have at it—unless it means you drop Nicky here while looking a little frantic. Then, you left without saying a word to us about where you were going. You didn't respond to any of us. We were scared something had happened to you. So, you do owe us for that."

Lindsay never raised her voice, but she didn't need to. Lena got the point loud and clear.

"I know you have a lot going on right now. For the first time, I think you are actually dealing with Gabe's death, and I'm proud of you. But is that really what sent you flying out of here last week, or did all of that have to do with J.C.?"

Lena and Lindsay studied each other across the table while Lena thought about what she'd said.

"I'm not sure what sent me out of here last week. The easy answer is J.C. And maybe that's the right answer. I don't know." Lena shook her head. "When I left, it was definitely J.C., but as the night wore on, everything seemed to point to it being about Gabe. But you know, I'm not really one for introspection, so a lot of this is guesswork."

She saw Lindsay and Mike exchange a smile. She responded with one of her own.

"I'm sincere in my apology. I hate that you were so worried about me that you had to reach out to someone else to make sure I was okay. That's not how we treat each other, and I am really sorry."

"Accepted," Mike and Lindsay said at the same time.

"Do you want to talk about it?" Lindsay asked.

Lena didn't even need to think about the question. "Yes," she said before she launched into a detailed account of the events of the weekend.

When she told them about the field and the penny, Lindsay cried with her. When she described the game and everything surrounding it, they were right there with her, experiencing the wonder of it all. But when she got to the parts about J.C., the telling became halted with bits and pieces coming out in a random way.

"Is he really who you want?" Mike asked. There wasn't any judgment in the question. It was just an honest curiosity she could understand.

And she hesitated in her answer—not specifically because of her conversation with her mother, but because when she was away from J.C., the obstacles seemed to outweigh her feelings.

"Yeah," she finally answered, "but it seems so very complicated."

"More complicated than this?" Lindsay asked, waving her hand between the three of them.

"It's all the same issues we've beaten to death," Lena said with a smile for Lindsay. "Except now, it's different because I'm in deeper."

"So, what are you going to do?" Lindsay asked.

"I have no idea," she responded.

"Well, I hate to break it to you, but before you go any further with this, you need to figure it out because it's not just you and J.C. in this," Mike said.

"Yeah," she said, looking away from them. "But I told him I was all in, and I meant it."

"With everything that happened this weekend, maybe you shouldn't have said that," Lindsay offered.

"Yeah, maybe not," Lena concurred. "Maybe not."

Lena dumped the Christmas presents Nicky had designated for her house on the counter before dropping her purse and keys on the barstool. She heard the ding of her phone but figured it was Lindsay, so she started back outside to bring in the rest of the presents.

After two more trips, she closed and locked the door before she made her way back to the kitchen. She contemplated putting everything away but decided on a glass of wine instead. When she finished pouring, her phone buzzed again, reminding her of the waiting text message. Hearing it was one thing, but finding it was another. Finally locating it in one of the boxes stuffed with clothes for Nicky, she triumphantly pulled it out.

"How the hell did it end up in there?" she said aloud into the empty house.

She read two identical texts that had her laughing.

J.C.: Are you home?

Lindsay: Are you home?

She typed a quick reply to Lindsay but decided to call J.C. instead of responding. When he didn't answer, she responded to his text.

Looking back to the pile of stuff on her counter and taking in the emptiness of the house, she decided to tackle it. She took another sip of wine and walked to the stack of presents awaiting her. She picked up the first one when she heard a knock on her door. Confused, she moved toward the front of the house, and as she turned down the hall, she could see J.C. standing there. She hurried forward, not at all holding back, and quickly unlocked the door.

"Merry Christmas," J.C. said, a big smile on his face.

"Merry Christmas," she responded, practically jumping into his arms.

She kissed him and then stepped inside the house. He followed her into the kitchen before he grabbed her again.

"It's good to see you," he said.

Her fingers found their way into his hair. She toyed with it, loving the feel of it in her hands. Smiling, she said, "What are you doing here?"

"Beer first. Explanation second?"

She laughed but complied, stepping away and grabbing him a beer. She picked up her wine glass on the way back to him, and he followed her into her small family room. Then, he pulled her down next to him on the couch. She leaned in and kissed him quick before she sat back and waited expectantly.

"How was the day?" he started.

"Good. Busy and crazy but fun."

"What time did they wake up?"

"Five forty-five, but we managed to hold them off until six. Then, it was chaos for about thirty minutes."

"Was it a free-for-all?" he asked.

She shook her head. "No. We make them go one at a time. But even so, they bug each other to hurry up on their next one, so it's like a well-orchestrated race to the finish. They have no idea what they've actually gotten until about three hours later," she explained. "Mike and Lindsay both have big families, so there are always tons of presents." She paused. "Probably completely different than your morning."

"Ah, yeah. I think I got home at five forty-five. And there were no presents until noon when my mom and I each had a Bloody Mary in hand."

Lena's eyes got wide. "You open presents with alcohol?" At his nod, she continued, "I've got to get Lindsay to bend on that rule."

J.C. laughed. "I'm kinda surprised Lindsay even has that rule."

"Me, too, actually. Something about being responsible adults," she said on a laugh. She leaned back on the couch, putting a little distance between them. "Rolling home so early in the morning?" She was teasing him, but part of her wasn't. The part of her leftover from the weekend had really wanted to be with him this morning, and she wondered if it were the same for him.

J.C. leaned back, too. He put his beer between his legs and scrubbed his hands over his face. "Yeah, it's been a hard couple of days."

Feeling her eyes narrow, she quickly turned away and focused on the wine in her hands. He didn't seem in any hurry to elaborate, and while she wanted him to tell her about it, she found herself struggling to get ahold of the funky feeling of jealousy careening through her.

"So, how did you end up here tonight?" she asked.

"Impatience," he muttered under his breath.

But it was loud enough for Lena to hear it. She watched him as he removed his beer from between his legs and placed it on the table before taking the wine out of her hands. She wanted to protest at losing her glass, but he pulled her on top of him, so she was straddling his lap. Then, his mouth and his hands swallowed any objection. She had no desire to say anything as all thoughts drifted from her mind when her body took over. He didn't let it last long though, and she tamped down on her disappointment when he returned her to her former position and retrieved her wine glass for her.

"Sorry," he said with a smirk. "But I was impatient to kiss you."

She laughed at the deflection of his earlier comment and took a hearty sip of wine.

"How was Christmas with your mom?" she said, deciding on an innocuous subject.

He smiled at her, and she knew he understood that she'd picked a deliberate topic.

"It was fine. Quiet compared to yours." He reached for his beer. "Did you get grilled about your impromptu weekend trip?"

She laughed. "The grilling took place on Sunday night when I got home. You didn't think Lindsay would let me go for four days, did you?"

He shook his head. "Nah. I would have loved to be a fly on the wall," he said.

Lena laughed, suddenly uneasy. "I don't know about that."

"So, was there a verdict?"

Lena looked at him, wondering where this was going. "On us?"

"Yeah," he said, still not giving anything away.

Lena could feel her brows draw together in puzzlement, and she knew he'd noticed as his finger moved to soothe the line on her forehead.

"I think the verdict was to take it slow."

"Hmm," he said.

He got up from the couch, taking his empty beer with him. Lena presumed it was to get a new beer, but she watched him as he walked into the kitchen. He returned with a beer but sat it on the table beside him. Taking her glass from her, he placed it beside his bottle. Then he twined their legs together and rested his empty hands on her knees.

Lena cocked her head to the side, waiting. With him in front of her, she was able to appreciate every expression crossing his face. His dark hair looked unruly, and she realized he'd been dragging his hand through it since he walked in, his tell of nerves. She was so used to confident J.C. that the person in front of her was a bit of a mystery.

"What's going on?" she asked.

He squeezed her knee. "I got accepted to Johns Hopkins."

It took her a moment to realize what he was talking about. Then, she threw herself into his arms, and in the aftermath, she marveled that he'd managed to keep them both upright on the table.

"I'm so excited for you." She kissed him soundly and then sat back on the couch. She couldn't contain her smile. "Jesus, J.C., Johns Hopkins," she said with some awe. "Go hard, or go home, huh? Couldn't settle for a state school?"

With her comment, she could see his mask of unknown emotion fall away. She didn't know if it had been apprehension or nerves or fear of the uncertain, but he suddenly graced her with the smile she'd come to think of as hers.

"I guess," he answered.

"You guess?" she said, laughing and rolling her eyes. "It's impressive as hell. You should be really proud of yourself."

She was giddy in her praise of him, and she could almost tell the moment her excitement overruled whatever it was he'd held at bay when he walked into her house. It lifted, and his relief was palpable.

She narrowed her eyes at him. "Why weren't you excited when you walked in here earlier? You seemed more stressed than happy."

He groaned a little, and when he ran his fingers through his hair again, she knew the excitement from seconds before had drained away. She stilled his hands with her own, so they were connected—hands, legs, eyes.

"Talk to me," she said softly in a tone she knew she'd heard from him often over the last couple of months.

He tilted his head back, his eyes seeking some unknown guidance from the ceiling, and she gave him some time. Then, she squeezed his hands, a reminder that she was there.

He dropped his eyes to her and gave her a small smile. "A year ago, when I started taking all the steps to do this, things were different."

She tensed slightly at his words, hoping his reluctance had nothing to do with her. Even after everything they'd shared over the weekend, she didn't want him looking at things with her in mind, especially considering her conversation with Mike and Lindsay.

"We were an organization. We lacked direction, and aside from doing things specifically related to Gabe, we weren't really impacting anyone else. But in the last couple of months, things have changed. As soon as we come up with a name..." He smiled at her then.

"Still?" she asked. "You still haven't come up with one?"

He shook his head.

"So, the paperwork I slaved over is still sitting somewhere, unsubmitted?" She gave him her best disappointed mom look. "Damn. Call it Playing for Hearts or Hope for Hearts. Pick something!" she scolded on a laugh.

He paused and tilted his head to the side. "I actually like both of those. It's better than what we've come up with." He let go of her hands and pulled his wallet from his back pocket. Withdrawing a tattered, worn cocktail napkin, he looked up. "Do you have a pen handy?"

She laughed as she moved away from him to get a pen. After returning from the kitchen, she looked over his shoulder as he scribbled both suggestions on the cocktail napkin.

"How long have you been carrying that around with you?"

He looked up at her and smirked. "Since the day we came to your office."

Lena laughed. She dropped her hand onto the top of his head, ran her fingers through his hair, and pulled gently on the ends. His head lifted, and she dropped a kiss on his mouth, like she'd been doing it forever.

"You're crazy," she teased.

He smiled as he folded his little napkin and placed it back in his wallet. He wrapped his arms around her legs, leaned in, and nipped at her belly ring. Then, he lifted her, turned them both, and landed on the couch with her straddling his lap.

He picked up his thread of conversation, as if they hadn't diverged. "We're on the edge of something big and far-reaching. If I walk away now, I think I'll regret it."

She sat there, stunned by his summation, knowing he was talking about their foundation, but she wondered, too, if it applied to them. She looked down at him, but his expression told her all she needed to know, and she relaxed completely.

"Is there any way you can do both?"

He sighed. "I doubt it, mostly because of the demands of both. I mean, I might be able to be here for events, but even that would get dicey. But the other part of it is that I'm kind of an all-or-nothing guy. I don't think I can only be half in because I'd never be okay with my effort, no matter what the expectations. I'd still have to live with me." He smiled slightly.

"I get that," she said.

She wished she had some good wisdom to spew at him or some fail-proof way for him to get to his decision. But she'd never been good at thinking things through, so she always just barreled ahead and then tried not to look back for lingering regrets.

"Do you have to make a decision right at this minute?" she asked.

"No, of course not."

"Then, for now, just enjoy the moment, enjoy the sense of accomplishment." It was simple advice and basically her motto.

You should live in the moment because you never really knew what life would throw at you next.

"Yeah," he said heavily.

"You'll know what's right."

She felt him relax underneath her. He leaned his head back on the couch.

"It's good to see you," he said, his hands starting to roam up and down her back.

She leaned forward, softly kissing him, trying to soothe his worry. The gentle gave way to deep quickly. She pulled away before she could get swept up in it.

"J.C.," she said. Then, she waited for him to open his eyes and focus. "You got accepted to Johns Hopkins!"

He smiled big. "Yeah."

"That's badass!"

His hands flexed on her hips as he nodded, his eyes all lit up. She couldn't resist his smile or her responding one, and she moved forward to take his mouth with hers, all her excitement for him rolling into the kiss. He pulled her closer to him, delving into the depths of her mouth. She reveled in it for a bit before she pulled away. She kissed him again before she stood and grabbed his hand.

She walked toward her room without even thinking about it. The only indication of its significance was a raised eyebrow from J.C. as she looked back at him when they walked through the door.

She didn't know how long it would last, but she didn't think about her mother's concerns or Lindsay's advice. She just followed what her heart was telling her to do.

Lena dropped her messenger bag and purse on the counter and hurried to her room. She'd run late from leaving work, so she was short on time. She attempted to contain her excitement about seeing J.C., but it had been three long, lonely nights since he'd cleared out of her house, and there was an unfamiliar giddiness about her.

Slipping off her heels, she quickly unzipped her dress and discarded it in the laundry basket meant for the dry cleaner. She pulled on a pair of skinny jeans and a black button-down shirt. She slid on her new over-the-knees black boots she'd scored on sale and hurriedly brushed her hair.

She heard the doorbell and tried not to race down the hall to see J.C. Hardly containing the shit-eating grin on her face, she walked very calmly to the door.

She could see the blue of his dress shirt through the window and almost moaned at the thought of him actually being dressed up. J.C. in nice clothes twisted her in a different way.

"Guess what?" he said when she opened the door.

She stopped herself from jumping into his arms and stepped back to let him in. "What?" she asked.

He paused in the doorway, taking his time looking at her. The smile remained on his face, but the look in his eyes changed. He stepped forward, right into her, and kissed her, hard.

He broke the kiss and rested his forehead on hers.

"Hi," she said before she moved her head to the side and dropped a light kiss on his mouth. "Good to see you."

"You, too. Seemed like longer than three days," he said.

She laughed. "It did."

They stayed like they were—foreheads together, J.C.'s hands locked on her hips, Lena's hands resting on his forearms. His hands flexed, and when he took a deep breath, she felt it reverberating through her, too, like his air was hers.

He shifted her back against the wall and shut the door with his foot. Then, his mouth was on hers again—opening hers, exploring, relearning—like the three days were really years of depravation. She settled into the kiss, her hands getting tangled up into his hair.

J.C. broke the kiss too soon, and Lena found herself holding back a groan of frustration. After lightly kissing her on the forehead, he grabbed her hand, and pulled her toward the kitchen.

"You still okay with meeting everyone out?" he asked.

Lena couldn't see his face, so she wasn't sure if he were as disappointed as she was with her early-in-the-week agreement to go out tonight. She just wanted to walk directly to her room and finish what they'd started in the hallway.

She managed to work up some enthusiasm when she answered with, "Yes, of course."

He released her hand. She made her way toward her purse and turned to head right back out.

J.C. stood, leaning against the archway, his legs and arms crossed. His hair was slightly disheveled from her hands running through it, and his dress shirt was untucked on one side. He was so hot and tempting, but the expression on his face made her pause.

"What?" she asked.

He shook his head. "I don't really want to go out," he said on a sigh, "but I told the guys we'd meet them."

She smiled, feeling mollified by his admission. Walking back to him, she stood just a little outside his reach, knowing if she stepped closer, they'd end up like they had been in the hallway. "What were you so excited about when you got here?"

He smiled wickedly. "You need to ask?"

"Ha-ha," she responded drolly. "You know what I mean. You had something to tell me."

The wickedness disintegrated, and he smiled. "Yeah," he said, "we decided on a name, one of your suggestions."

"That's awesome," she said. And she meant it, but she'd just had to work really hard to get the words out of her mouth because he was looking her over from head to toe.

She couldn't read him, but the something about the way he was looking at her reminded her of how Nicky looked when he couldn't figure out a math problem. It was as if J.C. were totally confounded.

He seemed to snap out of whatever it was that was bothering him. "Yeah. We submitted our paperwork—finally."

"So, are you going to tell me?" she asked, curious as to what they'd finally chosen.

"Oh, yeah," he said, smiling sheepishly. "Playing for Hearts. Max is working on a logo. It's official."

He pulled away from his lean on the wall and walked toward her. When he extended his hand, she placed hers in it. He gently tugged her into his arms.

"So, thanks are in order, I think," he said before kissing her on the top of her head.

"And you can throw away your little cocktail napkin?" she teased. "Or will you frame it?"

"You're funny," he said.

They both started walking toward the front door, seemingly resigned to their fate.

As they walked out the door, Lena imagined what it would be like to be able to share their days on a regular basis. She pictured every night being like this, a give-and-take of the day along with J.C. and Nicky bonding and laughing. Another amazing man as a role model for her son stood before her, yet she still couldn't let go of the worries expressed by her mother and her best friends. Perhaps if she had already dealt with Gabe's loss when she met J.C., then maybe they'd have seen that she could be ready for him.

But she understood right in that moment that her heart needed to heal before she could give it away. Suddenly, she wasn't sure if she had enough time to get there. And if she was feeling like this now, what would it feel like when she let him go?

This was why impulsiveness worked for her. *Why try to foresee the future when there might not be one to glimpse?*

There wasn't much to the location the guys had chosen. It was long and narrow with a couple of high tables and seats along the bar. The flat screen televisions everywhere added to the constant din of conversations. It was a typical college bar, and J.C. immediately knew it was something Lena had outgrown long ago.

He saw her tight smile and followed her gaze to Anna. He wasn't really up for the tension already surrounding them, but he'd committed and figured he could make it for a little while. Bryce, Fletcher, and Max were already there, too, and Lena's obvious happiness at seeing them made him relax.

"So, do we have to give you props for the name?" Fletcher asked before Lena could even sit down at the table.

"Yes," she answered with a straight face. "I've trademarked it."

For a split second, Fletcher looked like he thought she was serious. Then, he laughed. "Did you at least get him to throw that stupid napkin away?"

"Absolutely not. You guys should frame it."

"It would disintegrate," Bryce said.

"You're probably right," she concurred.

"You got the next round?" Bryce said before J.C. could sit down.

J.C. turned from the table and headed to the bar without even providing a response.

"I'll help," Anna said.

He wanted to groan but managed to smother it. He leaned on the bar, waiting for the bartender.

"I didn't realize Lena would be here," she said as she came to stand next to him.

J.C. turned to face her. "Why wouldn't she?"

"I guess I didn't know it was a thing."

"A thing?" J.C. questioned.

"Yeah. I mean, I just kind of assumed she needed someone to lean on during the weekend."

"Didn't we talk about this already?" he asked tiredly.

"Yep," she answered sarcastically. "I guess we already covered this."

"What can I get for you?" the bartender said, interrupting the staring contest they'd been engaged in.

J.C. placed the order and then turned back to Anna. "I thought this wasn't going to be a problem, Anna. We've been over this.

We both agreed we'd made a mistake, long before Lena was even in the picture." Frustration was evident in his voice and manner, and he tried desperately to rein it in.

"Yeah, a mistake. I got it. Although, maybe if you say it a few more times, it will really sink in."

J.C.'s eyes strayed to the table. Lena's back was to him, but Bryce and Max were subtly watching them. Anna's level of near hysteria began to worry him, and as he contemplated options, he saw Lena look over her shoulder at them. When she quickly turned away, he knew he had to do something.

As if on cue, the bartender brought their drinks, and J.C. paid.

He handed three drinks to Anna and grabbed the other three. "Let's get them their drinks, and we can go talk."

After they distributed the drinks, J.C. leaned in toward Lena's ear. "I'm going to go talk to Anna. I'll be back as soon as I can." He dropped a kiss on the spot right below her ear. Then, he looked up to see Bryce and Max attempting to ignore the kiss.

With too many problems to solve, J.C. turned away and grabbed Anna's hand, leading her outside to the street.

The whole minute it took for them to walk through the long, narrow bar, the refrain in his head beat, *I'm so fucked! I'm so fucked!*

He could feel Lena frustration, and he had no idea what to do about it. Instead, he and Anna sat at a high-top table lining the street and he waited for her to speak.

When Anna remained silent, J.C. started, "I'm at a loss. I don't know what to do to fix this. But I want to be with Lena. And we are friends who have worked together for a long enough time to know that we can't go on like this. So, what can we do?"

"I don't think there's anything we can do. I know you think what happened was a mistake, but at the time, I didn't."

J.C. ran his hands through his hair, tempted to pull on it in his frustration. "So, it's always going to be like this now?"

"Until you leave."

"Wow!" He leaned back in his chair, at a loss for any words to say.

They sat there long enough for J.C. to feel the pressure of being away from Lena while sitting with a girl he'd once had sex with. The description of Anna in his head felt wrong, but her little display tonight reminded him that this was what she wanted. She'd rather be a girl he'd slept with than a longtime friend he'd built something with. The realization saddened him.

"Well, I guess the next couple of months are going to suck for you because I'm not going anywhere, and we have a lot to do. You can figure out how you want to handle this while we're working. But tonight is the last time I'll walk away from Lena to tend to you." It was an asshole thing to say, but he knew Lena wouldn't appreciate this Anna stunt, and he was tired of having the same conversation.

He stood up, thinking about just walking away, but then he turned back and motioned for her to precede him back into the bar. When they got back to the table, it took J.C. one look at Bryce's face to know he was screwed.

Lena stood up without any provocation and looked over to him. "You ready?" she asked.

"I am," he said. "See you all later."

He followed Lena from the bar, the exact path he'd walked with Anna not fifteen minutes before. He reached out and placed his hand on the small of her back, grateful when she didn't flinch. They made it to his truck before she turned toward him.

"I think it's probably time for you to tell me what went on between you two. I'm too old to play these juvenile games."

"We slept together. It was a mistake. The moment it happened, I knew it was a mistake. And I thought she knew that, too." He wanted, needed, to say more, but he didn't.

Lena was silent for the ride back to her house, and J.C. wondered what was going to happen when they got there. He turned off the truck and quickly got out so that she couldn't run, solo, to her door. When she walked in and left the door open for him to follow, he took it as a sign. He just wasn't sure if it was good or bad.

She had two beers in her hand when he got to the kitchen, and he took one with a grateful smile in her direction as he leaned against the counter.

"Thanks," he said.

"You're going to need it," she responded.

He couldn't help but chuckle. "Sorry," he said, unsuccessful in his attempt to hold it in.

Their eyes met, and she gifted him with a reluctant grin.

Breaking their staring contest, Lena took a sip of her beer and sat heavily on the barstool. "What are we doing, J.C.?"

"Dating?" he stammered, unsure of the response she was looking for.

This time, she laughed. She tipped her beer up again, took a sip, and then placed it back on the counter. "Is it supposed to be this complicated?"

"I have no fucking idea," he said.

"You know what's not a complication?" she asked.

"What's that?"

"Sex."

He looked at her sideways and offered her a boyish grin. "I can definitely get on board with that."

"I figured," she said on a laugh.

Just like that, they tucked the complications away and reveled in the simple.

J.C. looked at his watch as he left their planning meeting. He was running late to meet Lena, so he pulled his phone out and typed a quick text. As he jumped in his truck, he couldn't help but smile.

The whole thing with Anna had made he and Lena pull back some, but they had been seeing each other when they could. It was every other weekend and Wednesday nights that passed too quickly while the time in between seemed to move in the other direction. The days apart were a mixture of anticipation and impatience while the time together was a study in passion and harmony.

Some days, he thought the reason things were so unbelievably good between them was because they had finite amounts of time to be together. He would get to miss her in between and then enjoy the time he was with her. He'd convinced himself that those limits heightened his desire to be with her, the whole absence making the heart grow fonder. It was really the only explanation he'd allowed himself to believe when he considered how much time he spent thinking about her during the times they were apart.

When they came back together, Lena would become an amazing audience as he shared his life with her. She was scary smart with numbers but would balk at any written word. She hated to read but would spend hours digging up additional research for him. They'd talk logistics for the screenings, and she would give him valuable input. She'd run financials for the organization based on what they'd done in the past and some of their ideas for the future.

They'd met for lunch one day, and she'd handed him a manila envelope when they were leaving.

"Just something for you to look at later when you're lying in bed, thinking of me." She had given him a mischievous smile before quickly kissing him and heading back to the office.

He'd been tempted to open it, but he'd put it away, deciding to wait.

He'd told her all of his medical-school planning would wait until his day was done when he was about to go to bed, so it wouldn't get mixed up with what he was doing. So, later that night, he'd pulled out the contents of the envelope. It had taken him a second to realize what it was. She'd taken the cost of attendance for Johns Hopkins and run the numbers for him, down to the amount of debt he'd have, depending on the amount of his loans. She'd even researched the length of time it would take for pediatric cardiologists to get established in different areas, so she could calculate his income. He'd smiled the whole time he studied it, marveling at all of the work she'd put into it.

On the last page, she'd written, *Just so you have all the information.*

He'd called her, laughing. "Don't you have anything better to do?" he'd asked as soon as she'd picked up the phone. His question had been greeted with laughter.

"Don't worry. Tax season is coming, and I'm about to get really busy."

He'd tried not to think too much about having to share her with clients for the next couple of months. He knew he'd be really busy at the same time with the heart screenings Play for Gabe had been planning.

With their time already limited, the thought of having to compete with work also was something he wasn't looking forward to. Even caught up in all of his life-altering decisions, Lena was at the forefront of his thoughts. And trying not to think about her or include their relationship in his pro-con list seemed to be an impossibility.

When J.C. arrived at Lena's house, he was surprised to see Mike's SUV parked in the driveway. He knew Mike and Lindsay were aware of whatever he and Lena were doing. But with soccer on a break and Nick's custody arrangements, he hadn't seen Mike and Lindsay since Thanksgiving.

J.C. contemplated leaving. Picking up his phone from the center console, he glanced at the last text he'd sent her, telling her he'd be late, and realized it hadn't been read. He'd talked to her two hours ago, so she knew he was coming.

He sat, indecision pulling him in two different directions. If he could have been assured of her reaction, he knew he would have walked right into her house, but he hesitated, wondering if she would be pissed. Not knowing what to do bothered him.

Looking at their texts from earlier in the day, he decided to take a chance.

Getting out of his truck, he eyed his backpack, the one he'd stuffed full of his clothes for the next day. Thinking it would be better to leave it for now, he made his way to the front door. He'd gotten into the habit of walking in, but this time, he knocked. When Mike answered the door a minute later, J.C. felt that inherent nervousness of meeting a girl's big brother for the first time mix with a possessiveness, which surprised him.

Although Mike looked frustrated, J.C. relaxed when Mike managed a welcoming smile.

"Hey, Coach Cal," Mike said.

J.C. paused at the moniker. "Hey," he managed, not sure if calling him Mike would be okay.

"Come on in."

Mike held the door for him, but J.C. held back and let Mike precede him into the kitchen.

Lena was sitting at the bar, her hands clasped in front of her. She was still in her work clothes, and the heels of her shoes were tucked onto the crossbar of the chair. When she turned her head to the side, the small smile she gave J.C. was forced. And that was how J.C. knew he'd walked into the middle of a heated scene.

Completely uncomfortable, he stood on the threshold of the kitchen and waited for someone to give him an indication of what he was supposed to do. Over the last few weeks, Lena's house had become as familiar to him as his own. He knew where everything went, and he moved freely. But now, with Mike in the space, he felt like he didn't belong there.

"I can come back," he offered.

He kind of hated both of them in that moment for making him feel like he was in the wrong for showing up when he was supposed to. But his words in the thick silence seemed to snap them both out of their funk.

Lena unhooked her feet and stood.

Mike said, "No, I was just heading out."

Lena walked toward Mike, and they fell into a natural step with his hand moving to the small of her back as they made their way out of the kitchen. J.C. continued to stand where he was. He heard them talking, but it was low, and he couldn't make out any of the conversation.

J.C. walked to the fridge and grabbed a beer. He heaved himself up onto the counter and was assailed by the image of Lena sitting in this position with him between her legs. Trying to drown out the image, he lifted the beer and took a long sip. He didn't want to think about how long it was taking her to return, but he found himself watching the microwave's telltale green digits clicking away the minutes.

Frustrated with her, he took another long sip, almost finishing the bottle. Bringing it down, he twirled it in front of him, eyeing the last sip. He lifted it but stopped when he heard her footsteps coming toward him, the clicking of her stilettos a drum in his ear. When she rounded the corner and met his gaze, he lifted his beer in the air in a silent toast before he took a large sip, his eyes never leaving hers. Neither of them spoke. The middle-school staring contest seemed ridiculous between them, but he couldn't bring himself to break the stare.

He wasn't sure how long they had been frozen in their corners, and although his little green numbers across the room beckoned to him, he kept his sights on Lena, hoping she'd give something away.

After what seemed like an eternity, Lena crossed the kitchen to the fridge. She grabbed and opened a beer. Turning toward him, she pulled the empty bottle from his death grip and replaced it with the new drink. Then, she came and stood between his legs. Her hands dropped to his thighs, but her eyes came back to his. In her heels, she was almost level with him, which allowed her to lean forward and plant her lips on his.

At first, he resisted.

He knew her. She would blot out the awkwardness of the last fifteen minutes with sex.

But with her lips hovering near his, her scent surrounding him, her hands rubbing his thighs, his resistance began to chip away.

"It's so good to see you, J.C.," she murmured so close to his mouth that he could feel the vibrations of the words skitter across his lips. She kissed him again. "I needed to see you," she said.

He wasn't sure if it was the proximity or the words, but he tilted his head, and his lips met hers in a kiss with punishing intensity. Their tongues tangled, their mouths intimately locked, but neither of them made any effort to get closer.

For the first time, J.C. really didn't want the kiss to lead to anything more. While he knew his kiss was laced with annoyance, hers tasted of apology—not for what had happened, but for what was coming. He ended the kiss, and placing his hands over hers, he forced her back, out of his space. Grabbing his lonely beer, he jumped down from the counter and made his way over to the barstool, leaving the expanse of the counter between them. He thought about all the ways to play the conversation about to happen, but he couldn't figure out if he was ready for the inevitable conclusion.

Lena turned toward him so that she stood directly in his line of sight, the five feet between them an endless ocean. "I didn't mean for that to happen," she said.

He got that. He wanted to push her, question her, but nothing came. He merely watched and took slow sips of his beer while she waited for some reaction. At first, she was contrite, but after he let the silence linger, he could see her ire rise. He really just wanted her to explain what was going on, to trust him enough to let him in.

He sighed, dropped his eyes from hers, and played with the label on the beer bottle. "Are you going to tell me what's going on?" he asked. In that moment, he knew if she shared it with him, he'd be cool with the last twenty minutes of being uncomfortable.

She waved her hand, as if she were swatting a fly or pushing away a silly idea. It was a small movement with so many interpretations that he saw out of the corner of his eye.

"Just something with Nicky. It's not really a big deal, but Mike and I needed to talk about it."

He nodded slowly. "Do you want to talk about it?" He knew the answer to the question and almost smiled thinking, *Ask a stupid question, get a stupid answer.*

"No. It's really nothing. Just typical parent shit."

Knowing what he did about her past, he wasn't surprised how effectively she'd been keeping him separate from the rest of her life. He really did understand her hesitation to let him into Nick's life in any way, other than as his soccer coach. Neither one of them were sure about anything, but how good things felt now. What would be the point of pulling Nick's emotions and feelings into the mix?

Like she didn't share J.C. with Nick, she didn't share Nick with J.C.

In the end, none of today should have surprised him. The fact that it did scared him because while he'd thought he had his emotions under control, today made him feel like he was in over his head.

He wanted to go with her explanation. He wanted to get back to the feeling he'd had on the drive over here, those highs of the last couple of weeks.

He felt her move toward him, and he lifted his head. When she got to his side of the bar, she turned his chair and moved into the space between his legs again.

"Why don't I change?" she said as her hands landed on his shoulders. Then, they crept up his neck into the depths of his hair.

He suppressed a groan. With his eyes on her, she smiled gently, trying to soothe his ego, he was sure.

"Then, I'll drive us out to the Key, and we can grab some dinner."

She leaned forward to kiss him. When he pulled back, she halted. She cocked her head and studied him. The crease between her brows appeared, and although he was tempted to smooth it out, he kept his hands where they were.

"I'm talked out right now, J.C. I just want to have some dinner and enjoy being with you."

As if on cue, his stomach growled, and she laughed, the tension between them draining away. He blamed the beer, but he acknowledged that what she was giving him wasn't enough.

The soccer preseason party had come at an opportune time, Lena supposed. It fell during one of those weeklong stretches when glimpses of J.C. were all she'd been afforded. Small moments of quick lunches, effortless phone conversations, and cute text-messaging were what she survived on from Wednesday to Wednesday every other week. She hated to admit it wasn't enough.

She watched him as he reached into the cooler and grabbed a bottle of water. He looked up as the cooler top banged shut and flashed a hesitant smile in her direction. They both looked around, watching intently to see if anyone around them had noticed their brief connection. It'd been playing like that over and over throughout the party—the connect and then hedge. She knew he didn't care, so his only reason for vigilance sprang from his concern for her. She got it.

This was a day they wouldn't usually see each other because she had Nicky this weekend. For that reason alone, having a small stretch of time to watch J.C. made her grateful for the party. Even if it meant only peeks, no touches, stilted conversations, just being in the same place with him somehow made her happier.

She had been surprised he'd shown up alone, but she had discovered through careful eavesdropping that Bryce would be arriving late. She felt oddly uncomfortable with even carrying on an impersonal conversation with J.C. as she imagined everyone would know what was going on between them if she so much as spoke a word to him. So, she'd been skirting around him, reveling in and loathing his presence.

Sarina's house sat on one of the many canals, which eventually dumped into the Gulf of Mexico. It was a prime piece of property and any kid's dream home. Aside from the main house, a guesthouse stood attached to the pool area, and beyond the screened-in deck stood a full-size tennis court. It was the perfect place for ten eight-year-old boys and their siblings to run around. The grown-ups got to sit on one of the patios and merely observe their children.

She and Lindsay stood on the dock, looking back toward the house, watching the controlled chaos.

"How are you holding up?" Lindsay asked, eyeing Lena over the rim of her plastic wine glass.

"I'm good. Thankful Sarina believes in adult beverages at kid parties. I still don't quite know how adults survive all this noise while sober."

"That is why we always ditch those people who invite us to dry kid parties," Lindsay said matter-of-factly.

Lena held her smile. "Well, that's typically not the main reason. Just usually a good indicator that we'll find a reason later."

Lindsay burst out laughing. "We're going to hell."

"No question," Lena said, giving in to the giggles.

"Is it hard to be here with him but not *with* him?" Lindsay asked.

Lena shrugged, not willing to explain her feelings to Lindsay right at this moment.

"He's been having a hard time keeping his eyes off you," Lindsay remarked.

"Really?" Lena asked, looking over at Lindsay with a surprised expression.

Lindsay looked at her like she was crazy. "Absolutely. What do you think?"

"I hadn't really thought about it."

"Mmhmm," Lindsay murmured.

Lena ignored her and allowed her eyes to find J.C. on the tennis court with the kids, managing their version of soccer tennis. He looked amazing in a pair of shorts, a T-shirt, and a pair of sneakers. Her body couldn't wait until Wednesday.

As she continued to watch the game, Bryce arrived with Fletcher and Max in tow. Her initial delight in seeing them vanished as she imagined the complications of their presence and her acting like she wasn't with J.C. For Lindsay, it didn't seem weird because she had yet to hang out with them together as a couple, whereas the boys hung out with them often enough to know they were together.

Lena took a fortifying sip of wine, trying to play out their reactions in her head.

"I didn't know the Apostles were coming," Lindsay said.

Lena didn't look at her as she replied, "Me neither."

Lindsay laughed lightly. "Well, this should be interesting."

Lena chose not to comment.

"Have you told him yet?" Lindsay asked.

Lena looked at her with widened eyes. "Told him what?"

"About Nicky?"

Lena took a deep breath and shook her head. "No, and I'm not going to. It's none of his business," she answered in a harsher tone than was needed.

Lindsay stepped back from her. She shook her head and then looked Lena in the eyes with a hint of derision. "What are you doing?"

Lena couldn't help but be taken aback by Lindsay's question and the leveled look. "What do you mean?"

"I mean, what the hell are you playing at? It's obvious that you have some deep feelings for this guy, but you act like he doesn't mean anything to you."

"Linds, I'm not having this conversation with you again. Just drop it."

"Sarina knows about Nicky, and so do some of the other parents. You need to tell him before he hears it from someone else."

Lena turned back toward the tennis court where the big boys had joined J.C. in the game. J.C. laughed at something, his eyes alight with humor that she could discern even from a distance. He looked her way at that moment, their eyes meeting briefly, and in that split second, the laughter faded from him, as if he could sense the tension in her. He turned away from her, and she was sorry for the instant change in his demeanor. She wondered briefly what had caused it.

Had he sensed the tension in her, or had he thought about being around her but not with her?

She couldn't begin to guess, their mind-meld failing her.

"Lena," Lindsay said plaintively.

Lena knew the tone. It was curiosity mixed with frustration, something she'd heard in J.C.'s voice recently.

"Linds, what? I'm not made for this. I'm not supposed to love anyone else." She didn't look at her best friend because she wasn't sure if Lindsay would call her on her bullshit or look at her with pity. Neither was appealing. "I don't want what you have. I don't want anyone else to mean so much to me that if he went away, I wouldn't know if I'd survive. And I already know he's going away. So, what's the point?" Lena drained her wine.

"You're so full of shit," Lindsay said scathingly. "And you're a selfish coward."

Lena stepped away from her, withdrawing, as if Lindsay's words were a physical blow. She moved toward the house, the other parents her destination.

But Lindsay grabbed her arm, and Lena turned back to her.

"If that's really how you feel, Lena, then you need to let him go."

Lena shrugged her off and walked back to the house, to a glass of wine, to mingle with some people who didn't know her so well.

J.C. extracted himself from soccer tennis when he noticed Lena scurrying from the dock. He'd been excited about the prospect of seeing her today, but the fantasy of the party hadn't come close to the reality of being in the same place but not being able to be anywhere near her.

He'd hugged Sarina and Lindsay, but Lena's greeting had been stilted and stiff, so he'd foregone the opportunity to wrap his arms around her. It was probably a good thing because he'd imagined it would have been difficult to want to extricate himself.

The last hour had proven even more trying as she'd chosen avoidance rather than hiding in plain sight—not that he'd expected her to act like they were a couple, but she didn't even seem comfortable enough to have a conversation with him.

He watched her skirt the outside of the tennis court and beeline for the guesthouse. It had to be relatively empty as it looked like most everyone could be accounted for. He followed her at a slow pace, stopping to chat along the way. When she stepped inside through the back door, he made an excuse of needing to use the restroom to extract himself from the conversation he'd gotten sucked into. He made sure everyone in the vicinity knew where he was going before walking in the back door.

He did a quick perusal of the small living room, and finding it empty, he headed for the hallway. The light from the bathroom peeked out from under the door.

Tapping lightly on the door, his body jumped with both relief and anticipation when he heard Lena say, "I'll be out in a second."

"It's me, Lena," he said.

He was happily surprised when the door opened immediately, and she stepped back to let him in.

He closed the door behind him, leaned back against it, and pulled her flush against his body. He didn't speak nor did he give her a chance to speak as he planted his mouth on hers and probed against her lips, looking for access. Lena opened instantly, melting against him. As much as he wanted to linger there, he knew it wasn't why he'd followed her.

Reluctantly ending the kiss, he moved her back away from him. "You okay?"

She didn't answer right away. Instead, she leaned back against the sink and brought her hand to her mouth, tracing her lips, almost as if she wanted to capture the essence of their kiss through the tips of her fingers. She steadily looked at him, wanting him to watch what she was doing. He reached out his hand and pulled her fingers from her mouth, needing to distract them both.

"You looked upset when you were talking to Lindsay. Are you okay?" he asked again, impatience mingled with his words.

"I'm fine," she answered distractedly. "You can't be in here with me," she said quickly, like she'd just realized where they were.

He rolled his eyes. "It's fine. You don't actually have to act like you've never met me. No one is going to think anything of it if you have a conversation with me." He hadn't realized until he'd said it that he was pissed at the way she had been acting toward him. The anger in his voice surprised them both.

"I can't figure out another way," she said, her eyes widening, as if she hadn't meant to say it.

He shook his head. "Whatever," he said.

He reached behind him and turned the knob, opening the door, and then he left without another word.

Needing a distraction, he headed outside, back to the tennis court. It was hard to think a whole lot with a bunch of kids vying for his attention.

Max, Bryce, and Fletcher had handled things while he was gone, but they immediately worked it out, so he was back in charge. He shot a grateful look in their direction.

An hour later, when dinner was called, J.C. was calm. He followed the kids into the dinner line and then left them to mingle with the adults. He'd pretty much gotten over the situation when Bryce sat down next to him. J.C. could tell by the look on his face that Bryce wanted to say something he wouldn't like. Bryce had a way of telepathically communicating his intentions to J.C. This moment, he looked hesitant and nervous, which made J.C. weary of the conversation. Instead, he continued to eat and let the burden fall to his friend.

"I'm confused."

J.C. couldn't help it. He rolled his eyes. "Why?" he asked.

Bryce looked back over his shoulder to where J.C. knew Lena stood—not because he had noticed or attempted to keep track of her movements, but because he could always sense when she was near him.

"Are you not together?"

J.C. wanted to laugh at the uncomfortable expression on Bryce's face. "Not around her son," was all he would say.

Bryce paused to take a bite of his cheeseburger. J.C. turned when he heard Lena laughing. She was sitting at a table with Fletcher and Max because, somehow, it was okay for her to be around them. Shaking his head, he looked back at Bryce.

"Is that why you didn't tell me about what happened to Nick?" Bryce asked.

J.C. set his burger down. "What are you talking about?"

Bryce warily eyed him. "She didn't tell you," he stated.

J.C. took a calculated deep breath. "B, you're starting to piss me off."

Bryce looked back over J.C.'s shoulder, presumably at Lena. Then, he picked up both of their plates and walked them over to the trash. "Let's go check out the dock," he said.

J.C. ran his hands through his hair, hating where this was going. He slowly got to his feet and followed Bryce out of the house. Neither of them spoke as they made their way to the dock. They sat on the end with their feet dangling. The night air settled in around them, the darkness a buffer. As always, the water soothed J.C. There were no rolling waves, and if you didn't know where you were, you could almost think the water was solid ground. J.C. sighed contentedly and leaned back on his hands.

"At school a couple of weeks ago, Nick passed out during PE," Bryce said.

J.C. felt the calm dissipate.

"The school called Lena and Mike, and they took him to their pediatrician. Following standard protocol, I guess, they also saw the pediatric cardiologist. He didn't find anything on the EKG, but because of the family history, they sent him for an echo." Bryce stopped speaking, and silence descended between them.

"And?" J.C. managed to get out. "What were the results?"

"Normal," Bryce assured him. "Everything was normal."

J.C. wasn't sure where Bryce's mind went, but he couldn't quite figure out what to focus on. Fear came first. The unbelievable fear that Nick could suffer the same fate as Gabe seemed to be overwhelming. Second came the confusion. *How could Lena have kept something like this from him?* They shared everything—or so he'd thought. But quickly on the heels of that, he remembered they'd shared nothing about Nick. Anger didn't hit until the first two had settled in, leaving little room for much else. But once there, it nestled in between the other two and expanded, pushing them out and away so that there wasn't any other emotion left.

As soon as Lena and Nicky exited the party, her phone buzzed with a text.

J.C.: I need to see you tonight.

She didn't fight the anticipation as it zipped through her. She gave a passing thought to the issue of Nicky being with her. Then, she responded.

Lena: Give me an hour.

The ride home seemed simultaneously interminable and quick. Nicky kept up a constant chatter, a blur of words strung together by an overtired child. He recounted the ten games of tennis soccer, highlighting virtually every point he'd scored. She smiled indulgently from the front of the Jeep, enjoying his tired ramblings. It kept her mind off of J.C.'s impending visit.

When she'd responded so decisively, she hadn't given herself an opportunity to think about having a man at her house when her son was home. She'd never broken her rule. It wasn't Wednesday. But J.C. always seemed to elicit odd responses from her. She couldn't quite pinpoint the reason for her capitulation. Maybe it was because of their abbreviated kiss in the bathroom, which had left her hungry for more of him, or her guilt for forcing him to leave her there without any explanations. Perhaps it was because she'd eaten with Fletcher and Max without even acknowledging J.C.'s presence. Maybe it was Lindsay's scolding of her on the dock and her insistence that Lena cut him loose. A hundred reasons bounced around in her head, but none more honest or poignant than facing the truth that she missed him in an insane, detrimental way.

She glanced at the time on her dashboard and calculated the remaining thirty-four minutes before he'd be standing at her front door.

Pulling into the driveway, she hurried Nicky into the tub and then into bed. His droopy eyes glazed over as she pulled his blanket up under his chin. She let the happiness of his existence hit her.

When he murmured, "I love you, Mama," she glowed.

She leaned forward and proclaimed her love for him as she kissed him on his left cheek, his right cheek, his forehead, his chin, and his nose.

"My good-night kisses," he said as his eyes closed, the pull of exhaustion winning.

"Yeah, baby," she said as she watched sleep claim him.

Lena stood up and turned on the bathroom light, leaving the door cracked. Then, she made her way out of his room. She stood in the kitchen, attempting to figure out a way to eat up the remaining minutes before J.C.'s arrival. She was nervous and excited at the same time.

Crossing to the fridge, she took out a bottle of water and moved toward the living room. As she sat down, she thought of the day. She'd needed to give J.C. a wide berth, and she was certain she'd succeeded. But she'd spent a lot of her time tracking his movements, watching him. She knew why she needed to keep him separate from her life in this house, but she had to admit, if she were going to expose her son to anyone, J.C. would be the one.

Lena jumped up from the chair, suddenly not comfortable with where her mind had taken her. She couldn't share Nicky to J.C. for a number of reasons. He was leaving. There was no way they could have a relationship while he was in medical school ten states away. And he was so young. If she'd been given a choice about parenthood, there was no way she would have chosen to be a mother at twenty-three. *How could she even think to put a burden like that on him, especially with a child who wasn't his and one who didn't need a father?*

She realized she was pacing and shook her head, trying to calm herself. She was horrified she'd ended up in her living room, thinking about Nicky and J.C. and family all in the same sentence.

Her buzzing phone thankfully provided the distraction she welcomed. She picked it up to read the text.

J.C.: Here.

Discombobulated by her wayward thoughts, she strode toward the front door, mindful of J.C.'s consideration to text her rather than beating on the door. She'd forgotten to turn on the porch light, but she could make out the shadow of J.C. in front of the door. Everything in her evened out now that he was here. She felt it all release, and she wondered why his presence always seemed to soothe her.

Opening the door, she stepped right up to him and practically threw her arms around his neck. He braced them both easily as she slammed into his body.

"Hey," she murmured as she rose up to kiss him.

She'd intended on something deep and sensual, her desire for him overwhelming her. But J.C. stepped away from her, leaving her empty.

Her head cocked to the side, and her brow furrowed with confusion. "You okay?" she asked.

She couldn't read his eyes in the dark.

"Yeah," he said unconvincingly as he held out his hand, indicating she should precede him into the house.

She turned and walked forward. The door closed softly behind him, and she resisted the urge to turn and face him as he crossed the threshold. The darkness in the hallway, which only provided a barrier, propelled her forward toward the bright kitchen. She needed to be able to see what he was thinking.

"Do you want a beer?" she said softly, mindful of Nicky sleeping down the opposite hall.

"No, thanks," he responded.

Lena was oddly off-kilter. J.C. seemed distant at best, angry at worst. She could feel something radiating through him, but she couldn't quite put her finger on it. Then, in the back of her mind, she heard Lindsay's warning.

Regardless of what it was, Lena knew she owed J.C. an apology. She stood in the middle of the kitchen, at odds with the space around her, fidgeting nervously. J.C. remained in the archway between the hallway and the kitchen, his shoulder braced on the frame. He watched her from his stance across the way, but he made no move toward her.

She studied him. Not sure how to break the silence, she walked toward him. Standing a few inches away from him, she waited. She wanted to make the move to touch him, but the closed expression on his face stopped her.

"You sure you're okay? Did something happen?"

J.C. continued to look at her, and the scrutiny of his expression increased her sense of unease.

As closely as she was watching him, she didn't even see him move until his hands were on her hips, and she was being pulled toward him and then flush against him. His mouth was on hers. His tongue delved into her mouth, exploring every inch, and she was lost under the onslaught of him. Her hands found their way into his hair, and she glued herself to his body.

It was exactly what she'd needed, what she'd been missing over the last couple of days. It was hard and fast, passionate and overwhelming.

Then, his hands left her hips and moved up to cradle her face. Everything about the kiss changed. He softened the pressure but continued to deeply kiss her. His hands turned gentle, and she felt something totally different, the shift subtle. She seemed to need this, too, and she melted into him, absorbed in the moment, in him.

J.C. pulled back, extracting his tongue from her mouth, hovering over her partially opened lips. His thumbs caressed her jaw on both sides, and she felt oddly cherished. He completely withdrew his mouth from hers, and then he leaned his forehead against hers.

J.C. and Lena stood in the same stance for what seemed like an extended period of time before his hands dropped from her face, and he stepped away from her. He looked at the ceiling, and ran his hand through his hair, shaking his head. He was reluctant to meet her eyes, his fear of the impending conversation making him long to be anywhere, other than in her house.

It has come to this, he thought briefly.

He knew she was studying him and wondered what she truly saw. For all the intimacies of the last couple of weeks, he hoped he'd preserved his ability to hide his emotions from her. Apparently, *she* had it fucking mastered.

He turned from her and walked to the fridge, rethinking his decision on the beer. He pulled one from the shelf and popped the top on the bottle before he turned to meet her confused eyes.

He leaned against the counter and took a deep breath. "What are we doing?" he asked.

He'd expected her to be startled or nervous, but instead, the look on her face looked more like resignation. Perhaps she'd been waiting for this. He didn't know what she was thinking, and it pissed him off.

"What do you mean?" she asked as she moved toward the counter and pulled out a barstool.

She dropped her arms on the counter and clasped her hands in front of her. Her pose was reminiscent of the day he'd found her here with Mike, and like a chain reaction, he realized what had gone down that day.

"Just what I said. What are we doing? I get that we're sleeping together. Is that all we're doing?"

"I don't know. I thought we were having some fun in there, too," she replied flippantly.

The kiss had quelled some of his anger from earlier in the night, but her response grated on the rawness of it, rekindling it.

"Fun and fucking. Perfect."

Lena's eyes widened, and he experienced a moment of glee because, as much as he'd let her in, she had no idea what an asshole he could be when he was pissed.

"Why don't you tell me what's really going on, J.C.?" Something in her gave way to conciliation.

"Why didn't you tell me about Nick?" he asked.

She drew in a deep breath, one he could hear and see. "Because it's really not any of your business."

Her tone had been so matter-of-fact that he felt like he'd been slapped. In a way, he had. Reality could be a bitch.

"Ah," he said. "Thanks for clearing it up for me."

"I thought…" She paused, fidgeting. "I thought I could go there, but I just can't, and I never said I would share him with you."

She truly believed that. He could see it in the way she looked at him.

"No," he agreed, "you didn't. You did, however, promise me a beginning."

She literally scoffed at his statement, and J.C. gripped the bottle in his hand so tightly that he was afraid it would shatter.

"You've never really acted like you're twenty-three until right now."

He laughed at her, but it sounded bitter, even to him.

"So, because I think I have a right to know about what's going on with you and your family, I'm acting immature. That's the frickin' pot calling the kettle black." He scoffed right back at her. "Fine, I don't have a right to know. But, shit, did you not even want to talk to me about it?" He could feel his hurt bleeding through his words, and he hated his weakness, that she was his weakness.

Neither one of them spoke for a moment.

"No," she said softly, like if she'd said it any louder, something would have splintered.

"No?" he asked.

"No, J.C. I didn't want to talk to you about it. I can't go there."

"What does that even mean?"

She took in a shaky breath. He heard it rattle through her, and he braced himself for what he knew he absolutely didn't want to hear. Whatever she was going to say, whatever her reason was, it was going to force him to make a decision he knew he didn't want to make.

"This"—she moved her hand between the both of them, highlighting the energy between them—"is just temporary. It can't last. So, no, I didn't want to share it with you. I didn't want you to know the fear of those couple of days. I didn't want you to be there to watch me go through that. I don't want to be bound to you any more than I am. So, no, J.C., I never even considered telling you."

"It's permanent, isn't it?" he asked.

Again, the look of confusion was on her face. "What?"

"The damage to you when Gabe died."

She flinched like he'd hit her, and he felt vindicated in his delivery. She tried to cover it with a shrug, like the only one of them who could be hurt was him. Her impenetrable heart didn't actually get hurt, her stance seemed to say to him.

"Look, I am sorry for the way I acted today at the party. It was silly. I shouldn't have acted behaved like that. I know you are mad about it, and I don't blame you. I just didn't know how to act with you outside of this world we seem to occupy. You have every right to be upset."

She got up from the chair and walked toward him. He tried not to, but when she reached out for him, he dipped away, like her touch would be too much. And he supposed it would. So, she stopped her progression and stood a few feet away from him.

"All this other stuff doesn't have anything to do with what we have," she whispered before she moved forward.

She wrapped her arms around his neck and kissed him. It was a dirty kiss, one that screamed sex with her open mouth and questing tongue. He moved into it for a moment before he pulled her arms from around his neck, held them pinned with one hand, and gently pushed her away from him.

His eyes met hers. "What we have is nothing I want."

He let go of her wrists, moved around her, and left her house without a second glance.

Maggie—2006

The church is silent even though people are spilling out between the doors and the sides and taking up the passageways. I have a fleeting image of the contents of a jelly doughnut leaking out the sides and bottom, like the delicate pastry can't handle the gooey mess.

I know a lot of these people. It's what happens when you grow up on a small peninsula. There aren't a whole lot of places to hide on this little strip of land. Maybe I should be comforted by all this familiarity, but I just feel cold, not really alive. My blood is flowing. I know it is because since Gabe fell in front of me, everything has been heightened. It's like, since he can't feel anything, I get to feel everything double. *How ironic.* I'm fairly certain I'm just as dead as he is, but all these emotions are hitting me and making me hyperaware of how horrible this is.

I've spent the last two days avoiding my parents and the Apostles. I can't take on their sadness. If I can't handle strangers' grief, imagine what would happen to my heart if I had to deal with the people who loved him.

And I don't ever want to look into the eyes of J.C. again. Oh my God, there's this eerie connection between us, and his grief would destroy me. Even though I know this and I can't stand to be around him, I think he's the only person of the hundreds around me who can actually understand what I'm feeling.

So, even though I have avoided him, when they bring the coffin in, I seek him out. I'm not surprised to find those deep brown eyes looking for me either. He gets it, too. He doesn't really want to have to handle my sorrow, but I am for him what he is for me—some crazy salvation in this desert of grief.

BLISS

He finishes his job, and I find myself scooting over, wiggling infinitesimally to make space for him. No one would think to question J.C. sitting with us.

When he sits, I feel this weight lift from my chest, like I can suddenly breathe again. My hand seeks his of its own volition. I grab his right hand in my left, and I feel his sharp intake of breath. I get it when a penny clatters against the wooden pew between us. I smile and am surprised to find it's a genuine smile. He quickly reaches over with his left hand and picks it up. He's embarrassed. I can feel that, too. So, I lift my right hand, place it in my lap, and open it, so he can see my own penny. He takes another breath, and he squeezes my hand. I cut my eyes to him and see a smile on his face. It slices through me, warming me in the coldest, deepest part of my being.

And it's right at that moment, I know. I know I won't always feel like this. When this child comes, I'll be able to love him or her. I know Gabe is with me because my heart fills with an indescribable love.

But here's the other thing. I know I don't ever want to feel this devastation again. I'm surprised at how easy it is to close down that piece of me that can love. I don't want a bigger circle. I don't want to allow anyone else in. I decide—in the space of a heartbeat, with a fifteen-year-old kid as my witness—that I'm never going to love anyone else. I refuse to do it.

When J.C. squeezes my hand again, I feel like he gets it. But when I walk out of this church, I hope I never see him again.

"Mama! What are you doing in there?"

Lena heard the door bounce off the wall as Nicky flung it open. She'd also heard the panic in his voice.

Rolling over to face the entrance to the room, she rubbed her eyes and tried to focus through the crumbles of dried mascara and eye crusties. Blinking a couple of times, she saw Nicky standing in the open door, his hair going in ten different directions all at once. He'd long-ago forsaken pajamas, and the sight of his sturdy little body encased in Pro Combat underwear dragged a weary smile from her.

"Why are you yelling?" she managed to push out through her raw throat.

He released his hold on the door and bolted toward the bed. Lena lifted the covers, and he climbed in next to her. Snuggling close, he wrapped his arm around her stomach.

"I couldn't find you. Why are you sleeping in here?"

Lena took a quick glance around as the events of the night filtered through the early-morning fog in her brain.

J.C. Fight. Vodka. Guest room.

"I forgot to put sheets on my bed, and I was too tired."

"Oh," he said, explanation accepted.

She made a note to strip her bed before he made his way into her bedroom today.

"I'm hungry, and I want to watch TV," Nicky informed her.

Lena smiled. Kissing the top of his head, she squeezed his body to hers. "Okay. But can you lie here with me for a little while longer?"

Nicky was a snuggler, so she really wasn't asking for much. But her request made him burrow in deeper, hugging her harder.

Ah, just what I need.

"I can still go fishing with Dad today, right?"

Lena almost groaned but managed to hold it in. She'd totally forgotten about fishing. It wasn't a big deal, but with the way things had gone down the night before, she could have used the distraction of Nicky all day. She could go to work, but somehow, the crunch of numbers didn't hold her attention like entertaining her son did. He sort of demanded her focus, whereas the numbers basically added and subtracted themselves. She could practically do it in her sleep.

"Maybe I'll go fishing with you," she offered up.

She couldn't see it but could feel Nicky's eyes roll. "You hate the worms and the fish and the smell," he reminded her on a giggle.

His belly rolling with the rumble of laughter made her smile.

"Besides, there's not enough room."

"Are the girls going?" Lena asked.

She already knew the answer. So far, the twins were as girlie as they came. She wasn't sure if it would change, but if a Disney Princess wasn't involved, they weren't either.

"No. Coach Cal and Coach B are coming," he gushed.

Lena felt her stomach plummet. Talking to Nicky had distracted her from the hollow pit growing down in the bottom of her belly. It had formed the moment J.C. grabbed her arms and pulled them from around his neck. The vodka had filled it in for a while. Then, Nicky had made her forget, and it was even better than the vodka. But it was there again, gaping, waiting to suck her in.

"Oh. Your dad invited them?" she asked, not that it mattered.

Yesterday, it hadn't mattered, and Mike had known it. Although it felt like a contradiction right at this moment, she was totally fine with J.C. spending time with Nicky outside of their relationship. She couldn't conjure up better role models for her son than the Apostles.

"I did. But I asked Dad first," he said proudly.

"Good, buddy. You should always check with us first," she reminded as she ran her fingers through his hair.

The silky texture reminded her of Gabe's hair. She had a fleeting image of soothing her baby brother by running her hands through the hair near his forehead. Its effectiveness never ceased through bad dreams, illnesses, and restlessness. He would crawl into bed with her and place her hands right where he wanted them. And she would comply. She'd forgotten about that, or she'd probably buried it. Shaking off the memory, she continued to run her hands through Nicky's hair.

"That feels good, Mama," he murmured.

She wondered if she could possibly convince him to fall back to sleep. She looked down at his heavy lids, taking in the curled-up, lush dark eyelashes. It didn't seem fair that her son had better lashes than she did. She could feel his body begin to sag.

Then, he startled awake and sat up. "We have to be at Dad's at nine thirty. And it was seven fifteen when I woke you up," he said with pride in his voice.

She only had one digital clock in the house because she wanted him to be able to figure out the time without the aid of the illuminated green numbers on the microwave. She felt herself smile again, thankful for his presence.

"You figured it out on your own?" she questioned him.

He rolled his eyes, and she stifled her laugh. She suddenly felt sympathetic for her mother. It really was an annoying habit when it was directed at you.

"Yes," he said.

She could imagine him at fifteen, answering her in the same tone.

"So, you have to get up."

"Okay, okay. Sheesh, you're so bossy," she teased. She rolled out of bed on the opposite side.

She began to make the bed, tugging and tucking, until it looked like it hadn't been slept in the night before.

She glanced around the stark room and found her memories of J.C. alive and well. Without the distraction of Nicky, she found she wasn't prepared for the emptiness she felt. The wide pit in her stomach expanded.

She'd kidded herself into thinking she could hold her emotions so tightly.

But in the early morning light, she realized she'd fallen for him. Those family thoughts of her, and J.C. and Nicky, she'd batted away last night had been real, a tucked away dream. Now, they were merely shattered fragments of a recent past she hadn't been willing to take a risk on or fight for.

She thought about J.C. saying she was damaged. She'd blown it off at the time as merely a low blow from a disappointed lover. *But what if it had been more than that?*

As hard as she tried, she couldn't quite relegate J.C. to that role. He was more than just a guy she had been screwing. He'd been her friend, her confidant, her hope. And that explained the presence of the pit. Really, it explained her actions the night before and his comment.

She thought perhaps he was right. She was damaged, probably permanently, and essentially, she was a coward. Somehow, it seemed easier to let him go now than it might feel later.

"Mama! I'm hungry!" Nicky yelled from the kitchen.

Not that he couldn't throw his own waffle into the toaster, she thought.

She left the room, pulling the door shut behind her, closing in the memories and the revelations.

J.C. had almost pulled out of the fishing excursion. He wasn't sure if he was up for being around Nick and Mike. He'd had a hard enough time getting Lena out of his head, and the thought of being around her family didn't seem so appealing. But it was always impossible for him to fight the lure of the water.

A couple of hours in, he was glad he'd come. The day was perfect with its blue skies and warm temperatures. What had happened last night wasn't really anything. With what he did, the people he'd met who'd survived their own personal tragedies, walking away from a girl should rate low on the misery scale. It only needed a little perspective.

And he could achieve perspective on the water.

After some time in the Gulf, Mike turned the boat back toward a sandbar where Nick begged him to stop. Bryce and Nick hopped off the boat, swimming the twenty yards toward the temporary island where a number of boats had moored. He and Mike started tidying things on the boat—tying off fishing poles, collecting trash, all the little nagging chores that came along with a day in the sun. J.C. watched Bryce and Nick emerge onto the sandbar and head toward the other side, exploring.

"You good?" Mike asked him, startling him.

"Yeah," J.C. answered, thankful for the hat and the sunglasses.

He hadn't spent any time with Mike and Lindsay and Lena together, not since he and Lena had dived into their relationship. But somehow, it seemed like Mike knew something was off, which surprised J.C. But since Mike had started down the path, J.C. decided to try to garner some understanding.

"So, what happened with Nick and the doctor?" he asked.

Mike studied him long enough for J.C. to figure that he wasn't going to answer. He shrugged like it was no big deal.

"She didn't tell you?" Mike asked.

J.C. shook his head.

"She really has the emotional capability of a twelve-year-old boy," Mike remarked.

He lifted his hat off his head and ran his fingers through his hair before he replaced it. J.C. couldn't determine if it was to stall or figure out what to say, but the comment made him smile.

"Yes, she does," he concurred even though he was fairly certain the statement had been rhetorical.

"When Nick was born, I spoke with the pediatrician about what had happened to Gabe. I didn't know a lot of details. Lena didn't talk about it, and we weren't close enough for me to ask." He sighed. "Maybe I should back up. I didn't even know what had happened aside from the fact that she'd lost her brother. But when the baby was born, Lindsay pulled me aside and explained everything. The autopsy had determined it was genetic. Even though they encouraged Lena to get tested, she refused—her whole ignorance-is-bliss theory. Anyway, Lindsay didn't want to betray Lena, but she wanted me to know they'd suggested we have the baby tested. After I spoke to the pediatrician by myself, I approached Lena to get her to agree to having Nick tested. It was a difficult conversation, as you can imagine. She became robotic. It was almost like Gabe never existed." Mike stopped talking.

J.C. looked away from Mike, behind him, toward the water. He inhaled deeply like he could somehow breathe in Mike's words and find some key to understanding Lena.

J.C. brought his attention back when Mike started talking again, "At first, she flat-out refused. And I am sure you know how damn stubborn she can be. We were at an impasse. I'm not sure what changed her mind. Maybe Lindsay?" He lifted his hands, trying to express his confusion. "I've never gone back to ask. But Lena came to me about a month later and said she would consent to the testing with one condition. She didn't want to know the results."

"What?" J.C. couldn't stop the word from coming out of his mouth.

Mike shook his head. "At the time, I was so relieved by the turn of events that I didn't push it. I scheduled the test and moved forward. But the night before the test, I went to her and asked her to explain. Why wouldn't you want to know? We were talking about her child. She said if he had hypertrophic cardiomyopathy she would live her life in constant fear. She would wonder if he should be playing or running or jumping, and she'd end up robbing him of his childhood and her of her ability to enjoy him. She acknowledged that she thought about having me tell her if the test was negative, but then she would know automatically if I didn't come back to her with the results. It was so irrational. I mean, if he had HCM, there would be things we'd need to do. But I couldn't change her mind, and I figured I'd cross that bridge if and when we came to it. The results were negative, but she never asked."

They were quiet for a while, the sounds of the water and the people talking and the boats' engines bouncing around them, while they festered in the silence of their separate thoughts of Lena.

"Anyway, when he passed out at school, we immediately went to the doctor and then the pediatric cardiologist and then the hospital for the echo. We did it all, and she did it with us. Trust me, I wasn't sure if she'd be able to handle it, but she was actually pretty amazing. I thought…" He looked away from J.C. and then back. "I thought it was because of you. She just seemed so much more mature. I know that sounds ridiculous to say about the thirty-year-old mother of my son, but it's true. She's an awesome mother. But she can be so fucking immature sometimes when we have to make hard decisions. She might not have told you what was going on, but if it had happened before you, she wouldn't have been there. She would have delegated it to me, you know? She just seems so much stronger than she used to be." Mike stood up from the captain's chair and rapped on J.C.'s arm. "So, whatever you're doing, keep it up."

J.C. smiled derisively. "It's over."

"What?" Mike asked, surprised.

J.C. shook his head. "I can't wait for her to grow up."

Mike studied him. "Believe it or not, kid, I understand. But I think you should know that she's grown up more in the last three months than the thirty years prior. I get impatience. But I think that when she finally gets there, she'll be worth the wait."

"I'm sure she will," J.C. concurred. "But she'll be worth it for someone else."

It had been a month since J.C. had seen her. It seemed somehow serendipitous for his first sighting to be at a soccer tournament. Even though their rooms were across the hall from each other, J.C. had managed to avoid Lena all of Friday night and all day on Saturday. He almost laughed when he thought about Bryce's horror at discovering that Lena and Nick were across the hall. It was a bit hard, knowing she was so close, but no harder than knowing she was in the same town.

He'd kinda thought he had moved on—until he had seen her in the lobby.

Maybe, he thought, *my avoiding tactic was the wrong way to go.*

Maybe he should have taken the smaller doses of her for the last month, so his first sighting wouldn't have knocked him for the loop it had.

It was what he was thinking about as he closed the door to his room behind him on his way to meet Bryce downstairs.

He turned around to find Lena walking out of her room at the same time. Neither one of them seemed to be able to move.

He recovered first. "Hey," he said in greeting. *Lame*, he thought.

"Hi," she said.

He took her in without meaning to, doing a head-to-toe perusal. She was in shorts that hit her mid thigh and a long-sleeved shirt that slipped off of one shoulder, showcasing the strap of a camisole underneath. He clenched his fists to keep from reaching out to her. But he wanted her, and it was overwhelming in its intensity.

Why couldn't he have been satisfied with what she had been offering?

He moved toward her like an invisible lead was pulling him. His hands were on her nape and cupping her jaw before he was even aware he'd changed his mind. He kissed her, gently at first, like he might have forgotten the shape of her lips. He relearned their contours, coaxing her mouth open for him. When his tongue found its way inside her mouth, he unleashed the feelings he'd held at bay for the last month. Her hands reached up, and she clamped them around his wrists as she moved backward, toward her door. She dropped one of her hands, and he felt the door give way behind her.

He followed her step for step into the room, never relenting in his kiss. He kicked the door closed behind him and turned her around, pushing her back against the wall. Releasing her mouth, he moved down her throat and across her collarbone, his hands finding their spot on her hips, while he tasted her.

"I missed this," she breathed, her mouth free.

He squeezed her hips, letting her know he'd heard without actually responding to her. He dropped to his knees, searching for his ring. He lifted her loose shirt and traced her stomach with his tongue, sucking the ring into his mouth.

"J.C.," she moaned.

Grabbing the ring with his teeth, he bit down, clicking it. "My ring," he whispered.

She chuckled. "Yours. For sure. You love that ring."

"Not the only thing about your body I love," he responded, grinning up at her.

He felt her stomach contract underneath his hands, her excitement amping up. He slid one of his hands up under her shirt and pulled the strap of her camisole down her arm, exposing her breast through the thin material of her shirt. His mouth moved up, and he nipped at her, leaving a wet spot on her shirt.

Then, it hit him—what she'd said. She missed *this*, not him. The realization snapped him out of his sex-hazed trance.

He abruptly pulled away and stood up, keeping some space between them. He ran his hand through his hair. "Shit, Lena. I'm sorry. I shouldn't have done that."

She looked at him warily. "I don't want you to be sorry," she stated.

"I can't do this."

She banged her head against the door. "You seemed to be doing it just fine." She smirked.

He smirked back. "Let me rephrase. I don't want...to want to be doing this."

She looked down at his pants and looked back up at him with her eyebrows raised. He couldn't help it when he laughed. She laughed with him.

"Why?" she asked simply.

"I just...I can't," he said, as if it pained him to admit it. And he guessed it did. He waved his hand between them. "It's not enough."

He saw her roll her eyes, and he wished so badly that it were enough.

She pushed away from the door and moved to him, wrapping her hands around his neck and through his hair. She left enough distance between their bodies to make him crave having her against him. As a seduction tactic, it worked. He thought he'd combust if he didn't pull her to him. But he thought about how he felt about her and how she didn't feel the same about him. And while he was so tempted, he wasn't sure he could survive her.

"Don't," he said, hating the way his voice hadn't sounded entirely sure of what he was saying, like he was trying to convince himself.

But there must have been something in his tone or expression because she released him.

"I want more than you want to give me," he said. He looked away from her.

There was more, but he didn't really feel like baring too much of his soul.

He pulled her into his arms. They held each other for a time—he'd never be sure of how long—before he kissed her on the forehead. Then, he tugged on her navel ring, flashed her a crooked smile, and left the room.

When the door closed behind J.C. with a gentle click, Lena made her way to the bed on shaky legs and sat heavily. Yet again, she'd messed it up and played it all wrong. She could have said a thousand things to him, but she'd immediately reverted to the physical because it was so much easier than dealing with all of her messy emotions.

Somehow, she had managed to avoid laying eyes on J.C. for four weeks. She hadn't even seen him when she had to pick up Nicky from practice once a week. It was almost as if he didn't exist anymore, like she'd gone back to a time when J.C. hadn't been a part of her life. His absence had made it easy to forget, except on some nights. Some nights, she couldn't forget, and she would sit in her room, her sanctuary, replaying their time together, over and over in her head.

It had taken her two weeks to actually ask Nicky about him. He'd assured her that J.C. was still coaching, but he had to leave early on Thursday nights. As far as avoidance strategies went, it was pretty brilliant. She wasn't sure how J.C. could do it, but he'd seemed to be fairly adept at making himself scarce. And she could admit, she'd wanted to see him so badly she ached.

It had taken her all of a second of catching a glimpse of him to know how much she'd missed him. And it didn't have everything to do with sex. She missed him and the way he'd soothed out all the bumpy surfaces in her heart and filled the gaping and yearning spaces. All the concerns she'd hoarded seemed so meaningless.

She wanted to chase him out into the hall to tell him that she'd been wrong, that she should have been more open, more willing to give him what he needed while she'd taken what she thought she wanted.

It wasn't the time or the place to have a conversation with him, especially after that humiliating encounter. But they did need to talk. At least, she needed to talk. It was time.

The quaking in her limbs subsided with her resolution. She made her way to the door. She walked across the hall and knocked.

"Is he here?" she asked when Bryce opened the door.

Bryce shook his head. "No. I don't know where he is."

She wanted to scoff but decided she didn't need to alienate Bryce any more than she already had.

Bryce looked at her with sympathy, but didn't offer anything up. She was so tempted to ask about J.C. She almost didn't, but she wasn't sure when she would get another chance.

"How is he?"

She wanted to know so much more than that, like when was he leaving for med school and how the final stages of the planning for the screenings were shaking out. He'd talked about a potential merger, and she was curious to know if it had panned out. But she couldn't get her mouth around the words, and she knew it wasn't fair to ask Bryce.

"He's good," Bryce answered.

"That's good." She looked at Bryce, meeting his eyes. "I miss him." It felt good to say it. She wondered why she could confess to Bryce but had, until this moment, been reluctant to acknowledge it to herself and certainly to J.C. when she'd had the chance. At first, she'd chalked it up to being lonely. But she was starting to see that it was so much more than that.

Bryce grimaced, as if he really didn't want to know how she felt about J.C. "I should probably keep out of this, but he's better now, and it'd be good if maybe you could make sure to give him space."

He winced a little, but Lena wasn't sure if it was because he'd betrayed something about his friend or if he felt bad telling her to stay away from J.C.

"Sure," she said. "I totally get it." She almost left it at that but found she couldn't quite keep her mouth shut. "It's not what I want, of course. But I understand."

"Do you?" he asked. "Because I'm trying to figure out why you're standing at our door."

"No, I don't." She almost turned around and walked away, but she felt like she owed Bryce an explanation, too. They'd become friends, and she'd betrayed that, too. "I want to walk away—I really do—because it would be so much easier. And I tried. That's what the last month has been about—trying to stay away—but I really don't want to."

"But what you want and what he wants seem to be two very different things."

"Were. They *were* two very different things. I just had to get there, ya know? I wasn't where he was, and I needed to get there."

"And all of a sudden, you're there now?"

It was a fair question, a good question, one she'd ask of someone who could crush her best friend's heart.

She looked away from him for a second and took in the hotel hallway where she found herself having one of the most important conversations of her life. Its grays and greens were everywhere, an interior designer's way to get everything to coordinate and match. Nothing in her world fit together in such a deliberate way. It was all fortuitous and untidy. And for the majority of her adult life, the chaos had allowed her to deliberately forget one of the most important people in her life, so she could avoid feeling the loss of him.

"There were things I let keep me from him, stupid little things that seemed to point to all sorts of reasons for us not to be together." She looked back at Bryce. "I get that now."

"Okay," Bryce said.

"That's it? Okay?"

"You're going to have your work cut out for you, explaining it to J.C. I don't want to be your guinea pig," he said with a wink.

"Fair enough," she said.

"I really don't know where he is right now."

"That's probably better. I have to get some things worked out first."

Bryce nodded.

"Thanks," she said. "For not judging."

"Don't thank me. I totally judge."

They shared a smile. Lena gave a little wave and turned to go back to her room.

"Hey, Lena," Bryce said. When she turned around, he gave her a big smile. "Look what I found when I came to answer the door." He held up a penny, and with a wink, he said, "You've got this."

Lena nodded and then turned away before he could see her tears.

Since the screening had ended last week, J.C., Bryce, Max, Fletcher, Anna, and Kyle, all been taking it easy, trying to do things that required little effort. That meant playing video games, drinking some beer, and sleeping. The night before, they had a post-event celebration at their favorite bar and decided today would be about watching soccer.

"You expecting anyone?" Bryce asked when he heard a knock on their apartment door.

J.C. looked over at him from the couch and shook his head before returning his attention to the soccer game on TV. He heard the door open and close.

"It's for you."

J.C. got up, turned toward the door, and then stopped abruptly, taking in his visitors with a look of surprise he didn't even try to disguise. "Hey," he said.

"Coach Cal," Nick said as he closed the gap between them and held out his fist for their traditional bump.

J.C. hit Nick's fist with his own and then looked back up to meet Lena's eyes. He couldn't quite believe they were standing in his apartment, even after actually touching Nick and knowing he wasn't a mirage.

"So, Nicky and I were wondering if you had plans today?"

J.C. looked over at Bryce, who was sporting a goofy smile. But at J.C.'s narrowed gaze, he shrugged his shoulders, like he had no idea what was going on.

"No, not really. What's up?"

"We have a party to go to, and we're hoping you can come with us," she said, like it was an everyday occurrence for her to show up at his home with her son in tow. "If you can. If you want." For the first time, she looked nervous about being there, the furrowing of her brow giving her away.

"Yeah, sure." He looked at how she was dressed in a yellow sundress. "Do I have time for a shower?"

"Of course," she said.

"I'll be quick," he assured her.

"Don't worry. We've got time. It's not for a bit."

He nodded. He should have moved, but he couldn't take his eyes off of her and Nicky—together, in his apartment, inviting him to go somewhere, with the both of them.

"Nick, how about a round of FIFA14 while J.C. gets pretty?" Bryce said, breaking the awkward silence and snapping J.C. out of his Lena haze.

"Cool."

J.C. finally turned and made his way to his room. He heard the game start up, and Nick started talking trash. He heard Bryce and Lena laugh. He was so curious about what was going on that he took a quicker than normal shower. He grabbed a polo shirt and his nicest pair of shorts, trying to match Lena's dress code. He pulled on his Sperrys and fixed his hair.

When he walked out fifteen minutes later, Nick and Bryce were engaged in a soccer war, and Lena was sitting demurely on the couch, messing with her phone. She looked up to J.C. and offered a tentative smile.

He smiled back, but he was impatient to figure out what this little visit was all about, so his smile came out looking forced.

"You ready?" he asked.

"Uh, do you mind if I show Nicky the pictures of Gabe?"

He tried hard to conceal his shock, but he didn't think he'd managed it because she sent a tentative smile his way.

"No, not at all."

"I've got a couple, too," Bryce said. "I think some of them are the same, but I might have some different ones."

"Thanks. I'd like that," Lena responded. "B, you are probably going to have to turn the game off though because Nicky won't move if it's on."

Her comment garnered a laugh from both of them, especially because Nick seemed to have missed the whole conversation. Bryce moved to the remote and pressed the Off button. When the TV faded to black, Nick turned around to look at them, like he'd just noticed there were people around him.

"Can we see the pictures?" Nick asked Lena.

Rolling her eyes, she nodded. "Yes. They said we could."

J.C. opened the door to his room but stood back, allowing them to go in without him. He turned to Bryce. "You knew about this," he stated.

"Not really," he said in a hushed voice.

"Whatever," he muttered.

He couldn't figure out what he was feeling about this unexpected turn of events. What he wanted mostly was an explanation, and he didn't see it coming anytime soon.

Lena and Nick took their time looking at the pictures. When they were done, the three of them left the apartment. Nick jumped into his car seat in the back of the car.

"So, whose party are we going to?" J.C. asked as soon as Lena pulled out of the parking lot and onto the street.

"The girls," said Nick. "It's a stupid pottery party."

"Nicky," Lena said in a total mom voice that made J.C. smile distractedly.

"Well, it is. And I'm going to be the only boy there."

J.C. turned in his seat and held out his fist. "I'll be there, too, buddy."

"True," Nick responded with his fist bump, which made J.C. laugh.

"The twins are six today. It's their party, but he makes it sound like there will be a bunch of girls when it's really just one additional one." She briefly looked over to J.C. before returning her eyes to the road. "I think we are in the throes of *girls equals cooties.*"

"I totally get that. I think I'm there, too," J.C. deadpanned.

"Ha-ha," Lena retorted.

Silence descended between them.

Questions ran through J.C.'s mind, but with the audience of one in the back, he was reluctant to voice them. He turned to look out the window.

After his encounter with Lena in the hotel room, J.C. had decided that his first inclination to completely avoid Lena was the way to go. It was difficult to be anywhere near her and not want to touch her or talk to her.

Except right now, he thought.

Right now, he had no idea what to say to her, and having Nick in the back was an amazing touch deterrent. He stole a quick glance in her direction. He hadn't seen her around Nick much. She was totally relaxed, like being in her Jeep with J.C. and her son was the most natural thing in the world.

She peered over toward him and caught him watching her. She graced him with a smile that seemed to explain something, but he wasn't quite sure he understood.

"It's a tradition. On birthdays, it's family only. I can't even remember when it started. I guess, in the beginning, when we first had Nicky, I wasn't really up for making new friends. But we wanted him to know his birthday was special." She stopped her explanation and cut her eyes from the road to look over at him. "Anyway, the actual birthday is family only—grandparents, aunts, uncles, cousins. But no one else. The twins have been dying to paint pottery, so that's where we're headed."

"I feel like there's something in that explanation that I'm supposed to just get," J.C. said.

Lena laughed. "I was kind of hoping you would let me off easy."

This time, J.C. laughed. "Yeah, that's totally not happening."

The pottery studio was situated near the hospital in a revitalized small section of town that boasted some upscale cafes, a couple of bars, and a high-end grocery store. They parked in a spot on the street, and J.C. followed Lena and Nick into the fray.

Even without Lena's poor attempt to explain the guest list, it would have taken J.C. all of thirty seconds to get it. He was greeted warmly by Lindsay and Mike and introduced to both sets of grandparents and one of Mike's brothers, his wife, and their daughter.

He and Nick picked out *boy* pottery to paint, and he took his seat at the kids' table, totally comfortable being the only adult. He wouldn't let his man, Nick, suffer at the estrogen table alone. Nick painted a pirate head, and J.C. stayed true to form by picking a soccer ball bank that he was fairly certain he would leave with Nick. He'd been tempted by a heart bank just because of Play for Gabe, but he didn't think he could handle the ribbing from Nick.

When they finished painting, they turned their pottery over and the group headed to one of the restaurants down the street.

Lena and Mike corralled the kids, leaving J.C. to pull up the rear.

"How are you?" Lindsay asked, surprising him.

He looked down at her and smiled. "I'm good. Thanks for letting me participate."

"Participate?"

"Yeah. Not sure if you budgeted for the extra piece of pottery," he teased.

"You're right. I think it might have broken the bank."

They took a couple of steps in silence.

"Do you get how big of a deal this is?" Lindsay asked suddenly.

J.C. smiled again. "I get it."

"But you're not impressed?"

"I never said that." He paused to gather his thoughts because he wasn't quite sure how best to say what he was thinking without offending her. "Look, I get it. She explained—well, sort of explained—on the way over. But I've done a really good job of trying to put this behind me. So, you have to understand..."

"Understand what?" she prompted.

"It's not as simple as she wants it to be."

Lindsay laughed, which was not the reaction J.C. had expected. He looked over at her, wondering if she'd been holding out on the adult beverages at the party.

She bumped into him with her shoulder. "Give her hell, J.C. Oh, and don't feel like you have to stay. Just have her back at the house for cake tonight," she said as she opened the door to the restaurant and joined the rest of the group.

Lena had saved him a seat and looked up at him hopefully as he perused the table. He went to join her, torn between being happy about being with her family and struggling with having to wait for her explanation.

He leaned over toward Lena. His mouth was so near her ear that he couldn't control his impulse to drop a kiss right below it before he whispered, "Can we get out of here, or do you want to stay?"

She pulled away from the contact but looked at him. "We can go, but we have to be at the house later for cake."

"What about Nick?"

"He's staying with Mike tonight. And I sort of prepared him for this possibility."

J.C. nodded. "Let's go."

They excused themselves from the table but not before Mike winked at him.

J.C. and Lena were silent on the walk to the car and on the short ride to her house.

Like a mantra in his head, he recited, *I will not touch her, I will not touch her, I will not touch her*, over and over until they parked and walked into her house.

"Do you want a beer?" she asked as she dropped her keys on the counter. "Because I am going to need a glass of wine."

"Sure, I'd love one."

She moved to the fridge and grabbed his beer. She popped the top before she walked over and handed it to him. He got lost for a moment in watching her. Flashes of their time together collated in front of his eyes.

She lifted her eyes up to his and smiled at him. "What?" she asked as he studied her.

"I think I blocked out how beautiful you are. It's all coming back to me now."

She laughed as a genuine blush tainted her face. Turning away, she chose a bottle of wine. J.C. got up and took it from her hands. He found the old-fashioned corkscrew that he loved to tease her about and opened the bottle for her. She handed him a glass to fill. Then, she turned and walked into the living room. He followed, choosing to sit across from her.

"It's good to see you, J.C.," she said.

He didn't say anything but observed her closely from across the length of the coffee table.

"And I'm really glad you were there today."

He leaned back, seeking space from the vulnerability he could see in her eyes. He would never have associated it with her as she'd cloaked it so well under all the layers of cynicism and impulsiveness. It made her seem more approachable and sweet and tempting.

All the fortifying of his heart that he'd done over the past couple of weeks toppled like a sand castle under the weight of a wave. What he felt for her was too much.

He stood up, suddenly unable to sit idle while waiting for her to say what he needed her to say.

"Any chance you can just tell me what today was all about?" His words were laced with his impatience.

She groaned and dropped her head to the back of the couch. "I'm trying to tell you that you're, like, my favorite person, and I'm pretty sure I'm in love with you."

Lena picked her head up off the couch and looked across the room. The stunned expression on J.C.'s face was kind of priceless.

"If you'd been more patient, I could have been more eloquent," she said sarcastically.

She forgot how quick he could move until he was across the room, and she was being yanked up into his arms. He cradled her face in his hands and kissed her hard. When he released her, she sat back down, her thoughts a little hazier than they'd been before he'd scrambled her brain with his lips, mouth, and tongue.

"The hard part's over," J.C. said as he sat on the couch next to her.

He turned her, so they were facing each other with her right leg curled around his left hip. She noticed he'd left space, like he didn't want to be too close to her.

"You think that was the hard part?" Lena asked.

"It wasn't?" He sounded genuinely curious.

"Maybe," she said on a shrug. "Maybe the conclusion is the hardest. But, shit, I feel like our journey to this point right here?" She waved her hand between them until he reached out and stopped it, interlocking their fingers. She looked up at him. "I feel like it was difficult to get here."

"It wasn't for me."

"Well, lucky you," she snapped.

He laughed. It was *her* laugh, the one that punched her in the gut and made all the doubts scatter like dead leaves in a gusty wind.

The smile lingering on his face soothed her. He brought his other hand up to her face, skimming across her cheek and along her jawline.

"Talk to me," he said.

"I thought you understood what I could give."

He lifted his eyebrow in question. He looked like he wasn't sure he got her point, but she wasn't quite sure either, and she had no idea if her explanation had made any sense.

"*Okay*," J.C. said, drawing it out, emphasizing his confusion.

"You're going to think I'm crazy."

J.C. chuckled. "Who says I don't already think that?" he teased.

"You remember the funeral?"

"Of course."

"We were sitting together, holding hands."

He nodded. "Yeah, it surprised me when you didn't know who I was when we met again."

"Well, I vowed to never see you again after the funeral."

"Okay," he said, a little shocked.

"It was too much. I didn't want to even remember the funeral. The first time I even thought about it was after everything had happened between us. It all kind of hit me then." She paused. "There was a moment at the funeral when I knew, as horrible as I felt, that I'd be okay. I mean, I knew I'd never be the same, but I accepted the fact that I'd get through it all. I don't know if it was because I was pregnant or what, but anyway, for a split second, I felt that.

"The next thought I had though was about what I'd let myself do or not do, and I vowed then and there that I wouldn't let anyone else mean as much to me as Gabe because I never again wanted to feel like I felt in that moment.

"And you were there, holding my hand, and the second I thought I'd never love anyone, you squeezed my hand, and I know it sounds stupid, but I thought you knew that, that you got it and me. And I didn't think you would push me to have more than that."

He looked confused. "Let me see if I understand. Back in December, when you said you were ready to give this a shot, you thought your version of a shot was the same as mine."

Lena nodded her head because, so far, he was spot-on.

"But your version was not to really go all in. It was to stick your toe in the shallow end."

"I mean, I think it was more than that. It was definitely more than that, but then there were all these complications and people expressing their doubts. I'd never done this before, so I just pulled back. But when I'd said I was in, I'd meant it. Don't you think that?" she asked.

"Yes. I think you were in up to maybe your waist." He winked at her, and she smiled because he did get it, and it was all very reasonable in the way he was explaining it. "But not when it came to anything outside of the two of us. In isolation, everything is easy."

Lena felt the first prickle of a blush, knowing the conclusion he was working toward would sound as crazy as she thought it did.

"I'm with you up to there," J.C. said.

"Do you get lost on the next part? The part where I didn't think you needed me to be all in because I thought you got the promise I made to myself at Gabe's funeral?"

"Yeah. See, I didn't understand or even know there was that part."

"I thought you got it—that I didn't want to love anyone like that again."

"But you already do—Nick, Mike, Lindsay, the girls. How did you think you could keep that promise to yourself, even in all that grief?"

"I didn't say it made sense." The prickle turned rampant, moving through her system, heating her from the inside out.

"So, what's different now? What changed? Why, today, are you all of a sudden willing to be more open?" He looked so earnest in his desire to understand.

She wanted to tell him she'd meant what she said in December. She just didn't execute it very well. "When you came here on Christmas Day and told me about med school, I felt like I'd been freed from having to go all in because you'd be leaving, and I didn't think I should or could do that to Nicky—or at least, that was what I convinced myself of. But it gave me a barrier. And keeping the two most important parts of my life separate from each other allowed me to keep my feelings in check.

"After I saw you last time, all sorts of things hit me. Up until that point, I thought I missed the companionship and the sex. But when I saw you in the hallway at the hotel, I knew it was you I missed. Even though I attempted to rein everything in, you owned my heart. From there, it was logistics."

"Logistics?"

"Explaining to Nicky mostly. And coming to terms with you leaving soon anyway."

He nodded his head. "Med school?"

"Yeah. Long distance? I just don't know how that can work when you are in med school."

"I deferred."

"What?"

"I was going to go, but we have so many things going on right now with Playing for Hearts that I just felt like I'd regret it if I went now."

Lena tried to fight her smile but couldn't quite pull it off. He laughed and pulled her toward him.

"You like that answer?" he whispered in her ear when she was buried in his arms.

"I do."

"Me, too." He pulled her other leg around him, so she was straddling him. Then, he pulled her in close, holding her tight, like he didn't want to let her go. "Any other things I need to know?"

"What about Anna?" she asked.

"Yeah, Anna. She's going to pull back this year, and then next year, when I go to school, she'll fill the void. She came up with it, not me. I will miss her friendship, but this break would have happened with or without you."

She sighed into him, content with his answer. "You still can't spend the night here when Nicky's here. I just don't feel right about it." She didn't think he'd give her a hard time, but she needed him to know it up front.

"Of course," he said. Then, he kissed her.

They stayed there, on the couch, for a long time, exploring each other, like they hadn't been there before. Then, he scooped her up and walked to the guest room. He dropped her onto the bed and came down on top of her.

"Why here?" she asked. She didn't really care right in the moment. She had more pressing desires.

As he undressed her, he answered, "It doesn't really matter where, does it? It's here, where we started."

He kissed her deeply again, and she forgot to think. His hands moved down her body, tugging on the hem of her dress and pulling it up, as he continued to stay buried in the depths of her mouth. He ended the kiss to pull her dress over her head.

"The elevator," she said breathlessly.

She didn't even have to explain what she meant.

He bent his head and kissed her under her ear. He continued down her body until his head was even with her navel, and he could mess with her piercing. When the ring was clamped between his teeth and he tugged on it, trying to push her to combustion, he smirked up at her.

"Soccer practice," he countered.

She laughed. He'd had to one-up her. He traveled even lower, and she forgot to think at all.

For the next hour, she was content to let him think he'd had the last word. When he filled her, her body felt satiated, complete, whole. When he kissed her, their breaths mingled, their bodies moving as one.

The hole in her heart left by the loss of her brother mended, forged by J.C.'s love and infinite patience.

In the aftermath, wrapped in his arms, exhaustion threatened to take her.

"The funeral," she whispered into his chest.

His arms tightened around her right before he chuckled.

He flipped her then and loomed above her. Staring into his eyes, she was suddenly wide awake.

"Do you know what I was thinking about at the funeral?" he asked, mischief dancing in his eyes.

She shook her head.

"I don't want to ruin your moment of profound connection, but when I was sitting next to you at Gabe's funeral and you took my hand, I got lost. I spent the whole ceremony thinking that the star of my teenage fantasies was holding my hand. When I squeezed your hand, I think I was trying to remind myself where I was, so I could keep my body under control."

She wanted to be horrified, but the whole scene made her giggle.

He laughed with her. "Right? What kind of guy sits through his best friend's funeral, lusting after his best friend's big sister?"

Lena laughed harder. "You're right," she managed to say between giggles. "You just ruined my moment of profound connection."

They continued laughing.

When the moment faded between them, the serious expression on his face concerned her. She moved her hand up to his cheek, caressing his face.

"What?" she murmured before she reached up and placed a gentle kiss on his mouth.

"You got me through the funeral. I knew people around me were grieving, too, but I just felt like my loss was so much more than theirs—until I sat next to you. And then I thought, *Maggie Pryce understands. She gets that I'll never be the same.* And as much as I was sad for you, it made it easier for me to deal with it. When I saw you in September, I knew."

She thought he was going to continue, but he didn't say anything. He continued staring at her, like he was trying to tell her something without saying it. Then, something shifted in his eyes, and she knew he was merely trying to find the right words.

"Knew what?"

"That I was supposed to love you. I love you, Lena. I can be patient and give you the time you need to come to terms with what's between us. I will give you time to figure out how Nick and I are going to work out our relationship, which is something you are going to have to let us figure out. And we can figure out med school together."

Lena didn't say anything. His declarations were swirling all around her, and for a moment, she thought she wouldn't be able to breathe under the onslaught of them. But when she took a breath, it came easier, like all the doubt and fear had been released, and all she could feel was his love for her.

"I love you," she said.

He smiled at her. "And it so wasn't the funeral. It was the regional game, in the parking lot, by the little shed."

"Okay, okay," she said, laughing again. "You win. That was the beginning."

"That's right, Pryce. And there's no ending for this story."

320

EPILOGUE

J.C.—Five Years Later

"Whatcha doing out here?" Lena asked me as she wrapped her arms around my waist.

I could feel her rest her head on my back and inhale.

Breathing you in, she always said.

"Just taking a moment," I responded, placing my hand on hers and leaning into her.

"I'm so proud of you."

I laughed. "Yeah, I got that from your damn speech that made me tear up in front of all my friends. Totally negated the cool factor of adding the MD to my name," I teased her.

But it was true. She'd almost brought me to my knees with her glowing words about me in front of everyone. She'd brought down the house actually. I didn't think I was the only one who had almost lost it. She'd included all of us in it—Bryce, Fletcher, Kyle, Max, and even Anna. It was this amazing piece of literature that had detailed everything we'd accomplished over the last five of years.

She'd started it as an all-hail-J.C. speech, but it'd turned into this letter of love to all of us for our work in the name of Gabe. I knew she hadn't meant to go there, but like everything with Lena, once she let go, she wouldn't hold back.

Recently, we'd added the forty-fifth state to our list of states that mandated EKGs for all student athletes participating in high school sports. Our little movement had gone national. It had been difficult to continue to be a part of Playing for Hearts while I was in med school, but we'd worked it out.

The door opened, and we turned in unison to see who'd found us.

"I tried to entertain her, but she wanted you," Nick said, walking toward us and depositing his little sister, Penny, into my arms.

At thirteen, he'd attempt to play it off like he couldn't be bothered to play her, but when no one was watching, there wasn't a more attentive big brother.

"Hey, Little Bit," I said, kissing her on the tip of her nose.

"Daddy." She giggled.

In some crazy twist of fate, Penny looked just like her Uncle Gabe. Lena and I didn't comment on it often, but his imprint was all over her. She might be the most spoiled three-year-old in the world. Between the twins, who treated her like their own personal Barbie doll; her godfather, Max, who didn't come to the house without a gift for her; and Nick, who doted on her, she didn't want for anything. I dreaded the teenage years when all this spoiling would surely come back to bite us in the ass.

"Were you giving Nicky a hard time?" Lena asked, leaning over. She kissed her cheek while she reached and pulled Nick into the circle.

Even after five years, I hadn't been able to break Lena of calling him Nicky. And he and I'd tried hard. I'd continued to attempt to convince her of how uncool it was, but this was Lena I was talking about. It was kind of difficult to convince her to do something she didn't want to do.

"I want cake," Penny said.

"Ah, I forgot about the cake."

"You can't forget cake, Daddy."

"You're right. We should probably go have cake," I said even though I was reluctant to leave the quiet of the patio.

It had been a long four years, and the thought of not having anything pressing to do now was pretty awesome. I imagined I'd start feeling twitchy as I waited for my residency to start, but for right now, being here, with our family, felt as close to heaven as I could get.

322

BLISS

We made our way into the house, all connected, touching in some way.

Bryce came over first, grabbing Penny from me.

"Uncle B, it's time for cake," she squealed, nearly jumping from my arms to his. Penny might love Bryce more than she loved cake.

Everyone must have heard because they suddenly gravitated toward the kitchen. It was amazing to look around at our family. My mom and Lena's parents had driven in yesterday. Kyle and Anna had come from Jacksonville a few days before because we'd rolled a board meeting into the weekend—two birds, one stone. Max, Bryce, and Fletcher still lived here, which was awesome. They were basically a permanent fixture at our house. Of course, Mike, a very pregnant Lindsay, and the twins rounded out the group.

As I looked around, I was overwhelmed.

We had all been taught to be excited for the milestones of our lives—graduations, births, weddings—right? But no one ever prepared us for the unexpected tragedies we would have to face. And sometimes, those tragedies could change the shape of your life. Some people wouldn't survive. The blows they had been dealt might change who they were, and they couldn't face their new reality.

It could have happened to us. We could have buckled under the weight of our grief when we'd lost Gabe. We could have lost each other and chosen to let go of the special bond we had. We could have let Gabe's death be another tragedy.

Instead, we'd turned it around and used it as an inspiration to carve out our own paths, to help other people. I couldn't pinpoint the moment, but I'd always be proud of the outcome.

I turned my head, and Lena caught my eye. In the din of the conversations around us, I could only hear and see her. She purposefully walked toward me, the glint in her eyes making me smile. At the same time, I braced myself because I knew that look. She had something up her sleeve, and she'd just decided to share it with me.

She wrapped her arms around my neck, her hand tangling in my hair, before she pulled me toward her and planted an open-mouthed kiss on me in front of everyone. And even though I could hear the catcalls of the boys and the laughter of Lindsay, I let myself get lost in Lena.

She ended the kiss and smiled up at me. And I knew I was in trouble.

"So, I have another announcement to make," Lena said to the room at large, but her eyes never left mine, and her arms stayed wrapped around my neck.

The conversation in the room halted, except for Penny, who continued to carry on a running dialogue even though no one was really listening.

"J.C. and I are expecting."

The room erupted with cheers and congratulations.

But I just looked at my wife, shaking my head, smiling. "Seriously?" I asked.

"I was going to wait until we were alone later, but I couldn't resist. Pure impulse," she whispered, a wide smile on her face.

I laughed. It was something of a joke between us. Whenever she did something that caught me off guard or surprised me, she would blame it on impulse.

Lindsay came up to us, all smiles, and wrapped her arms around us. "How did that happen?" She giggled.

Nick said from right behind her, "Aunt Linds, you know what my mom used to say. Ignorance is bliss."

We all laughed, except for Lena, who got really quiet. She looked around at everyone gathered in the kitchen, rejoicing at all that we had.

"No," she said, all serious, "not ignorance. This—*this*—is bliss."

ACKNOWLEDGMENTS

Sometimes, you can't find a way to say something you've already said in a different way, even when you claim to be a writer. I already had a concept for *Bliss* when I heard the story about my child's soccer coaches. Theirs is a story that deserves to be told.

> When they were sixteen, one of their best friends and teammates collapsed during their soccer practice and later died. Tragic, right? But here's the amazing thing. They started a scholarship fund while they were still in high school. They raised money by hosting cornhole tournaments, silent auctions, and anything else they could think of. And they raised $35,000 over a couple of years! Then, they placed five automated external defibrillators at youth athletic fields that needed them.

> But they weren't satisfied yet.

> So, they came together often over the next few years and began to put together a nonprofit organization, Who We Play For, whose mission was to fight sudden cardiac arrest, the number one killer of student athletes. WWPF brings together heart-screening groups from across the country. They have provided free or low-cost heart

screenings to more than 49,000 kids and have detected more than 60 heart conditions.

I approached them with something like, "I write romance novels with some sex and happy endings, and I would like to use parts of your story in my next book."

Over the last year, I got the opportunity to spend time with them and participate in some of their endeavors, and I really got to know them. They are dazzling!

Kieran, Evan, Megan, Zack, and Zane—Thank you for sharing your stories, embracing my idea, challenging me to think bigger, introducing me to Bethany, and providing my children with amazing role models. I look forward to watching you continue to not only *live the dream*, but to also inspire others, reach new heights, and blaze glittering paths.

Thank you to Dan, with whom I share a love of *Star Wars* and *Batman*, for my amazing cover and your infinite patience. I hope to create many more book covers with you.

Thank you to my editors—Heather Whitaker, for her first look at my book, and Jovana Shirley, for her last look at my book. I know it is a stronger book because of your contributions.

Thank you to Mamor, editor extraordinaire—I appreciate not only your advice on my book but your encouragement, stories, and belief in the project. My life is richer for having met you.

And to my girls—Patti, Brandi, Jen, and Gwen—Thank you for everything, like reading, commenting, encouraging, pushing, loving. You are incredible women who each provide me with a little something different. If I ever get all of you in the same place—look out, world!

To Fatty—Thank you for your support and your belief in me.

To my readers, *Bliss* has a happy ending, but not all stories do. So many families have lost loved ones to sudden cardiac arrest.

I challenge you to join the fight to end these preventable tragedies with a heart-screening organization in your community.

They call themselves Who We Play For now because they learned at a young age that you represent something bigger than yourself, a lesson many will never learn in life.

Who do you play for?

ABOUT THE AUTHOR

J. Santiago is a graduate of Villanova University and the University of Pennsylvania. She gets her love of sports from her fifteen-year career in the field and a houseful of boys who love to play. A former English and history teacher, she understands and embraces the power of stories in our lives.